I0583439

RUNEWAVE

JOSEPH LANGLEY

LCCN: 2025917965
ISBN: 979-8-9998187-0-6
eBook ISBN: 979-8-9998187-1-3

Cover Illustration by Yulia Zhuchkova
https://www.artstation.com/avalach

Gavin's Notebook Illustrations by Katelyn Jobinger
Stelli's Runewave Illustrations by Joseph Langley

For Danae, Ian, and Olivia,
whose friendship and feedback never fail to cast
Mirrorwaves in my heart.

A list of potentially upsetting topics, themes, and subject matter found within these pages has been included on page 388.

Reading is one of the most profound undertakings anyone can make. More profound, however, is the constant and difficult project of taking care of yourself.

Take care of yourself, everyone. The world needs you.
~Joseph

RUNEWAVE

1

At the edge of the Zenithian Swamp, rain could sometimes sound like weeping.

Droplets caught the wide leaves of the Aycmor trees, weighing down their ends, picking up particulates of brown sap and growing heavier, heavier until the leaves bent and curled to release them. They fell to meet the darkened water below, sliding between the Feltwing fronds, bogged down by dark blue slime that swirled in absent rivulets through the murk.

There, nestled against the backdrop of the bog, a village stood. It balanced on wooden stilts, its crooked, charactered homes held above the crystal waters of Lake Vithim. The water glistened sapphire in the blue light of the sun, caught cacophonous with round ripples by the falling rain. The edge of the swamp was no mystery to the lake; the dark sifting sunken slime-filled bog churned a sour line in the water from which the town kept a safe distance.

Yet both these waters caught the rain like little punctures to their flesh, and the infinite pattern of ripples spread forever across both bog and lake. Patches of still water were few and far between. In the bog, the twisted trees and sifting foliage and hanging leaves and whispering boughs left patches of water beneath them still as death. In the village, the eaves and awnings and slanted roofs did the stilling. Careful carvings carried water through rain gutters, pooling droplets toward the corners of the roofs, where they dripped, dripped, dripped through chains of tiered wood until they reached the lake below.

This rain, this trickling. These careful carvings, and their whittling. All of it could sometimes sound like weeping. Whether it did or not, of course, depended on who listened.

Gavin listened, and heard the weeping of a dead man. He sat on the floor of his house which stood like any other house in that village, stilted above the azure lake, collecting its water and dripping its tears below. He braced himself on the planks behind him with a right hand that had only three fingers, the other two long ago cut off. His dark beard clung ragged, cut by a knife, if cut at all. His hair hung half before his eyes, strands heavy and matted. He wore a light brown smock of hand-spun fabric, the sleeves rolled up to reveal hair-covered arms. He sat there, still.

And he chose to listen past the weeping. He heard the iridescent overlap of crackling laughter and teasing fire. A sound that was bright, and pure, and gleaming, and made the weeping forever worth it.

It was the sound of his children, happy.

They were playing a game of Zvaloor, hunched on either side of the gameboard; a long wooden basin of water, with goal posts at either end, and little rocks and debris placed in the middle as obstacles. The raft, as it was known, drifted in the middle, kicked around by symmetric ripples.

His daughter, Rose, tapped the water by the raft. A stamp of ripples expanded from where she touched, as if placed there by colorless ink, able to texture and shape the surface of the water. They picked up the raft, which rose and spun on her wave, around a rock. "Ha!" She exclaimed, jumping forward and tapping again, her old ripples fading away, these new ripples redirecting the raft forwards, cresting faster than the last.

His son, Bloom, lunged and tapped the water in front of the raft. Ripples expanded from his touch, but they were inverted, leading with the troughs. When they collided with Rose's ripples, they deconstructed, leaving the water still. In a flurry of motion, both kids started tapping the water, rocking the raft back and forth in the chaotic current of their overlapping attempts.

Gavin smiled, and let his eyes wander. The room was full of plants, all carefully grown under his care. A pale-blue vine that trailed in the hinges of the front door, through the rafters above. *Cyril vines... go taut when disturbed...* It hung down along the walls, to help hold up shelves for more plants. A bright golden flower with blade-shaped leaves, a tiny blue flower that twinkled like a star, a bulbous fruit that grew to ripeness and faded to death, all in the span of a day. A drooping stalk that glistened with slime. *Nurrii Stalks... Perfect to add to morning bread... As long as you add water, of course. Raw, and it just might stick your teeth together...*

"Dad, dad, did you see? Did you see?"

Gavin blinked, eyes back on the game.

"Did it go in? Did it go in?" Rose was practically bouncing from her skin, little button nose stretched by her wide, excited eyes. The roots of her hair were coming in blonde against the otherwise black tangle. The sound of the dead man's weeping threatened to overpower the rain. He swallowed, hard.

"Tell me it went in. It *totally* went in."

Gavin laughed. "What do you think, Bloom?"

His son stared down at the board with a cocked head. The boy was gangly, already tall for his eleven years of age, yet sat with the unassuming posture of someone who wished that he weren't. "I think," he said, folding his arms, "it went in, but Rose was too excited and knocked it back out, so it shouldn't count."

Gavin laughed again. "A strong argument! Hmm..."

"Dad, *please*, that's not in the rules! You can't do that!"

"Well you guys did *beg* me to be the judge, which means I can do whatever I—"

Rose leapt at him, her weight throwing him back. He laughed, catching her as she squirmed to try and get a hand over his mouth. Strong though she was for an eleven-year-old, he could have easily pushed her off. He didn't. Her hand slapped over his mouth, and she sat up in his lap, triumphant.

"Ha! I'm the judge now, and I say it's my point!" She exclaimed. Gavin sat back, eyes wide over Rose's hand, trying to look scared.

"Okay," Bloom said, dropping a stone into a bowl on Rose's side of the board. "Fine…" he tapped the water, kicking up the raft on a burst of rapid ripples, casting it down the board. He tapped around it, guiding it past rocks and debris—

"What!" Rose shrieked as the raft approached her goal. "No fair!" She leapt off of Gavin, slipping her finger into the water. The raft started to spin in place, currents and ripples sloshing together.

"Foul play!" Gavin exclaimed. "There's been an attack on the judge! There has to be a rule about that somewhere."

Bloom reached forward and tapped twice, quickly, once on each side of the raft. It surged in one direction, before the ripples of his second tap caught up and *crashed* it in the other, spinning straight towards Rose's goal—

Rose shrieked, poking her finger down on the water in front of her goal and leaving it there. Instead of casting ripples outward, her finger *pulled* the water towards it, stamped circles *appearing* at full extension, before shrinking into the point of her finger. The moment the raft hit these backwards ripples, it slowed to molasses, stuck in place as if the water itself had become sap, or syrup. Gavin's heart jolted at the sight, and the sound of weeping in his mind grew louder.

"Rose," Gavin said, right as Bloom exclaimed—

"Hey! No fair!"

"That's enough," Gavin sighed, moving forward. "You know the rules, Rose. No Runewaves."

"But dad, Zvaloor is *basically* like using Runewaves, it's the same thing!"

"No, it's our *compromise*," he said. "Look. It's about time you both head to bed anyway. We've gotta wake up early tomorrow. You're coming to the shop with me."

"What?!" Rose exclaimed. "I thought we were staying with Aunt Dezma while *you* went to the shop!"

"I know, that is what I said yesterday, but sometimes plans have to change," Gavin smiled at her. "Besides, I've been cultivating some cool new flora I want to show you guys. Ever seen a *glowing* flower before?"

"What!" Bloom perked up. "Dad, that sounds so cool! How does it glow?"

He started packing up the Zvaloor board, sliding a thin water-tight wooden sheath through notches on the side, to cover up the top. "It's a process called bioluminescence. I've only ever seen it once before, in these creatures—well, amoeba really— from the swamp, but—"

"Wait, dad!" Rose grabbed his hand as he reached for the rock-filled bowls, going to pour them into a leather pouch. "Who won? We need to count."

Gavin laughed. "It's just for fun, Rose. No need to worry about a winner," he poured the stones into the leather pouch, taking the other bowl and combining them, making it impossible to tell who had more. "Think of it this way—you *both* won. Because you had fun playing! Right?"

Rose sighed, rolling her eyes. "We always count a winner when Dezma lets me play people at the tavern."

Gavin ruffled her hair. "That's because when you're playing other people, she wants to let you show off. You can beat other people. Just don't beat Bloom. You're his *ally*, no matter what."

"I think I won though, for the record..." Bloom muttered. Rose and Gavin both glared at him.

"You did not!" Rose exclaimed.

"The *point* is," Gavin lifted the board, reaching to place it on a shelf, spinning to try and find one not already holding a plant. He failed, eventually giving up and sliding the board into a corner. "You both love each other, and I love both of you, so we don't try to win against each other. We try to win *with* each other. Because sometimes, we're all we've got. Okay?"

Rose squared her jaw and straightened her back. Bloom sighed and fell against her, holding her up.

"Good, now come on, let's go wash your hair before bedtime."

They both groaned, rolling free of their poses. Gavin laughed, grabbing each of their hands, leading them through a door at the side of the room. It opened into a cubby-hole of a bathroom, covered clay buckets serving as latrines, a deep stone basin taking up the back half. A singular plant kept the room company, hanging in a pot from the center of the roof, its long black leaves drooping well beneath its clay home. Gavin reached up to a slat on the wall, dug in his nails, and wrenched downwards. Something shifted with the sound of grating wood, and a little panel opened up. Rainwater began trickling through a shallow gutter that ran on the inside of the wall, whisking this way and that until it dripped and splattered into the stone basin.

"Come on now," he murmured, sitting on the side of the basin, patting the spot beside him. "This doesn't have to be so dreary."

They begrudgingly joined him, hopping up to reach the side. With slow, careful hands, Gavin leaned Rose back, letting her shoulder-length hair droop behind her into the water that now filled the basin. She closed her eyes as he worked his fingers into the knots and tangles of her hair, pulling them free as gently as his deft fingers could manage. The soft splashing of moments like these brought him comfort. The comfort of a familiar ritual. The comfort of familiar sensations. The familiar feeling of the specific consistency of Rose's hair as he worked out her tangles. The specific sound of thickening water sloshing at his movements. The specific aroma of the specific dark-leafed plant he kept hanging in their bathroom. The specific hardness of the basin under his tailbone. He was comfortable here.

Like washing away the stressors of life. Covering up, if just for a moment, the sound of the dead man's weeping that crawled up the back of his neck.

He helped Rose sit back up, reaching over for a mortar and pestle sitting by the edge of the basin. He plucked a dark leaf from the plant above, grinding it with thick, round motions. Rose's leg bounced impatiently, but she didn't try to leave. There was a time not so long ago when Rose would have resisted this ritual. Gavin didn't like the fuss he'd had to make to get her to accept it. But some things were necessary.

Once ground, he took some of the fine, sticky powder from the mortar, coating it on the pads of his fingers. He held them up, wiggling them, grinning. "The Bugaboo's gonna getcha!" He reached for her hair, grabbing it with a gentle touch, working his fingers around to tickle her scalp. She laughed, flinching away, curling up from the tickling.

Her laughter bubbled into his chest, and he laughed too, as the powder on his fingers took to the wet strands, dark black color sticking, covering the subtle blondeness of her roots that had grown out since their previous dying session. Once done, he turned to Bloom, fingers stained black, holding them up like claws with a playful sneer on his face.

Bloom shrieked, sliding away from him on the basin's edge, holding his hands up. Gavin lunged forward, Bloom pinwheeled, almost falling in—

Gavin caught him, still laughing, and lowered him back into the water. He washed away the dark stain from his fingers, then began working out the tangles in Bloom's hair. It didn't take quite as long. Bloom had fine, short little locks that wanted to stick out in every direction, much to his chagrin. Gavin leaned him back up, ground a second leaf, and worked the dark color into every little sign of the boy's natural blondeness peeking through.

"There we go," Gavin said. "All ready for bed now!" He led them from the bathroom.

Rose sighed, craning her head up at him. "Do we have to sleep right away?"

He paused, reaching over to part two large leaves that hung down from separate plants, and looked out the window. The blue sun set on the line between the bog and the cerulean lake, reflected two-fold. On the left, the light died in dark slime. On the right, it shone beautifully, reflected in the soft waves of pure water.

His heart wilted, flower petals curling up inside him. "It's really late, Rosebud," he said. "The sun is setting."

She pouted. "Barely!"

He laughed, squatting down to her level, giving her hand a squeeze. "Look, Rosebud. I don't wanna keep you locked up. You go to sleep tonight, and come with me to the shop tomorrow morning. But then, while I'm working, you can do *whatever* you want. Go be a kid. Both of you. Play with Nell's daughter, beat people at Zvaloor, I don't care. As long as you're safe, I don't care. Okay?"

Rose's eyes went wide. She squealed in delight, jumping up and down. "ALL DAY??"

He laughed. "Until I close the shop for the night, yeah. All day. I promise."

"Yes yes yes!" She threw her arms around Gavin's neck, leaving the ground, hanging from him. "You're the best dad ever," she mumbled into his neck. He laughed, nearly falling backwards, hand going to her back. He stood up, letting her down.

"I don't know about that," he said, leading them into their bedroom. It was small and cramped, slanted roof coming down to the floor on one end, nearly too steep to accommodate the bed. Gavin had to duck. There was only one shelf, pushed up against the far wall, with a couple poorly sewn stuffed animals, a crooked wooden chest, and a few hand-bound books.

"True," Rose said as she climbed into the bed. "But you *would* be the best dad ever if you told us a bedtime story."

"That wasn't part of the—"

"I wanna hear the one about the man-eating plant lizard again!" Bloom exclaimed.

Gavin laughed. "I've told you that one at least five times already!" The way Bloom looked at him, eyes wide and pleading, melted his heart. "Alright, fine. *One* story. But you'd better not be yawning tomorrow. I can't let you guys run around on your own if you're too tired to escape the Bugaboo if it finds you."

Bloom and Rose crawled into bed. Gavin tucked the ratty furs under their shoulders, making sure they were snug and tight.

"Bubbles!" Bloom squealed, reaching out his hands. *Crrr-rooooooaaaak.* Gavin craned his neck up, smiling. A large light blue toad clung upside down to the roof, staring at them with wide little eyes. *Crooooaaaakkkk.* It hopped straight for Bloom. He caught the creature in his outstretched hands, pulling it into a slimy hug, laughing as it wriggled up into the warm space between the two kids, rooting around until it sat with large hind legs tucked up around its head. Rose and Bloom giggled, poking at it and petting it.

Croak. It sounded satisfied. Bloom and Rose looked at him

expectantly. He crouched at the edge of their bed, eyes drifting to their small round window, watching the faint ebbing of the sunset through the rain.

"Deep in the Zenithian swamp, there are all sorts of beasts that most would consider... terrifying," he lowered his voice. Bloom and Rose shivered, looking at each other with excitement. "One such beast is the Zar'thul, a massive, lumbering creature with vines for arms, rows of wicked thorns for teeth, and a twisted pollen tongue. All who see it run in fear. The Zar'thul comes out right when the Carrow Wolf moon nips at the Tuft Rabbit moon's tail, called to hunt by some forgotten primal urge. They feed on flesh, and blood, and once they catch your scent they will not stop for anything until they eat you!"

Bloom and Rose gasped, huddling in fear, eyes wide. Bloom hugged Bubbles tight. Gavin smiled.

"On one particular night, a young princess was lost in the woods. She had nothing but her wits about her, and her knowledge of the swamp. She was doing an amazing job, finding the few sources of fresh water, staying away from the sinkholes and grasping vines. But then she looked up. The Carrow Wolf and all his dark, curving teeth caught up to the Tuft Rabbit in the sky, and the world was bathed in purple."

Gavin started talking faster as the tension built.

"She knew what that meant. The Zar'thul would come out, and hungry it would be. She heard it lumbering, and saw its massive maw. She ran and ran, ducking under vines and hopping over sinkholes, terrified, but confident in what she knew. You see, there are these algae covered ponds in the swamp, rare and hard to notice. But the princess was cunning. She saw one, and dove underneath, knowing that these particular ponds had pockets of air trapped deep beneath their scum, where creatures could breathe, and hide from predators up above. She crouched down there, breathing the limited air beneath the pond all night as the Carrow Wolf devoured the Tuft Rabbit in the sky, as the Zar'thul stomped and hissed above, unable to find her. Her stomach rumbled with hunger, her mouth parched with thirst, but she knew... she knew that all she had to do was wait. Wait for the Carrow Wolf to finish his meal."

Bloom and Rose breathed low and steady, the sound of near sleep. Gavin stood up, looking down at them. So peaceful. The rise and fall of their shoulders cozy and calm. He continued in a whisper.

"But when she thought it was safe and emerged from her hiding place, the Zar'thul was still there. Its maw was shut, its vine-like arms curled up around its torso. It looked at her, and she looked back. The thorns that served as teeth, they didn't look so vicious. The tongue of pollen, not quite so thirsty for blood. And as it walked up towards her, despite its horrifying visage... she didn't run. She raised a hand, and gave its oblong maw a pat, and smiled, because she knew the Devouring of the Tuft Rabbit Moon had concluded in the sky, and so the Zar'-thul was safe."

Rose let out a subtle snore, one of her hands tucked under the warmth of Bubbles' belly.

"And that's the story of why the swamp is not your enemy," Gavin breathed. "Nor is it your friend. It is a force of nature. A brilliant wonder. A thing to be respected, and admired, and understood. Because if you do, maybe it won't be so vicious."

He brushed the hair from Rose's cheek, and pulled the fur tighter around Bloom's neck.

"Sleep well, my Raindrops."

He stood, stepping quietly from their room, shooting one last glance over his shoulder before shutting the door with the barest of clicks. He made his way across the darkened room, picking his way through the chaos of plants and shelves, ducking into the bathroom. He washed his own hair in the still full

12

basin, with far less care than he had given his children. He ground another leaf, and rubbed in the powder, staring at himself in his reflection in the water. Dark pits sagged beneath his eyes from lack of sleep. His hair hung, dyed black, in unkempt curls that hugged his eyebrows and hid his ears. His beard grew curled and tangled and annoyingly blond. He pulled a narrow drawer open from the wall, which had previously been seamless and hidden, withdrawing a knife. He used it to slice free his beard, hands slow and steady. He only nicked himself a few times.

His reflection stared back at him through the hair-water mixture now in the basin. The shaving job was horrid. Uneven, not quite shaved to the skin. But at least it wasn't obviously blond. He tucked the knife away in the drawer, pulled the drain on the basin, flipped the rainwater shutter closed, and left the bathroom.

He grabbed a wide topped clay pot, hefting it under his arm, heading for the back door. He ducked through it, free hand on a beam that supported the roof to keep him steady. A small lip sheltered him from the rain.

The tiny back patio overlooked a long stretch of the lake, running lengthwise and not quite straight between his home and the swamp. He smiled at the dark tangle of branches. Wyllinic bugs hummed the melody of twilight. Rain pattered through the wooden rain chains hanging at the corners of the roof.

He turned, looking along the outside wall of the house. A row of Isingrass grew in boxy planter pots, balanced on the narrow deck. Droplets of rain fell at even intervals through careful carvings along the outside wall, carried down from the roof to keep up consistent irrigation.

The grass itself was yellow-green, each stalk starting thick, before splitting into a thousand hair-thin strands at the top.

Within the split-ends sat little pods, brown and hairy, at various stages of growth. Gavin leaned out along the line of grass, hands carefully turning over the pods. Those ready for harvest had a particular swelling to them, as if meaning to burst, coupled with a darkening to their undersides. He picked those that were ready, tapping them gently against his elbow until small fissure cracks formed, before dropping them in the pot. He returned indoors, grabbed a cloak, and threw it over himself, flicking up the hood. With a final glance, and a half-veiled smile to his children's door, he stepped outside.

The night air was crisp. He breathed in the smell of rain. Natural. Comforting. It smothered him, in the way a parent's embrace reduced the world to a pinprick, and whispered that the blindness of peace didn't conceal the horrors he feared that it did.

The sounds of a dying man's weeping crawled out of his ears to disagree with the night air.

His three-fingered hand gripped the rafter that stretched from his wall to the overhang above his front deck. The deck dropped off in front of him, without a railing. Below lay the cerulean waters of Lake Vithim, deep color fading to a pale white as the Tuft Rabbit Moon rose to replace the sun. The space between buildings was left clear and open, roads of empty water sparkling with raindrops. He turned from those roads, looking instead to the boards which balanced precariously over the gaps. He took careful steps along those, huddling in his cloak as the raindrops pattered the fabric.

It would have been slow going, to traverse these makeshift bridges, tucking himself up beside buildings, working his way around the roads the long way, all while clutching a heavy pot of Isingrass pods under one arm. But Gavin's feet were practiced from thousands of journeys. They knew where the boards would creak, and avoided those spots.

"Gavin?" A heavy voice called up from the side, cutting the rain. "S'that you?"

He turned. Someone walked along the water-road. The water rippled around his feet in concentric hexagons, interrupting the pattern of raindrops. The hexagons followed his steps, expanding until they faded into the chaos of the falling raindrops. "Nell?" He called back. The man had no hood, his heavy brown beard curling with a bright smile, his usually frizzy hair tamped down by rain.

"Get down here!" Nell called, jogging over and reaching up a hand. Gavin took it, a wan smile warming his features at the kindness. He stumbled down, close to Nell, making sure to keep his feet on the inside of the rippling hexagons. Nell knelt, putting his palm to the water's surface. The hexagons pushed outwards against the natural ripples of the rain, giving Gavin ample room to stand. The slight rise and fall as each hexagon passed beneath his feet made him a bit queasy.

"It's no time to be without a Standwave," Nell said, walking with him down the water road. Gavin measured his steps to keep pace, careful not to take a step off the patterned ripples. Walking on someone else's Standwave always felt like riding on a raft that didn't carry him along with it.

"It never is."

"Aye. I'm surprised you don't slip."

Gavin laughed. "I never do."

They walked in silence for a few steps.

"How is it you never get tired?"

"Hm?"

"With two kids. My one has me feeling like the Tuft Rabbit after a Devouring. Ha!"

Gavin chuckled with him. "Who says I don't get tired?"

"You never look it!"

They took a slight turn, walking at a new angle between the

houses. There weren't exactly clear-cut roads in the village. Not in the same way bigger cities to the west would have them. Instead, each building simply sat above the water, and sometimes the buildings formed straight lines, and other times the gaps turned this way and that, splitting in every possible direction, or coming to dead ends. The townsfolk knew where they walked, and Gavin didn't have to ask where Nell was going, any more than Nell had to ask him.

"Moons forbid I ever find out what it feels like to 'look tired,' then." He grinned sidelong at his companion. "I've just never been *not* tired enough to give you a comparison."

"Suppose you're right," he replied. "But nah. I don't buy it. You love those kids too damn much."

Gavin laughed under his breath. "There's the trick, Nell. At the end of the day, when I can barely walk, and the Carrow Wolf's got me in the ass, I just feel satisfied. Another day they got to smile, and laugh. Another day they're happy. I've been where I can't afford to be tired. I'll take tired every time."

They walked in companionable silence. The houses around them grew more sparse, making way for more and more open water. Gavin's eyes darted to each nearest deck of wood, his mouth going just the tiniest bit dry. The Standwaves pulsed beneath his feet. Out, to a fizzle. Out, to a fizzle. Out, to a fizzle...

"I like that," Nell said. "I'll take tired, too. It's worth it."

"It's worth it," Gavin echoed. His thumb stretched over the space where his fingers should be. He could feel the bones, pressing up against the thin layer of flesh that had grown to cover his wound. Uneven. It had been an uneven cut. "It's worth it."

A clearing opened before them as they reached the village marketplace. Vendors packed up for the night, sliding lids into boxes, pulling leaf-curtains around to cover their stall windows. Lights played in the water, faint glowing colors waffling up from concentric parallelogram ripples around the fronts of the stalls. Gavin watched one woman, heavyset, hair pulled back and covered by a wide hood, kneel to touch a faint blue glow coming from the water. The parallelograms collapsed towards her hand, and the water stopped glowing.

Nell and Gavin made their way around the marketplace, heading for a large building at its end. The largest building around. While the other buildings weathered the weather, this building imbibed it, taking in the rainfall and scattering the droplets across a scale-like pattern of carved shingles. The water seemed to dance as it cascaded through, reaching a row of ten wooden rain chains that flanked the entryway, and spiraling its way down to send little ripples through the lake.

"Might Nona be free of her chores tomorrow?"

"Aye, she could be," Nell said. "If she's given an exciting enough reason to finish 'em early."

"I suppose that's for her to judge," Gavin chuckled. "I promised my kids they'd get to play tomorrow. It's about time they had a day off. Between helping Dezma wait tables, and helping me around the shop, they've been a busy bunch. I thought maybe they could run around with Nona for the afternoon."

They stepped between the rain chains, and Nell pushed open the door. "Aye," he said. "She'd like that, I think. I'll see what I can finish extra on my own, to help free her up."

"No need to take on more work to your shoulders," Gavin said. The percolating aroma of warm stew rushed across his face, soft murmur of voices twisting between the crackling of a merry fire. Above the subtle din rose an upbeat melody, plucked free from a lyre.

"Ha!" Nell guffawed. "We both know you're doing twice the work in the shop without them. Can't imagine running that place with only a hand and a half."

"Gav!" Dezma, the tavernkeep, waved from behind the bar.

Her grin stretched across her wide face, rendering her well-muscled stature warm and welcoming.

"Hey Dez," he called with a grin.

"He's here?" Another voice called.

"Oh, thank the Moons!"

"He's here! He's here! He's here!" The chant echoed from voices all around, as people raised their glasses above their heads.

He laughed, shouldering past pats on the back and loud hurrahs to reach the bar.

"I ran out of Isingrass earlier this evening," Dezma said. "Tell me you have some, or they might cook me into the stew and serve me for dinner."

He slid the pot over the counter. "Fresh as they get," he hopped up on a stool.

"Rinna still at it?" Nell asked, craning his head through the crowd. Gavin followed his gaze, as the crowd cheered and clapped with the ending of a song. Seaglass clinked, glasses raised. He could just make out two women embracing in a side hug at the far end of the room, before bowing to the audience.

"Goin' late today," Nell muttered.

Dezma chuckled. "Way you talk about her, I'd say you were still working up the courage to tell her you think she's pretty."

"Aye," Nell grinned. "Still am."

A faint smile came to Gavin's lips, even as that whisper of the dead man's weeping echoing in the rain outside worked its ugly fingers deeper.

"Better do it soon," Dezma said, with an air of gravity. "Fifteen years and a kid don't make up for kind words."

Nell's grin widened. "Half the town tells her every time she plays a song. Can't let her head get too big."

Dezma snorted. She hefted the clay pot onto the right half of a double-basin scale, adding small round stones until it balanced out. It took twelve stones. "Nine stones," Dezma nodded.

"Not bad."

Gavin nodded, smiling. Three stones had been subtracted, to account for the weight of the pot. Dezma pulled a bag up from under the counter, counting out four green Seaglass scales and one purple, sliding them over to Gavin. He pocketed them.

"Isingrass tea refills in five!" Dezma shouted over the din. "I'm only making one more batch!"

"And thank the Moons for that!" Someone shouted.

"Aye!" The crowd echoed.

Gavin laughed. "Keep making your tea and you'll be able to buy the kingdom."

She turned to a large basin beside her, behind the counter. Reaching up to the wall, she cranked a lever, which shifted open a shutter on the roof. Water trickled through, making its way down into the large basin. "If only it were for sale," she grunted, reaching into the clay pot and withdrawing a couple Isingrass pods. "Maybe if I give Cindeere some tea, he'll stop trying to conquer us."

"Aye," Nell said, still watching the performance across the room, elbow up on the counter. "It'd be more than anyone else is doing about him. They say his armies run as far east as the Saxtile passage."

Gavin puffed his cheeks out, raising his eyebrows. "That far?"

A new song started up, raucous and cheerful. Feet thumped on the ground, in perfect rhythm despite the chaotic, drunken huddle of the audience.

"It's no night for all that worrying," Dezma said, throwing the Isingrass pods in the half full basin. They floated, drifting around in the current formed by the incoming water. Once it neared the top, she cranked the lever back, shutting the flow. The surface of the water flickered with tiny circles at her touch, rippling outwards and snapping over top one another. The water started bubbling, then steaming. She reached back for another Isingrass pod. "Though I do have to ask—you have any extra Alimin, Gav?"

He frowned, raising his eyes to the sloped interior of the roof. Long logs set in triangular beams kept it aloft. Gray logs, thick and sturdy. Those would be Grendlewood logs. There were only a couple Grendles left in the swamp—five he could think of. He was sad to see Grendlewood used for support beams. Grendles were massive and beautiful, with roots so large you could crawl through their insides, look up at the trunk and watch as veins pumped nutrients into the leaves. He blinked.

"I should, yeah," Gavin said. "Vargus giving you trouble?"

"Not so much yet," Dezma said. She tossed another pod in her cauldron, and tapped the surface of the boiling water. The ripples shifted, pulling the edges of the circles until little concentric stars filled the bubbling, boiling water. The Isingrass pods released a faint pink hew, which danced along the star-shaped ripples. "But the Silverscales should be swimming through next cycle, and you know how Vargus are when I have meat in the pantry."

"Aye, and I've got extra nets this year, we're planning a big haul."

Gavin nodded. "I can bring some tomorrow. Never can be too careful."

"Last thing I need is to lose a finger right before the Full Festival," Dezma said, grinning and raising an eye down at Gavin's hand.

That deathly sound on the back of his neck crawled its way down his shirt, across his spine. He shifted in his seat, shrugging his shoulders. He chuckled, trying to scare the sound away. It didn't work. "They'll eat it, too," he said. "Heartless little bastards. Love them though. Have you seen the way they help each other up across crevices? It's quite ingenious—"

The tavern doors banged open. Gavin jumped, the sound of the rain's weeping overwhelming him, his hands going clammy, goosebumps rising. Not a single other head turned. Voices kept rising and falling. Dezma chuckled under her breath.

"Never change, Gav. Never change." But as she looked up from him, her face darkened. The corners of her lips turned inward. Her shoulders stiffened. A wave of silence rippled through the tavern, emanating from the door, until even the music faded into silence.

Gavin's eyes followed Dezma's. A woman walked towards the counter, cloak hanging heavy, dripping with rainwater. A bow and quiver of arrows hung over her shoulder. She threw back her hood, the ends of her hair waterlogged, hanging down around her neck. She had wide, dark eyebrows, and a small face, with small purple eyes.

Her expression stormed like the clouds. "A hundred troops," she called out. "Marching towards us."

Voices buzzed to life, worried, as people shot looks back and forth.

"What do they want with us!"

"Cindeere? He's this far east?"

"How many?"

"Let's send 'em packing!"

"Who's the—"

"How do you—"

"Shut up, all of you!" Dezma shouted over the din, coating the room in a ringing silence. "Let Mourra speak. Here," she grabbed a mug from the shelf to her side, leaning down, sniffing the pot of Isingrass tea, before dipping the cup in and scooping it full. She handed it to Mourra, who smiled at her, clutching it in both hands, closing her eyes, taking a deep whiff.

"It's not Cindeere," Mourra said. "They fly the banner of King Arnall."

A bit of a twinge entered Gavin's chest. He thought of Bloom and Rose, cuddled up in bed. The sound surged on the back of his neck. His fingertips tasted the stale remnants of Twitillic sap, as if it still coated them, still stuck his thumb against his palm, still dripped through the space between the uneven stubs on his right hand. He got to his feet, slow and shaky. *Everything is okay,* he told himself. *Nothing to worry about...*

"Bitin' Moon curse those scabbers!" Nell grunted from the bar. *Scabbers.* Gavin swallowed down bile. Kingsmen deserved the slur, but if Nell antagonized them too much, if he gave them too much of a reason to interfere in the town... "What're they doin' this far east of the war?"

"I don't know that they're normal scabbers," Mourra said, taking another sip of her tea. "There's no reason for them to be this far east. But all the same... They'll get here as the Carrow Wolf rises."

The most alarming silences didn't just mark the absence of sound. They *buzzed*, like a Swamp Hound waiting to strike.

"What'll we do?" A voice called from the crowd. A heavy face, with dark stubble, a bit of grease staining his torn collar. "I've got three little ones at home, I-I can't let them get mixed up in all this—"

Dezma raised her hands, and all the eyes turned to her. "Nell and I will go speak with them as they arrive. It's just a couple pompous idiots with a flag. We'll figure this out."

Nervous laughter sifted through the room.

"Besides," she grinned. "Tea's ready. Drink your fill, and I expect a pile of Seaglass on my bar before I get back."

Dezma made for the exit, walking through the crowd. Gavin stumbled back as people moved forward to the basin behind the bar, dipping their mugs to refill. They did so now with tired arms and scared glances. Worried whispers took the room. Gavin slipped to the back door, pausing to listen at the cusp of the rain.

"What if you don't come back?"

Dezma chuckled, a dark noise from the back of her throat. "If I don't come back, then you've got your answer all the same."

She passed through the front doors. Gavin swallowed, and left through the back. The sound of the rain. It all depended on who listened.

Gavin listened, and heard only the weeping of a dead man as he ran back home to his children.

STANDWAVE

The Basal Tone of Standwaves solidifies water, allowing the user to walk across it. Standwaves are, for most Runecasters, second nature.

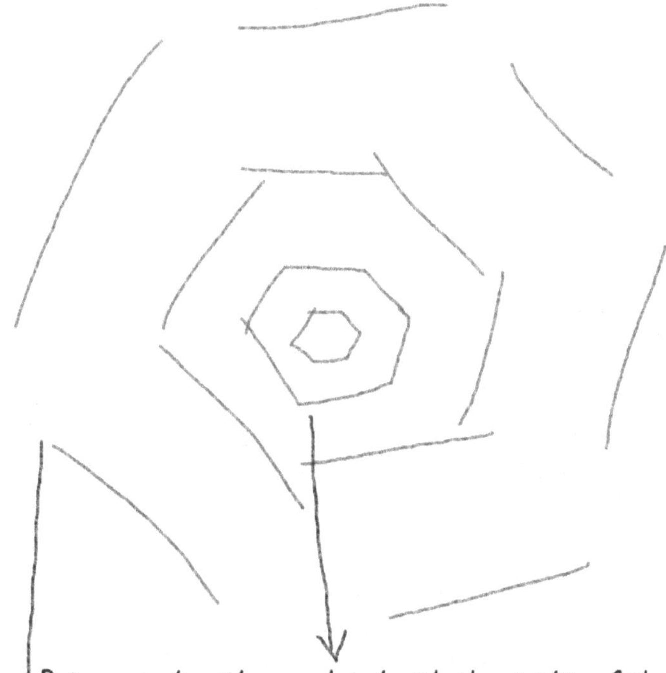

Potency is directly correlated with the rigidity of the runic shape. For Standwaves, that means hexagons.

As the Standwaves expand past regidity, the effect wanes.

Trained Runecasters should find it easy to maintain Standwave rigidity through hundreds or even thousands of ripples.

2

An empty lake made many noises. Obvious were the whispered hissings of the Wyllinic bugs, and the whistling of the wind. More subtle was the slight sloshing of water, and the shadowed crossbow snap of raindrops dripping to its surface.

Most would struggle to consider this sound. Those bugs, and their hissing. The wind, and it's whistling. Even the water, and its sloshing, or the rain, and its dropping. All if it could quite easily blend into silence...

Unless the empty lake had the right listener. Then a deeper quiet emerged. The quiet of the conversation the bugs were having with each other. The quiet of the song the wind was singing. The quiet of the dance the water was dancing to the beat the rain was playing. The empty lake made many noises, but in some respects the empty lake made one noise, of endless voi—

Thud. Thud. Thud. Thud. One hundred soldiers marched across the lake. Each step shocked the unstill surface, pulling the dancing ripples into one hundred rigid hexagons. *Thud. Thud. Thud. Thud.* The Standwaves drifted, fading patterns blurring together behind the uniform lines of soldiers, hanging in the water like a stain of grease in white clothing.

On the horizon before the company of soldiers, the Carrow Wolf Moon rose, hueing the word purple. Its crescent silhouette appeared as teeth, and at its center glowed a purple beacon, an eye that never left its prey. In the newborn light of the Hunter, the General held high a fist.

And with a final thud, the soldiers all fell still.

To someone with a good ear, the not-so-empty lake still sang with hidden music. The company of soldiers stood like a rock in the center of a half-full glass goblet with a wetted edge, and while it was true that the firm edges of the Standwaves at their feet suffocated any undue movement, the right listener might hear a new hardness in the lake's singing.

Lieutenant Stelli listened, and heard the weeping of her dead brother.

She stood in the line of soldiers, right behind her father; the General, the man who had raised his fist. Her height brought her no higher than his broad shoulders, though her chin-raised, back-stiff posture elevated her presence almost to match. She had her hair tied into a sharp braid that wrapped up into a bun, pulled so tight it angled her features, sharpening her nose and gaze, setting her mouth into a firm line. A Canine hung at her waist: a wicked white baton made of bone, its sharp pointed handle widening into a club-like base. It gleamed in the purple light of the rising moon. She stood there, still.

And she chose to keep listening to the sound of weeping. She narrowed her eyes, scanning the landscape. She heard the dark and menacing tangle of the Zenithian swamplands to her left, felt the leaves of the curled and broken Aycmor trees drooping, shaking, shivering against the jumps and drops and runnings of the rain and the wildlife. She heard the silence of the village that clung along the bog's edge, its buildings looming through the haze of hissing rainfall, wooden and twisted. Its very presence precluded a visit, dark demeanor weighing on the woman's eyes and ears. The water crested softly beyond the company's Stand-waves, and she watched the water dance. The rain punctured its dancing, playing the drumbeat of weeping like needles through flesh.

Out of the fog, the dancing water shifted into swirling hexagons beneath the feet of two shadowy figures who ghosted forward amidst the rain. The song of the lake helped them move, their Standwaves but another rhythm in the natural order.

Behind the Lieutenant, soldiers mumbled and shifted their stances.

"Be still," she breathed. "Even a nothing town like this one could hide our quarry."

One of the men spit into the water at his feet, its liquid subsumed into the pulsing pattern of his Standwave.

"Hold." The General said. As he spoke, a new pattern surged around the edges of his Standwaves: interlocking diamonds, unfolding like geometric flower petals in the water. The Echowaves caught his voice and amplified it across the lake.

He had a sort of regalness to him. His dark stubble cut his chin, and his graying hair rebelled against the falling rain, curling around his ears. He held a long staff in his hand, which jabbed against his Standwaves, and stood as tall as him. At the top, a hand-carved Carrow Wolf howled towards the sky, green paint smeared into a scar across its left eye.

The figures in the haze stopped their movement, features obscured by the darkness and rain. The leader had long dreads hanging down past her muscular, broad shoulders. She clutched a straight-edged Longtooth: a sinister and sharp polearm of bone, longer than she was tall. "We don't often see visitors," the woman called. "Let alone Kingsmen, so far from the King's Steppes, with the King's war nowhere in sight."

"My company is tired from a long march," called the man with the Carrow Staff. He continued the flickering of those diamonds in the water, casting Echowaves to take his effortless words and project them loud and menacing. "We invoke the right to quarter."

"We have few beds, and little enough food for ourselves," the woman hedged.

"We have no beds, and carry less food. As Kingsmen, we have the right to quarter. As peasants, you have the honor to host."

"And what guarantee do we have that you are Kingsmen? What is your name, General?"

Standing just behind him, she *felt* the bristling of his back, the sharpening of his posture.

"I am the General of Stillness, Hero of Sparrow's Ford, Savior of the Southlands, and Prime Runecaster of the Realm. My name belongs to King Arnall, but many call me The Wolf."

"And yet... General," she spoke the title as if it tasted sour in her mouth. "You're at least three Devourings from the Steppes, and further still from battle. I struggle to understand your reasons for needing quarter. It sounds like your predicament is your own doing, leading your company this far east without proper food stores, or knowledge of the area enough to gather."

The General stepped forward out of rank, raising his fist again to indicate he wasn't to be followed. A nervous energy bubbled inside Stelli's chest. Her eyes darted between the two hazy figures. The woman in front, armed with that wicked Longtooth. The man behind held some sort of long sharpened weapon, hard to make out in the haze of the rain. Her eyes flicked back to the General, tracking his movements. Her mind did little spasms, playing out scenarios in flashes—the woman attacking, the two of them surrounding, Boundwaves in the water, Slashwaves for his neck—

She quieted her worries. If the strangers attacked, her father would simply kill them.

The General brought his staff up under the leading woman's chin, lifting it to make her meet his eyes. She glared back at him. She had an impressive frame to her. Large muscular arms. Thin, firm mouth. She held her Longtooth with a calm, calculated ease. Despite the staff under her chin, and the General glaring down at her, she did not flinch.

A begrudging, savage respect bubbled in Stelli's gut.

"You don't need to threaten me," the leading woman said. "I know I can't refuse you. I know that you will take your quarter whether I agree or no. You will have your houses, and your food. But I also know that you Kingsmen care about your arbitrary reputations, and if you murdered a woman here in front of your company when she hadn't so much as lifted a finger, they would think you had lost control. So forgive me if I fail to muster adequate respect, knowing that—"

The General wrenched his staff to the side, cracking her in the shoulder. Again, not a flinch.

"At worst, you'll just give me a couple of bruises," she finished in a low voice that somehow carried across the entire field of soldiers. Stelli found that she couldn't take her eyes off the woman, even as she stepped to the side in an exaggerated bow, and swept her arm out to the village. "Your quarter, sir," she said. "Might I return to tell my neighbors of your plans, before you show up to toss them from their homes?"

The General shifted his foot forward and tapped the water at the edge of his Standwave. The edge of the hexagon rippled free, pushing past the bounds of its shape, twisting into concentric parallelograms that rippled out from a central anchor ripple. The anchor ripple *burned* with reflected purple moonlight, like fire flickering along a line of alcohol soaked cloth. As the General's eyes shifted up for the village, the light shifted forward, the anchor ripple pushing through the rain spattered waves away from him, illuminating the terrain. The ominous energy of the buildings faded like cobwebs at the touch of the light, their squat, hobbled demeanors flashing with the pathetic truth of their small, slanted, deteriorating selves.

The light faded thirty paces away from him, and the haze returned. "Give us those closest to the swamp," the General said.

"Make haste."

"I am sure battle hardened Kingsmen can manage if we don't," the woman shot back.

"Go," the General spat. And the figures faded back into the haze, walking as shadows amongst the rain filled air. "Lieutenants, your rounds."

Stelli turned from the village, moving amongst her ten soldier unit. Her hands shook with the slightest nip of cold as the rainwater brushed against the creases of her first finger and thumb, the only two of her fingers uncovered by her glove. She shook with something deeper, too. Something in the snap of the General's voice. She calmed as she got to work, and followed his order.

She knelt stiffly next to the first man in her unit. She grabbed the hem of the thick gambeson at his shin, wrenching it up to reveal his lower legs and ankles. A tight-strung shin-sheathe wrapped from calf to bridge, leaving the heel open and exposed. She felt along the cloth, checking the knots that kept it affixed, making sure no gaps of skin poked through, searching for the telltale red stains of chafed, broken skin. Seeing none, she jerked the gambeson cloth back down over his legs, and continued down the line.

"Hold your breath, York," she told the sixth person she checked, prodding around a dark red stain in the white fabric. The man tensed, his entire body going rigid, and starting to shake. She undid his knot, unwrapping the cloth as slowly as she could, yanking a little bit to make it detach from the congealed blood beneath. His skin pulled back, little strands clinging to the coarse cloth. It was right above the bump on his ankle, where a fold in the cloth scraped with each step, chafing the skin. She bunched up the cloth and held it beneath the wound, careful not to let even a single drop of blood fall into the water below. With her other hand, she reached into a pouch at her belt.

York muttered something under his breath. Stelli's eyes flicked up to his face. Clenched eyes. A tear, staining the corner of his chin. The skin of his cheeks curved unscarred in the pale moonlight.

Stelli ground a paste into her fingers, thick and sticky like mucus, and pressed it to his chafed skin. She felt his muscles tense, felt his involuntary intake of breath, as a little stifled sound of pain escaped the corners of his lips. The noise invaded her, sinking her stomach beneath the waves and trapping it there. She hated this part. But then it was done. The paste took to his wound, hissing as it melted his skin back over itself to stop the bleeding. He gasped even more when she pulled the cloth tight and wrapped it back up his leg.

Around the company, more stifled sucked in breaths and whimpers shifted between the tense, straight-backed soldiers. Stelli finished her rounds, checking every ankle and lower leg. She reached one woman in her unit in particular, and felt her insides squirming. Short cropped hair, slight frame. She carried no Canine, preferring instead a long, straight-bladed Dewclaw, along with a smaller hunting knife, both sheathed at her hip. Though her demeanor remained locked in just as professional a stance as any other, the faintest curl flitted across the corner of her lip. They came face to face, eyes meeting for a long silent moment, parted only by rain. *Tess.* Stelli's heart thumped upside down in her chest. She swallowed, and then knelt, reaching for the cuffs of Tess's gambeson, pulling them up, fingers probing the wrapped cloth, searching the bump in her ankle, the skin just above the wrapping. Nothing. Stelli puffed out a breath of relief as she stood up, turning back—

"Moons cursed waste of our time…" one of the soldiers muttered. It was Seban, head cocked to look sidelong at York, who wiped tears from his eyes. She could imagine his pain. Like a pair of glassblower's tongs gripping his skin, yanking it into place, and shoving it in a kiln until it hardened. It took *hours*.

"Seban," she whispered, pausing in her steps. Rain caught her cheeks and neck, trailing into her stiff gambeson. "Would you like to repeat that?"

"No, Lieutenant Stelli," he said, looking away, towards the village.

"Hm," stepping up to him, slow and deliberate. "But now I'm curious." Her eyes flicked briefly to the General as he paced down the line of soldiers. "What, exactly, is a waste of time?"

Seban raised his chin, though it quivered. "Nothing, Lieutenant Stelli. We can't afford to disrupt our ranks by allowing blood into our Runewaves."

She gripped his shoulder in a cold hand, lingering until he met her eyes. She gave him a firm nod. The General needn't know about Seban's affections for York, nor his outburst. He was loyal. Something in Seban's pained gaze softened as he understood her mercy. She turned back to face the front and clasped her hands behind her back just as the General approached their position in line.

The Carrow Wolf stalked forwards along the dome of the sky, its color beginning to swallow the smaller Tuft Rabbit, which whimpered at a slower pace. The Tuft Rabbit never impressed in the same way as the Carrow Wolf. It was small, and pale white, leaving little impression on the sky. But its tail drew eyes. Its tail stretched as far as it could hop, marking its journey, a gorgeous sparkling of star-like light.

Beautiful. And easy to track.

The General raised his hand, palm open this time, and one hundred feet once again beat against the dancing surface of the lake. They passed between the buildings, stringing out into a line to filter in along the empty water roads. The pale reflections of eyes shone between rickety wooden shutters. The swamp loomed larger in front of them, a backdrop to the village, dark trees catching glimmers of the Carrow Wolf's purple light, the reflection appearing to Stelli like eyes and teeth and claws in the haze. The hiss of the Wyllinic bugs became the sinister buzzing of a million tiny wings lurking in the bog.

And then she did see figures. Shifting shadows, naught but glimpses between buildings. The eyes glaring out between shutters became darkness, each crack in the splinter-filled windows empty, lifeless, motionless. Instead, her eyes locked onto hooded men and women and children, carrying their possessions away, giving the company a wide berth, abandoning their houses.

Nobody greeted them once the movement stilled. For a brief moment, one hundred soldiers stood in the silence of rainfall, near the humming of a swamp, flicking their eyes in nervous anticipation towards all the dark crevices of the swirling slime just paces from where they stood, noting the drooping fronds, the twisted trees, and the painful, unnerving stillness.

She felt that stillness in her bones, in the way that the houses *felt*, their lights inside extinguished, no signs of life save for the dying twirls of smoke that came from the odd chimney.

Even the smoke was beaten to stillness by the rain.

The General called out units, pointing them towards buildings, and away the soldiers marched. They stepped on the half-submerged, rotting boards that made up the first steps of creaking staircases leading from the lake to the buildings, reaching up to the rafters of the low hanging roofs to pull themselves free of the water. He pointed Stelli and her unit towards a group of houses a little further away. They trudged over, Standwaves rippling at their feet. A sturdy, wooden mudskiff bobbed in the gentle current beneath one of the houses, moored by a thick green vine. The woman with the Dewclaw at her belt, Tess, stepped towards that house, throwing Stelli a sidelong glance. Stelli gave her an imperceptible nod. She vanished inside the house above the rocking mudskiff. The other members of her unit moved away without so much as a grumble—

"Lieutenant Stelli!" The voice snapped the air, like the ending of a waterfall.

She tensed, turning to the General. Her father. "Yes, sir?"

"With me," and he strode away.

"Denetha, wavepit," she called out. "York, rest. Seban, share his quarter. The rest of you, run through the first forms before eating." Hopefully she would rejoin them in time to eat, but with the General, there was no guarantee. Her unit rushed to fulfill her request, a few of them stifling groans from their already relaxing muscles.

She caught up to the General, clasping her hands behind her back, falling into stride. Walking beside him drew out a strange sensation. Beneath her feet, the water flickered and toiled with the General's Standwaves, each of his steps looking more like stamps onto parchment than water, locking in the hexagons, dissolving any wayward ripples that might have been in the way. Indeed, Stelli's own Standwaves that she projected with each step were challenged, rolled over by the force of the General's hexagons, forcing her to stay close to him, to rely on his Standwaves, lest she fall into the water.

The drum that she kept beating in the back of her mind faded with the leaving of her Standwaves. That's really what it felt like. A *drum*. As if the back of her head, the inside of her head, were the palm of her hand, the water the taut surface of her mental instrument. It rubbed the inside of her head raw, gave it blisters. But it made beautiful and useful music beneath her feet. In some ways, she supposed, it was a relief to stand beside the General and need only his Standwaves to walk.

But her body could not relax. Her shoulders couldn't slump. Her mind rushed, and her heart refused to slow. She kept her eyes trained on the General's every movement, his very presence raising the tiny hairs of her arms and drying her throat, because she knew him. He never wasted an opportunity to test her, and she would not be found disappointing. Not to him.

They came to the edge of the pure water. Three steps in front of them, the first striations of dark blue slime twisted between long drooping fronds that skipped just above the murk, sometimes half submerged. The song of the swamp buzzed loud now, eclipsing the sound of rain. She could hear a faint croaking, overlapped with the buzzing, and the creaking. It sounded like the murmured call of a cliffside. The tempting crackle of an open fire near fingertips. The seductive flirtations of the void.

Her father spun and swung his staff.

She leapt away and leaned back, the staff passing just above her chin. She began the beating of the drum before she had even landed, pushing out Standwaves from her feet and skipping away on her back foot as the second swing came her way. She struggled with the Canine at her waist, ducking a third swing from the staff as the General pressed forward.

The fourth swing she caught on her Canine. The song of the swamp snapped with the clacking of wood on bone. She shoved the blow to the side, skipping another half step back, Canine held, guarding, warding. He stared, impassive, his heavy eyebrows scrunched in focus. He shifted left, and she shifted right. No anger infused his posture. Just calm calculation. His staff had much longer reach than her Canine. About double. And beyond that, his arms were longer than hers, though that mattered less while he gripped the staff in both hands, as he had for all the strikes so far. His legs stood in a striking stance, spread apart, ready to lunge or retreat at a moment's notice. Hexagons emanated from where each foot touched the water. She had to keep an eye on those. One lunge, and he could shift his patterns, trick her with Boundwaves, or catch her off guard with Slashwaves—

He lunged again, staff swinging high. She jumped back—

Her foot caught on the raised ripple at the edge of her own Standwaves, ankle twisting with the awkward elevation, her form shattering. The General pressed, staff slamming for her weaker side. She twisted, swinging her Canine for the deflection—

He spun the staff the other way, predicting her motion, and—CRACK. She tumbled to the water, hands and feet now both casting Standwaves to hold her weight. She squeezed her hands to fists against the hardened water's surface, feeling the tickle of a multi-pronged leaf against her palm. Her side smarted. Stupid. *Stupid.* A skilled Runecaster never kept her Standwaves going when she leapt.

She shoved her fists against the water's surface, pushed herself to her feet, picked up her Canine, stumbled, righted, raised her head, and stared at the General. He looked down at her, staff at his side, a slight frown on his lips. The tips of his dark hair stained with gray. His nose looked like a melting blister. She grit her teeth, hand squeezing against the Canine until her knuckles went white.

"Again," she growled.

"Tell me," he whispered, turning away from her to look at the swamp. "What you thought of the woman who welcomed us to the village."

She squeezed her eyes shut, sucking in deep breaths, fighting down the strange sensation in her throat. The strange sensation that came from standing so close to him. The strange sensation of all the pain and effort in the back of her mind washing away, as his Standwaves pushed under her feet, and held her above the water. She swallowed, eyes flickering open, a bit of heat rising on the side of her neck. Stelli had examined that woman quite closely. She hadn't been able to take her eyes off that woman. The General must have noticed somehow. He always noticed.

"I respect her," Stelli said, forcing a neutral expression. The Canine twitched in her right hand. She wanted to swing it, while he was talking. She *itched* to swing it. To see if she could catch him off guard for once.

A grunt. "Good. And the town?"

"Too many of my unit have already dismissed it," she whispered. "So far out of the way. Absent from half of our maps. They think we're chasing a tail that has no moon, that this hunt will bring us nothing. But..."

The song of the swamp buzzed above the rain.

"If I were hiding, this is where I would hide."

This time, *she* swung. She swung as he nodded, as he looked away. Her Canine whizzed in the air, straight for his chin. He ducked and spun, twirling his staff to catch her second blow, deflecting it, carrying her momentum to the side, spinning to crack her in the back and send her to the water—

She ducked, rolling with her Standwaves, using her body to cover the water as she did so. In the back of her mind, a rhythm danced. Subtle, strong, solid, like the rhythmic beating of a drum. Consistent. Hexagonal. She slammed her mind into the center of the rhythm and tugged the corners of that hexagon, rounding them and wrenching it inwards—

She came to her feet soaked but standing. The General lunged with his dominant foot, pressing the attack. Stelli stepped back, out of his measure, the blow whistling the air and spiraling back the few strands of loose hair that had fallen free of her tight braid.

But it didn't connect. A smile spread to the corner of her lip.

The General looked down at the water. A new pattern stamped the water, circles rippling in towards his feet, over and over again. As if a rock had been dropped in the water, yet instead of casting its ripples out and away, it pulled its ripples towards itself. He growled. She lunged now, his legs unmovable pillars, locked by the Boundwaves she had hidden under her roll. She struck for the neck, converted the strike into a jab to the gut, and when he dropped his hand to catch it, she spun the Canine, fell to the back foot and raised the weapon because his one-handed counter was aimed for her head—CRACK, she blocked his staff.

It nearly staggered her. Moons, his strength was impenetrable, despite his old age, despite his bound feet, despite swinging with one arm. She grit her teeth and stared him in the eyes. A small growl emanated from deep in her throat. A redness surged inside as her muscles strained in the bind, legs supporting back supporting arms.

She pretended to bend a little as he brought his second hand up, pressing down on her, using his extra height and weight to dominate, even if he couldn't take a step—

But he overcommitted. She felt the moment he leaned into it, expecting to break her. Felt the moment the scales tipped entirely in his favor. And she didn't try to resist. She tilted her Canine, allowing his full pressure to snap free, crashing out of the bind and off the Standwaves to her side. The moment the weight left her she *lunged*, swinging as hard as she could, inside his guard, exploiting the fact that he couldn't leap back out of her short reach—

CRACK. Her Canine slammed into the side of his jaw.

She stumbled back, breathing heavily. He stayed in his position, head to the side, looking down. She grinned, leaping forward to swing for his neck. He caught it, arm outstretched, the bone of her Canine vibrating in the air.

He chuckled, deep in his throat. "Well done."

Warmth filled her. She smiled, letting out a surprised breath. She'd—

WHAM. His knee hit her gut. Bile rose in her throat as she doubled over, stumbling backwards, Canine dropping from stiff fingers. Her bleary gaze fell to the water.

A single burst of ink-like blood streaked the water, catching the punctures of the rain, spiraling with unseen currents. It *wormed* its way through her Boundwaves, catching along the lines of her pattern like they were veins, pulling it apart like an insidious spider destroying its own web. The General rolled to the side, giving himself time to recreate Standwaves on a patch of water untouched by the blood, coming back to his feet. He looked up at her, and she saw her mistake. A bit of blood, dribbling down the side of his chin.

He licked it off before it could fall into the water at his feet, and then spit at her, swinging his staff at her legs—CRACK. The world tumbled as she tipped and whirled down. She shoved a hand down towards the water, that far off drumming in the back of her head her last chance to stay above. The Standwaves formed beneath her in a flash, but even as the patterns formed, the blood the General had spit pulled them apart—

And she fell right through. Frigid water shocked her breath free. She couldn't breathe. She couldn't. Breathe. Mud gripped her right shoulder and hand like fingers; the coarse water rushed around her, spiraling through her ears, into her nose, across her eyes. She flashed out her hands, dragging herself up until her head broke the surface, her braid a heavy weight across her back. She spluttered and gasped for breath. Her father stood over her, far enough back that the blood he had spit into the water didn't infuse his own Standwaves. Just hers.

"I'm glad you made that mistake," he whispered. "Many Runecaster's never learn, until it is too late. But now you know. Blood is as much a weapon as it is something to be feared. Never make an opponent bleed, unless you are ready to kill them."

He turned and stalked away, leaving her to thrash in the water. She stroked away from the spiraling blood and slammed her hand down on the water to cast new Standwaves. This time, the hexagonal crests proved helpful, giving her a solid handhold with which to lift herself.

Once standing, she kicked the ripples, uncaring for how the hardness of them dug into her bare foot. Stupid things. Her ankle pulsed with pain where it had twisted. She felt along her sides, pressing lightly on the tender skin around her ribs.

She grabbed her Canine out of the water. She dripped onto her Standwaves. The droplets stayed somehow separate from the water beneath, puddling atop the puddle. As she turned and walked back towards the village, her Standwaves followed her steps, abandoning the water droplets to rejoin the lake.

She passed between the houses and into the village, forcing herself not to limp. Soft voices bristled between raindrops. Steam sifted into the air, soldiers warming their hands and feet in wavepits. Soft lights played from the water around the edges of houses, elegant, parallelogram Mirrorwaves casting a pleasant glow.

"Lieutenant!" Her unit came to attention as she arrived. She flicked her eyes to take in the four houses they had been assigned. Small. Slant-roofed. Moss coating the wood of the walls around the corners. Rain trickled to the corners of the roofs, falling through rain chains that dangled in the light breeze. The ramshackle walkways of wood between the houses seemed close to falling apart. And unnecessary. It brought a sour taste to her mouth.

She looked back to her unit. Eight members. One missing. Seban glanced her up and down, a worried frown on his lips. York couldn't quite meet her gaze. The others tactfully avoided staring at her right arm. Though the rain had washed free much of the mud, dirt coated her cloak, clinging between the cracks of her elbow and lower arm.

"At ease," she replied.

They all relaxed, sitting back down. They'd constructed a small wavepit—stones, arranged in a tight circle, to contain their Runewaves. It was offset from the center point between the houses. Judging by the darkness of the opaque water, she guessed it hadn't been shallow enough anywhere else. She approached, sitting amongst them, leaning forward to warm her hands...

Moons. No steam. She grit her teeth, slamming her hand into the water, stamping it with tiny, interlocking circles that sloshed it back and forth: Steamwaves. In moments, warmth bathed her hands and face. She closed her eyes, basking in the sensation.

"Sorry if it was because of me," Seban muttered after a long moment. "I thought he wouldn't be able to hear."

"I was not being disciplined." She didn't care to open her eyes and see their disbelieving looks. Her Steamwaves crackled with a pleasant sound that washed away the damned silence she was sure had taken the circle of soldiers. But silence had a nasty tendency to escalate. That bubbling built in her ears, *rushing* inside of her. The warmth on her hands and face burned, yet they shook as if freezing. She couldn't hear. She couldn't listen. Maybe the others were talking. Maybe they were talking about *her*. Talking about things they couldn't understand. They didn't live with this. They didn't live with this. *They didn't live with this.* She missed the soft, strange sensation of her father's Standwaves, washing away her own beneath her feet.

She stood up, shaking condensation from her hands. "Eat," she said. "Then sleep."

She stalked from the clearing, making her way to the house that had the mudskiff beneath it. She vaulted the distance up to its deck, reaching a hand to grab the moss covered lip of the roof, and slipping up to the door. She didn't turn around. No voices followed her.

But eyes did. Sometimes she couldn't care. She ducked through the low-hanging entryway. A strange smell assaulted her, floral and angry, a disgusting mesh of all things that grew.

She wrinkled her nose, glancing left and right at the hodge-podge of shelving. All the shelves had pots on them, balanced precariously, displaying the most eclectic assortment of flowers, herbs, strange vines, beansprouts, and half a dozen other things that Stelli couldn't even begin to recognize. The swing of the door felt weird. She moved it back and forth a bit, cocking her head at the vine twisting among the hinges. Dried leaf residue coated the floors, pushed into the corners, or crushed under feet. To her right, a door led to a corner room, the roof hardly leaving space for the bed and shelf shoved against the opposite wall. The room to her left looked like the bathroom, though Stelli couldn't imagine relieving herself in the archaic chamber pots, or bathing in the crude, stained basin.

She made for the middle door, tucked in next to the fireplace. Another tiny room. With another bed.

"Not out there with the others, Tess?" Stelli said, standing in the doorway. Tess glanced up. She looked small, without her cloak and gambison, and knives at her waist. The short hair and thin frame made her appear younger than she was.

"I can't bear to hear their conversations when you aren't around," she whispered.

Stelli frowned. "What do they say?"

The woman stood, pushing past Stelli and moving to a spot on the wall where two large, hanging leaves covered a small window. She pushed them aside, staring out at the unit. "They think the General is lying," Tess whispered. "Or to be more charitable, they think he is wrong. They don't believe we will ever find this man we hunt, no matter how many backwater villages we search. They don't believe he exists."

Rain sounded different from inside a home. The initial falling grabbed the wood like a knock, before the trickling soothed the hardness of the sound. "I wish they would talk to me about those things," she whispered.

Tess jerked her head around. "Me too. You could punish them."

They locked eyes for a long moment. Stelli looked away. "Yes. But also... I get it."

Tess kept staring at her. Her eyes drifted down along her muddied cloak and arm, lingering on her side, and then her ankle, before returning to her eyes.

"It hurts, Tess," she whispered. "I should hate him. I should hate him so much."

Tess stepped forward, grabbing Stelli by the shoulders. Her eyes somehow burned with intensity and smothered her with their softness all at the same time. "Stelli."

"I'm bruised in all the places that won't show," Stelli whispered. "And he calls it a lesson."

"Stelli—"

"I finally got a blow back on him today. My reward was the mud—"

"Stelli." Tess's hands squeezed so much it hurt.

"When I hit him," she hissed. "He said '*well done*'. All it took was two words, and I felt warm instead of angry. Moons, Tess, I *still* feel more warm than angry—"

"Stelli," Tess's gaze finally cut through. She blinked, focusing on the woman's thin face. Her voice was urgent and soft, like a knife reflecting the stars. "You can hate him. It's okay to hate him," she whispered. "You just can't let that hate make you forget why we're here. You haven't heard a child scream. Haven't seen a mother bludgeoned to death in her own home. If there is even the slimmest chance that the General is right about the man we hunt, if he truly has the gift to cast Runewaves through blood, the war will be over. Cindeere will *lose*. We could kill his entire army without so much as a second glance at the red water. You know that right? You haven't forgotten? I know it's easy to hate the General, and that's okay, but he is also *right*—"

The rain knocked hard on the roof. "It's okay," Stelli said, chin quivering. "I'm sorry I scared you. I don't hate him."

"It's okay if you do," Tess said.

"I don't hate him," Stelli shook her head. She wiped her eyes. "I don't."

"I'm glad you talked to me," Tess said with a small smile, cocking her head.

Stelli nodded, sucking in snot, taking a deep breath. "Yeah. It just gets hard sometimes."

Tess yanked her into a stiff hug, taking her breath. She froze, but the hug stole her posture, untensed her body, slumped her shoulders, relaxed her mind, and slowed her heart. She let her head bury into Tess's shoulder, let her eyes squeeze close.

"I've got you," Tess whispered. "I've got you right here. You don't have to be strong all the time. Only when he needs you to be, and that is *not* always, no matter how much it feels like it."

Stelli wept into her friend's neck, finding all the ways she could fit her body closer against Tess, seeking warmth in her every crevice. They stood there together for a long, long moment, alone and unobserved, save for the discerning gaze of a light blue toad which crouched upside-down in the shadowed rafters above them, and listened.

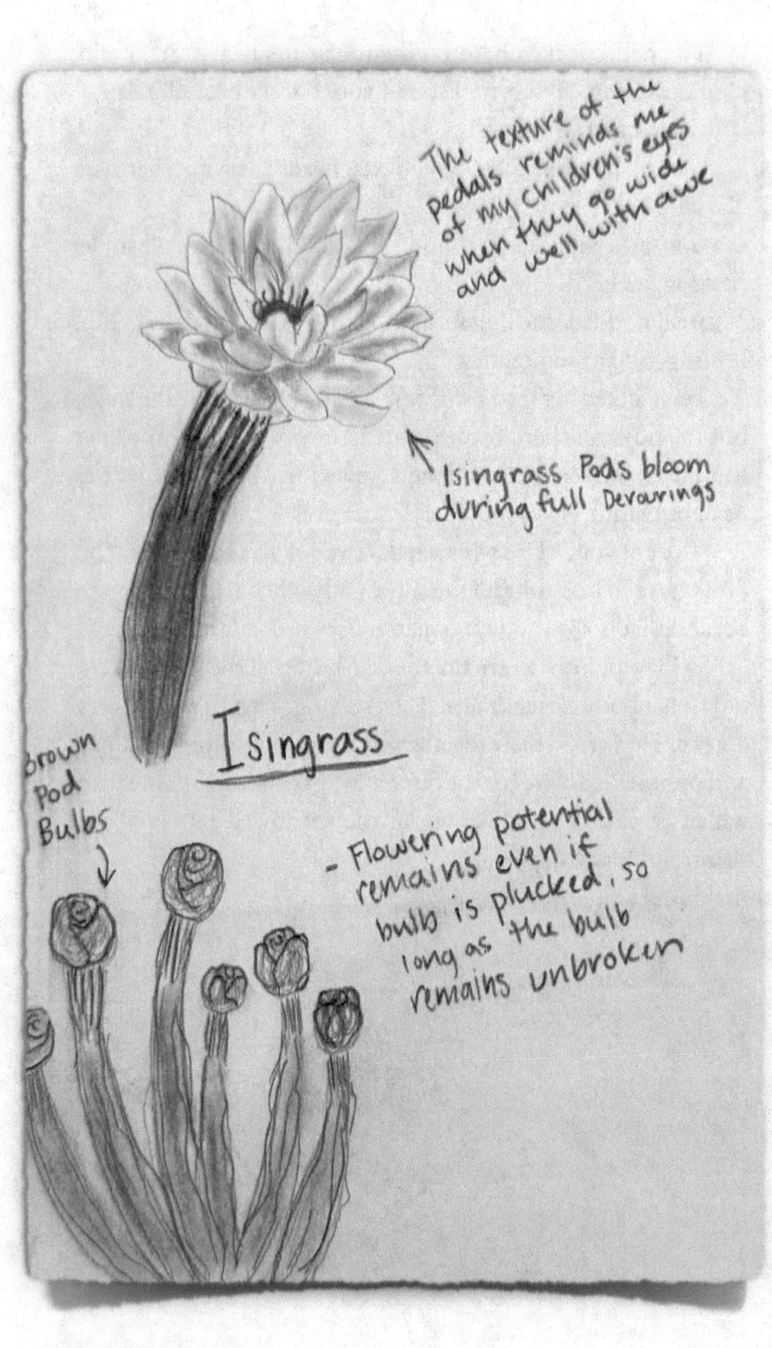

The texture of the pedals reminds me of my children's eyes when they go wide and well with awe
Isingrass Pods bloom during full Devaurings
Isingrass
Brown Pod Bulbs
- Flowering potential remains even if bulb is plucked, so long as the bulb remains unbroken

3

The sound of weeping only grew as the night went on. *Everything. Is. Fine.*

"Try and get some sleep, okay?" Gavin whispered to his kids where they lay in the corner of the quiet, suffocated interior of Dezma's tavern. He tucked them in with his cloak, leaving his arms bare and nipping with cold. They didn't have any more blankets. It would have to do.

"Da..." Bloom muttered, grabbing a corner of the cloak and pulling it up under his chin. "When can we go back to our house?"

"Soon," he whispered. "Soon. I promise. It's just some passing Kingsmen, they'll be gone soon, and everything will go back to normal."

"Do I still get to play tomorrow?" Rose's voice drifted, half asleep.

He smiled, though inside his heart withered, petals falling off and trailing to the pit of his stomach. "Yes, my Rosebud," he whispered. "All you want. Nona will be right here too. Think of this as a fun sleepover."

Rose murmured something, but the words were imperceptible. Her little cheek pressed into Bloom's shoulder as they snuggled into each other, wrapping the cloak as tight as they could. He smiled down at them for a long moment, before turning and looking around the room.

He needed the Moon's damned weeping to go away. It was

like an itch that always danced just out of his reach. He swallowed and stood up. Work. Something to take his mind off it. He needed something to take his mind off it.

The quiet voices of other parents calming their children played over the trickling of rainwater on the roof, and the dying crackles of the fireplace. Dezma's broad-shouldered shadow rushed around in the darkness, kneeling next to families, rushing to grab them warm bowls of soup that simmered above the coals, or make-shift blankets from her curtains and washrags. Gavin stepped between sleeping figures, careful to keep his footsteps quiet, intercepting Dezma as she returned to the bar.

"Hey," he whispered. She looked up at him. Her strong face drooped with dark bags, eyes bloodshot. "You need sleep."

"No more than the rest of them," she grunted, stepping past him, grabbing one of the last few bowls from her shelf behind the bar, ladling it full with a dwindling amount of soup in her cauldron. "Half the folks haven't had supper, and their food belongs to the King now." She turned, trying to go past him again. He grabbed her shoulder.

"Let me help," with his other hand, he took the bowl from her hand. She barely resisted. "Who needs it?"

"Visae," she muttered. "And Jerome, and Bregga, and the poor Maisa girl. The Vennilans don't have bedding. I still want to search the town, make sure no souls are without shelter—"

"No soul would think to sleep in the rain before knocking on your door, Dezma," he said. "You've done that work a thousand times before tonight. *Rest*. I'll handle it."

She stared at him for a long moment. Truth was, his own bones felt ready to break, his chest high strung, his heart wilted and congealed into a thorn so thick it felt fit to burst through his skin. But there was no way he was sleeping any time soon. So he smiled at Dezma, and she gave a small little smile in return. "Thank you," she muttered, and moved off.

He brought the soup to Visae, kneeling by his huddled figure, breathing soft words of encouragement. The older man smiled, expression warming through the chapped lips and downcast gaze. Gavin moved on. Jerome nodded at him, thanking him by name. Bregga looked terrified. She had a child, no more than twelve or thirteen Devourings past, clutched up under a privacy cloth, where she crouched against an overturned table that had been pushed against the wall to make room. She took the soup in one grateful hand, setting it gently on the ground beside her, rocking her child in a soft grip.

She bit her lip, looking up at Gavin. "Does... does everyone have warmth for sleep?"

He hesitated. "Not yet," he whispered. "One family is without, but I will find—"

"Take this," she held out the privacy cloth, revealing her young baby, feeding at her breast. She shook the cloth in the air, not quite meeting his eyes. "They need it more than me, I-I feel terribly selfish, I—"

Moisture prickled Gavin's eyes. He smiled, and kneeled next to her. "Bregga," he took her hand and pushed it back down towards her child. "Keep him warm," he whispered. "We all need him to be warm."

Tears filled Bregga's eyes now. She wrapped the child up again, hugging him close.

Gavin moved on. He had no time to linger, even if his thoughts buzzed. *The Vennilans have nothing...* he shook his head. Soup for the young Maisa girl. *Name... name...* He made his way to the family, huddled together, very awake in the corner. The girl was the youngest, around fifteen or sixteen. Old enough to understand the situation, not old enough to understand how to deal with it.

"Here you go, Jen," he remembered the moment he knelt at her side, handing her the soup. "Eat up. And," he glanced at the parents with a twinkle in his eyes. "Try and sleep. Mom and Dad would appreciate that."

They chuckled, and he moved off. Bedding. Bedding. Where to get bedding. If only he was at home; Gurrengie leaves made great blankets, if you could get past their smell. They were soft, and absorbed the warmth of the sun during the day—

His mind flashed to his shop, running a mental list of his inventory there. He *might* have Gurrengie leaves in the back room. They had some use for wrapping wounds, given their thickness and softness. His shop wasn't far. Just a few buildings over, right outside the town square. His hands shook. He'd have to go outside, risk... risk...

He found Nell near the center of the room, huddled with his wife. They had their heads together, whispering softly while their daughter, young Nona, slept curled against them.

"Nell," he whispered. "Rinna. Sorry to interrupt. Can I steal your husband for a moment?"

She cracked a tired smile. "Steal him for longer, before he convinces me to take up arms against our new house guests."

"I wouldn't *actually* do it, not on my own," Nell muttered.

"Come on," Gavin said, yanking Nell to his feet, taking him over closer to the bar, away from sleeping families. He grabbed Nell's thick, corded shoulder, giving it a squeeze. "I need your help."

"Aye," the man said. "I figured."

"The Vennilans don't have bedding," they looked together over at the family slumped in the far corner, three bodies packed together, heads turned inwards. "They're the last ones. We're out of ways to improvise here, no more washrags, or cloaks, or curtains."

"Aye..." Nell stroked his beard, staring at that shivering family. "We could set a watch of people with the ear for Runewaves to keep a Steamwave going at their sides for the night. Not a blanket, but'll keep 'em warm enough."

Gavin pursed his lips. A good option, that he hadn't considered. "If we can find people willing..." he trailed off. "My other thought, I have these plants at my shop—"

Nell chuckled. "Not sure if they would be keen to sleep under leaves, Gav."

But these are *warm* leaves!" He hissed. "Soft, too. We could tie a few together, make a nice blanket for them."

Nell glanced back at his wife and daughter, folding his arms, biting the corner of his lip. "Nay, look, I'll start the Steamwaves, and find someone to replace me when I tucker out."

Gavin rubbed his eyes, stifling a yawn. "Right, okay, if you're sure," he mumbled. "How is Nona?"

Nell squeezed his shoulder. "She's fine, Gav," he murmured. "Worry about yourself. You've done enough."

He grimaced. The weeping. If he tried to sleep, he would hear the weeping again. "Here I was saying that to Dez just a few minutes ago."

Nell raised his eyebrows. "Aye. You're a smart man." He shoved Gavin back, and moved to help the Vennilans. A few steps, and Gavin slumped down to the small patch of hardwood next to the sleeping forms of his children. Hardwood. It bit his back, his feet, unrelenting. Knotted and coarse. He put his hand down on it, chin shaking. Grendlewood. Used for the floor, too. It was, of course, the sturdiest wood to build a tavern from. To build any building from. He watched Bloom shift, snuggling closer to Rose. She snuffled. It brought a warbling smile to his lips. But the weeping whispered along the edges of that smile. It pulled at his lips, crawled into his mouth, and down his throat.

He reached into the breast pocket of his tunic. He pulled out a little drawing, done in a childish hand and smeared with fingerprints. The face was clear enough to make out: curled hair and bright eyes, even if they weren't exactly where they should be. Funny. He missed his wife, he did—the feeling was acute and sharp. More than missing her, though, the drawing made him miss Bloom and Rose. He gazed at their small sleeping forms through tear-streaked eyes and missed them. Because even though they were right here, he wasn't making them smile, hearing them laugh, feeling their little wriggly, wily selves tackle him to the floor. That absence echoed in the weeping of the dead man that curdled in the back of his mind. It told him that he would never hear his children laugh again.

The flower in his heart had deeper roots than his despair. He would always, always love his children more than he would fear losing them, and yet the more he loved them, the more he would fear losing them. So the flower's roots grew deeper, and his heart's pedicel forever unfolded new petals to wrench apart that despair and carve space for beauty. The Carrow Wolf Moon bled the world purple outside, pulling and tugging to rip the petals free. He bowed his head into his knees and shook with the force of infinite petals growing through infinite despair.

The tears fell. They caught in the straggled remnants of his beard, finding their way down to patter on the Grendle floor beneath him. His shoulders shook. He stifled the stiff sobs that wracked his body and threatened to burst him. The... the parchment the drawing was on, it was... was... *stripped Sweetleaf...* He squeezed himself tighter, shaking. *Take a Sweetleaf plant, pull gently on the base of the stem...* His teeth dug into his lip. *Gently, because you don't want to...* He pulled his head back, seeing the drawing through tear-stained vision. *Don't want to hurt the leaf...* the tears fell hot and thick now, as he tucked the drawing back in his breast pocket with shaking hands. He tried to wipe them away, but more came to replace them.

Around the room rose the stifled noises of other families sobbing too. Together, in the cacophonous silence of the dark tavern, the weeping sounded like rain.

* * *

"Hey," Gavin knelt next to Jen, who hunched in a corner, knees pulled up to her chest. Her parents had both left for the day, out to harvest in the Sliffitan swathes just around the side of the swamp. Though his eyes hung with leaden bags, and his shoulders and back ached from a fitful night of sleep, his mind felt sharper than it had the night before. Still, if he didn't talk, didn't move... He pushed it out of his mind. He remembered the Maisa family, including why the girl wouldn't be out in the fields with her parents and siblings. "How are you holding up?"

She grunted, and didn't turn towards him.

"Holding up enough to grunt at me, I'll take that." Behind him, the shrieks of children at play bent the air. It brought a smile to his face. Chaos and stress weighed heavy on the shoulders of adults, but tell the children to go wild, let them mess with furniture they've never before been allowed to move, and they would smile to no end. "Did you know I'm a Bloodfoot, too?"

That got her attention. She peered at him, with wide, curious eyes.

"Rhythms are all wrong in my head," he shrugged. "Truth be told, I can't even hold a Standwave."

"It's not such a deal," Jen said. "I'll manage someday. Ma's teaching me."

He sighed, settling down into a sitting position beside her, back to the wall. In the middle of the room, Bloom, Rose, and Nell's daughter crouched on either side of a pile of furniture they had constructed, throwing wads of bedding over before shrieking and ducking for cover. "And maybe you will. It's not impossible. But the water will always be stormier, for you and I."

"I never did nothing to upset the Moons. I been a good kid. Ma says the Carrow Wolf is testing me, seein' if I'm prey or not.

I'll show 'em. I'll show 'em I'm not prey."

Bloom stumbled over a chair leg as a big wadded curtain came flying towards him. His little eyes went wide, but he planted his feet, held up his hands, and *caught* it. Laughing, he ran at the barrier and leapt over it, whacking Nona with the curtains. She shrieked and ran around, his little legs chasing right behind her.

"There's a kind of rodent in the swamp that can't swim," Gavin whispered, watching his children play. "Her little paws aren't made for it. Her fur weighs her down. If she tried to swim, and I've no doubt that she could learn if she was forced, she would never be as quick as the critters who live in the water. A Snyrsnout would chomp her up."

"Huh?" Jen looked confused.

He smiled. "But this rodent—they're called Bounders, by the way—they *thrive* in the swamp. It's the best habitat for them. The trees are dense enough for them to leap from bough to bough. They've learned that the Cyril vines are natural snares, so they arranged them around the trees to catch birds and little lizards to eat. They're hunters! But not like the Flipped-clingers or the Snyrsnouts. They do it their own way, and because of it, they have one of the largest populations in the whole swamp."

"Are you sayin' I shouldn't try to learn Runewaves? Ma would kill me—"

Gavin shook his head. "Not necessarily. I'm saying the Moons gave us heavy fur and tiny paws. If we try to swim just like everyone else, we'll drown. But if we learn to leap, and use the Cyril vines to our advantage... what could stop us?"

Nell's daughter grabbed the curtains out of Bloom's hands, and the chase reversed. Rose hopped up and down at the side, cheering them on. Jen nodded, eyes distant. "I like that," she muttered. "What could stop us?"

He grinned. "Only one way to find out, right?"

She nodded, hesitating for an awkward moment, as if more words were lingering on her lips. "Thank you," she said, pushing herself to her feet. "Maybe I'll try that. See if I can compete with Da."

Gavin laughed. "Do it!"

She moved for the door. He watched her leave, thoughts abuzz. The Maisa family needed to be more like plants and animals. No matter how much an environment tried to blot out the sun, plants would always find the crevices they needed to climb in order to be illuminated. Funny how humans so often found ways to overthink their growth towards the sunlight.

He shook himself, standing. The floor of the tavern was littered with makeshift bedding, where families had slept. And would sleep again, tonight. And the night after. For however many more nights they were all forced to exist like this, suffering together in a single room. Nell had gone to trawl along the edge of the swamp for fish and small critters to fix for dinner. Most adults were out the same as him, doing what they could for the town in a time of chaos.

Gavin couldn't stomach the thought of going outside, though cold pinpricks took his skin. He missed the sun. He glanced out the front windows of the tavern. The marketplace bustled with soldiers going stall to stall. About half the normal vendors were still out there, wares hanging from wooden posts, cheerful calls and bright smiles strained by the militant nature of their customers. He tried to pick out any symbology on the soldier's vests or armaments. Tried to see if any carried banners. But through the narrow windows, in the packed bustle of bodies, his eyes detected nothing.

He tried to swallow down the sound of weeping on the back of his neck, and failed.

"Dad! Dad!" Bloom's feet clomped on the hard floor as he

ran up and slammed into Gavin's legs. "Dad!"

Gavin laughed, turning from the window, rustling his son's hair. "What is it?"

Bloom thrust his hand in the air, holding an Isingrass pod between his small fingers. "It fell off! Rose and I found it on the ground by the Isingrass."

"By the Isingrass? Where's Dezma hiding Isingrass in here, what've I been doing, bringing it to her all these Moons?"

"I dropped by your shop," Dezma called, poking her head out from the small storage room behind the bar. "We were running out."

"But *look* dad!" He waved the pod in his face. "It never falls off in our house!"

He took the pod, turning it over. "That's because Isingrass pods don't fall off their shoots!"

"But it did, it fell off!" Rose exclaimed. "Right Nona? It absolutely fell off." She puffed out her chest, nudging Nona in the side, who cocked her head up at Gavin and grinned, nodding.

"We'll see about that," Gavin said. "Show me where you found it. We've got a mystery on our hands!"

Bloom led him by his hand, scampering over to the back room where Dezma sorted jars and crates, taking inventory. Sure enough, by the side wall, about five clay basins of dirt-logged water harbored the tall, multi-stranded Isingrass plants. Behind him, in the entrance of the door, Rose and Nona scampered up to look in.

"Sorry to crowd your space, Dez—our big scary warden here says these Isingrass pods are trying to escape their cell."

Dezma cracked a smile, shifting to the side. "So he tells me."

Gavin knelt, and took the stalks between his fingers, using a light touch and feeling up the sides of the plant. The stalks didn't really *split* into hair-thin strands, he knew. They started that thin from the bottom; the strands were just held together by a complex root system, spurted up from the ground as one mass, before contact with the air allowed the individual strands to separate. He shook the top of the Isingrass stalk, watching the thousand little strands jostle together.

"I don't know guys!" Gavin said, voice teasing. "Isingrass pods don't just get up and hop away." He waited for a dramatic pause, then spun around, hands up in claws, face contorted. "Which one of you did it?" He hissed.

Bloom squealed, falling onto his back and dragging himself away. Rose giggled as Nona shrieked, jumping back, the noise dissolving into laughter.

He plodded forward in a squat, one foot at a time, claws up. "Who did it? I'll getcha!"

Bloom laughed, running back to Rose and Nona, hiding behind them.

"It wasn't us!" Rose squealed.

"Promise!" Nona said.

He plodded right up before them, glaring down at them, contorting his face—then dropped the posture, frowning. "Unless..." he held up the pod Bloom had given him, looking at it with wide, fascinated eyes. "You know, there are rumors about these pods... Dark rumors..."

"Woah!" Bloom tore away from Rose, grabbing for it. "I want one now!"

Gavin laughed. "I haven't even told you the rumors!"

"What are they?" Bloom cocked his head.

"I've heard they withhold a wild sort of beauty," he whispered, turning the pod over in his hand. He angled his face down, so the dim lighting of the windowless storage room cast his face in shadow. "And that in the light of the Tuft Rabbit's death, they bloom into a rose so beautiful that nobody can resist taking a whiff."

Bloom's face lit up. "Dad that's *SO COOL!* Can we see?"

Rose cocked her head. "But there's no Moons down here, Da, how could it have just fallen off?"

Gavin frowned. "That's a good point…" He threw his hands up in claws, looming over Bloom. "It must have been you!"

Bloom screeched.

"Or one of you!" He pounced towards Rose and Nona, who fell backwards in a tangle of limbs, laughing.

"But," he turned back to Bloom. "I *could* show you… Dez, the next Full Devouring is, what, a couple nights away?"

"Something like that," she said, scribbling something on a parchment, with a long feather quill. He recognized the feather. It came from a migrating Eerie, which nested in the north.

"Tell you what," he knelt down next to Bloom. "When that next Full Devouring comes, I'll let you guys stay up late, and I'll make sure we have Isingrass nearby so we can see how beautiful the flowers are. How does that sound to you two?" He glanced at Rose, looping her in.

Bloom leapt at him, squeezing his neck. Gavin caught him in the hug, laughing. "Okay, okay, woah—" Rose and Nona slammed into him too, throwing him to the floor, the hug turning into a wrestling match as they tried to pin him down. Laughter bubbled in his chest, the sound of youthful mirth infecting him, spreading the petals of his heart, stealing the heaviness of his wilting. Rose and Nona sat on his arms, Bloom perching on his chest, throwing his hands in the air, triumphant.

"We got him!"

"We got him!"

"We got him!"

Dezma glanced down at him above her paper, smirking. He gave as much of a shrug as he could. "Alright little hairless Bounders, you got me, but it's time to get off, that's right, there we go…" he stumbled to his feet as they backed away, laughing. "I've gotta help Aunt Dezma here with the preparations for tonight, go on, run along and have fun—and no more trying to steal Isingrass pods! We need those!"

They disappeared into the main room, giggling without mercy.

Gavin dusted himself off, looking over Dezma's shoulder, reading her scribbled numbers and grimacing. "Only a day and a half? That's a grim estimate, no?"

She shrugged. "The General claimed more than his soldiers needed. He paid us for it, but his entitled ass doesn't realize that if he's taken all our vendor's supplies in town, there's nowhere closer than Angar's Ford to buy more food, and that's a three day journey. My numbers here only account for what Nell and I and a couple others have stored up. It's possible we could find extra around the village, but we'd have to go knocking."

"It might come to that," Gavin said in a dark voice. "You know everyone in town would help us."

"Some already have," she sighed. "I hope Nell can net us extra. It'd push the headache down a couple days, and by then they may have left. It'd help if the General wasn't so damn mysterious about why he's here. Walking around with that green scar on his staff, refusing to tell me his name, calling himself 'The Wolf'—"

Gavin's mouth went dry.

"—as if he's hunting through the damn sky at night. If it wouldn't get us all killed, I'd stick my Longtooth up his ass just to make him look how he sounds."

Gavin tried to swallow, but he couldn't, each gulp reaching for the saliva in his mouth and not quite finding it, like a fish flapping its bottom lip in the air after being taken from the water.

The sound of children shrieking echoed in from the main room. Gavin jumped, the sound of weeping filling his entire back, his arms. *It's laughter.* He took a deep breath. *Laughter.*

"Oh well," Dezma said, turning around. "At least they're

having fun—" she came up short, seeing him. "You okay?"

He swallowed again. *Green scar... The Wolf...* "Yeah," he whispered. The weeping. The weeping of a dead man hanging over his neck. It wouldn't go away. "I'm okay. I'm fine."

She gave him an odd look. Blinked. Then turned away, hefting a large sack on her knee, handing it off to him. "You're thinking too much. Here. The Maisa's brought in extra Sliffitan, we'll need the whole sack seeded before dinner."

He followed her, the world around him numb and colorless. He blinked a few times as his hands fell into a familiar pattern, working the Sliffitan. The... the long, feather-like stalks had seeds hidden along their stems. To extract the seeds, he had to flick his fingers along the soft downy barbs of its body, scraping free the seeds into a bowl. Squeeze too hard in the flick, and the barbs would pluck free of the stem, falling in amongst the seeds, and adding more work to the process. Too light, and some of the seeds would stick in the barbs, forcing him to pluck them out one by one.

Sliffitan. Seeding Sliffitan. He knew how to do this. His breathing came easier as his hands worked, each feather sifting through his fingers like grass in the wind. *It will be okay. Everything will be okay. I'm safe here. We're safe here.*

"Dad!" Rose bounded up to the opposite side of the bar. He swallowed and blinked, looking up, picking out the last few seeds from the feather in his hands. "Dad, Bloom is worried about Bubbles." Her eyes were wide and watery as she clambered up onto a barstool.

He closed his eyes for a long moment, collecting himself. *Not will be. Is. Everything* is *still okay.* "Rosebud, I'm sure the nice soldiers staying in our house won't touch Bubbles. He'll be fine."

Rose shook her head, tears flying to the countertop. His eyes flicked to the pile of chairs and tables the kids had been playing around. Bloom sat in the middle of the floor, tears openly falling down his cheeks, hands on the Grendlewood floor like leaves plucked from a tree. Nona stood by him, glancing up at Gavin with the furtive, lip-biting demeanor of guilt. "Nell doesn't think the soldiers are nice!" she said. "Nona, tell Gavin! Nell thinks the soldiers are mean, and that they might hurt Bubbles!"

Nona looked away.

"I'm sure Nell didn't say the soldiers would hurt Bubbles, Rosebud," Gavin said. "The soldiers have everything they asked for, they have no reason to hurt us more."

"They have no reason to hurt us at all!" She shouted. "That didn't stop them!"

Her words rang against the air. The couple other families in the room quieted, turning to look. Gavin's hands shook, still holding an empty Sliffitan feather. He set it down, moving around the bar, pulling Rose into a hug. She buried her head against his chest, little arms squeezing him so hard.

"Dad," he looked over. Bloom stood a few steps away, sucking up a glob of snot into his nose. "I wanna go make sure Bubbles is okay. Can we go?"

"No!" He sucked in a breath, biting his lip, shaking his head. He extracted himself from the hug, kneeling down, taking both his children's hands. "We can't go back to our house right now," he whispered. His heart withered, and he felt the petals tearing free. It took everything he had not to let his own chin quiver. "Okay? We just can't. I know you're worried about Bubbles. Truth is? I am too. But we're gonna have to be worried together, okay? There's nothing we can do for Bubbles right now."

"It's no big deal," Dezma said. "They're just cowards with a symbol. I can go talk to them if you want, Gav. See if they'll let us bring Bubbles here."

He opened his mouth to deny—

"Please! Pleasepleaseplease—"

"Thank you so much Aunt Dezma I'll do *anything* to make it up to you—"

Dezma laughed, slapping Gavin on the shoulder. "Don't worry so much."

His hands shook.

"I'll go right after I finish readying supper," she said, smiling down at the kids. "But you'd better leave your dad alone, I need his help."

They nodded, bouncing away, as if every care in the world had been solved. He stood up, numb, the world buzzing around him. He walked back around the bar. Picked up another feather. Squeezed his eyes shut. Plucked a few seeds into the bowl...

"Gav..." Dezma's hand shook his shoulder. He blinked. "Gav. You look like it's you with the Longtooth up your ass. What's up?"

He shook his head. The air took on a new consistency, when words had to be said, and he wasn't ready to say them. It grew thick and deafening, clammy and stale. It blocked his vision and drained him pale.

"You can't go, Dez," he whispered.

She furrowed her eyebrows, plucking the last few seeds from a feather of her own. "What do you mean?"

"It's too dangerous," he whispered. He felt Dezma's gaze against the side of his face like a hot iron. He squeezed his eyes shut. "The General, the... the Wolf, you called him... he's here because of me."

MIRRORWAVE

Mirrorwaves reflect or absorb light. Skilled casters can amplify even the barest moonlight into a brilliant glow.

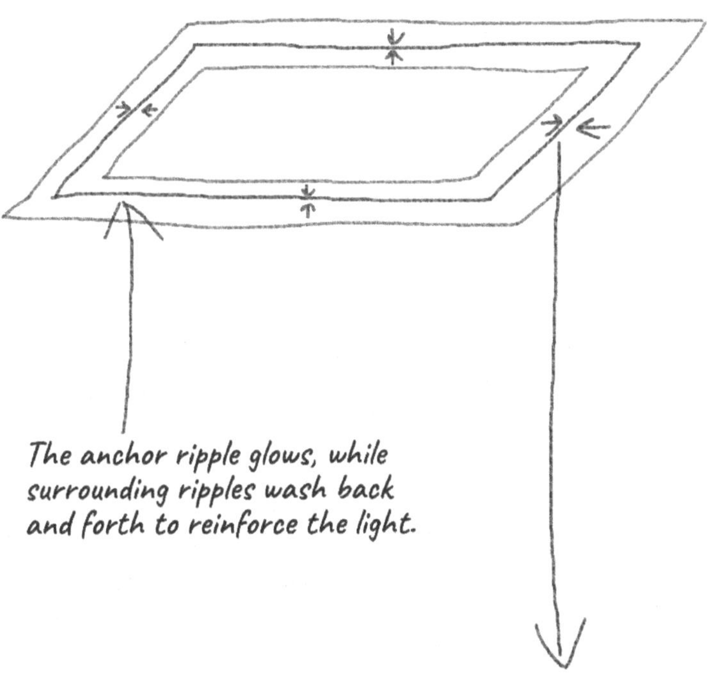

The anchor ripple glows, while surrounding ripples wash back and forth to reinforce the light.

Subversive Mirrorwaves cast out instead of in, as if the outer ripples are stealing the light from the anchor.

4

Who are you, little guy?" Stelli sat on the edge of her bed, hair a mess, side of her face creased from sleep. She could feel some of the strands of her poofy hair brushing the slant of the roof just above her. Knots of hard muscle tweaked with her small movements, just beneath her shoulder blades, along her shins and forearms...

Crrrooooooooak. A light blue toad clung to the wall, about the size of her head, its large fat legs bunched beneath it. It stared at her with wide, beady eyes. *Crrrrrooooooooaaaakkk.* It sounded indignant. Almost offended.

"Did you crawl in here from the swamp?" She muttered, blinking at it. Her heart thumped against her ribs, a little quicker than normal. She moved over to the window, pushing aside the leaf covering that kept it closed. A chill breeze came in, brushing her bare arms. "Come on, little guy," she said. "Out you go. You want out, right?"

Croak. It sounded final, determined, and didn't move. She frowned, moving to her pack, pulling out her gloves, keeping an eye on the toad the whole time. Her gloves left her index finger and thumb exposed. Skin contact with the water made casting Runewaves easier, so Runecaster tradition had developed around gloves that left two fingers exposed. Now she cursed that tradition. Could toads have poisonous skin? Or slime, or something? She'd prefer a direct assault from someone with a weapon. At least then she would know how to fight back. She flexed her hands against the gloves. She took a deep breath.

And she lunged, closing her hands around the toad's hind leg as it tried to hop away. It kicked and scrabbled at her palm, wrenching against her, stronger than she expected. She pulled it against her chest, falling into the bed and clutching it there as it writhed and scrambled, hind legs thrashing in her grip. Slime oozed against her exposed fingers, coating them, an icky stench contorting her nose. She didn't let go.

It calmed after a few seconds. She kept her grip along its back legs, holding it out in front of her, breathing heavy. "Okay, little guy," she breathed. "Not very friendly. I'm just trying to help you out."

She moved to the window, reaching out her arms, elbows squeezing between the narrow wooden gap. "Be free," she breathed, and threw the thing out towards the water. It landed with a splash.

She shuddered a breath, backing into the room, sitting down on the bed, and looking at her slime-covered gloves. She wrinkled her nose, pulling them off, setting them on the small shelf by the bed.

Her eyes fell to the askew chest and scattered books, one shelf lower. She pursed her lips, hesitating for a moment. The bruises along the lower side of her right shin ached. She slid one of the books free onto her lap, flipping it open, holding away the two fingers on her hands that still felt slick and sticky with slime.

The book was full of drawings, scrawled in a messy, child-like hand, done in vibrant yet scattered color. The pages were *thick*, the space between the membranes bloated with various dyes. The first few pages just had indistinguishable messes. But further in, the smears took on shapes. Faces, in the mess—with off-kilter eyes too large for the heads, and mouths that looked alarming in the way they curved.

Then features came into greater focus. A family, standing hand in hand. Four people. A father, with light messy hair, a clean-shaven face, and bright brown eyes. His smile lit up the drawing, and he had little leaves and twigs sticking out of his hair. He held hands with a woman, a mother, smiling just as bright. At either side of them was a son and a daughter, really young. The daughter was drawn with a goofy outfit on, strange little boxes and blobs of color. The son had thin little lines on his face that resembled some sort of over-large mustache.

Tears prickled Stelli's eyes. The family looked so happy. So content. She couldn't take her eyes off the way the father smiled. She drank in every corner of his smudged countenance, filling in the gaps, hand shaking where it gripped the page.

She forced herself to flip to the next one. Her smile faded from her lips like the final fall of a corpse's chest. Fire. Darkness. Miasma. Color. Meaningless shapes. She flipped quicker, searching for more drawings, searching for that happy, perfect family again.

Eventually the people came back. But there were only three of them, and they were drawn with dark hair this time. The father still smiled, full of joy and love, and the kids still had silly lines and colors across their faces, and the paper was crinkled and torn and loved just like the rest of the book. But it carried a *weight* to it. The heaviness of a missing mother, a missing life. Everything must have changed.

Her eyes drifted down to the father's right hand. She couldn't be sure what brought her eyes there. Some dark portent of her periphery. Some dread-induced calling of her subconscious. Breathing, on the back of her neck. A swirling green scar, in the un-breathing of her drowning self.

The father only had three fingers on his right hand. The index and middle fingers were missing. She flipped back and forth between the drawings of the father, picking out facial structure, the hair color, the eyes, the nose. With each glance, the thudding of her heart against her chest grew stronger, louder. A tear flowed over from her eyes, plopping down against the paper, adding her own mark to the emptiness of the drawing.

She cried, because that man with the bright smile, that man who loved his kids, might be her father's target. Which would make this house the house of the most dangerous man to have ever lived.

She slammed the book shut, shoving it on the shelf. She grabbed her Canine from under her pillow, holding it close at her side. Breathing, like the panting of the Wolf, sending stiff drops of sweat and drool down her neck. A little shiver ran up her spine. The prickle of eyes, slanted and narrow, purple and gleaming in the night. *Watching her.*

She scoured the rest of the shelf, jiggling the latch on the chest until it popped open. A small bowl greeted her, full of small black... Dead insects, with long antennae and way too many legs. Next to it, some mashed up colors, probably from berries of some sort, and a few different sticks of wood with rounded ends. She moved on, flipping through the other books. More drawings, more drawings... she didn't allow herself to linger. She could *hear* the breathing behind her, feel its drool catching in the tiny hairs of her lower back—

"Lieutenant?" Tess stuck her head through the door. "The unit is ready to run through the forms."

Stelli blinked, stilling the shaking of her hands. "You lead today."

"Lieutenant?"

"You heard me," she whispered, standing up. "Go, be Lieutenant for the day."

"The General—"

"I'll speak with him."

Tess hung like a Tuft Rabbit in the Carrow Wolf's maw,

short hair still around her head, mouth a fragment open. "Yes, Lieutenant," she whispered. And darted from the building.

Stelli moved into the main body of the house, looking at it with new eyes. She held her Canine up close to her chest, ready to strike. The way the leaves hung from the plants on every available shelf, the shadows they cast... all those nooks and crannies looked to her like sinister hiding spots. Her eyes flicked to a long, thin wooden basin, covered by a panel slid in between carved grooves. She knelt next to it, pulling free the panel, slow and careful.

A flat plane of water, with rocks and debris strewn about, goals on either end. Two bowls held smooth stones, about equal. She—

Sffffft. She jumped and spun. A vine, twisted in the rafters above the front door. One strand hung loose, swinging in the slight wind of the open window. She stared at it for a long moment, eyes flickering to the shadows at its side, calming her heartbeat. Her knuckles went white against her Canine.

She turned to the room Tess was staying in, opening the door, glancing back and forth. Still. Dark. The predawn blueness of early morning sifted through a leaf-covered window. A bed tucked up against one wall. Opposite the bed, a desk with a few drawers, low to the ground, and chairless. She scanned every corner of the room before moving to it, sliding open the drawers.

Papers. Drawings of plants, with descriptions. A ream of parchment, full of more drawings of plants and animals, and pressed flat samples of leaves. A book, bound with a cord. She thumbed through it, finger slipping on the moist edges as the parchment bled. It told a silly story about a princess running away from a huge lizard in the swamp, with a pollen-tongue, and thorns for teeth, and vines for arms. She tossed it back in the cabinet. She double and triple checked the room, pulling the cabinet away from the wall, checking under the bed. There, she found a few more wooden boxes with sliding lids, revealing a variety of different game boards inside. By the window, she found a jar, full of mold. Something told her the mold hadn't been cultivated by accident.

She grunted, turning, surveying the room one last time, shaking her head. *It's not enough...* she thought. *It could be nothing, just a coincidence... But three fingers... How many men had only three fingers on their right hand...*

Thump-thump... her heart, against her chest. *Thump-thump...* She forced herself to breathe. She took slow steps. Back, into the main room, ducking under the doorframe. Every inch of her exposed skin prickled with phantom pain. Every shadow glinted like the sharpened-edge of a Dewclaw. *Thump-thump...* Every plant dripped with toxins in her eyes, and she could feel their promise in her bloodstream, see the blackened, dead eyes and blue lips and haunted cheekbones... *Thump-thump.* She returned to the corner room, with the slanted roof, ducking under the doorframe. She grabbed the book with the drawings.

Thump-thump. She flipped through. *Thump-thump.* The father's smile, that haunting, beautiful, loving smile, stared at her, taunted her. She ripped the page out. Kept flipping. Paused on every drawing of the father. Tore them out. Until she had them all. She set them flat, tucking them under her shirt, their cold, crinkled presence a vice grip on her heart.

She moved to the bathroom with slow and cautious steps, acutely aware of the space around her. She threw back her hair, tying it into a messy ponytail. There was no water to wash with. Stupid outskirts town. Plumbing hadn't spread from the Steppes yet. Or perhaps this town was just too poor and sad... her eyes drifted to the only plant that hung in the bathroom. She stood, peering at it, reaching up a hand to run along a drooping leaf. It left a little dark residue on her fingertips. Against one wall, balancing on the edge of the basin, sat a mortar and pestle. She picked it up. The bottom was stained black. She glanced between the stain and the hanging leaves.

And then the large stone basin. Bending down, she could see little elements of dark powder around a large drainage hole, thick stopper attached to a chain and rolling free to the side. She pulled the drawings from under her shirt, handling them with slow care. *A happy family, blond hair... The father, blond hair, five fingers on both hands... Blond hair... blond hair...* She flipped to the last few drawings.

The father. Three fingers. Dark hair. She looked back up at the plant, and then at the basin, tucking the drawings back under her shirt. The children looked so young in the drawings of them with blond hair. Young enough for the timelines to match up. Rain chains spiralled with droplets of water on the roof, and the sound reminded Stelli of her dead brother's weeping. *Moons.* The timelines, the dyed hair, hiding in a far away town... Why else would a father move far away and dye the hair of his entire family, if not to hide?

She moved like a marionette, controlled by strings. Strings of drool, hanging from the half-open, tooth-filled maw of a wolf, blown forward by its rank breath. She grabbed her cloak and threw it on. Ducked out of the small door, eyeing the vine that still dangled before it, making sure not to touch it. She turned the door handle with her Canine, avoided the door frame, and hopped from the deck to the tranquil lake below, beating Standwaves into the water. Mingling soldiers sitting around Wavepits, stretching before their morning forms, gave her strange looks as she strode away from them. She straightened, and didn't return the looks.

Soon the prickle would leave her back. *You hate him, right?* Soon the panting would leave her neck. *You should hate him.*

Soon he will love you.

She passed into the marketplace. About half the stalls were

empty, but some vendors leaned across their wooden counters, or sat back on stools which rocked up and down on Standwaves. Colorful cloth hung down low above their heads, shielding them from the sun. Soft words drifted on the light wind, but they were tense, difficult words, strung tight by tension, and the faces of all were taut and worried.

The drawings prickled under her cloak. She stepped up to one of the vendors, a heavyset woman with hair pulled back under a hood, heavy cheeks sallow under bright, piercing eyes. She had beautiful woven scarves and hats hanging along a clothesline, which matched the colors of the flickering Mirrorwaves that bordered the stall where it touched the water.

"Good day, Miss," Stelli said, leaning her elbows on the counter, ducking under the hanging hats and scarves. "Sorry to bother. Any of your colleagues selling plants, local flora...?"

The woman affixed her with a clear gaze, glancing up and down her cloak. She sniffed.

Stelli held out a hand. "Lieutenant of the seventh unit under the General of Stillness."

"What do you need plants for?" The woman warbled. "Your General gone and took all the ones for eatin'."

"I'm not asking about plants for eating," she whispered. "I'm asking about plants with purple flowers and low hanging vines, plants with big drooping dark leaves. Good for dying hair, perhaps."

The woman just stared at Stelli, under her hood, eyes sallow, lids hanging low.

Stelli sighed, reaching into a pouch at her waist, pulling out a couple purple shards of seaglass.

"Got his own shop, he does," the woman grumbled.

"Where?"

The woman kept staring. Stelli sighed, pulling out a few more purple shards.

"Just a few buildings in from the tavern."

Her heart pattered faster. "And where's the tavern?"

The woman waved her hand at the big building off to the side of the marketplace, a building with a high sloped roof, and carved scale-like shingles that shone with droplets from the previous night's rain.

"Thank you, miss."

The woman scoffed as Stelli walked away. "Where's the tavern... Moons..."

She straightened her back to knock off the scorn, pacing around a few other market stalls, and ducking into the narrow path of exposed water between the buildings, to the side of the tavern. She drew her Canine from under her cloak, glancing around every building, eyes even tracing the low shadows in the narrow spaces between floor and lake.

No movement. Never movement. But the man with three fingers didn't need movement. The man with three fingers could be anywhere, ready to kill her without a second thought.

She ducked out into a wider road, glancing back at the marketplace. People mingled. She could see other soldiers passing through, marked with the deep purples of the Carrow Wolf, no doubt instructed to look, to search, to make themselves seem as innocuous as possible.

She had no eyes for the other soldiers. She drank in the prickle on her spine, and the panting at her neck, and the teeth waiting to sink into her flesh. *You hate him. Soon he will love you.*

She found it. Long beams holding it out of the water, a wide covered deck extending from the front, below an open window with brilliant flowers and drooping vines hanging out amongst the wooden slats and supports. She steadied her breathing as she stepped up to the door, clutching her Canine. *Breathe in. Thump-thump. Breathe out.*

She threw it open, lunging in, eyes flashing side to side. Plants hung *everywhere*, filling the open space, taking up every bit of room on the walls. The light cast in through the open door and wide windows sent shadows blooming from every drooping leaf, painting monstrous shapes on the jagged foliage of the walls. She ducked around vines that stretched across boards nailed into the ceiling, pushed aside leaves as large as her torso, looked under wide-petalled flowers and around large clay pots.

She stumbled against a countertop, jumping, tensing, clenching her open hand against the wood... but it was just a countertop. With a creaky looking gate at one end, leading to a backroom. A rickety chair sat behind the counter, in front of a lockbox, and a large leather bound tome, with yellowing pages.

Heart hammering, she kicked open the door to the backroom, ducking through.

It dripped with humidity, slamming her in the face. Thin wooden walkways traced between troughs of water or dirt, and large open slats in the walls cast bright, filtered light across the miasma of bushes, small trees, sprouts, vines, flowers—every type of plant imaginable. She ducked along the wooden walkways, glancing side to side.

Drip.

She jumped, spinning for the noise. *Drip, drip.* Drops of dew pinged down from the end of a drooping leaf. She forced herself to take deep breaths, reaching out with her Canine to move aside fronds in the way of her path, or vines that hung too low.

Nothing but plants. She started to breathe easier. Laughter bubbled in her chest, emerging as a low chuckle in the empty room, her only audience a symphony of flora. Here she was, muscles tense as a Grendlewood's bough, heart pounding fast as a pitched battle, in a room full of *leaves*.

A room that *might* belong to the most dangerous man in the world.

Or a silly man with silly children who liked to draw mustaches on each other.

The prickle washed across her back, purple eyes roaring over her consciousness. She heard the Wolf's voice growling angry diatribes in her ear, felt the bruises on her ankles and back swell with pain. She spun her Canine, turning and emerging into the main room.

She flipped open the large book on the counter, eyes dancing along the words. *Sensiili Magdolin—sold in the market of the Third Partial of the 71st Full to Sandra Bennex, a saleswoman from the Steppes...* flipped back a page... *Cyril vine—sold out of shop on the Twelfth Partial of the 70th Full to Nell...* She flipped back a few pages, scanning more and more neat, numbered, and dated lines, each showing the log of a different sale. She slid her hand under the left ream of pages and flipped it to the start, scanning for a date, heart pounding...

Fourth Partial of the 68th Full. The 68th Full. This upcoming Full would be... the 75th... which made the start of this log...

Just under seven Full Devourings ago. *Exactly the right amount of time.* Her hands shook again. She stuck her tongue out the side of her mouth, carefully ripping free the opening page, with that first date. The sound of the paper ripping rent the silent air of the shop, each little follicle of fibrous paper popping free one by one. She folded it, and tucked it in under her shirt with the drawings.

The shadows looked sinister again. She lifted her Canine, and strode for the door.

It was time to speak with her father.

He had chosen a home to quarter in no more grandiose than any other. Lodged at the very edge of town, it sat squat and crooked, with a creaking dock built out from its side, absent any boats. Brown, craggy fishing nets hung from posts, dried out in the sun. A few crabs skittered away from her feet as she pulled herself up onto the stairs that lead to the door.

She pushed it open. Her heart pounded for a new reason this time. She held up her Canine, ducking through, looking around. A fireplace sat dead, unlit. A warm rug of thick, full fur laid out across the ground, a couple carved rocking chairs sitting still against the wall. A dark wood table, low to the ground, sat next to round sitting mats of woven fabric. An old, rusty harpoon balanced on pegs on the wall, next to a crudely knitted fish, with gangly little eyes. It reminded her of the children's drawings.

A door on the right was open. The General sat at a desk. Every few seconds, something rattled next to him, wood and rope grinding together, scraping, chafing, bucking.

"It's interesting," the General said, not even looking up. "How a pet thrown from a window, no matter how wild it once may have been, will starve."

She stepped forward into the doorway, eyes landing on the desk. A large light blue toad, about the size of her head, bucked and reared, trying to jump out of a wood and rope trap. It looked uninjured, but its eyes bugged out, and its feet scrabbled for purchase against the jumble.

"It bothered me," she said.

"If we killed everything that bothered us we'd have few things left." Now he did look at her. The prickles rushed along her back, and she felt the panting on her neck. "But if we *catch* them..." he lifted the trap, pulling the rope taught, giving the toad room to sit. "And feed them," he held out a handful of little brown bugs. A few of them crawled around his hand, finding the crevices of his knuckles and fingernails, as if trying to hide from their fate. The toad's tongue shot out between the rope, once, twice, three times, slamming into the General's hand, lapping up the insects. One tried to run up his arm.

The tongue snatched it before it could even hope.

"It's amazing what they'll do for us," he said. "I understand the contempt you feel for things that shouldn't require your attention. I feel it too. But you can't let that contempt blunt your mind. Everything can be useful, no matter how insignificant."

She balled her fists, insides worming with shame. "Must everything be a lesson?"

"Was I wrong to observe your love for learning?"

She stalked forward. "I do everything you ask—"

"Lieutenant—"

"It doesn't matter how effectively I succeed, how much I aid your hunt—"

"*Lieutenant.*"

"I know I'll never be my brother," she hissed, tears filling her eyes. She yanked the papers out from under her cloak and shoved them into his chest. "But I do *everything* you ask. And you still call me Lieutenant."

He put his hand over hers, looking down. The boiling shame in her gut twisted with joyful glee at the surprise on his face. He worked her fingers away, sliding out the bundle of papers, looking at them one by one. She sucked in her tears, the sound of paper scraping on paper the only sound to fill the room.

He looked up at her. *Truly* looked at her, then tepped forward and pulled her into a hug. A warm embrace. She scrunched her eyes and pressed her head into his shoulder, tears pouring from the slits of bunched skin that her eyes had become.

"Good girl," he whispered into her ear. "Good girl." He gave her one last squeeze, before moving for the door. He hesitated, lit by the sun in the doorway. "Organize patrols around the town," he whispered. "Cut off access to our quarter. Nobody leaves the village until we have our quarry."

Her father left. The toad kicked and jumped at its cage. The pained rattling continued.

5

Dezma's fingers stopped, Sliffitan feather dead between them. "Why?"

He stared at Bloom and Rose. They looked so relieved, so happy, sitting in a little circle with Nona, laughing and falling into each other. He forced himself to keep husking the feathers. He swallowed. Bloom's laugh squeaked through his nose, while Rose's chortled in her chest. Focusing on the noise helped still his hands, pushing away the sound of that dead man's weeping.

"The General used to have a son," he whispered. He pulled a few seeds off the feather in his hand, little soft blades slipping between the gaps where his two missing fingers should be. "Skilled with Runewaves. Wanted to be a teacher, way I remember it, not a warlord like his father."

"You used to live in the Steppes," Dezma breathed, seeds pinging into her bowl. "Right?"

He nodded. "Grew up there. Married there. Had my children there," his voice trailed off. "Became a widower there." The Steppes had such interesting flora. He could still smell the Rock Roses. Compared to the scents of the swamp, their sweetness sickened him.

"The General's son?" Dezma prompted.

Gavin nodded, snapping his fingers back into motion across the feathers. "Between deployments he would go around and teach the local children how to use Runewaves. Simple stuff, really. Nothing remarkable. Bloom and Rose were so young, barely toddling around, but Rose's eyes lit up so bright when she got a chance to play with Runewaves. She would always go watch the lessons, drag Bloom along, and sometimes join in..." He swallowed a lump in his throat. "Something went wrong one time. One of the other neighbor kids got too ambitious, cut himself with a Slashwave. His blood filled the water. Everyone fell in. Even the General's son couldn't move away quick enough. Half the children didn't know how to swim yet, and there they were, all spluttering in the water. All except Bloom and Rose."

"They got away in time?"

"No," Gavin whispered, watching them laugh. "They stood on the blood."

Gavin had never known Dezma to fall so still. He felt her presence like a corpse, cold and frightened of what came next.

"Course, the General's son saw this," Gavin continued, hands starting to shake. "Showed up at my house that very same night. Begged me to let him train my children. *Begged*, Dezma. On his knees. Told me they would change the world one day. That his father would make them heroes."

Dezma's silence drew the words out of his mouth, each stumble of his tongue like a step towards some unseen void.

"He would have taken them, Dezma," Gavin whispered. "I could see it in his eyes. He was so afraid. As if there were hands gripping his neck, squeezing until he got what he wanted. He would have done anything, Dez. Anything."

He felt the weight of Dezma's gaze on the side of his neck. "You..." something hitched in her voice. A mix of awe and intrigue, the word hanging in the air, turning over itself. "You killed him?"

"And I would do it again," Gavin swallowed bile, staring at Bloom as he laughed that squeaking laugh, wrestling with Rose over something Gavin couldn't see. "I would do it a thousand times again if it means I get to see them happy."

He finally looked up at Dezma.

Storms brewed behind her eyes. Angry storms. The kind of storms that smothered the Carrow Wolf in the sky, and tore the stars asunder. She pursed her lips, and flicked her gaze to the door.

"I thought about running," Gavin said, hands cold against the Sliffitan. Frigid numbness etched his joints. "When the soldiers first got here. I knew there was a chance it was the Wolf. I keep the mudskiff packed and ready, just in case. It would have been easy, to just take the kids and leave town, right then. But when I woke them up, I... Dez, I *promised* Rose that she could play today... And what are the odds, random Kingsmen... I've done everything to make the trail cold, covered our tracks, dyed our hair, moved all the way out here... I-I didn't want to overreact, ruin everything for nothing, and it all happened so fast, I-I..."

Nona tackled Rose, and they rolled around on the Grendle floor, shrieking with laughter while Bloom clapped on the sidelines.

He bowed his head between his frigid, numb hands. "This is the only home they remember," he whispered. "I don't even care that I've put the town in danger. I just want them to be happy and free."

Dezma's well-muscled arm wrapped around his shoulders. She gave him a firm squeeze. "We all need them to be happy and free," she said. "It's worth it. Okay? *It's worth it.*"

"Uh oh," A voice rose behind them. Cold air drifted through the back door of the tavern. The smell of fish swam against Gavin's wet eyes. "That doesn't look like dinner making."

Gavin gave a weak smile, straightening up, wiping his eyes. Nell stomped the rest of the way in, tossing the door closed. A couple fish hung dead over his shoulder, silver scales dripping with dew. He slapped them down on the bar, opening his right hand to show a row of orange eggs, packed tight in a long, thin sheathe. Incisions ran down the fish guts, the insides emptied save for the meat. The gills were still red and raw from bleeding.

"Fresh bones for a fresh soup," Nell flicked up a fileting knife from his belt, slicing into the head with a clean angle, holding it still with his other hand. He glanced up at Gavin, then Dezma, then back at Gavin. "You alright?"

Dezma looked at Gavin, raising an eyebrow. He took a deep breath. Talking felt easier now. His hands no longer felt so numb.

"Gav's a wanted man," Dezma grinned, ducking into the pantry and coming out with a large barrel under one arm, and a bung starter in the other. "The baddest outlaw in all the Kingdom."

"Ha!"

"I'm serious!" Dezma took her mallet and tapped along the bung stave, loosening the plug of the barrel. "Ever heard of the time the Bugaboo made the King pee himself? That was him."

Nell grinned, turning the fileting knife over and slicing just below the head, down the fish's ribs. "Stole the King's underpants, did he?"

"Oh yeah. The General would have his head if he found him."

"Aye! Maybe I should turn him in meself, snatch a hefty bounty."

A lightness surged in Gavin's stomach, regrowing the petals of his heart. His hands found their motions again, pulling seeds free of their pods. Dezma slid Nell a smaller bowl over the counter.

"Right," Nell stacked large chunks of the meat in the bowl. "Starch?" Dezma ducked back into the pantry and came out with a jar, tossing it over. Nell caught it and sprinkled fingerfulls of the powder across the fish in the bowl. "He actually after ye?"

"Yes," Gavin whispered. "But I'm more worried that he's after *them*," he motioned with his head towards the children. They hadn't seen Nell come in yet, they were too busy piling on top of one another, rolling in a mess of limbs and laughter.

Nell's fileting knife thunked into the hard wood of the bar. "Not after we kill him he ain't."

"Don't do anything stupid," Gavin mumbled. "He doesn't know that I'm here, or—"

"He might," Nell sliced off a thick chunk of meat from the next fish and added it to the marinating bowl. Despite his anger, his white knuckled grip and reddening face, the cut was precise and perfect. "The boys'n I got stopped on the way back in today, buncha Scabbers asking why we were comin' into town. Patrols, I reckon. To keep you in."

He swallowed, fingers shaking over the feathers again. "He can't know. Not for sure. I'll just, just lay low, if he doesn't come up with anything he'll have to leave—"

"Dad, dad, dad," Nona careened around the bar and slammed into his legs, wrapping her arms tight around his waist. "Dad I'm so sorry please don't be mad at me I'm so sorry—"

"Woah, woah," Nell said, returning the hug while trying to keep his fish-covered hands from touching her. "Sorry? What's all this sorry business, what did ye do this time—"

"I told Bloom and Rose about what you said last night about the soldiers and what you wanted to do to them and then they got scared the soldiers were gonna hurt Bubbles and now Gavin is mad at me and I'm really sorry—"

"Shhhhhhh," he rubbed her back. "I'm sure Gavin's not—"

"It's okay!" Bloom bounced over, hopping up on a barstool, pulling Rose up with him. They balanced, both on the same stool, a gangly mess of sibling. "It's okay because Dezma is gonna go get Bubbles for us so nobody will hurt—"

"Nay," Nell said, glancing between the kids, Gavin, and

Dezma, stepping back from the embrace. "Nobody's goin' over there, it's too dangerous, not with—"

"I'm sorry," Gavin whispered. His hands were numb again. "Us adults were talking, and we... we decided we can't go over there, okay?"

"WHAT?" Bloom screeched. He tore away from Gavin's grip, spinning on Dezma. "You *promised!*"

She looked away. "I'm sorry."

Bloom's eyes filled with tears. "But... but dad, what about Bubbles?"

"Bubbles will be fine, Bloomstalk," Gavin said, forcing as much soft conviction into his voice as possible. "The mean soldiers will be gone in a day or two, and then we'll see Bubbles again—"

"HE'S NOT FINE!" Bloom shouted, tears pouring down his cheeks.

Gavin rushed around the bar, gathering Bloom and Rose into a hug, squeezing them as tight as he could. The tighter the hug, the tighter his throat, any words swallowed by the gravity of his children's tears. What could he say? How could a father break his children's heart? Grow calluses on his petals strong enough to withstand the broken shards of their childhoods? His burden. His burden. His burden. *It's worth it.* He squeezed them tighter. "The world isn't fair," he whispered. "It's not fair at all. But we'll get through it together, okay?"

"It's not worth it," Bloom mumbled into his chest. "Not if Bubbles is gone when we get back."

"Shhhhhhhh," Gavin rubbed their backs in slow circles, weathering their shaking shoulders and stifled sobs. Each wave crashed against him, their erosive force striving to tear him free of his foundations. But petals couldn't be eroded. They drank, and so he breathed, and so he kept hugging them. "Shhhhhh..."

The rest of the afternoon passed through blurred tears.

Bloom and Rose shot him hurt glances from the corner, huddling in his large cloak. Gavin pulled seeds off Sliffitan feathers, each one rolling under the pads of his fingers, numbing him like needles. He thought of the glorious moment when the General and his troops left the town, and they could stumble in amongst the wondrous smell of his herbs and flowers, and Bloom and Rose could hug Bubbles again, and snuggle up with him to sleep. He thought of the smiles they would have on their faces. Which made him think of the red rims of their eyes, where they sat in the corner, and the shaking of their little limbs as he had hugged them.

Nell and Dezma didn't talk much, beyond brief instructions, handing over ingredients, trading jobs. But they eyed the doors with furtive glances. As townsfolk returned, slow, family by family, from whatever work they had gotten to during the day, their apprehension grew. Dezma jumped when someone entered. Nell muttered a curse under his breath, fingers slipping on a slice of fish, dropping it to the counter.

Eventually Gavin finished husking all the Sliffitan feathers. Dezma showed him how to shape little cakes by wetting the seeds and rolling them together. The hard grains stuck together well. Dezma had cobbled together a vegetable broth, setting it to boil in her large cauldron. The steam filtered through a metal grate balanced atop the large pot, filling the room with a delectable aroma. Gavin placed the rolled Sliffitan cakes on the grate to steam. A new smell joined the broth, weaving into the melody of dinner—warm and whole, like the underbelly of a lizard basking in the sun.

Chatter filled the tavern, just like it would on most evenings. The chatter was muted. The soul was sucked free. Excited mutterings and thrown back glasses of Isingrass tea were replaced with dark recountings of tired, stressful days. The words sifted through Gavin's ears like worms, burrowing and twisting through his brain. Even the aroma he couldn't quite enjoy, a sour underpinning spoiling the taste on his tongue.

Nell added the fish to the stew as they finished marinating. The chunks of meat made satisfying hisses as they plopped through the bubbling, Steamwaving water. Dezma sprinkled in spices, waving her middle finger in slow circles above the broth. Under its point, the water bucked and jostled, little concentric stars rotating out and interlocking in complicated little swirls. The steam faded as these Tastewaves replaced the Steamwaves. On the metal girder, golden yellow Sliffitan cakes sat, lumpy and malformed, yet crisp.

Dezma hefted the cauldron, large arms clamping around the base. She shuffled out from around the counter. "Get your sorry asses over here," she called. "Dinner's ready. Eat up, and things won't look so bad."

Chuckles rose, as families crowded forward for their servings. The cauldron was big enough for four or five people to gather around at a time. Dezma handed out bowls to eager hands. People used the bowls as ladles, scooping for the fish. Clinks rang out as families bumped bowls, going for the juiciest looking morsels, laughing together as they divided the soup with light-hearted competition. There were enough Sliffitan cakes for each family to have one. Sad fingers broke the cakes into twos and threes, letting the pieces slip with soft warm murmurs into the soup, absorbing the surrounding flavor.

Gavin balanced three bowls on his arms, bringing the servings to his still disgruntled children. His heart withered from the thought of their broken gazes, and their trembling, but his mind felt numb from feeling.

Bloom and Rose leaned into each other, exchanging whispers. They jolted upright as he approached, eyes bright, smiles sheepish. He smiled a half-quirked lip back at them, raising his eyebrow. Rose's nose curled, and she pulled back into herself, again looking angry.

He settled down next to them, crossing his legs, setting the bowls down on the floor. Soft steam wafted against Bloom and Rose's round faces. Rose turned away, but followed the bowl with the side of her eyes.

"You heard Dezma," Gavin said, nudging the bowl closer to Rose, grinning. "You'll feel better if you eat."

She sniffed. Gavin laughed, scooting the bowl closer, wafting the steam towards her face. She laughed, falling backwards into the wall. Her stomach let out a grumble, and her laughter doubled. She grabbed the bowl and lifted it into her small lap, holding its warmth against her.

Bloom picked out the chunks of fish with his hands, popping them in his mouth. His eyes went wide, cheeks puffing out as his jaw worked to grind the food.

"Careful," Gavin chuckled, taking a measured sip. The warmth surged on his lips. He puckered them a bit, closing his eyes as the spice flushed his throat, filled his bones. It almost quieted the weeping in his mind. But not quite. His eyes darted to the door, and the window just above his head.

"Fnksyu," Rose said through a full mouth, tears brimming as she swallowed. She gulped down the soup in big mouthfuls, sucking the stringy veggies over her chin, ignoring the mess it made. "Itshrllygd fnks dad!"

He cocked his head, blowing over the surface of his soup. The taste itself left something to be desired. Dezma had made the broth without proper ingredients, using tastewaves to replicate the tang and spice. For what she had been working with, on such short notice, it was remarkable. But the fishiness still overpowered the flavor. And while Tastewaves could bring out the flavors of spice, his nose didn't run, and the heat died after a few moments of each sip. He craved a lingering burn, one that would stay with him, cleanse him, purify his insides. Still, he couldn't complain. Dezma was a brilliant cook, making the best of a bad situation, and already he could hear the worry lines sloughing free of the townsfolk's faces, as the warmth and flavor melted them into comfort.

"Can we go to bed now dad?" Bloom said, a blue hand-like leaf clinging across his lip, the empty bowl at his feet. "I ate my dinner, I'm ready for bed now."

He scrunched his eyebrows, finishing his bite, cocking his head. "I suppose," he said. "There's still quite a long while before the Moons rise though."

"We know!" Rose said, wiping her eyes after swallowing her last bite. "We want to sleep so that the time will go faster and the soldiers will leave sooner."

He smiled, heart tired. "Okay, Rosebud. That sounds like a plan." He took another sip. The fish and Sliffitan cake were gone, leaving just the broth in his bowl. Rose and Bloom snuggled back, clutching Gavin's cloak around themselves and curling into each other. Gavin swallowed, watching them. They scrunched their eyes closed, and started breathing slowly. He took another sip, and then another. Rose let out a little snore.

"I guess I should feel lucky," he said to nobody in particular, taking another sip. "That I have children who can fall asleep so fast. It's really quite a magical thing."

They didn't stir. Another sip. The warmth was running out, and dread crept back in.

"But you know," he took another sip, not wanting to finish. "Instead I just feel kinda sad. Here I am, eating dinner all alone, without anyone to keep me company. If only my children were awake. I do love talking with them so very much..." No more warmth. The last sip passed down his throat.

"Oh well," he said with a sigh, gathering the bowls and standing up. "I should probably go help them with dishes. I sure hope my amazing children aren't trying to trick me by pretending to sleep. I *will* be keeping an eye on them, you know."

He hesitated, watching them for a long moment. Their faces stayed impassive, their breathing calm and uniform. He raised his eyebrows, nodding slowly to himself, and then made for the counter. Dezma, Nell, Rinna, and Mourra all collected platters, Dezma politely shaking her head and holding up a flat palm, refusing the Seaglass chips people offered her.

"Here," Gavin said, taking a load from Mourra's arms, smiling at her. She stood about a head shorter than him, hair long and flowing around her waist. "Let me."

"I've got it! Go take the load off Nell's back we all know lugging fish all day's made his arms weak—"

"Hey!" Nell barked. "At least I'm not still caked in the eyes from sleeping all day—"

"And saving your sorry asses in the process," Mourra finished in a sing-song voice, sliding behind Gavin with an armful of bowls, and dumping them in Dezma's large bucket of suds. "Maybe the soldiers will leave in the night, and I'll let you all go on believing they're still suckling our tit the whole next morning."

"I think we'd feel that, love," Dezma called out, grabbing a plate and scrubbing it with a frazzle sponge. Gavin felt a little spike of pride at the design—made from a specific type of abrasive moss in the swamp, its spines did a good job at scraping the grime off without causing too much damage. "Whether you did your job or no."

Gavin grabbed another frazzle sponge, pulling up one of the bowls and working it into the residue that had accumulated.

"I'm sure I could numb it for you," Mourra called out, smiling at someone and taking their platter.

Dezma laughed, a big bellow that Nell joined moments later, followed by the rest of them.

"Woah woah woah," Nell squeezed past Gavin, stepping up

to Rinna, leaning around her and putting his hands under hers to help lift the bowls she was carrying. "Since when were you trying to steal my job—let the cook do his own dishes for once—"

"Oh were *you* the cook?" She said with a sidelong glance and a grin, ducking through his side hug, stepping back and putting her hands on her hips, leaving him with the full weight of the dishes. "That explains some things."

"Aye—but don't be too quick with that tongue o' yers, Gav and Dez helped too."

"That must be why it was edible," Rinna's mouth twitched in a barely resisted smile.

"Moons forbid, your own husband bein' good at cooking." He squeezed back past Gavin, dumping the bowls in the bin. Gavin tried to crane his neck, keep an eye on his children in the corner, but he couldn't quite see between the throng—

"Oh come now," Rinna said, sliding more bowls off the countertop, smiling and nodding at people as they brought them up. She handed them off to Gavin, who handed them to Nell, who dumped them in the bin. "If all we cared about was good cooking, we'd all be married to Dezma."

Everyone laughed again. A sound that normally would have comforted him, except that he had just had a horrifying thought. *Pretending to sleep, worried for Bubbles...* Had his children snuck out? He tried again to see the corner. Was that his cloak, on the ground? Was it empty? *Moons!* His heart spiked—

CRASH. The doors slammed open. Gavin's world tipped over, a hand whipping against his shoulder and tossing him to the ground. He rolled towards the bar, ducking underneath it. Dezma moved in front of him, bumping against the grinding pot and sliding it to give him cover.

The room fell still as death as the doors creaked back shut. Footsteps thudded on the Grendle floor; the marching of soldiers. One pair broke from the others. Lighter steps, but somehow more distinct, like the pitter patter of rain on a roof, the weeping kind of rain, isolated and alone yet somehow multitudinous and everywhere.

"What," came the voice. "No applause for a hero?"

The voice chilled him. Chilled him the way that the courage of saying difficult words drained the feeling from fingertips and sucked the sensation from the underside of tongues. So slow and deliberate. So full and inevitable. Like the final bit of water falling from a waterfall.

Gavin's breathing stuttered. He swallowed it down. Forced it even. Still. Quiet. His horrifying thought just moments before turned itself over, and he wanted with everything he had for it to be true.

"General," Dezma said, leaning over Gavin. Her elbows thunked into the wood above him. He craned his head up, seeing nothing but the underside of the smooth Grendle grains. "If anyone else marched into my tavern with six armed men, I would draw my Longtooth to defend from a mugging."

"Lucky for you, I am not anyone else."

The collective bated breath of the room suffocated his ears. Muttered words and frightened gasps rose with the thuds of footfalls and the cracks of Canines on wood. His heart filled his throat. He stayed still, tucked in an awkward tangle of limbs between Dezma's legs and the bar. To move was to die. He closed his eyes, and felt a tear trickle down his cheek. But inside, he already knew. He knew he was right, that his children must have snuck away, not understanding the danger.

Saving themselves. By accident. *Moons.*

"To be blunt, sir General, I would have preferred the mugging," Dezma said, voice low.

"You may yet get your wish," the General replied. "There is—"

"Yes yes," Dezma cut him off. "You're looking for someone. Don't think we haven't noticed the patrols you've set around the edge of town, and the soldiers you have marching up and down our roadways. You think this someone is in the town, and now you've stooped to searching families in their bedrolls while they ready themselves for sleep. I would have thought brigandry was beneath you, sir General."

"If I thought of things as beneath me I would still be harvesting Harrywick beans in Vaelor."

Gavin's hand clenched and unclenched in a fist.

"Perhaps the difference between you and a brigand is rather thin," Dezma said.

A slow burning rose in the back of Gavin's head, like a swarm of Vargus picking at his brain. He shook against the wood of the bar. Hope. Hope. Hope. It didn't feel like hope. It felt like tense muscles and fear, like sweat and a quivering chin.

"Sir," a voice snapped the air, cutting through the room. "There's only one little girl in here, but she's got the wrong hair, and there ain't no twin."

"Aye, and you'd better keep your hands off her or I'll make sure you never have hands to touch little girls with again," Nell called out.

"Leave her, Nibbin," the General called. "It's not her."

Gavin sagged back against the bar, pulling his knees up against his chest. His muscles unlocked like a Cyril vine with its base slashed. He was right. They snuck out. They snuck out. *Moons above they snuck out.*

"A kid," Dezma scoffed. "Comparing you to a brigand was too generous."

"What would you prefer, tavernkeep? A lazy king who lets Cindeere tear through your town and murder your young, or a brigand with the power to stop the bloodshed?"

A long silence. The floor beneath the bar grabbed at his

hands with sticky tongues. His shoulder hurt. There was no good place for his elbows or knees.

"Look, sir General," Dezma replied. "I don't really care about your war. I give people drink, I tell jokes, and I find folks some entertainment after a long day's work. Kill as many of Cindeere's men as you want out on the battlefield. We'll probably cheer you on," Gavin felt Dezma shift over the bar, leaning in. "But if I know anything, it's the people in this room. I know who they loved when they were kids. I know how it went when they confessed. I know every bit of unrequited yearning in this town. I could tell you what everyone lays awake thinking about when they can't sleep. If we had a wanted criminal in our midst, I'd have seen it in their eyes long before you came waltzing in with your Canines and your thinly veiled threats."

Something slammed right above Gavin's head. His eyes flinched shut, and he curled further into himself. "You might want to start hoping they've outsmarted you, tavernkeep," the General growled. "Or none of you are leaving town."

Pain, it seemed, had a tendency to drag seconds into an eternity. One spot in particular, not quite the tip of his right elbow, but just below it, *burned* from the pressure where it jabbed into the side of the bar.

"S'that drawn by a child?" Dezma said. "Rather crude for a wanted poster."

"One of my men found it in their Quarter," the General whispered. "Unless you mean to tell me that a child in your town is drawing pictures of wanted criminals from the Steppes *by accident.*"

Another tear leaked from Gavin's eye.

"All I can tell you is, that man doesn't live here," Dezma whispered.

"If I were anyone else," the General whispered back. "I would make you bleed for every lie that left your lips." He paused.

"You're lucky I'm not anyone else."

His footsteps marked his leaving, but they paused before the door creaked shut. "It's only one family. A small price for freedom and happiness, hm?"

And the door slammed shut. For the first time since the General's entering, a true silence emerged. It was the silence of Gavin's creaking limbs as he pulled himself from under the bar and staggered forth, wanting to uncurl but instead clutching his body tight around himself. It was the silence of everyone staring. It was the silence of him stumbling over to his cloak, empty on the ground, and pulling it to his chest, fabric pressing between the severed bones of his two missing fingers.

Dezma stepped over to him, kneeling at his side, wrapping her large arm around his shoulders, giving him a squeeze. He pulled the cloak into his face, tears leaking into its coarse fabric.

"It's worth it," he said, no more than a whispered plea. "Right?"

She stood. "We need a plan," she said, voice low. "We need a plan!" She repeated louder. Her voice bounced off the edges of the room.

Nell cracked his knuckles into the bartop, one by one. "Aye. I've wanted a crack at these soldiers the moment they came through here. Their Wolf's already got one scar across his eye. What say we give him another?"

"Sounds fun to me," A young, female voice. *Jen.*

"Count us in," called the Vennilan's from the far corner. "They're asking for it."

"Aye. Let me get a few punches in," called Jerome.

"I'll never forget your kindness," Bregga called. "I don't know what I can add, but whatever it is, I'll add it."

"Aye!" Another voice, to his left. "They can't push us around!"

"We'll fight for you!" Another voice, in a far corner.

"We'll fight, we'll fight, we'll fight!" Voice, everywhere, all around, rising one by one like chimes struck alone, until their collective leftover ringing warmed the air with harmony. A cold chill struck Gavin in the chest, rushing up his arms, a mix of warmth, and love, and disbelief. Tears caught his eyes. He grabbed his cloak, which felt cold against his fingers, cold and empty. He threw it around his shoulders.

"Right," Nell called. "A plan then. Jen, Jerome, you two see what kinda weapons you can scrounge, makeshift some Long-claws from your scythes, whatever works. We'll needya on the front lines."

"Aye!"

"Anyone got a mind fer Runewaves, you'll be waitin' to catch 'em out when our front line retreats."

Gavin squeezed his cloak tighter, stumbling back away from the crowd. He swallowed through a dry throat.

"Retreat?" Jen called. "What happened to giving them new scars?"

"Aye, we won't do that by being stupid," Nell slapped his hand down on the bar. "I thought about this all night. You get them angry, get them to chase you through the roads. *Our* roads. They'll get strung out. Easy pickings for my fishermen up on the roofs, trawl nets ready. It'll be the best catch of the year."

"I need help," Gavin whispered. "I need to find Bloom and Rose."

The voices fell silent. All the heads turned to him. He swallowed again, hands sweaty. Time ticked away in the back of his head.

"I-I have a mudskiff, with supplies packed and ready. At my house. That's where they'll have gone, anyway. Back to my house. T-they have a pet toad, and t-they were worried... Anyway, I just need to get there. And fast. But there might be sol-diers in the way, a-and—"

"Aye," Nell cut him off.

"I'll come with you," Dezma said.

"Count me in too," Nell grunted. "Just give me time to get the lads set up on the roofs."

"You're leaving?" Jen's voice warbled. "Running away?"

He looked at the floor, where the slit under the front door played with the slightest bit of twilight. "It's too dangerous," he croaked out. "For them."

"As he should!" Bregga called. "We all need his children to be safe. Right?"

"Aye," Nell called. "It's worth it."

"We're settled, then?" Dezma called. "Tonight, the Wolf goes hungry, and the Rabbit goes free!"

And the voices of the town echoed in unison.

"Aye!"

STEAMWAVE

Steamwaves manipulate temperature: the Basal tone expands the circles, heating the water, while the Subversive tone contracts the circles, capable of even freezing the water if the caster is skilled.

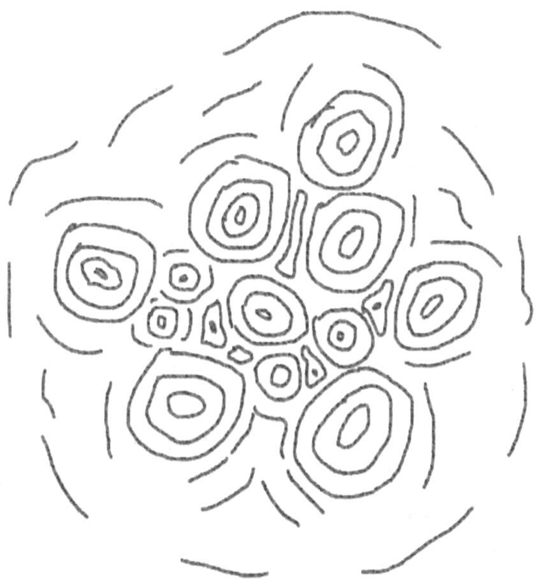

Perhaps due to their evaporative nature, Steamwaves have the least rigid shape. Loosely, Steamwaves are small circles, though their power is transferred through the corellary ripples in between those cast.

Clever Runecasters can Twicecast Steamwaves with Mirrorwaves, using the steam created from the heated water as a canvas for the light to project loose, flickering images.

6

Skin stretched between Stelli's splayed fingers as she leaned forward off the rickety wooden deck and planted her hand atop the lake. Little lappings of water caught in the slight divots of that skin, cold and sporadic and irregular. She cocked her head to the side, raising her chin, hair falling free strand by strand from behind her ear.

In the back of her mind, the first rhythm began. She played it slow and deliberate, and could feel its edges in perfect definition. The water vibrated against her palm, hexagonal ripples pushing up against her skin like a father's fingers on the back of a skull, pressing down and spreading, slowly, slowly, until the fingers reached their maximum extension and a ghost sensation cast the feeling onwards.

One.

She pushed off the wooden deck and wobbled into a handstand atop the water as the hexagonal pulses of her standwave lifted her and lowered her, lifted her and lowered her. The regularity of it, the soft tickle. The way the water rolled, the way the pattern played up her arm, through her neck, in the back of her head. The thought of those fingers, pushing their slow pressure on the back of her skull...

A soft tingle took her mind. Not quite warm, or cold. Not quite real. She could breathe, and she could rise, and she could fall, and she could breathe, and she could breathe, and she could breathe...

At the tip of her thumb, she wove with the tingling, and started playing a second rhythm. She played this one a bit faster than the first. The beats fell in discordant syncopation, off kilter and conflicting. But she didn't think about that. She let her mind fuzz, she let the patterns roll against the palm of her hand, and allowed the discord to coexist. This new rhythm was the rhythm of Boundwaves. They whisked around her thumb, then caught the tips of her other fingers, allowing the water to stretch and bend, yet stick to her hand. She still had to balance, of course. But now any drifting current or natural wave from the wind wouldn't disrupt that balance. She would simply take her little sticky patch of water with her.

Two. She took a deep breath, steady, as she beat her mental drum in two different time signatures simultaneously.

The next rhythm came slow as molasses, and existed behind the other two. She didn't so much *play* it as she did remind it to keep playing, every few seconds. It required her to hit the other side of the drum in her mind, and focus in a different way. Her arm shook, and a bit of pain etched around the fuzzing. But even so, a flash of satisfaction wormed through her gut, as the light around her eyelids faded, her subversive Mirrorwaves stealing the brightness of her surroundings.

Three. Another deep breath to calm her heartbeat—

She wobbled, rhythms sliding through her mind, the beating of her heart throwing off the other patterns, distracting her—she tried to throw her weight to the side, but overcorrected, as the water wobbled, then gave way, her Standwaves faltering—

SPLASH. She twisted under the water, swimming back to the surface, throwing up a hand to grab the wooden deck of the strange, plant filled house. She could feel tall seagrass of the lakebed in her feet, around her legs. She kicked it off, pulling herself the rest of the way onto the deck.

She flicked her hands along her arms, legs, and shoulders,

drying off as best she could, before throwing her warm cloak around herself and going inside. The fireplace crackled with slowly dying embers. She sat down hard at the hearth, back prickling with the warmth of the fire, eyes meandering between the various bizarre plants that adorned the walls.

"Always only three," she said. "I felt better that time though. I didn't wobble at two."

"You're hiding from something again," Tess whispered from the shadows. "The General would say that wolves do not hide."

"You're in the shadows," Stelli said, eyes scanning through the room. They locked on a leaf, which twitched in the wind. But they were inside. There was no wind. "Are you not a wolf?"

"There's a difference between hiding and not wishing to be seen," Tess stepped out from the other room, tossing a seed through the air. It landed on the leaf, and made it drift, as if in a breeze that was not there. She walked over and plopped to the hearth, right next to Stelli. "What are you hiding from?"

Stelli stared out the window, through a tiny gap between drooping leaves. She could just barely see the Tuft Rabbit Moon making its way up the sky, pale light leaving plenty of room for the stars. "The General will have him soon."

Tess nodded. "Everything will change."

"Yes."

"Your brother's death, justified."

"Yes."

"No more orphaned children. No more dead siblings. No more sacrifices. No more war."

"My father and brother will be heroes. *I* will be a hero. The Moons will hunt above a kingdom that cheers our names."

The Tuft Rabbit's tail gleamed bright in the sky.

"Why hide from that?"

Stelli's eyes rimmed with moisture, distorting her view of the

Tuft Rabbit, taking its component whites and pale blues and spreading them into stretched lines, like gashes of starlit blood. "I don't know," she whispered. "It's everything I've ever wanted."

Tess wrapped an arm around her shoulder, giving her a squeeze. "It will feel better once the wait is over," she said.

Stelli closed her eyes, letting herself fall to the side, against the other woman's warmth. Her careful posture broke, just a little. The embers sent flickers of heat along the inside of her neck, up her cheeks.

Hiss... Stelli's eyes flicked open. Tess tensed beside her, hand dropping to the knives at her belt.

Pale white steam flickered and twisted past the window, blotting out the view. It poured through the crack under the front door, sneaking up along the sides, twining through the leaves and vines of the plants on the walls and obscuring the space. Stelli leapt to her feet, drawing her Canine.

"Another test for you?" Tess breathed.

Stelli shook her head. "No," she replied. "He's too busy for that now." She moved to the door with slow steps, holding her Canine out in front of her. The flickering, coiling steam brushed the air of the room with a familiar, humid texture. *Steamwaves. From outside.*

Crreeeeeaaaaaak. Not from the door. From behind her, in the other room. The room she slept in. "Guard my back," she whispered. "I'm going out the front."

"Right here," Tess breathed in return, right behind her.

Stelli jabbed her Canine into the handle of the door, twisting and pushing. It flew open, rattling on its old hinges. Steam *poured* in, cascading through the opening and rising to the ceiling, flickering around the rafters. She stepped into it, flicking her Canine from side to side, casting brief swirls of open space in the steam. Water, rippling. Sky, alit with stars. The pale light of the Tuft Rabbit shone like a lighthouse through the steam.

She paused, weapon held ready, warding. Her mind whirled with her father's tests, her father's training. She let sound overtake her perception. The slightest of ripples. Water, cascading over water. She stepped, slow, cautious, forward onto the narrow deck of wood that spanned above the lake. Most Runecaster's couldn't cast from very far away...

She took a moment to watch the twisting of the steam, to listen for the center of its rising, and calculate the position of the Runecaster. She went from stillness to movement with the speed of a viper, sliding the Canine to the end of her grip and swinging with one hand for extra reach—

CRACK—a cry tore from an unseen throat, stifled, broken, full of pain. The steam stopped billowing, and vision began to return. She wheeled her Canine up by her head, expecting a return stroke—

The steam cleared just enough for her to see the target. She froze, eyes going wide. A little girl. Curled over on Standwaves, just below the deck. Hand clutching the side of her face, and her nose. Red blood welled between the girl's fingers, mixing with tears on her cheeks, carrying down droplets to the side of her jaw and chin, where they...

Dripped, dripped, dripped down, into the water below. Stelli lunged forward to catch the girl before she fell in, watching as the blood filled her Standwaves, spiraling along the hexagons, pulling at the edges. Her hand closed over the girl's arm, and she wrenched back—

The girl stumbled to her feet, standing on the red hexagons that continued pulsing under her feet despite the blood in the water.

Stelli's world numbed. She heard the screaming of the pale moon above her. The stars became eyes. Angry eyes. Devouring eyes. Phantom hot breath rushed along the back of her neck, and prickles wracked along her spine. She could feel the skin of the girl's arm, beneath her hand. Every little detail. Down to the tiny hairs, and the slight bump just above her wrist.

The Standwaves still worked.

She almost collapsed.

A little girl. The most powerful Runecaster in the world is a little girl.

She pulled the girl up to the dock, hand a vice grip around her wrist, dragging her through the door and slamming it shut. She glanced around. No sign of Tess.

"What do you think you're doing?" she hissed at the girl, crouching down to her level.

The girl twisted, wrenching her wrist free and stumbling back. She stuck up her chin, hand still clutching her bloody nose. "I'm looking for Bubbles," she said, words slurred, yet defiant. "You have him, and I want him back."

Behind her, the soft scraping of footsteps gave way to the shadowed form of Tess, shuffling forward with a young boy held firm in her grip. She tutted, clicking her tongue against the roof of her mouth, as her eyes passed across the little girl. "Hitting a child, Stelli? How could you."

"I hit the Runecaster hiding in the steam," Stelli said. "Who then turned out to be a kid."

Tess raised an eyebrow.

Stelli swallowed, mind flashing. *A kid. A kid. A kid.* "Who's Bubbles?"

"Our toad," Bloom said, holding back tears. "A blue toad, da calls him a Wandering Warrighast Toad. His name is Bubbles and we love him very much, you didn't hurt him, did you? Did you?"

Inside, Stelli winced.

Tess sighed. "A *toad*—"

Stelli jerked her head, just the slightest amount. Tess fell silent.

"I saw Bubbles," she whispered. "He's a nice little toad. We're gonna go get Bubbles for you, okay? Here," she reached out a hand towards Rose's face, hesitating. "May I?"

Rose watched her, eyes wary, but lowered her hand. Stelli took the soaked edge of her cloak, and wiped away the blood with a gentle hand. "Shhhhh, that's right," she murmured. The nose didn't look broken. The blow had landed along the cheek, cutting the skin just above the lip. It would leave a nasty bruise, and certainly would hurt, but she would be alright. "Sorry about that nastiness, I didn't mean to hurt you."

Rose's eyes shone confused, glancing around at the tall women surrounding her. "Y-you'll bring us Bubbles?"

Stelli smiled, and nodded. "Yep! Just stay right here, okay? We'll be right back."

She grabbed Tess's arm, dragging her into the cramped, cleared out study. She left the door open a crack so they could still see the kids, watching them run to each other and embrace.

"What in the Carrow Wolf's maw is going on?" Tess hissed. "Why are there children trying to kill us?"

"They're not trying to kill us," she hissed back. "They live here, Tess. It's their home. Bubbles is their pet, and this morning I threw him out the window."

Tess blinked.

"But that's not important," Stelli said. "The girl, Tess. She bled when I hit her, and her Standwaves didn't lose their power. The blood tried to tear them apart, and it failed. I watched it happen."

Tess's eyes changed, snapping into focus. "Just like her father."

Something boiled in Stelli, under the surface. Something that wormed in her gut, made her feel nauseous, something that crept up the side of her throat, poking her esophagus, sharp and ready to pierce.

"It makes so much more sense," Tess whispered. "The three-fingered man has fled for seven Fulls. How would the General have turned him to our side? But children..."

Stelli didn't swallow. The feeling crawled into her mouth, jabbing her tongue.

"He's a monster," Stelli said, words mumbling out as if her mouth was full of spiders.

Tess grabbed Stelli by the shoulders. "Who will still save the world. This changes nothing."

Stelli squeezed her eyes shut. She swallowed. Her mind buzzed with a hidden, painful numbness. "Keep them here," she whispered. "I'll go get my father."

Tess nodded, and they walked back out into the main room. The two kids looked over, eyes bright and excited. "Did you find him, did you find him?"

Stelli knelt down. "When we took our quarter, we have protocol. Do you know that word, protocol?"

Rose frowned, cocking her head. "No?"

Stelli smiled. "It means that there are things we always have to do. One of those things is to clear a house of any animals inside, to make sure we don't end up hurting them."

"Okay..."

"So Bubbles isn't here," she said, watching in pain as the children's eyes sunk and shattered. "But I know where he is. So I can go get him, okay? You just sit tight right here, with my good, nice friend Tess. I won't be long."

They both nodded in the over-exaggerated way that only a child could nod, their hair bouncing. "Be quick," Bloom blurted. "Da will be really mad when he realizes we're gone."

Stell's mouth flickered a smile. "Don't worry, I'll hurry." She nodded at Tess, then darted out the door. She found the easy rhythm of Standwaves in the back of her mind, throwing them down at the water as she walked. Her eyes jumped to the main body of the town, flicking down the long paths between houses, water glistening purple in the light of the just rising Carrow Wolf. Patrols of soldiers marched along those paths, their feet casting out hexagons, angry Canines held firm in their hands. Every opening had a group of soldiers. The whole of the General's company marched to keep the town contained.

She found the General marching with a group of six soldiers, entering the district of houses nearest the swamp.

"General," she intercepted him.

He paused, holding up a fist. The six soldiers around him stopped, eyeing her warily. "Lieutenant."

"We must speak," she said. "In *private*."

"These men are trusted. Nothing you have to say can't be heard by their ears."

"You might change your mind once I start speaking."

"I might not."

Stelli balled her fists, glaring at the six men. A few had twisted, horrible little smiles on their faces. All of them looked at her, and all of the looks felt condescending.

"Children, Father," she whispered. "Have you always known it was the *children?*"

The soldiers laughed, the noise echoing over the rippling of their Standwaves, twisting between the sagging wooden houses, wrenching her gut. She squeezed her nails into her palm, forcing herself to breathe deeply, staring the General straight in the eyes.

He chuckled too, just a couple bursts, quick through his mouth. It burned her. It burned her, because she saw in the tightness of his mouth, and in the posture of his shoulders, that the chuckle wasn't genuine. It burned her, because she knew he was exactly aware how much his chuckle would hurt. It burned her, because even though she knew all that, it still burned. And that made it burn all the more.

"Go," he waved at the soldiers. "Rest. She won't have anything to say that you don't already know. I want you awake and ready by the Devouring, just in case the Rabbits try anything."

"Yes, sir!" They said in unison, stifling their laughter, though sparing a few more amused glances between Stelli and the General as they spread apart and walked away.

"Walk with me," he said, turning and striding between the buildings. She scampered to catch up, feeling the familiar whispering of her Standwaves, as they wavered at the intersection where they ran into the General's. Somehow, as if by some deep instinct, the General's Standwaves seemed to *reverse* when they collided with hers, taking on the subversive tone, deconstructing with her waves and leaving stillness in the water, forcing her to scamper forward even more, hopping the gap, and using his instead of her own.

Her breathing came a little easier, in the embrace of his sturdy Standwaves under her feet. She grit her teeth, fighting the calming buzz of his presence.

"You lied," she said, forcing her fingers free of fists, uncurling them like she was snapping open a clam.

"You believed me," he replied.

Shame and embarrassment rocketed through her mouth, leaving her tongue heavy.

"We're hunting *kids*."

"We are."

"Do you not hear how monstrous that sounds?" She wanted to cry, but she forced herself not to. Her father could not see her cry. Her fingers curled, but not towards fists, towards claws, claws that wanted to wrap around her own shoulders, pull herself into a tight little ball, hide herself from the panting at her neck and the eyes on her back, because Moons damn it all, how could she have been so *stupid*? The three-fingered man could have just fought back, could have just refused to help, and what would her father have done? Tortured him until he broke? And what if he never broke? Stupid. Stupid. Stupid. It didn't make any sense, unless the most powerful Runecasters in the world were *children*, who could be manipulated, convinced to fight... *You believed me.* A tear slipped free, and she slapped it away, hoping her father hadn't noticed.

The General turned them down a narrow path between buildings, forcing them to duck around dangling rain chains. From their vantage, they could see a swathe of open water, across which soldiers marched in patrols of three. In the gaps of their Standwaves, where the ripples died, the Moons shimmered a glorious reflection. The pale Tuft Rabbit, with the purple Carrow Wolf nipping at her long, trailing tail.

"So many people misunderstand the Moons," her father whispered, his voice twisting between the soft ripples of their footsteps. "Every night during the Partial Devouring, the Wolf feasts a little more, and the Rabbit comes closer to dying. People know what it is to fear death. So they pray for the Rabbit, and spit on the Wolf."

The sky danced in its reflection, shifting water playing the chase in a brilliant miasma of purple and pale white light. The Carrow Wolf was magnified in that dark water, its outline shining like a silhouette, craggy surface gleaming its spines and shadows like teeth around a glowing purple eye. The Tuft Rabbit looked small. But its tail was big. Its tail stretched across the reflection, twinkling with a hidden mirth, even as the purple swallowed her.

"So yes, my daughter," he whispered, eyes glowing in the reflection of the moons. "The Wolf is the monster of the sky. But who stops the horizon, which swallows them both?"

Her hands shook, as the Carrow Wolf Moon sunk its teeth into the backside of the Tuft Rabbit Moon, smothering three quarters of its color from the sky. The Partial Devouring happened slowly, like a painting torn from its folds. The pale light of the Rabbit seeped blood across the stars. She squeezed her eyes shut, but the colors told the story against her eyelids just as well as a thousand night skies.

"I have them in my quarter, with Tess guarding them," she whispered. "The boy and the girl, who can cast their Runewaves through blood. I saw them do it. You were right, father. They can stop the horizon," she quivered. "Are you proud of me?"

His hands landed on her shoulders gripping them. She felt his breath on the back of her neck, felt his gaze running up her spine. "Yes," he breathed. "I am proud of you. I have *always* been proud of you. Come. Let us save the moons from the horizon."

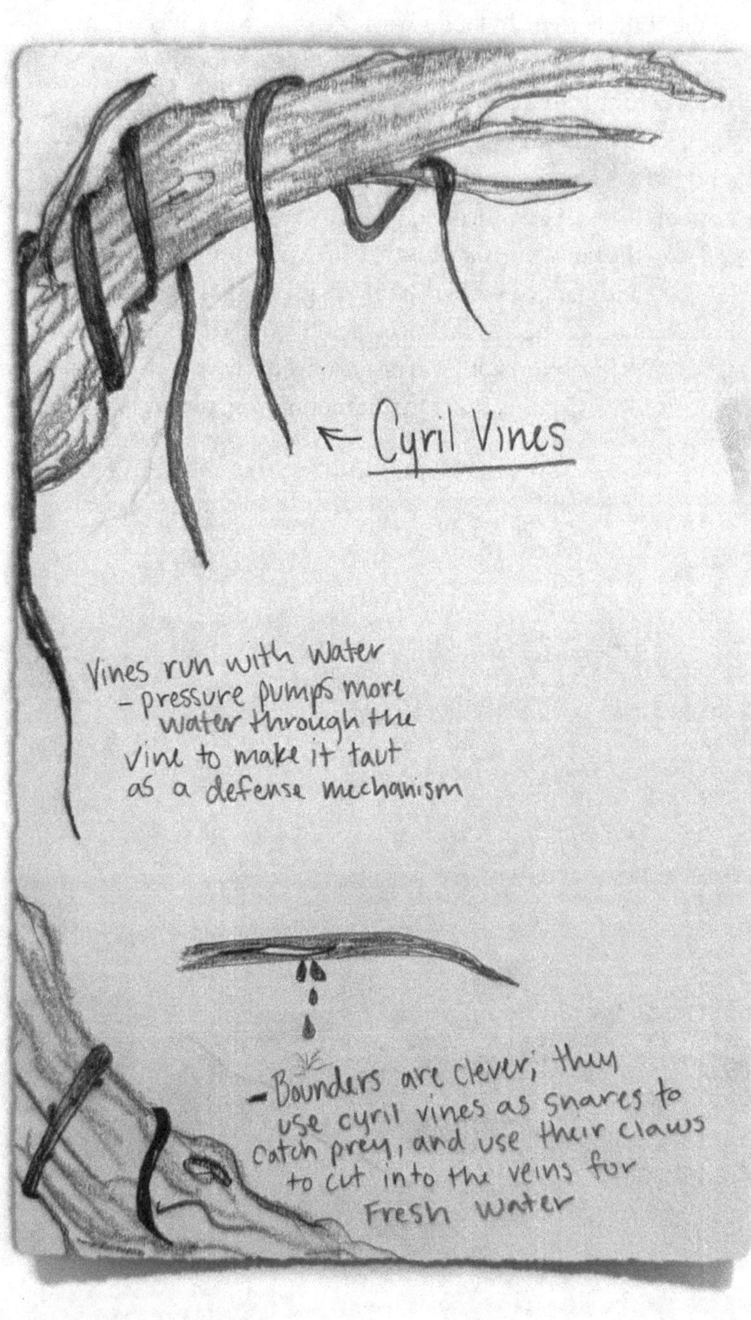
← Cyril Vines

Vines run with water
— pressure pumps more
   water through the
vine to make it taut
as a defense mechanism

— Bounders are clever; they
   use cyril vines as snares to
catch prey, and use their claws
   to cut into the veins for
   fresh water

7

Gavin knelt in the shadow between two houses, hood thrown over his head, eyes locked on the darkness that clung along the waterways before him. Soldiers moved, their footsteps slow, deliberate, sinister. They walked in groups of three. One member of the group cast Standwaves, hexagons rolling out from under their feet to eclipse the other two, leaving their focus free. Every few steps, the other two knelt and tapped the water, twisting the edge of the hexagons into circles that pulled inwards, like whirlpools without the depth and spiral. The result was a wall of Boundwaves in the water, encircling the town, preventing passage.

Nell's hand clasped his shoulder. He turned, meeting the grizzled fisherman's eyes. They shared a smile, and a quick hug. Nell gave him a soft pat on the back, before standing and stepping out of the way for Dezma. She pulled him into a hug too, crushing his ribs into his lungs, but making him smile all the same.

"Go get 'em," she whispered in his ear. "We'll meet you at your house to send you off."

And then they both were gone, slipping down onto the water, moving between the shadows of the buildings like specters of their dead village.

"Hey!" One of the guards called. "What are you doing out this late?"

"Gotta talk to your General," Dezma's voice called, ringing

out above the quiet trickles of the lake. Gavin turned, reaching up above him, pushing off the deck and climbing onto the roof with slow, precise movements. The wood creaked beneath him. The cut shingles pushed their hard edges into his palms.

"Under the Moons?" The guards shot back.

"What do you think happens under the Moons this close to the swamp?"

Gavin moved to the edge of the roof, eyed the gap, and stilled his breathing.

"Ma'am, why do you have a weapon?"

"Maybe because of what happens under the Moons this close to the swamp."

"You need to turn around—"

Gavin leapt, landing with a thunk and a rattle on the house beyond. He tensed, hesitating, laying flat against the slope of the roof and praying his dark cloak would conceal him in the dim purple light of the moon.

"Ma'am if you don't turn around, then—"

His voice cut off in a gurgled shout of surprise. Goosebumps shot across Gavin's arms at the noise, the noise of a man reaching for air and finding blood instead. A second scream sounded, cut short. A third shout, a shout for help, broke through the air, panicked and scared, coupled with frantic footsteps across the water.

In moments the third, too, was choked off, and the silence of the lake returned. He slipped over the rooftop to the other side, foot catching in the gutter to stop him from sliding off. He scanned the momentary stillness of the shadows below.

The lake rippled in the silent wind. He felt it playing around his ears. It filled him. Days had passed without him hearing the lake, and now the way the water danced and the wind whistled felt... muted. Deadened. Like a ball of cloth shoved down the lake's throat while it drowned.

He let his eyes grow used to the lake's natural movement. The slight light reflecting from crests and troughs, the miniscule swaying of the stilted houses, the way they creaked, the way the water smelled against his nose... No people. Nothing inorganic. He moved like rain, lowering himself from the roof to the deck below, keeping his hand on the rafter for support. Strange, he thought, how utterly foreign such a familiar place could learn to become. The way the window shutters sat, the swaying of the rain chains in the wind, even the forlorn tone of the wooden creaking... all of it kept that uncanny sound of weeping squirming across the back of his neck.

Another shout. Voices. Suspicious patrols come to investigate the disturbance. He kept his gaze forward, stepping down a familiar route, quickening his pace, feet sliding through familiar footholds, head ducking beneath all the same beams and low hanging roofs it was used to ducking under—

Bu-wooooooooo Bu-woooooooooooooooo. A horn sounded in the distance, low and droning. The timbre of the air shifted. The weeping on the back of his neck washed down his spine.

Bu-wooooooooo Bu-woooooooooooooooo.

Voices rose as one, breaking through the sound of the horn, hoarse and tangled and scattered, but full of spirit. The sound shook the lake, gave the water a new kind of ripple, one that he couldn't see as much as he could *feel*, in the way the water brought the sound washing against the rickety wooden supports of the houses, in the way a thousand tiny water bugs shook free of the underside of the wood and hopped as one away from the wordless call.

He felt something strange in the presence of such a noise. A welling behind his eyes. A melancholic resignation. He ducked around the last corner, and made it to his house. The low slanted roof. The leaves covering the window, in place of shutters. His hands found the familiar handle, turning it, pushing open the door with a soft creak, leading with his shoulder.

Behind him, the voices and the horns snapped in half, and bent into the chaotic noises of open combat.

He stepped inside, looking around. A long purple sliver of light cast deep into the room, framing his stretched shadow. He reached up, feeling along the Cyril vine that twined among the door hinges.

He took a step forward, using the vine where it glided between the rafters as a guide. "Bloom?" Another step. "Rose?" Another. "You in here?"

"Shhhhhh," murmured a low, feminine voice from behind him. He came up short, sharp metal tickling his windpipe. "Don't scream. They might hear you." He watched the sliver of purple swing shut at his feet as the door closed, severing his shadow. *Thunk...*

"You sound so young," he croaked, trying not to swallow. "Too young to be mixed up in all this."

A soft laugh tickled his ear. He couldn't bear it anymore. He swallowed. The Dewclaw at his throat pricked at the movement. "You sound old," the voice whispered. He felt her movement as she leaned down, directly by his ear. "And scared of change—"

He yanked down on the vine. It tensed against his finger, going rigid—

WHAM. He ducked and spun as the door slammed into the woman, thrown open by the stiff twist of the Cyril vine. He heard the Dewclaw clatter and dove for the sound, hands closing around the hilt of the knife as he rolled and raised it in shaking hands. Where. Where. His eyes scanned the darkness, locking on every shadow beneath every hanging leaf and wide-petaled flower. His back hit the far wall, shelf jabbing him with its corner. A pot wobbled against his back, spilling a bit of soil down his shirt. He could feel the leaf against the back of his neck. *Nurrii Stalks.* He could tell from the texture. *Little pores on the side of the stalks emit a sweet slime, great for morning bread—*

Steel flashed from the darkness. He swung at it wildly, metal shrieking on metal as the knives clanged together. He leapt back along the wall, knocking over another pot which shattered on the ground, spilling dirt across the floor, ducked a third swing, then threw the Dewclaw up to catch a fourth. His assailant's smaller knife slid into the Dewclaw's crossguard, inches from his fingers, and *Moons* he tried to still his hands but his body shivered against his will—

The woman loomed above him, her face a sliver of pale skin in the moonlight. She twisted her knife. His breath left him as the Dewclaw spun from his hands with her clever movement. Her knife slashed into his right thigh. He curled down, hands jumping to the wound as he fell backwards, dark dirty blood spilling over the gap in his fingers. He dragged himself along the floor, forcing breath in and out of his lungs, fighting back the tears that rushed in his eyes at the pain, the pain, the *pain—*

He saw through his water-filled vision the woman standing above him. Long mottled cloak, patterned in a strange way that dazzled the eyes. Her face looked even younger than her voice. A sliver of an expression played on her mouth, the slightest frown, below the widest brown eyes. Then his gaze shifted to the shelf right beside her. Nurrii Stalks, balanced precariously where he'd knocked into them earlier—*as long as you added water. Raw, and it just might stick your teeth together.*

He kicked the shelf with his uninjured leg, snapping it off the wall. The pot crashed down, slamming into the woman's side, shattering against her and coating her in slime. The plant fell to the floor, a jumble of long, drooping stalks, lathering the wood with its juices. He scrambled backwards as the woman tried to lunge for him. Her foot caught in the sticky slime at her feet, pitching her forward. He rolled to the side, repressing a shout at the pain that lanced through his leg with the sudden motion. He forced himself to his feet, gasping, favoring his left side, looking down at the woman on the floor. She wrenched at her leg, trying to get it unstuck—

He grabbed the Dewclaw from the floor and hit her in the side of the head with the hilt. She collapsed, still. The Dewclaw fell from his shaking hands. He checked the woman for a pulse. Found one. Turned towards Bloom and Rose's room, leg trailing blood. He felt light headed. Black spots danced in his vision.

Screams sounded outside. Breaking. Crashing. *We'll meet you at your house to send you off...*

He scrabbled at his cloak, ripping off a strand at the bottom, nails digging into the fabric, teeth clenching as he leaned into the tear. He pulled it tightly around his thigh, watching the blood soak it through even as he tied it off. He let out a thick breath. Flicked his cloak back down, hiding the wound.

A shout. Right outside. The clacking of wood on wood, each parry and blow like stings of a hornet in his head. Water crashing. Splashes. *No time.*

He poked his head through the door, forcing a smile, slipping in. Bloom and Rose huddled together on the floor by their bed. The skin around Rose's nose and upper lip was bruised purple, a shallow gash still leaking blood down her chin. Tears traced across the marred skin.

"Oh, Rosebud," he rushed forward, forgetting the pain in his leg, pulling her into a tight embrace. "Shh everything is gonna be okay, Dad's here now—"

He pulled Bloom into the hug too. They both trembled against him. He rubbed his fingers into the back of their hair, tracing small circles on the right at the top of their necks. "Everything will be okay. Okay? Everything will be okay."

They burrowed into him, holding him, hiding from the world in his arms. He could feel their tears against neck.

"Dad," Rose sniffled in a tiny voice. "Are you mad at us?"

"Oh, Rosebud," he murmured. "I could never be mad at you. Just breathe, there you go, I'm right here, I'll always be right here..."

No more horns sounded. Something splashed, cut off by an angry bellow and a flurry of clacking wood. Something shook the house. He kept rubbing his thumbs through his children's hair, murmuring in their ears.

"It's time to stand up, okay?" Gavin murmured, helping them to their feet, still holding them close. "One step at a time, there we go..."

"Da where are we going?" Bloom said in a shaking voice. "What's going on? What are the horns and the—"

"Shh," Gavin whispered. "I know the noises are scary. I know. I'm scared too. But it's going to be okay. We're not gonna let the things making the noises find us, okay?"

He bent down, putting his shoulder up against the bed. His vision filled with black spots as he grunted, sliding the bed to the side. It screeched. His hands found a wooden indent in the floor, pressing into it, popping up a stray board. He slipped a few fingers beneath it, pulling, wrenching free the boards. They came off easy. Through the gap, below the floor, his mudskiff rocked in rippling water, cresting up and down, up and down.

"Remember the story about the princess and the Zar'thul," Gavin whispered, helping Bloom down into the mudskiff. "The Princess knew about the scary things, and found a way to hide from them until it was all okay. We're gonna be like the Princess."

He moved to help Rose down. She resisted him, looking over her shoulder as a scream tore through the air. A bloody scream. The kind of scream that tore a throat, the kind of scream that didn't end with breathing.

She had tears in her eyes. She focused on Gavin's, a gaze crystallized between father and daughter. "What does that sound mean Dad," she asked, chin quivering. But he saw it in her eyes. She knew what the sound meant. "Can we help them? We should go help them—"

Gavin fought the tears, fought his mouth so it wouldn't curl down and twist under the onslaught of his emotion. "This is the best thing we can do for them," he whispered. Then, in a weaker voice. "The *only* thing."

Rose looked at him, tears cascading down her cheeks. Her little eyes darted across his face, flitting around like bugs in the rain. She gulped.

"We have to go, Rosebud," Gavin couldn't keep the thickness out of his voice. "We have to."

"Okay," she whispered. She let him help her down into the mudskiff.

He hopped in after her. It tipped and rocked with his landing. He had to duck so the rise and fall of the water beneath them didn't knock his head into the floor of their house. He maneuvered around his children to the flat stern of the mudskiff, climbing over the large pack of supplies he kept stocked there, avoiding the large potted plant by the starboard railing, and grabbed the singular oar.

As the mudskiff crested out from under the house, one last thought occurred to him, falling against him like a deluge under his skin. He paused, looking at his two children, huddled in the bed of the mudskiff. So small. They looked back at him with such trust. Tears built under his eyes. He turned, grabbing the lip of the deck at the back of the house, and stretched his arm up to grab a single plant from one of the planter boxes.

A tall stem that split into a thousand little strands, all to carry a singular, brown, unassuming pod. He settled back into the mudskiff, tucked the Isingrass amongst their other supplies, looked up to the swamp, and pushed off the house, sending them adrift towards the embrace of the Aycmors.

BOUNDWAVE

Boundwaves are my favorite-- father always says they are the one Runewave with an accurate name, as the basal tone allows you to bound and the subversive tone leaves your enemies bound.

BASAL TONE

SUBVERSIVE TONE

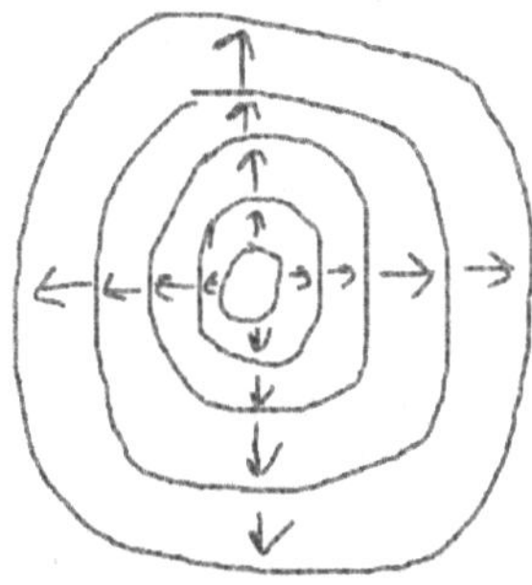

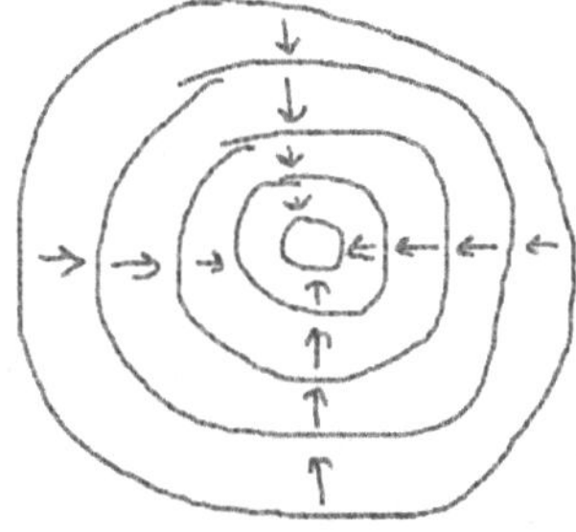

The Basal tone is rarely used in battle. Launching into the air is quite dangerous, and casting Boundwaves through an enemy's Standwaves requires Twicecasting Subversive Standwaves and Basal Boundwaves, which most struggle to accomplish.

Subversive Boundwaves make the water sticky. They are the most useful wartime Runewave, as they can lock down and disable combatants with no risk of drawing blood.

Clever combatants can circumvent Subversive Boundwaves by bleeding themselves. Beware.

My father uses Basal Boundwaves to vault around the battlefield, leaping over opponents. I don't know how he manages such precice control.

8

Stelli listened to the lake, half a step behind her father. Its dance was muted and still. No rain played a beat. The wind brushed her hair, but not enough to whistle. Most would find it hard to consider this sound. It all could so easily blend to silence...

But Stelli listened. Stelli heard the sound. She considered it, turned it over in her head, and felt its singing on her heels. A mournful melody, something sick and sweet. Or something that once had been sweet but now was sick, some heat and pressure pushing down against its motion, squeezing discord from a symphony, yet still it sang... Sang, in the buzzing of the Wyllinic bugs basking in the patter of the swamp's wings, all the noises building into one emotion thumping in her chest. It overwhelmed the prickling against her spine, and suffocated the panting breath on her neck. Half warmth, half anger, now turned to something else she couldn't quite define. She found every step heavier, the closer and larger the swamp loomed, the more they approached the house, the end of the hunt...

Excitement. Infectious, like the way her stability wiped free beneath her feet with each step she took beside her father, replaced and reinstated just as her stomach lurched, ready to fall.

Bu-woooooooo Bu-wooooooooooooooooo—

A shout, and a snap. *Breaking.* The lake hummed. CRACK. CRACK—a scream. She jerked her head towards the noise, but behind her—CRACK. Another shout. The world rose in chaos, splashing and shouting, breaking and cracking. Wood slamming against wood, the slashing of metal on metal, movement between the shadows, movement on the rooftops. Stelli saw some great shape loom in the sky, backlit by the stars, a shape with a thousand little strands and arms, thrown from a roof. A surprised shout rose moments later, the thudding and cursing of tangled limbs.

Her hand dropped to the Canine at her waist, but an arm clamped her shoulder. "Irrelevant," her father hissed. "*Come.*"

She staggered after him as he dragged her away from the battle, away from the horns, away from the screaming. She heard the tearing of flesh, the sounds that came from a bleeding throat. She could *feel* those sounds, even more than the humming of the lake at her feet.

Bu-wooooooooo Bu-woooooooooooooooooo.

"They're *dying*—"

"So are the soldiers at the Saxtile Passage," he didn't slow.

Children...

I'm proud of you.

She followed him. Her father's words arranged the poking, piercing sensation of her loyalty and love into a single sharpened steel hook, which yanked her along behind him. The pain satisfied her, and it was easy to do nothing but let the hook drag her.

I'm proud of you... Yank.

She followed him. CRASH. Wood splintered, windows broke, doors flew open. Resting soldiers started to wake up, stumbling from their quarters with Canines in hand, wiping sleep from their eyes, looking around in the dark in confusion and fear. Stelli ducked with her father past a line of soldiers, rushing forward—

CRACK. A staff swung from the roof, clocking one of the soldiers in the head as two peasants leapt from the rooftops, swinging with wild, unpracticed form, weapons no better than walking sticks and grain scythes. Stelli caught the battle in backwards glances. Soldiers closed on the peasants, six on two. They rushed, stringing out—

Blood spread in the water beneath them, taking their Standwaves. Hands reached up from the murk beneath the dying ripples, wrenching the soldiers through the water, throwing elbows into noses, thrashing and kicking and yelling. Stelli's mind flashed through a million days of training.

Training to fight enemies who avoided blood, and used Runewaves. The peasants didn't care. They swam, and grappled, and threw their elbows like knives, and fought with steel farm tools that cut with rusty edges. They used what they had.

The hook in her heart yanked her around to face forward. She walked with her father. They reached the house. Her father stepped up on the deck, Stelli just half a step behind. Something made him hesitate—

CRACK—he spun at the last moment, catching the blow of a wicked Longtooth lancing for his neck. He stepped backwards and leaned away from the second blow as a woman stepped from around the corner—

Movement, from the rooftop. A burly man, throwing something with many arms, no, not arms, *ropes,* weighted at the ends, splaying against the sky and crashing towards her father.

I'm proud of you.

Stelli threw herself forward, ramming into her father and pushing him away. The net crashed over her instead, weighted ends slamming into her side, the momentum sending her careening off the wooden deck towards the water. She pushed Standwaves down beneath her, landing hard on the hexagons as they expanded. Her breath puffed out. The tangled rope obscured her vision, squeezed her arms to her side. One of the weights fell off the side of her Standwaves, plunking into the water. The full weight of the net bore down. Her cheek pressed the hard edge of one of the hexagons as the pulse passed beneath her. She caught her breath, squirming against the rope, managing to turn herself over, get a hand against the water, lift herself just a little and raise her head

Her father danced, fighting both the man and the woman at the same time. Stelli knew the woman. The long dreads, the fierce expression, the Longtooth. She knew the man, too, and recognized the harpoon in his hand. Her mind flashed with memories of their shadowed forms, standing without fear in front of an entire company of soldiers.

They might as well have fought that entire company now.

Her father's staff spun in a blur as he skipped across the water, hexagons vanishing and flashing to life with each step. The woman darted forward to try and get behind him, but he stayed in step with her, keeping the two opponents at his front, staff always just a shade too quick, deflecting the woman's Longtooth, crashing against the man's harpoon. They drove him further from the plant-filled house, every step he took in that direction met with a lunge and swing, forcing a deflection, a backstep, a growl.

The area was clear around Stelli. She struggled with the net. Her own weight pinned her left arm beneath her. It tingled and throbbed as each pulse of her Standwave rolled into her, bruising, shoving veins and nerves and blood and skin against bone. She rolled over, hooking a finger into the net, pulling it against her Standwaves. She held the constant rhythm of the Standwaves in her head, adding a second, more frantic rhythm over top of it, forcing them both to coexist in discord. Triangles swirled under her hand, the ripples pushing together and *forcing* a gout of water to lance into the rope, severing it. She felt the weight shift, but she still... couldn't...

The man jumped back, diving under the water, and the woman dueled her father alone. He leapt forward, his staff a flurry, the clacking of wood on wood ringing over the air as the woman back-stepped, her Longtooth just a little bit slower each time as she guarded against his blows. But the man hadn't been defeated, he'd dived under, why—

The hexagons under her father's feet lurched to life, coming in more frequent intervals, pushing beyond their natural decay as the man tried to pull himself up out of the water behind him. The Standwaves shoved into the man's chest while his legs were still in the water, pushing him backwards, his body tipping towards the lake as the heavier water grabbed his legs and tried to suck him under. He scrabbled at the ripples, throwing a hand behind him and casting Standwaves of his own, which pushed into his back, stopping his movement. Her father's Standwaves slammed pulse after pulse into his chest—

Stelli got her hand around another weighted connection of the net, using Slashwaves to tear through it. She kicked at the net, trying to stand but still finding herself restrained.

The woman swung at her father while his Standwaves expanded, feinting high before flipping the blunt end of the Longtooth low towards his legs. He dropped one hand from his staff, catching the Longtooth, grappling for it as the woman threw her shoulder forward, staggering him back.

The man twisted up behind them, rolling onto her father's Standwaves as the rhythm of the hexagonal pulses faltered. He sprinted forward, harpoon raised to stab her father in the back. Her father twisted, fighting the woman's grapple to wrench the Longtooth around and deflect the harpoon. The water twisted from hexagons beneath their feet, rolling inwards and rounding at the edges into Boundwaves, locking all three of the tangled figure's feet in place. Her father used his staff one handed to slap away the harpoon and twist around to batter the woman's head, once, twice, the blows not carrying much force, but still eliciting grunts—

The harpoon sunk past her father's guard, slicing his leg—

Stelli got another strand of the net severed, the water roiling in triangles to cut her free—

Blood dripped from her father's leg, towards the water, as the woman tried to twist away—

The water shifted beneath her father's feet, his Boundwaves inverting, reversing their effect. The water shoved him upwards instead of holding him down. He flipped through the air, wrenching the woman's Longtooth out of her grip, throwing her off balance, landing behind the man.

She saw the man's eyes as he moved to turn. They were wide and determined and frantic. Even through the distance, she saw the weight of a full lifetime in that look. Love and stress and worry and care and hope and anger and hard work, etched in the slight creases of the skin around his eyes, the scraggle of his long hanging hair. A fisherman nobody, who did nothing but love at the edge of a swamp—

Her father jammed the Longtooth up through the man's chest, jutting out under his neck. The white bone of the blade gleamed with dark red blood. The space filled with a red haze. The air. The water. The Runewaves.

She saw the fisherman's eyes as he crashed under the surface. They were empty.

The woman bellowed, lunging forward, her feet finding no purchase on the blood filled water as both she and Stelli's father fell into the chaotic jumble of red and disappeared under the surface of the lake. Stelli's hands went numb on the net, her shoulders feeling its weight a thousand-fold. Her half-crouched position, ready to stand, faltered, and she fell forward onto her knees, staring at that spot where the three figures had disappeared.

Her father crashed back through the surface of the water, hands scrabbling on Standwaves that formed at his touch, dissolving in moments from the bleeding of his leg. He turned and swam for the house, grabbing fistfuls of the water during their brief moments of solidity, using them to propel himself forward before the blood washed his grip away.

The woman crashed out of the water in front of him, grabbing the rafters of the house and yanking herself up, Longtooth back in her hands. Her father must have dropped it to swim. This woman, it seemed, could out-swim him even with a weapon in hand. She spun, standing firm before the door, Longtooth warding him farther away. He grimaced, treading water. One of his hands disappeared beneath the bloody surface.

For a moment, all was still. Stelli's hands hung numb in front of her. The hook in her heart wrenched and tugged, rising bile in her throat, threatening to choke her, choke her if she didn't throw up, choke her because she could see what her father was doing, felt the same resource hanging heavy at her own belt... She glanced down at the pouch there, the pouch full of a particular kind of ground up berry that could stop bleeding in a painful little pinch...

The woman didn't know. The same excitement from earlier rose in Stelli. It roiled in her throat, and cascaded up into her mouth, bending her forward as her stomach wretched and heaved into the lake, the vomit remaining atop her Standwaves, soaking into her clothes, pushed around by her hexagon ripples.

Throwing up didn't help. She still felt so relieved. Even as her father swam back through the blood filled water, dove beneath the surface, and came back up with his staff. Even as he created Standwaves on a patch of clear lake, pulled himself to the surface, and stalked forward around the pooling red. Even as the woman stepped forward onto the water, Longtooth held ready, anger in her eyes like brewing storm clouds.

She felt relieved, because she knew how the fight would end, and she was happy about that. It made her about ready to throw up a second time.

The woman stepped forward, left foot far behind her right, Longtooth held high and aggressive. She wasn't stupid. She didn't charge him in anger, or throw over-zealous swings that would give away her intention. As with the beginning of any duel, they probed. Her father extended his reach, swinging up from his low stance in a lunge, which she caught with a lifting of her elbow, lowering the tip of her Longtooth in the way of the strike. Her riposte came with a wide sweep, carrying her father's weapon through. He went with the strike, lifting his arms high to angle his staff towards the water, an insurmountable bar to ward away the woman's blow.

And then she disengaged, stepping back, Longtooth held high by her head, grip firm and untested. She stood between him and the house, mouth set in a thin, determined line.

He leapt forward. She danced back. He lunged, she deflected, their blows clacking together only a few times before they broke apart again.

Her father shifted his right foot to the side, slamming it down on the water just beyond his Standwave. The water boiled, little Steamwave spirals pulling free strands of vapor from the water. Then the patterns shifted. The spirals grew, shifting into rigid parallelogram Mirrorwaves, and through the mist—

The purple light of the Carrow Wolf above reflected, coating her father's visage, playing through the tendrils of mist around him. His form flickered with unclear shapes, the fangs of wolves, the burning glare of the hunter, a thousand arms and staffs flickering and flashing.

When he dashed forward, there was no telling where his next blow would land in the chaotic miasma of reflected light and mist as her father thrice-casted: Standwaves, Steamwaves, and Mirrorwaves, simultaneously. The tavernkeep shouted as he came at her, ducking and parrying strands of reflected purple, her staff passing through shadows and mist—

CRACK.

The first blow landed to her side. She took it, wincing, throwing her Longtooth in a wild counter stroke through the mist. It caught on something, but her father's terrible presence didn't slow. The water beneath his feet *danced*, the dissonant shapes of his Runewaves meshing together, as natural as the ripples of the rain—

CRACK.

This time, to her shoulder. She staggered to the side, ducking down, holding her Longtooth up by her head in a desperate attempt to shield it—

CRACK.

To the back of her head. He was behind her now, the reflecting light playing in the mist to make him appear as if he still stood at her front. Her knees buckled. She fell, catching herself on one hand, throwing a desperate one-handed blow behind her—

CRACK.

To her wrist. She screamed for the first time, Longtooth falling from her hands—

CRACK.

She spun to the Standwaves, unconscious. She didn't bleed a single drop. She just lay there unmoving. Her father stepped back, and before even dropping his thrice-casted Runewaves, began casting a fourth, leaving inward-rippling circular Boundwaves beneath the woman to hold her still. Only then did he drop his miasmic shifting of steam and light.

Moons... Stelli watched him with awe. *He is the best Runecaster in the world.*

He stepped towards the house. "Stelli," he said. "With me."

I'm proud of you. Her numb hands obeyed him, extracting

herself from the net. She stumbled over, pulling herself up next to him at the door. He threw it open, stepping in.

"Next time," he said, chillingly calm. "Be useful."

She bowed her head, stepping in behind him. The hook twisted, winding up the skin of her heart. "Yes, father."

The house was silent. The chaotic jumble of floral smells attacked her nose. Something else wove with the scent. Blood. The tang of blood. She blinked, taking in the main room. Fireplace, embers dead. A broken pot, dirt spilled across the ground. A body. Her heart flashed. A body. A tangled cry spilled from her throat as she ran forward, scooping Tess into her arms, feeling for a pulse.

Thump-thump... thump-thump... Stelli closed her eyes, squashing the tears. *Thump-thump... thump-thump...*

A door creaked. Her father moved into the next room. Stelli waited for the screams of fear, the struggle.

Silence.

Her father stalked back out. Ducked through another doorway. A crash, as furniture fell over, breaking on the ground. He checked the bathroom.

Silence.

He reemerged. She had never seen such a silent face. Every etching of his mouth, the lines by his eyes, all in dangerous equilibrium. Like the sharp edge of a Dewclaw, balanced on the bridge of a nose. He stepped out the front door. Stelli swallowed, hefting Tess up in her arms, staggering after him, coming out onto the deck.

Her father grabbed the woman by the back of her hair, lifting her from the water. She thrashed in his grip with weak movements, lulled and dazed by the growing bruises on her face, and her swollen lip. She threw a punch. Her father caught the hand, spinning her back to the water and locking her in with Boundwaves. She thrashed against them, but it was no use.

"Could have at least given me a fair fight," she hissed.

He put his foot on her stomach, leg tensed, ready to crush her lungs.

She spat on him. It dripped in his stubble.

"Where did they go?" He growled.

She started laughing. He dropped the Standwaves beneath her, shoving his foot down into her chest, pushing her under the water. She submerged, eyes going wide as she thrashed to get back up—

Her hands slammed into Standwaves. From the wrong side. She thrashed, turning over to stroke away from him, to where his Standwaves weren't—

He dropped them, lunging down and yanking her up from the water. Halfway through the surface, he slammed Boundwaves down around her, the patterns locking her in half submerged.

"Where did they go?" He whispered.

"Harvesting harrywick beans," the woman spat. "In Vaelor."

He shoved her under again, this time maintaining the Boundwaves on two small circles right around her hands. She tried to pull herself down, to swim away. The Boundwaves yanked her back. Her eyes went wide. So wide that the red part of her eyes showed around the whites, so wide it contorted the skin around her nose, pulling the veins into definition.

Stelli shook. She couldn't move, save for the shaking.

I'm proud of you...

Her father stood above the woman, hands clasped behind his back, watching her drown.

I'm proud of you...

He let her surface into Boundwaves, keeping her locked in place. She heaved for breath, delirious and wild.

"Where. Did. They. Go?"

She closed her eyes, closed her mouth, opening it moments later to shovel in more air. She gave no response. She just breathed.

"I know how long a woman can hold her breath, tavern-keep," her father hissed. "You're not even close."

He shoved her back under. She didn't struggle this time. Just floated back up, cheek pressed to the underside of the Standwaves, body drifting with the light current of the lake, hands on the Boundwaves holding her in place.

A father's smile...

He stared down at the drowning woman under his feet. Her dark skin was staining purple, the tips of her fingers paling. He let her head surface. She barely breathed.

He knelt above her, two fingers snaking out to squeeze the sides of her mouth. A bit of blood welled from her lip. He wiped it off with a thumb, a gesture so tender and sickening it curdled Stelli's stomach.

A father's hug...

"No no," her father said. "None of that now." He ripped free a strand of the woman's old waterlogged cloak, balling it up, holding it above her mouth. "You said it yourself," he whispered. "You know everything about the people of this little town. Don't tell me you've forgotten."

She coughed, blinking her eyes open, locking him with a gaze stronger than should have been possible. "Go ahead..." she said, voice hoarse and broken. "Coward."

He smiled a grim smile as he tied the torn cloak around her head, and shoved the balled up portion in her mouth as a gag. "Who knows," he whispered. "Maybe you're weaker than the women I'm used to." He shoved her back under.

And sealed her away. He knelt there, staring down at her. Still as water on a rainless night. Wind flickered his cloak in the air, though the ends stayed heavy with wetness.

And the seconds ticked by.

I've always been proud of you...

Her mind pieced through the last few days. Her father had a problem. He didn't know where his target had escaped to. *Children*—the thought curdled in her head. Her father always had a problem. She always found a way to solve his problems. He loved her because she solved his problems.

The toad. The plants. The storybook, about the princess and the Zar'thul. The notes about the swamp, in the three-fingered man's office. The mudskiff, bobbing underneath his house... she turned around, peering into the dark water beneath the house.

No mudskiff.

"He probably fled to the swamp," Stelli said, the hook carrying the words from her throat. "He was obsessed with it; I saw it in his notes. That's where he would go."

Her father's head turned slowly to look at her.

"Tess fled war for years," Stelli whispered. "She knows how to survive in the wild. She knows how to track. She knows the kinds of trails people leave. S-she can..." the second ticked by. The tavernkeep was still beneath the water, fingers blue, face turning purple. "Tess can track them down. If anyone can, it's her."

Her father walked over to her, leaving the woman drowning beneath his Standwaves and Boundwaves. He leaned down, taking Tess from her numb hands. She let go. He lifted Tess in his arms, like a cradle. "How sure are you?"

Stelli swallowed, staring up at the grizzled, gray-haired face of her father. "Tess will find them."

He nodded. "I'll find her a medic," he said. "Evaluate the damage. You'll be in charge of the company in my absence as I enter the swamp. You've done well," he reached out a hand from under Tess's body, cupping her chin and giving it a squeeze. "And you've salvaged this mission. But I won't give you another chance to waste my time being stuck under a net. Secure the town for when I return."

He disappeared into the darkness of the village, lugging Tess. And the seconds ticked by.

Stelli got to her feet, her numb body stepping down into the water, listening to the dying, final shouts of the bloodshed in the distance. The screams were fewer and farther between.

She hated how much his words filled her. Filled her with the desire to make him proud, to show him that she wouldn't mess up again. Her mind shifted into a new mode, a mode filled with numbness, a mode that needed to figure out how to fulfill his request. She had to find the remaining soldiers. Figure out how many were alive. She stepped towards the noise.

I'm proud of you. Was he still proud of her? Would he ever be again?

The woman hung under the water, body floating up against the Standwaves. Her dreads drifted around her head, twisting like seagrass. Stelli stepped around the body. Once she knew how many of her soldiers were alive, she could...

She kept looking back at the drowning woman. Even while drowning, she didn't look small. Her hands, stuck in the Boundwaves at the surface of the water, looked ready to lift the entire lake and hold it between her gentle, impenetrable fingers. The creases of her closed eyes twitched, skin bunching in fear. Stelli somehow felt that she knew this woman. Because in the fear of her creased eyes, she could tell there was something else. A non-fear. A confidence. An ability to look into the eyes of the General of Stillness, the Wolf, Stelli's father, and decide to fight back.

Stelli looked away, back at the town, taking more steps towards the dying battle. But in her head, instead of figuring out how to organize the company, instead of figuring out what her father would want her to do with all the soldiers on her own, instead of wanting to make him proud, a single other thought surfaced.

I wish I could do that.

She spun and ran for the drowning woman. The hook tore her apart inside. She ran anyway.

She brought her nails to her forearm, tearing through her skin, drawing blood. She pressed it to the Boundwaves. The blood surged and tore at the circles and hexagons, interrupting their rhythm, leaving them inert. Stelli reached through the lake and pulled the woman from the water. Her entire world shook. The colors of the sky bent around her vision as tears filled her eyes, because she couldn't believe what she was doing, she couldn't understand, but the pain in her heart felt so *right*—

She turned the woman over, propped her up on a knee, and hit the small of her back with an open palm. Her body spasmed, coughing. Stelli held back her hair, giving another quick hit to the back. Another cough, full of expelled water. Another hit. Another. Another. Another—

Breath. The woman's chest heaved, muscles spasming against Stelli, hand reflexively clenching into a fist against her cloak. "Wh... what—" She turned her head, and saw Stelli. Her eyes widened. She bucked against Stelli's grip, twisting away, stumbling across the water on half-formed Standwaves. She tripped, falling to hands and knees. She crawled to the expanding pool of blood that marred the lake and shoved her hands down elbow-deep in the red.

The blood worked at the edge of her hexagons, and she wobbled. She backed up, lifting her hands and watching as the red water trickled away between her fingers. Her broad shoulders rose and fell in heaving breaths.

Stelli took a few steps closer, hesitant and slow. The woman turned around to look at her. Her eyes didn't quite see. They saw something else. Something distant and whole. A warbling smile played in her countenance. A smile that flickered through her entire body like thunder through storm clouds, rumbling her apart, drawing tears to her eyes, and lightning to her arms.

"Nell has a daughter," she whispered, blood filling the creases in her hands. "Look... Look how much he loves her."

Stelli paused her advance, watching the woman with weary eyes.

The woman looked back, seeing the everything behind Stelli, and then seeing Stelli. Stelli couldn't quite match that gaze. She couldn't quite lift her eyes far enough.

"How could he do this," the woman whispered. Her eyes swirled into angry focus. "How could you do this?" She lunged at Stelli. Stelli staggered back, arms out to brace for the woman's addled charge. Strong as she was, the woman was too close to death to resist. She slumped into Stelli's brace and fell against her, holding her shoulders in a weak grip.

"You know where the family went," Stelli whispered, supporting the woman's weight. She shifted, and stepped back.

I'm proud of you. A cold flash, a twist of the hook, yanking her towards the abyss of the swamp.

She looked up to meet the woman's gaze and didn't flinch. For the first time in as long as she could remember, she felt a savage burst of respect for herself.

"You know where the family went," she repeated, swallowing. The world around her didn't quite feel real. The hook tore chunks of flesh from her heart. She spoke the words anyway. "And I know how the General hunts. We can stop him, and save your friend. If we work together."

In the delirium of the woman's near death, her eyes focused into Stelli's, and her lips twisted into a bloody smile. "A traitor," she whispered with awe. "Perfect. Let's hunt a damn Wolf."

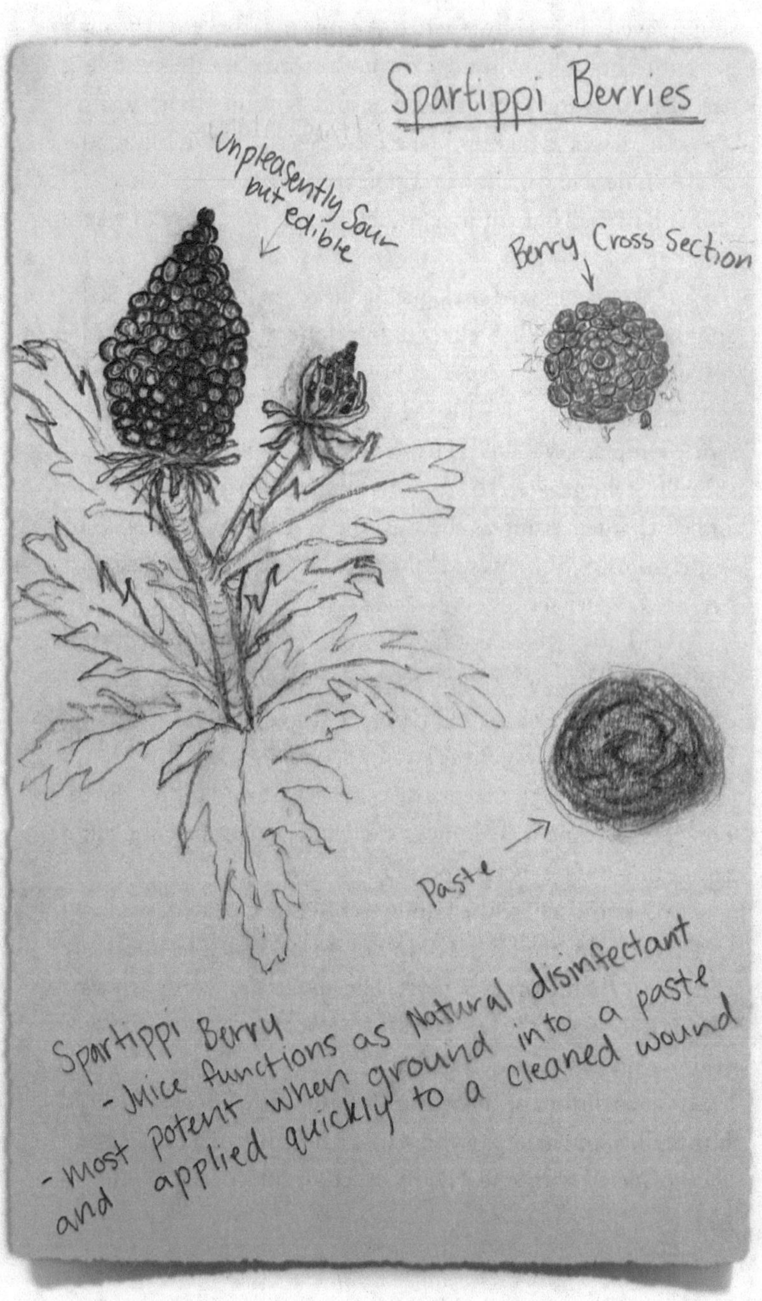

Spartippi Berries
Unpleasently Sour but edible
Berry Cross Section
Paste
Spartippi Berry
- Juice functions as Natural disinfectant
- most potent when ground into a paste and applied quickly to a cleaned wound

9

Gavin guided the low-bottomed mudskiff through the dark blue slime of the bog. Heavy leaves drooped above the quiet family, letting down soft drips of old dew, which fell just heavy enough to not be water, and stuck to what they hit just quick enough to not be sap. The only glow that broke through the tree cover filtered in soft beams of purple light, which caught the heavy stillness of the bog water and reflected a shimmering green.

The smell of moss and shadows hung in the air, a stench that lingered in clothes and nostrils, and clung like wet fabric to skin. On their mudskiff, though, a second smell drifted through that heavy fabric. A wide and ominous odor, like a decaying compost pile coupled with age old mildew. It followed the mudskiff like a cloud, emanating from the wide leafed presence of the Alimin plant, growing from a pot at the vessel's center. Insects buzzed and flitted through the swamp air, but as the mudskiff approached and carried that stench, the clouds parted with a sound like tearing parchment, peeling away to try and flee the Alimin. Most of them escaped. A few flew too slow, careening into lethargy as the odor washed across them. Every few minutes, the soft croak of a toad broke through the buzzing of insects.

Gavin held up his hand. One of the bugs landed on the end of his finger. "Here, little guy," he cooed. It was heavy and large, tens of little legs pulling at his skin as it crawled around between his fingers. Its eyes took up most of its head, wide and angular and multi-faceted, each little cone visible and spinning. Its long sleek body had a dark blue black sheen to it, rounding through the thorax and abdomen. Two long antennae stretched from its head. A stinger pulsed at the end of its abdomen, pushing in and out of a long, sleek sheathe.

"Da, da it's got a stinger!" Bloom said, leaning in, cocking his head. "Da can I touch it?"

He laughed a low chuckle. "Not the stinger, Bloomstalk. But you can hold it. Here..." he rested his hand on Bloom's small wrist, coaxing the bug until it stepped on to Bloom.

The little boy stared at it, eyes wide as the Moons. "What is it?"

Gavin lifted the oar again, slotting it into the notch at the stern, sculling lightly across the top of the water. The ooze swirled towards the oar, trying to stick, flickering with blue bioluminescence as it got excited. He yanked the oar away before it could latch on. His eyes traced the landscape around him, searching. To their left, two large Aycmor trees twisted together, leafless branches tangled forever, embracing even in death. A touch of relief spread through his hands as he guided the oar: these trees were the first landmark that showed he had led them down the right path.

"The Hearts of the Swamp," he whispered, turning back to watch the creature crawl on his son's hand. "They're called Swamp Hounds. Beautiful little hornets, aren't they?" Another stroke in the bog water, another yank away from the slime. The mudskiff crested onward.

"Will it sting me?" Bloom had his hand up in front of his face, watching the large wasp poke and prod around at his knuckles.

Gavin smiled. "Only if it smells a flower. Flowers send Hounds into a murderous frenzy. Best to keep it away from Rose," he glanced at his daughter, curled up on the blankets he had stocked under a little lip of wood at the bow. Her eyes were squeezed shut, asleep. Bloom scooted away from her, mouth opening to form a little 'o'. Gavin laughed. "Kidding, Bloomstalk. Rose might be our little flower, but she doesn't smell like one."

"True, she's stinky." The Hound hopped up off Bloom's hand and buzzed away, wings flitting between purple beams of light.

"Hey now," Gavin said. "Don't make fun of your sister while she's sleeping. There's no fun in that."

Bloom laughed, hands dropping to his lap.

"You should try and get some sleep too," Gavin whispered. "You've had a long day."

The smile faded from Bloom's lips. Gavin focused on the movement of his wrist, leading the oar in little figure eights behind the mudskiff, kicking off the slime, and propelling them forward. Let the wrist go, and the hand follow. Let the wrist go, and the hand follow...

"Can I ask you something, dad?" Bloom crouched next to Gavin at the stern, looking down as the oar disturbed the bogwater. The blue slime congealed at the cutting of the oar, spinning and clumping together as Gavin jerked the stuff off with each movement.

"Of course," Gavin said. His heart hadn't uncurled its petals since they left. Maybe it would someday. He felt bags under his eyes, like raindrops begging to fall. And his leg throbbed. "Anything."

"Is there gonna be a home for us to go back to?" His voice quivered with the words.

Let the wrist go, and the hand follow... The mudskiff crested on... "I hope so, Bloomstalk," A tear made it past the bags under his eyes, rolling down his cheek. "I didn't want to leave."

"Then why did we?"

Another tear. Gavin felt it on his chin, hanging for a moment before it fell. "Because keeping you two safe is more important than anything else in the world," he whispered. Another tear. This one found the corner of his mouth. "To me."

Bloom leaned into him, wrapping his arms around Gavin's torso, burying his head in his shoulder. "You're the best dad ever," Bloom whispered, squeezing tight. "You are home."

The tears broke, body numbing, lip quivering. He wrapped his free hand around Bloom, squeezing back, forcing slow breaths in and out, even as his lungs wanted to jolt, and the tears poured down his cheeks, across his mouth. His hands shook.

Let the wrist go, and the hand follow. *Breathe.* Let the wrist go, and the hand follow. *Breathe.* Drops of dew clunked down from the drooping Aycmor leaves, plopping onto the mudskiff with a thunk, or hitting Gavin in the shoulder, or slapping against the oar. A new genre of rain, heavy and slow and calming and meditative. Let the wrist go, and the hand follow. *Breathe.* Let the wrist go, and the hand follow. *Breathe.*

Bloom's breathing slowed to match his, and they grew steady together. He felt the moment his little boy fell asleep. The slightest nodding of his head, the way his arms felt, the sound of the breathing, all of it. He knew his kid. He pulled the oar from the water, slow and careful, scraping the slime off with the starboard railing before setting it down. He grabbed a blanket, and tucked it around Bloom's shoulders where he slept.

Walking didn't feel good, even the couple steps down their small vessel. Pressure on his right leg sent lancing pain up through his chest, and down to his ankle. He grimaced, checking again that Bloom and Rose were asleep, before rolling up his pant leg to look. The makeshift, torn-cloak bandage was stained a deep, dark red. He dug into the pack of supplies, withdrawing his jar of Spartippi berry paste, his Ralaf leaves, and sliding over one of their water pails. He made sure to keep three stocked and fresh at all times, covered with a lid that slid through grooves at the top.

He took a deep breath, and unwrapped his leg. The wound oozed warm blood across his hand. He shifted starboard, running through a mental list of predators in the swamp. *Blood hunters... blood hunters...* The Zar'thul hunted under the light of every Devouring, even partials. Not a problem for tonight, the Partial had passed hours ago. The Hounds hunted the smell of flowers. Snyrsnouts and Bounders were opportunistic hunters, laying in wait for prey to stumble upon them. Vargus went crazy for blood and flesh, but they abhorred the smell of Alimin, so on the boat he should be safe. Bluotaes Birds would come to watch when something bled, but they were not hunters—

A three-toned caw sounded above Gavin, each note distinct and existing together in discord, one note propelled deep from the throat, one as a trill high above, the other as a chirp through the middle. He glanced up with a half smile, eyes finding the source of the noise perched in an Aycmor branch above him. The creature carried a long plumage of faded black and green that seemed to vanish into the canopy. For a moment, as the leaves shifted in the light breeze, it looked as if this bird carried the entire swamp as its tail. It cawed again its three-toned caw, and adjusted its plumage.

Gavin gave it a nod, looking back down to his wound. As he lifted a mug from the supply pack, filled it with as little water as he could, and poured it over the wound, he couldn't help but feel the gaze of that bird, and see his wound as if looking upon it from the vantage of a tree branch. So small, and insignificant. This wound was not a bother to the machinations of the swamp. All would be okay.

He took a Ralaf leaf and rubbed some of the dirt and grime free. More blood gushed out, but the grime faded after a few passes, revealing the laceration. Not deep. Certainly not life threatening, unless it got infected. The Bluotaes Bird cawed again, and Gavin felt calm as he continued his work. Moons, how he'd missed this feeling. In the swamp, despite the Wolf nipping at his tail, despite the danger all around him, he heard not the barest whisper of weeping.

He washed his finger in what little more water he felt they could spare, before dipping it in the Spartippi berry paste, and rubbing it into the wound. It stung, but the stinging felt distant and irrelevant to him. He finished by tying the Ralaf leaves into a tight bandage over the wound.

That done, he packed away the supplies, and stared with a heavy gaze at what they had. Three buckets of water. His survival pack, a large cloth satchel, containing various jars and bags of useful flora. One jar of Spartippi berry paste. Maybe three or four more applications of Ralaf leaf. Three days of dried rations, though that shouldn't be an issue, he knew which plants and animals could be eaten here in the swamp. Ground Burria for sickness, five doses. Rhondrum thorn antivenom, more than enough for the occasional accidental prick. And a little touch of Morri, a poisonous stalk that numbed nerves, useful for taking away pain in small doses.

The dropping of that heavy water from the Aycmor leaves picked up in speed, plop, plop, plopping into the bog around their little mudskiff, building a cascade of noise. The buzzing of the insects shifted, snapping and darting. Dark masses of flying bugs swarmed across tree boughs and trunks, clamoring over each other, or fighting for space. Gavin turned his gaze upwards, shading his eyes against the water that found its way trickled down through the tree cover. Bloom and Rose, tucked in under the bow, dodged most of the soaking. In minutes, the chilled water found its way through Gavin's cloak, weighing him down with wetness.

The mudskiff drifted in the water, bumping against a root that stretched up to peek from the murk. Vines hung down from the trees' boughs in wide loops, reaching up across to other trees and clinging through beams of soft purple light, which now twinkled with drops of rainwater. Gavin hunkered down lower in the mudskiff, smiling at the vines. He followed one in particular up to a dark hole in the side of a tree, and spotted a flash of eyeshine, which drew a wider smile from him. Across the root, little dark shapes undulated their pincers as they crawled towards the mudskiff, falling over one another, a few of them getting slammed away, spinning to the bog by an unlucky drop of Aycmor drip. *Vargus... flesh-eating parasites... don't leave an open wound uncovered at night, or you just might get an infestation...*

Gavin shifted to the center of the mudskiff, grabbing the wide leafed Alimin plant and sliding it towards the root. The couple of Vargus that had made it to the edge of the mudskiff shook, hopping away from the plant, turning tail and running. Some of the nearby Vargus on the root quivered, staring and paralyzed by the stench. Gavin smiled at them, jerking his head back at the tree, raising a hand to shoo them towards where they belonged. He noted the piecemeal bark around the Vargus den. It looked like paper in the hands of an angry child, all the little pieces clumped back together with sap. No other creature churned the bark quite like the fury of the Vargus as they devoured regretful Bounders and small birds that wandered too close.

He shifted over with slow movements, trying to mitigate the rocking of the mudskiff, and checked on the Isingrass. It looked so brown and dull against the greens and purples and blues of the swamp, despite the plethora of muted colors around him. He checked it for bugs, making sure the tiny needle-point ends didn't snap with the weight of the rain. Still, the extra moisture would do well for them, so long as it saturated the soil. He arranged the plants next to each other, so the Alimin would shield the delicate Isingrass stalks with its larger leaves, yet still allow drips to reach the roots.

All that done, he looked to his children once more, smiled, pulled his hood up over his head, and curled up against the stern, finally ready to sleep.

It came for him in phases. The first, a fitful process of feeling the sounds of the swamp around him, the wriggles of insects against the bark, the croaking of toads in the distance, calling and responding to each other in deep throated conversation. The second phase of sleep came in the form of wondering. Wondering what those toads might be talking about. He swore, in his half-asleep delirium, that their croaks sounded like words. Warnings, he thought. Warnings, like the far off soundings of horns... *bu-wooooooo.... Bu-woooooo....* No... No.... He rolled over, knocking his head on the railing, squeezing his eyes shut. No horns. *Imagination.* He knew the swamp, understood it. The toads used their voices as territory markers, methods of setting boundaries for their hunts, not... not *warnings*, what could they be warning about—

The third phase of sleep wormed deeper into his mind, invading his dreams. *Green scar.* The head of a wolf, carved in a staff, planted in water that bled. He heard its howling once or twice in the night, jolting awake, listening and letting the buzzing of bugs and the dripping of rain and the soft splashing of creatures in the water lull him back to sleep. *He knew the swamp. He knew the swamp. Nothing howled in the swamp. Wolves didn't belong in the swamp.*

He woke to shimmering blue light refracting through rain covered leaves, casting long shadows across the swamp waters. He rubbed his eyes, feeling the cavities beneath them, as if the darkness of his lack of sleep manifested as holes bored through his skin. He checked their supplies. Checked the Alimin, the Isingrass. Looked down the bog river, to make sure no wolves loomed in the night. Bloom and Rose still rested, huddling into each other in their little covered cavity. He let them sleep, cracking the three fingers of his right hand, and the five of his left. He unwrapped a bit of their dried rations, ripping off a small piece of dried flatbread and jerky, munching on it as he stretched. His wrists hurt, sore from the sculling of the previous day.

Bird song rang out with the rising of the sun. Not the bright and cheerful birdsong that one might hear from the herons of the Steppes, nor the long and sorrowful tones that could be heard from the village. These were the croaking pesters of the swamp fowl, squeezed free from low hanging bills and wide chests of the semi-aquatic Berlyrr Birds and the angry, territorial Perching Cranes atop the tree cover. Gavin smiled despite himself, hearing the sound. The Berlyrr Birds sounded like his kids when he didn't feed them, and the Perching Cranes sounded like indignant parents.

He shook himself free from the siren song of the swamp fowl, lifting the oar and slotting it into the notch at the stern. His wrists protested at first, but as he fell back into that slow, rotating movement, casting the oar in little figure eights, the burning died down, letting him work. The mudskiff drifted off the root where he'd moored in the night before, once again cutting through the bog.

It didn't feel so much like a bog during the day. The bright blue light of the sun lit the landscape with a genuine glow. As Gavin traced the trees and foliage with his eyes, he saw the critters darting around, saw the movements of the bugs in the air, saw the darting Bounders as they ran along branches and hopped between boughs. The rain still fell, though it had let up in the night, lowering to a pleasant trickle. It dripped between leaves in little calming waterfalls that cast symmetrical ripples in the river below. Even the slime retreated in the daylight, hovering just under the surface, clinging less to his oar.

"Hey, little sleepyheads," Gavin said in a sing-song voice, as the mudskiff meandered through the bog. He kept his eyes trained on the path in front of them, standing sideways, turned to the right to look while his left hand kept the oar moving in the water. "So many beautiful things to see! So many awesome vines, and trees, and moss! Look at that moss!" He grinned as they coasted past a patch of water covered in greenish yellow moss, spiky and abrasive.

"Dad," Rose grumbled, turning over and pulling the blanket over her eyes.

"It's Frazzle Moss!" He exclaimed, reaching out the oar and wiggling it through the water by the moss. The Bogslime curled to glowing blue life. As the light bathed the Frazzle Moss, it puffed up, rotating outwards to display a row of tiny frazzles. He smiled down at it. "It's got a cool relationship with the Bogslime—when predators approach, the Bogslime lights up. The moss sees that as a warning, and displays its frazzles, thus protecting itself from the predators. Sometimes smart Snyrsnouts will chew on agitated moss to clean their teeth. They prefer Snotslime though."

His children didn't take the bait. Rose yanked the blanket down, staring at him for a while. He spared a glance. The bruise was dark and purple. Her lip looked just a little swollen. She had a confused, disgruntled look on her face. She glanced at the moss, and her face hardened. She turned back to her alcove, scooting to face away from him, and putting her head in her hands.

Bloom got up, groggy and slow, blinking at the moss. He hugged himself, wincing as a thick droplet of water fell from an Aycmor leaf above, sticking to his cheek as it slid down.

"Here," Gavin said, pursing his lips at Rose. He paused his sculling, tossing a roll of rations over. "Eat a little bit, both of you. One piece of flatbread, one strip of jerky, but no more for now."

Bloom blinked again, taking out his share and chewing, nose curling at the taste. He nudged Rose. She huffed, shifting around, bonking her head on the underside of the seat, flinching, rubbing her head, and taking her food.

The mudskiff kept drifting on.

Gavin felt a dual weight settling on the air of the swamp. The constant sounding of birds grew sinister in his ears, and the dripping of Aycmor leaves felt ominous and heavy. He scanned the terrain, noticing a large bush, with leaves that sagged under the water, showing just their curling tips. He frowned, slowing the mudskiff to a pause. That was a Wondor Willow, technically a kind of tree, though its trunk was wide and stout, and never grew taller than a man's knee.

A Hound slapped against his cheek, leaving behind a bit of mud as it recoiled and flew onward.

Rose giggled.

"Hey!" He got the oar moving again, in those consistent figure eights, guiding the mudskiff around the Wondor Willow. "I thought you were upset at me, now you're giggling because I'm funny?"

She bit off a big piece of jerky, bowing her head down and letting her ragged cut of hair fall around her face. "You're not funny, you just *look* funny," she said between mouthfuls. "Like you have poop on your face."

"What!" He put his free hand on his hip, spreading his shoulders and holding up his chin. "I do not look like I have poop on my face, what are you talking about?"

She giggled more. Bloom pointed at his face. "Dad, I think you *do!* That was a Hound, right? I didn't know Hounds could poop so much while flying!"

"Actually," Gavin blurted. "They *do* poop while flying! It's really cool—they use their poops as little markers, so their hive can follow their trail. But their poop is like a turquoise color, and it's actually equally pee as it is poop, so—"

Bloom and Rose both howled with laughter. "I knew it I

knew it!" Bloom wheezed pointing. "Dad, you *have* to see, come on, look at it, look at it."

He reached up to his cheek, using the pinky of his right hand to slide off the mud. He looked down, and the smell hit him. Like old, rotting pollen. His mouth fell open. "It *is* poop!"

Bzzzzzzz... A Hound landed on his hand, little front legs working in the turquoise slime that coated his finger. *Bzzzzzzz...* another one landed next to the first, then a third. The first one took off.

"You smell me, huh?" He said, holding the hornet up by his head, smiling at it. "Hope I smell good to ya, but there are no flowers here."

"Dad those stingers look really big," Rose looked on from the back of the mudskiff, eyes wide. She looked up, following as three, four, five more Hounds darted through the air, whisking towards Gavin's hand to sniff the defecation.

"Don't worry Rosebud, they won't hurt me," he said, though he did keep his hand a safe distance from his face. "They're my friends."

Rose *shrieked,* crouching down and leaping to the side, rocking the mudskiff. Another glob of turquoise slime slapped against the wood. The Hounds flew in small circles, rushing in and out, more and more bits of turquoise coating the brown wood of the mudskiff. Bloom went a bit green in the face, sitting up straight and stiff as excrement trailed through the strands of his hair.

"That's right, just stay still," Gavin whispered, kneeling slowly. Five Hounds clung to his hand, crawling over each other. He could feel their little legs grabbing his skin with soft needles that couldn't quite puncture. One of them crawled for his sleeve. "Don't move, okay?"

Bloom and Rose both sat bone still, eyes following the hornets as more and more flew around the mudskiff, a couple landing in Bloom's hair, or on the deck around them. None stayed for very long, but as soon as they took off, more replaced them. The buzzing eclipsed any trickles or bird song, drowning out the whisperings of the swamp.

"I thought you said they weren't dangerous, dad," Bloom said, eyes straining upwards to try and see in his hair. One of them crawled down onto his forehead. Bloom scrunched his eyes shut, shaking.

"They aren't," Gavin said, reaching his left hand slowly for the oar. "Don't worry."

"Then why did you tell us to stay still?" Rose gulped.

"Well," Gavin kept his voice calm as he maneuvered the oar to the deck, scraping off some of the turquoise poop onto the flat end of the oar. "Put yourself in their shoes. You have a really potent venom, but hurting people is no fun, so you don't want to use it. You just want to go around and find beautiful flowers, and live your peaceful life in the swamp," he scraped off another bit of poop. "A big giant comes in, flailing around. It smells weird. Not like a flower, but weird enough to draw your attention. You don't want to hurt it, but if it starts smashing your houses, trying to hurt *you*, or waving a delicious looking flower in your face, well, you might not have a choice."

Bloom nodded. The Hound crawled down onto the bridge of his nose, front legs fiddling with his eyelash. It paused, then turned and launched off, flying away.

"Right now, there's nothing to be scared of if you stay still," Gavin said, scraping more poop, ignoring the sensation of little legs landing and pushing off his right hand. He kept the pinky held out to one side, letting them cling to it if they wished. "They're just curious, is all. They've marked us, and we're trespassers in their territory."

"When will they go away?" Rose squeaked, squeezing under the seat at the front of the mudskiff, holding a blanket over her head. A Hound landed on her leg, and she squealed, jerking it to the side. Gavin tensed, but the Hound just leapt away and flew off. "I don't like them."

The oar started filling up with congealed turquoise defecation as he tried to clear each new dropping. Of course, it wasn't perfect. The wood stained blue beneath each one, and slime still clung through Bloom's hair, and on Gavin's hand. "Stay still, Rosebud," Gavin reminded her. "They're just checking out their buddy's trail. They'll move on."

As time passed, the swarm started to thin. With each two that flew onwards, only one landed to replace it. Bloom quivered as three or four Hounds crawled on his head. A particularly large one pushed a strand of his hair to the side, maneuvering on his scalp. Bloom stayed as still as Gavin had ever seen him, eyes building with tears. The Hound crawled down the side of his head, pulling itself over his ear, sticking its head down next to the hard cartilage by the lobe. Tears fell down Bloom's cheek, and a little whine escaped between his closed lips.

"Shh," Gavin whispered, taking slow, small steps forward, sliding his feet, and watching as Hounds buzzed away from his large presence, scattering into the air. "It will all be okay, Bloomstalk," he reached out his hand, three Hounds still clinging to his pinky. The Hound in Bloom's ear moved further, its whole body curling under the outer lobe. Bloom wasn't breathing properly. His eyebrows contorted, mouth shaking, tears streaming down—

"Shh," Gavin rested the flat of one of his fingers against Bloom's earlobe, gently nudging up under the Hound's face. It recoiled in Bloom's ear, raising its front legs in a warning. Gavin paused, staring at its little conal eyes, breathing deep and slow. He watched Bloom's breathing slow to match his. "Shh," he whispered again, moving his finger closer to the Hound, just a little bit. An invitation, not a threat. He smiled at it.

It crawled forward onto his finger. He withdrew his hand.

The Hounds started taking off and flying away. Soon Gavin had only the one on his pinky, before that one too abandoned him, vanishing into the miasma of the swamp.

"There we go," Gavin said, moving to pick the turquoise glob out of the boy's hair, before scraping it onto the end of the oar. "You okay, Bloomstalk?"

He blinked a few times, staring at the mirage of Aycmor trunks. "W-why did it feel so tickly," he whispered. "Like they had little fingers…"

"Well," Gavin said, kneeling at his side. "That's probably because Hounds have little tiny hooks on the bottoms of their feet, called tarsal claws, that they use to cling on to irregular surfaces," Gavin scrunched Bloom's cheek. "Like you!"

"I'm an irr… irregular surface?" Bloom stuttered out, eyes going wide.

"Yup!" Gavin said with a big smile. "You're all bumpy and lumpy, rough terrain for their little feet," he walked his hand up Bloom's cheek towards his ear. "I bet they saw your ear and thought *ooooh*, a big ol' cave! Time to go spelunking!"

Bloom laughed, swatting at Gavin's hand.

"Not many people can say they've had a Hound try to jump down their ear-hole and live to tell the tale," Gavin said, laughing back. "You're a champion. One of a kind."

Bloom puffed out his chest, grinning.

"We *are* going to want to get this poop off the mudskiff though." Gavin surveyed the wood, little clumps of turquoise and light blue, half-scraped stains dotted all around.

"Will they come back?" Rose whispered.

"Maybe," Gavin said. "They just searched us. We smell like them now. But if we move too far, or pass near a different Hound hive—"

"There's *more than one*?" Rose shrieked.

"There are thousands, I expect," Gavin said. "But we'll be fine, as long as we get the poop off before moving…"

He glanced back the way they'd come, an idea striking him. Hounds may be harmless in the absence of flowers, but the General had no way of knowing that. If he could draw the hornets behind them, covering their path…

"I don't like the swamp," Rose whispered, still hunkering under the seat.

Gavin smiled a sad smile. "Don't judge it too soon, Rosebud. I haven't even shown you the cool stuff yet!" He knelt down, and began scraping free poop with the oar again. Once he'd gotten the biggest chunks off, he balanced the oar on the side of the mudskiff, careful not to let any of the turquoise substance fall into the water. He pulled the lid off the Spartippi berry paste, using its edge to scrape free the rest.

"Won't they still smell us?" Bloom whispered, legs pulled up against his chest, looking up at the tree cover. The leaves bounced as raindrops fell between them, like a complex natural rain chain.

"They could," Gavin said. "If we didn't have this handy little guy." He slid the Alimin plant to the center, gingerly breaking off a leaf, and folding it in half. It cracked, a little juice coming from the leaf. He moved around the mudskiff, slow to manage its rocking, and rubbed the leaf along the edge.

Bloom wrinkled his nose. "I don't like that smell either."

"But this one will keep the bugs away!"

Rose shifted forward, ripping off a leaf of her own, and tucking it behind her ear.

"Be gentle, Rosebud," Gavin said, moving back to the oar. "But here, if this would help you feel better, you can have this one," he handed Bloom the folded leaf he'd just used to rub down the mudskiff. Bloom took it, also tucking it behind his ear.

Gavin took the lid of the jar he'd used as a scraper, carefully transferring the globules of wasp dung from the oar to the lid, setting it securely by the stern, next to where he stood while sculling. He left a little bit on the oar. Before lowering it into the water, he reached out to a nearby tree, and scraped the oar against a low hanging bough, leaving behind a turquoise blotch.

And on the mudskiff crested, his wrist falling back into the familiar motion. Let the hand go, and the wrist follow... Let the hand go, and the wrist follow... Let the hand go, and the wrist follow...

Every few minutes, he lifted the oar from the water, let it drip dry, then scraped a bit more excrement onto the oars end, and rubbed it on a nearby tree, or hanging frond, or vine. After about an hour of travel, he'd used up their supply.

He could already see more and more Hounds flickering through the air, darting between branches and leaves, swarming in the space behind them. Hopefully, they would create a wall of buzzing hornets that no sane man would dare try to cross through. He pushed off, rotating his hand, getting the oar moving, and left the swarm of Hounds behind.

Bloom and Rose didn't talk much, beyond little whispers to each other. Gavin tried a few times to point out cool plants that they passed—a big green flower on the side of a tree with sharp needle-like thorns on its petals, and a tree growing from the side of another tree, its limbs comically reaching for the water and the sky like a sideways natural bridge. But they didn't bite. Bloom hunkered in the back, staring out at the foliage and murk as they sailed past it. He kept rubbing his ear. Rose had her little sketchbook out, but the container of colors that Gavin had made her from mashed berries and other natural pastes remained closed.

"Hey, Rosebud," he whispered, keeping his wrist moving back and forth, back and forth. He hit the seat next to him with his free hand. "Wanna join me?"

She glanced up at him, stared for a long moment, before

walking over, hand on the side of the mudskiff for stability. She plopped down, looking out at the swamp, away from him.

"What's up?" He whispered. Let the wrist go, and the hand follow...

"What do you mean?" She said, still not looking.

"You're mad at me," he said. "I wanna hear about it. If you aren't ready to talk, I understand, but I'm here for you and—"

"You're hiding things from us," Rose blurted, twisting around to look at him. "You're not telling us something because 'I'm an adult and I know best and I don't want to scare the kids' but we're not little kids anymore either! And it sounded *really* bad back at the town! And I don't even know if we're ever going back or if I'll see Nona again or if she's even *okay*, and we never even found Bubbles, and now we're in this gross swamp and there are big scary bugs trying to eat us and I'm *not* dumb enough to not be scared dad! I'm even *more* scared because you won't tell us what's actually going on and that makes me think it's even worse than you're telling us."

Let the wrist go... and the hand follow... He sighed. Another petal peeled off from around his heart. "You know how I joke about the Bugaboo?"

Rose shifted around to face him all the way, looking up with wide, tear-filled eyes. She nodded.

"It's real," he swallowed. "And it's chasing us."

Rose hugged herself tighter. "What are you talking about?"

"It's a fierce, fanged beast," Gavin said, eyes drifting towards the tiny fragments of the sky, visible through the leaves. Patches of blue, mixed with white clouds. His voice built with the description, adding an exaggerated, sinister undertone... "With huge curving canines, and a mean, evil green scar across its eye. The blood of its last kill drips from its mouth, and it stalks through the night looking for little kids to *gobble up!*" he lunged at Rose, sneering, right hand a three fingered claw above his head.

She jumped back and laughed, sending the mudskiff rocking.

"You're making that up," Bloom said from the bow.

Gavin looked over. "Okay, fine. The gobbling up little kids part is made up. And the blood."

"But not the big, and mean, and scary part," Rose whispered. She looked like she was about to say more. The weight of the conflict in her eyes hung heavy over Gavin's heart. He gave her the slightest bit of a nod. Rose looked away.

Gavin knelt, picking up the oar, letting it drip dry before balancing it on the starboard railing. He scooted forward, wrapping both his kids into a big hug. "I won't let the Bugaboo get us. I won't. Whatever it takes. Okay?"

Rose squeezed him back. Bloom shook against him.

"Make sure..." Rose whispered, swallowing. "Make sure they don't get you either, dad."

ECHOWAVE

In terms of shape and rigidity, most find Echowaves the hardest to master. The shape is complex, and must be exact to achieve the desired effect. Basally, Echowaves enhance and reflect sound. Subversively, Echowaves absorb sound.

Skilled casters can increase and decrease the level of sonic amplification/dampening by extending and contracting the corollary diamond-shaped ripples.

10

Stelli crouched in the crook of a twisted dark tree and watched her father march into the void. Fifteen soldiers accompanied him, holding a tight formation. Their Standwaves pushed harsh hexagons through the dark blue slime of the bog-water. As each ripple passed, the slime congealed and glowed, blue light warbling against the underside of the canopy. The touch of the light curled open the slug-like bodies of a peculiar moss growing along the bank of the river, revealing rows of frazzled spikes, surging and receding with the passing of the glow. The soldiers held their Canines ready, eyeing the moss like it were a beast stalking them as they marched.

Tess led the way. She walked with a limp, crouching every few steps to check the water. The air buzzed. Not just with the wings of the swamp, the hissing of its beasts or the croaking and chirping of its frogs and birds. Not with the sloshing of the heavy bogwater at the marching of the soldiers, or even the shifting of the tavernkeep beside Stelli.

For Stelli the air buzzed with something else. It buzzed like the sword blade buzzed as it spun in the air for a strike. It buzzed like the soft current of the lake as it washed up against the bogwater, crashing over it and receding, time, and time, and time again. It buzzed with the ringing in the back of her head, and the nausea in her stomach, and the utter wrongness of looking down at her father from the boughs of a tree without walking by his side and feeling the comforting wash of his Standwaves supporting her from beneath.

I'm proud of you.

The tavernkeep shifted forward, leaning over a tree branch to peer through the leaves at the movements of the soldiers. "You didn't lie," she grunted. "That's a start."

"And you've refrained from nibbling the hand that feeds you," Stelli muttered back, "even if you won't stop squawking at it."

"Come on," the tavernkeep bumped Stelli with an elbow as she slid down the backside of the tree. She hefted a heavy pack over her shoulders, supplies gathered from Gavin's abandoned house. Stelli didn't feel bad. Gavin should be grateful if he made it back home to feel the loss.

Stelli dropped beside the tavernkeep, hefting her own stolen pack. Her mind came down on the water in a subversion of Boundwaves, pulling the water outwards to soften her landing. She slid the circles into hexagons with the same seamless thought, lifting her leg to take a step—

A Longtooth wavered beneath her chin. The gleaming white blade reflected the pale darkness of the swamp. "Lead the way," the tavernkeep whispered.

Stelli swallowed, eyes crossing as they drifted to the sharpened bone end. She met the woman's hard gaze. She saw nothing but sure, calm, fierce drive. "I don't know where I'm going."

"I'll tell you," the tavernkeep said, jerking her head off to the side, where the bog water hung between thick ferns and low hanging vines. "But you step first."

Stelli glared back. "Afraid, tavernkeep?"

In their shared looks, something *burned*. The hard lines of the tavernkeep's cheekbones, the scrunch of her eyes, the set of her mouth. All of it angled forward into that one, indomitable gaze. "Follow the edge of the mudbank. Don't step on the ferns. And as funny as it would be to watch, duck under the Cyril vines. I can't have you hung before I need you."

The constant rhythm of the Standwaves in her mind buzzed with pent up energy. The water vibrated beneath her heels. Her hand twitched towards her waist—

She shoved it down. Turned. And faced the void.

In the darkness of night, the branches of the twisted trees looked like fingers of some great monster, each trunk a wrist, the very water they stood on the breathing shoulders. The gaps between the drooping leaves, vines and murk-filled foliage loomed like gaping maws. The light of the flickering Bogslime at their feet underlit the terrain with rippling, eerie, refractions. At the edges of the glow, that moss prickled the air, and the spines it displayed felt like eyes opening to stare at the pair of women as they passed.

If Stelli could feel in that moment, she would have been afraid. Instead she just walked onward, Longtooth pressing into her back, mind reeling from the upside down wrongness of the moment. Her mind snapped like the repeating hexagons beneath her feet, seeing over and over her father stepping away from her into the swamp. In her mind, she walked with him.

She didn't. Her body shook. She fought the nausea.

The mudbank warbled between the low bushes and trees, leading her in an arch. With each step, the hook twisted in her heart, and she could breathe a little less. The rope grew a little more taut. Too many steps, and it wouldn't be the hook falling out, it would be her heart tearing free of her chest. The Longtooth pricked the back of her neck. She swallowed, and kept stepping anyway.

The bog water felt *sticky* under her feet. Each step ignited a new tiny candle of bioluminescence under the water, left to flicker out when she stepped away. Each tiny candle burned the moss at the river's bank, stripping open its form to display the thorns within. She ducked under a vine. The fading light of the slime illuminated the side of a tree, casting shadows through a dark hole. Pale eyeshine reflected back. Chills invaded Stelli's forearms. She flicked her gaze down, watching the patterns of the Bogslime. It shifted between foliage in some unseen current, catching the edges of her steps and agitating to life. Little hopping insects flocked around the light. She slapped one off her shin-sheathe.

"Don't step there," the tavernkeep whispered.

Stelli froze, foot in the air. A log drifted in the murk. The tavernkeep grabbed Stelli around the shoulder, squeezing her still. The log drifted closer.

"Snyrsnout," the tavernkeep breathed in her ear. "Stay still. It will pass."

The log's image shifted in Stelli's sight, bark becoming scales, knots in the wood becoming eyelids, narrow end becoming a tapering snout. It barely disturbed the water as it passed them, crawling up onto the mudbank with long, thin claws. It pulled with it a tail longer than Stelli.

The hand left her shoulder. Stelli stepped forward, cautious, ducking between two more trees. "Any other dangers I should know about?" She said, voice wry.

"Everything."

She grunted, eyeing the mud, eyeing the bark, eyeing every twig and leaf and bush. She saw a plant with a little fuzz on its branches, which she could imagine rubbing off to sting, or hardening to pierce. She saw swarms of bugs falling over each other on trunks, and she could imagine them devouring her flesh. She saw wasps the size of her small finger flying through the air, and could imagine how much a jab from their stinger would hurt.

"When will the General rest?" The tavernkeep asked.

"He won't."

"His men will need to."

She estimated the time, glancing up to check the sky. She saw only drooping leaves flickering between the boughs like scales adrift in the wind. A pale purple-white glow flickered between tiny gaps in the canopy. The Partial Devouring had passed. She had watched it, sitting with her father. Soon the horizon would devour both Moons, and daytime would come again.

"Soon," she said. "He won't let them rest past daybreak."

"He'll drive them to exhaustion."

"Yes."

"That's stupid."

Stelli shrugged, eyeing a dark gray rodent-like creature that crouched in the bough of a tree. "Only if he needs them alive."

"Why bring them at all?"

"To learn, I expect," Stelli whispered. "If one man is bitten by a venomous snake and dies, then they will know to avoid that snake. If another is hung by a vine, they will know to avoid those vines. His biggest disadvantage in this hunt is knowledge. Dead men will fill those gaps."

"Surely they resent him, then," the tavernkeep said, voice hard. "What happens when they mutiny?"

Stelli snorted. "They won't. It would take more than fourteen resentful soldiers to bring down the Wolf."

"There were fifteen."

"The fifteenth will never mutiny," she said. "She will learn all she can about this swamp, until she's pulled out your man by his roots and delivered his children at the General's feet."

The tavernkeep grunted. "Cut over the mudbank," she said. "Until you see the river. We should be well ahead of the General by now."

The mud squelched against the tight cloth that wrapped her foot and ankle, finding the gaps, wet and hard against her heel. The mudbank should have smothered life, but somehow desperate fronds stretched up like the hands of a person buried alive, and pale white maggots squirmed against her toes, and little rodents scurried between copses of these miraculous plants, nibbling at their feathery edges. She ducked a low hanging branch and came face to face with a large spider hanging in its web. She edged sideways, grimacing at the wetness of the ground. She breathed a sigh of relief once she stepped onto Standwaves again in the brown water of tidepool-like ponds on the other side of the mudbank.

"The fifteenth, the one you say will never mutiny," the tavernkeep said, splashing down behind her. "Is she the guide?" The pressure of the Longtooth at her back guided Stelli onwards. She saw the river where it sludged through the trees. Bog-slime and mud congealed over the thick, sturdy tree roots.

The air buzzed. "Yes," Stelli whispered, ducking along the side of the river. Up ahead, two leafless trees grew as one, their branches twisting in a dying embrace, suffocating each other with love.

"How skilled is she?"

"Very."

The tavernkeep grunted. Stelli passed underneath the two dead arboreal lovers, glancing up at the smooth curve of their trunks, the way they collided, in passion and finality.

"We need to rest," the tavernkeep said.

Stelli rested a hesitant hand on the coarse gray bark. "Smart," she whispered. "You already used me as a shield against the swamp. If you push me to exhaustion, I might mutiny." She turned to meet the tavernkeep's eyes.

The Longtooth hovered between them, its point warbling. The tavernkeep looked so tired. Eyes drooping. Mouth sagging. Her gaze had lost some of its surety, etched with haunted thoughts and exhaustion.

"Or," Stelli said, walking forward until the point of the Longtooth jabbed her stomach. "Is one resentful woman not enough to bring you down?"

"I'm the one holding the weapon," The tavernkeep whispered. But the tip sagged, unsteady—

Stelli lunged, grabbing the shaft in a burst of movement, spinning past the blade, yanking the tavernkeep forward, and lancing out her right foot to plant Boundwaves in the water. The tavernkeep cursed, yanking back on the Longtooth, trying to step away but finding her feet stuck. Stelli rolled her elbow up and around the tavernkeep's head, wrenching it into the crook of her arm and twisting the Longtooth free, bringing the point up to the other woman's neck. The skittering feet of a thousand little critters fled as the flurry of Runewaves sent the bog slime aglow beneath them.

She hissed in the tavernkeep's ear, hand shaking on the Longtooth. "I betrayed the Wolf, because someone has to, before it becomes impossible," she fought the tears in her eyes, held on to the rope attached to the hook in her heart, and yanked back on it for dear life. She meant the words to be fierce and firm. What came out was a desperate plea. "Don't make me change my mind." She twisted her hand, spinning the butt end of the weapon towards the tavernkeep's head. She raised a hand and caught it.

Stelli stepped back, letting go of the weapon, and shifting her Boundwaves to Standwaves. No need to drop the woman in the river. That might kill her. She turned away, hoisting herself into the tangle of branches, swinging her pack over a bough so it hung free in the air, clinging on by the strap.

The tavernkeep hesitated at the base of the tree, crouching and scanning the smooth, unblemished gray roots. Stelli watched with an absent gaze, half-crouched in the shadows of the branches. She had an impressive neck, thick and corded, lines of muscle running down into her shoulders. Yet her hands moved so delicately across the bark, shifting mud and leaves, plucking into tiny divots. The tavernkeep nodded to herself, and something in the nod comforted Stelli. She'd made a mistake, she realized. Lunging into unknown territory, climbing a tree. The tavernkeep's words echoed in the back of her head. *Everything*.

Stelli shook her head, tracing the bark around her with her eyes. The interlocking branches twisted like forgotten words. They felt wise beneath her touch. Wise and dead. Grown too close together, and burned in the afterimage of their own, one, perfect whole.

The tavernkeep clambered into the branches beside her, hoisting herself with one arm, while holding a bowl steady in the other. It glowed with the shimmers of aggravated Bogslime. Instead of sloshing free, the water pulsed with concentric stars: Tastewaves.

Stelli snorted, looking away. Her eyes lingered on the spot where the dark river emerged from the shadows. It had a light current, flowing deeper into the swamp. Trees and foliage grew amongst the currents, adding slight rapids to its edge, where the water either vanished against mudbanks, or became ponds and small cutoff streams. Hard to tell in the swamp, where the water ended and the ground began. If there even was ground. Sometimes the rocks shifted in the slight breeze, betraying themselves as bushes, or leaves. Sometimes they got up and scurried away.

Here by the river, the harsh purple of the Carrow Wolf Moon cast through the canopy in shimmering beams of speckled light, painting little patches of clarity against the trickling water.

"I am afraid of you," The tavernkeep whispered. She had the bowl balanced on her lap, spinning her middle finger through the water. With each subtle stir, the water and the Bogslime separated a little more, pulling apart like a throat taking in air for the first time in too long. Stelli didn't speak. Just watched the woman, in all her tiny movements.

"I remember you," The tavernkeep continued. She reached into her pack, and sprinkled something into the water. The

Runewaves shifted, stars popping into bubbles. "Out of all the soldiers in the General's company, I remember you."

Stelli furrowed her brow.

"Standing there, right at the front," The tavernkeep continued. "The way you looked at him made me sick. Like he was your god. Frightened of him. In love with him. Full of him, his every command and word. I saw it in the other soldiers too, but for some reason you..." she shook her head. "You were different. I thought to myself, she... she's someone to worry about. She would die for him. She would kill for him. She would sacrifice her very identity to become his weapon."

A three-toned bird call rose in the distance.

"I'm not often wrong about people," the tavernkeep finished.

Stelli shifted, the branches uncomfortable against her. She didn't speak. Soft steam drifted from the surface of the bowl, playing in the canopy. Stelli tensed as the aroma hit her, pleasant and warm.

"I know you don't still work for him. It wouldn't make sense to let me live, give me false hope, and then kill me later. But I saw the way you looked at him then, and I see the way you look at him now," she turned with heavy brows to return Stelli's scrutiny. "And it scares me. Because in the morning, when he comes around the bend in the river, I don't know what you'll do."

The soft buzzing of the swamp rose around them, and then fell again. Stelli watched as a glob of sap collected on the edge of an Aycmor leaf, before plopping down into the river. The tavernkeep shifted closer to Stelli, holding out the bowl.

"Food?"

Stelli grunted looking at it for a long moment. Somehow, the Tastewaves kept the Bogslime at the bottom of the bowl, leaving the top half shimmering clear. A mix of string vegetables and some unidentified meat conglomerated together at the top, floating in the bubbles of the steaming water. The tavernkeep tapped the water again, and little concentric stars brightened up the display, reaffirming the pleasantness of the aroma.

Stelli took the bowl from the tavernkeep's hands, not meeting her eyes, and took a small sip. The warmth of the bowl comforted her hands. The light from the irritated Bogslime glowed up from the bottom of the bowl, filtering through the bubbling stew. Illuminated pops caught her face as she tipped it. She puckered her lips, swallowing the grainy vegetables as she sucked them in over her chin, and handed the bowl back to the tavernkeep.

"You have a plan, then," she whispered, voice creaking from the heat of the soup. "Scared that I'll disrupt it?" The tree hurt, all the little knobs bit her shoulder blades. But somehow, the lingering aftertaste of the soup sifted the discomfort through a gossamer sieve.

"No," the tavernkeep whispered. "I can get us through the swamp. I can find Gavin, with enough time. But when it comes to dealing with the General, you're my only plan," she took a sip of soup. "That's why I'm scared."

Stelli took the soup as the tavernkeep handed it to her, staring down at the bubbling, star-shaped ripples. She lifted it under her chin, and spoke through the steam as the aroma found her. "You don't need to be," she said, but it was hardly more than a whisper. She tried to say it again. She couldn't.

They ate the rest of their soup in silence, passing the bowl back and forth until only the dregs of the Bogslime remained at the bottom. The tavernkeep arranged herself for sleep with the Longtooth at her side, planted firmly between the tangled branches. Stelli made sure to lay facing the other woman, with her hand resting on the Canine at her hip. The weapon was next to useless in a direct fight against the tavernkeep's Longtooth: Canine's were designed for Runewave skirmishes where one could not afford to draw blood, not duels against bladed weapons.

Still, the weight of it comforted her, the heft of its hitting end that she could imagine weighing down her wrist...

Her body split into little pieces as she fell asleep, sifting through the woven branches beneath her, passing into the dead lover's embrace... Something tickled her arm, she jolted, slapping at it, heard a hiss and a scurry and felt the tree branches shake... Vertigo slammed her as she saw below, sifting brown water... She grabbed the tree branches, shifting to be stable, eyes blinking closed again... Something felt *wrong*... Her head spun and twirled, a vast emptiness expanded behind her, as if she stood on the edge of everything and faced away from it. But, with her eyes closed, the end of everything expanded in front of her too, and... but there *were* things, the branches under her back, the tickling of a bug's legs on her cheek that she had to leave there, because to brush it off was to move, and somehow moving didn't feel quite possible—

I'm proud of you—

A twig snapped in her palm, and she felt its hard edges dig into her flesh, pushing little breaks and brambles in her skin.

She blinked her eyes open, and felt alone. More than alone. Emptiness filled the space around her, and stole her breath. She lifted a palm to her face, blinking. Light played off her eyelashes, trickling through the Aycmor leaves not far above her head. Her thumb brushed a bump on her cheek, red and raw. Its itching pulse pumped through her jaw whenever she shifted it. She pushed herself to sit up, groaning, running a hand down her aching legs, massaging the inside of her thigh, under her knee. Another bump of skin, hardened like a callous, but *so* itchy.

"Morning," the tavernkeep's voice broke through her morning dreariness. She crouched further down the tangle of limbs, staring down the river. Her face sagged with exhaustion, but her shoulders were steady, Longtooth unshaking in her grip.

Stelli checked her pack, making sure none of the tight clasps had come undone in the night. She slapped a large hunch-backed black bug off the metal, but otherwise found her supplies in check.

"We need to kill his guide," the tavernkeep said.

Stelli's eyes flicked over. She swallowed over a dry throat.

"Without her, he'll be stumbling blind. But we need to get her alone."

"He won't let her alone," Stelli whispered. "Not as long as he needs her."

"Then we'll have to somehow separate them."

"He might even keep her on a leash," Stelli's voice dripped with bitter tar. "If you want to kill her, you'll have to kill him. And—"

"Yes yes," the tavernkeep snapped. "Even fourteen soldiers wouldn't stand a chance against the Wolf. I know. Why did you save me then, if there's nothing we can do?"

"Fourteen soldiers can't defeat him, no," Stelli whispered. "But I know of two children who could."

The tavernkeep turned to stare at Stelli, eyes hard.

"You know, don't you?" She shifted forward on the branches, lip curling down at the discomfort. "What they are capable of? I could train them. I know how the Wolf fights."

"They're eleven."

"And if they are the only solution?"

The tavernkeep kept her eyes locked on Stelli for a long moment before turning back to the river. "As soon as children become a means to an end, we have already lost."

Creaking birdsong wove through the branches around them, as the blue sun rose.

"I don't believe that separating the guide is impossible," the tavernkeep said. "They aren't joined at the hip. What do you know about her? Habits, tendencies, things we can exploit?"

"I need you to swear to me one thing, tavernkeep—"

"Dezma," the woman snapped.

"Dezma," Stelli whispered. "I need you to swear something to me."

She met Stelli's eyes, that hard, overwhelming gaze encapsulating Stelli's essence. "What?"

"If your way fails," she whispered. "We go with my plan."

Dezma worked her jaw, grinding her teeth.

"If we don't use them, he does," Stelli whispered. "Don't you think it would be worth it?"

"Fine," Dezma spit. "But only if you swear you'll do what you can to make my plan work."

"I swear it."

Dezma nodded. "Then I swear it too."

Stelli sat back. "She knows the ways of nature better than anyone I've met. But she's never been here. She knows the signs of what is poison and venom, but not the specific examples of such here. She knows how to distinguish between what is threatening and what pretends to be. And she knows how to take the necessary risks."

"You know her well."

"She's also aware of patterns," Stelli said. "I would guess that she's picked up on some sort of tell. Something your friend does that cues her onto his tail. If we could figure out what that tell is, we could disrupt it—"

"Gavin won't be going on foot," Dezma murmured. "He's got a mudskiff. I hadn't thought of that. How could she possibly follow him?"

"If she knows he's rowing..." Stelli shrugged. "Even I could follow a river."

Dezma lowered herself from the tree, landing with a soft splash, before reaching up and unhooking her pack, hoisting it up on her shoulders.

"You might want to use subverted Echowaves," Stelli called

down. "The Wolf will soon be close enough to listen."

Dezma looked up, raising an eyebrow. "Subverted..?"

Stelli dropped to the water, lowering a hand. First, her Standwaves, to catch her. But then, where her hand touched the water, a new pattern emerged. Soft, like the unfolding of a flower, composed of diamonds.

The world went silent. Not a single buzz of an insect, nor the rippling of the water. The softest creak of a bone or a tree limb vanished. She raised her hand, moving it above the water outwards. The diamonds unfolded further in a large circle around them, leaving the water in the middle still, save for the Standwaves directly beneath them. The soft rippling of the river returned to them. Every few seconds, a soft buzz zipped by, as an insect flew through the circle of petal-diamonds in the water.

No birdsong. No everpresent, ebbing and flowing of tiny wingbeats.

"Subverted Echowaves," Stelli said. "More specifically, Echowaves cast with a Subverted Tone. They dampen, rather than echo. Some people call them Dampeningwaves, but I find that clumsy."

Dezma just stared at her. Looked down at the Echowave diamonds, the pattern flipping back and forth, petals opening in both directions. She stepped across it, staggered, eyes going wide, before stepping back in. She opened her mouth. Closed it again. Knelt, and stared at the pattern.

"Can all the waves be Subverted?"

"Yes."

Dezma stood back up. Blinked. Shook herself. "Fascinating."

Stelli shrugged. "Whatever you were going to say before, talk freely."

Dezma shook herself, stepping up to the perimeter of the circle of Subverted Echowaves, shooting nervous glances down the river. The subtle current trickled around Dezma's Stand-waves, dragging the pattern away, before a new pulse came to replace them. "I was thinking about this slime," she muttered, bending over, poking at it with the end of her Longtooth. Where she touched, it clung, congealing as she pulled her weapon away. "It reacts to touch, clumping together." Dezma jerked her head further in the river.

Stelli followed, looking down. The slime drifted in little stringy clumps pulling apart, before finding another bunch to stick to. Down the middle of the river though, it meandered in little spirals, following a disjointed path. The line of this abnormal pattern trailed through the murk, back the way they came, and further on down the river.

"Stern sculling," Dezma whispered. "One oar, off the back of the mudskiff."

"Disrupting the slime," Stelli murmured.

Dezma slashed her longtooth through the line, sending up a spray of water. The clumps scattered, swirling back into a more ordinary pattern. "If we follow behind him, we can break the trail."

"Tess will know by now that he's in a boat, and keep following the river."

"What decision will your father make when the river splits?"

Stelli frowned, trying to think, while at the same time allowing the two different rhythms of Standwaves and Echowaves to coexist. "He might split his group. If he doesn't expect an armed conflict, better to cover all the bases."

Dezma smiled, jerking her head upstream. "Come on then. No reason to wait for him."

They walked together in a bubble of silence, broken only by the rhythmic splashing of Dezma's Longtooth slashing the water, and the soft ripping of jerky as Stelli bit into some of their dry rations. Twicecasting emptied the strongest of stomachs.

Especially a subverted Twicecasting. The rhythm of the subverted Echowave fell in abject dissonance to the sordid, placid, consistent Standwave, making it difficult to maintain such a stable beat when contrasted with such a miasmic one. It gave her a headache.

She focused on ripping the meat apart in her mouth. She missed Dezma's soup.

Bzzzzzzz... The loud wing beats of a hornet slammed through the edge of their bubble of silence. She blinked, her eyes following its large body up as it flew out...

She stumbled to a stop, eyes staring towards the side of the river. *Bzzzzzzz....* Another one darted through the Echowaves. *Bzzzzzzzz...* and a third. "Dezma," she whispered. Another splash sounded behind her. "*Dezma!*"

Dezma backed into Stelli, knocking her stumbling a few more steps forward. She hardly noticed. Her eyes flicked around her, along the side of the river, on the trees, and the leaves, and the hanging vines. Her Subverted Echowaves fell away.

And the sound of a hundred thousand hornet wings assaulting the air blasted through their ears, eclipsing the peaceful silence of their walk. The hornets were *everywhere*. Coating every tree branch. Swarming in the air in front of them. Landing on leaves, before taking off and surging across the river in clumps of two or three, legs battling for domination on their new perches.

"Moons," Dezma breathed.

"Gonna make me walk through there first?"

Dezma shook her head, backing up. "Think they can defeat a Wolf?"

"I wouldn't bet on it," Stelli said, ducking away from the swarm, staggering after Dezma towards the underbrush before the dark haze of hornets took the river. Their feet found footholds on quickly formed Standwaves in the tidepools of a mudbank as they ducked vines, and slid between trees.

"Damn," Dezma cursed. "Damn!"

"Keep your voice down," Stelli murmured, eyeing the ground around them. "We have no water for silence."

"We can't break that trail," Dezma hissed.

"And they can't follow it," Stelli glanced through the foliage at the swarm, which only seemed to grow in numbers. It really did cover the entire river.

"We'll need to circle past the swarm, follow the river from a distance, like before," Dezma whispered. "You're right. This shouldn't change anything, as long as we can meet back up with the river before them, and wipe out enough of the trail. Unless the swarm continues past the fork..."

"We should wait and watch," Stelli whispered.

"And let them gain on—"

"We can move faster than them," she shot back, looking towards the river. "Better to know what they do than guess."

Dezma locked that indomitable gaze upon her once again. "You aren't going to see what you hope to see."

Stelli's jaw twitched. "Maybe the hornets will sting him," she whispered. "Maybe we'll get to listen to his screams as they fade into death."

Dezma's look held for long, painful seconds. The gaze tore her open, stripped her bare, left her small and frail and sniveling. Her maybes clung like droplets of sap from the Aycmor leaves, moments before they became just another part of the muck.

"Okay," Dezma whispered. "You're right. It would be useful, to watch and see."

The air between them burned, and their eyes were moths.

The fire burned out.

Dezma turned away, and moved off back towards the river. They found a copse of ferns, set back from the buzzing of the swarm. They crouched low and peeked through the gaps in the leaves. They breathed slowly, their exhales tickling the feathered greenery like wind through hair. Though they crouched on puddles of water in the mudbank, there wasn't room to cast an Echowave. Stelli's Standwaves eclipsed the entire puddle beneath her, hexagons rigid and locked.

Not that it would matter. The buzzing dampened all else.

You aren't going to see what you hope...

I'm proud of you...

He stepped from around the bend in the river, tall and imposing. His strong jaw cut along his gray stubble. The staff in his hand glowered at the landscape like the very moon in the sky. His eyes stormed, curled and beady and black under thick brows.

At his side walked Tess. Short hair. Mottled cloak, which didn't quite blend into the dark greens of the swamp like it did against the natural blues and purples of the Steppes. Her eyes darted at the surface of the water, scanning it. She bit her lip. Her hand fidgeted with the cloak, as she watched the General's face harden.

The company of fourteen men straggled behind them, disgruntled, disquieted, worn but all alive. The General paused before the swarming insects and stared up at them, face hardening into a firm line. Stelli leaned forward, not breathing, her world again shaking and shifting, flipping like a sword's edge. She stood on the edge of nothing and everything. All she would have to do is step forward, and she would be in the everything. His face... his face... *I'm proud of you—*

Stone cold eyes, over an emotionless countenance.

"How dangerous are they?" He growled, loud enough to carry over the buzzing.

Tess took a few cautious steps forward, pulling her hood low over her face, crouching low. She cocked her head as one of the hornets buzzed right in front of her, and then three more circled her head, before darting off.

"I'm not sure, General. I'm not familiar with this species. But hornets of this size, and this many of them... the potency of the sting doesn't really matter. If they attacked, we would die."

"York," the General barked. "Forward."

The frightened young soldier stumbled out of the ranks, eyes wide. He looked at the General. Stelli saw him shaking. Her eyes drifted down to his right foot, where the tight wrappings of his cloth covered up a stiff, hardened bump. Her hands felt the blister as it formed, felt the sticky mucus coating her fingers as she rubbed it down on the skin...

"Sir," York said. "Sir General, you know that I would never disobey you, I-I have always, *will* always, believe in the cause, b-but certainly even you can see—"

The General raised his staff, pressing the head of the wolf into the space between York's shoulder blades. His head cocked to the side, smiling down at the younger man. A look of love, of care, of... of pride... Stelli knew that look. She'd seen that look, directed at her. It hit her like a physical force, coating her skin in goosebumps. Her world flipped sideways, her visual perspective wrong, all wrong. Nothing was behind her. The hook. The hook had just been trying to drag her back to everything. And she'd made it. Everything was *right there*, in that look in her father's face...

York gulped as the wolf's head staff pressed into his back, pushing him forward a few steps. He looked up at the raging swarm. Stelli's heart closed in a clamp of steel. York glanced back at the General one last time. The General smiled, and gave an encouraging nod. The company of soldiers stood with their chins up, their shoulders straight. She picked through their faces. Many unfamiliar. One of them... *Seban.* He saluted, a stiff gesture, his second and fifth fingers up to the sky. A second soldier joined the gesture. Then a third. Then all of them. York's eyes shook as he looked between them, filling with tears.

He turned and stumbled into the swarm, ducking his head, holding his hands above his eyes, palms pressed so hard into his skin that Stelli could see the whites and reds of his worry wrinkles contorting his otherwise smooth face. The hornets slammed into him as he got in the way of their flight patterns, some bouncing off and starting to circle, others clinging to his cloak, crawling up his back, across his hood, over the hands that covered his eyes, their little legs picking at the spaces between his fingers, stingers pulsing in and out of their abdomens. His shoulders shook, his whole body shook, the Standwaves that held him up burst with an uneven frequency, wobbling him in the water, moving with the current. He fell to his knees with a muted splash, as more and more hornets darted down towards him, crawling up his sleeves, along the hem of his pants, under his chin, and on his neck.

Stelli forced her eyes to stay open. She couldn't bear to close them and wait for the screams.

Wait for the screams.

Wait for the screams...

York let out a surprised little guffaw, holding his shaking hands away from his eyes. He staggered to his feet, turning his hands over and watching as the hornets pulled at the fabric of his cloak, tickled his eyebrows, and then flew away. At first just one or two, with three more to replace them. But then three or four abandoned his skin, and only one or two landed. He spread his arms, tears streaming down his face, a grin plastering his mouth as little joyful giggles left his throat.

The sound of his laughter soon eclipsed the buzzing of the swarm.

The General waved the rest of his soldiers forward, and once again marched into the void.

11

"Alright Raindrops," Gavin whispered, as the pale hew of the Tuft Rabbit slowly slid its filter over the world. His heart struck his chest with painful blows. His head twitched over his shoulder every few minutes, eyes straining the shadows. Night had a way of bending the patter of Aycmor drip, curling it sinister. "Keep your eyes out for the biggest tree you can find."

He wasn't worried by the patter of the Aycmor drip. That sound was as natural to him as the rise and fall of his chest, the slight whisper of air through his nose as he drifted asleep at night. No, it was the sound behind the sound, the sound that he only heard because he knew it was impending. The return of the weeping of the man Gavin had killed. The Wolf, and all his soldiers, who were no doubt crashing through the swamp to try and find him. He cast his eyes at the dark curling Aycmor boughs, at the infinite interlocking of their leaves drifting with the passing of raindrops between their wide surfaces above him. *I'm sorry,* he thought. *I'm sorry to bring such a monster under your canopy.*

He grit his teeth and guided the mudskiff through the river with light swirls of his oar, sculling off the back. The river narrowed as the swamp grew denser, trees pushing in on either side and casting long shadows. He had to duck the low hanging vines. Each circle of the oar brought the sound of thick trickling to his ears.

He forced himself to breathe.

"Big trees?" Rose whispered. Whispering felt right, when

the night came. As if any noise would alert the Wolf to the Tuft Rabbit's presence in the sky, and draw it out sooner. "What for, Da?"

"Is the Zar'Thul gonna come out?" Bloom's voice shook. "We should find an algae pond like the princess did!"

Gavin chuckled. "Good memory Bloom. But if we got in an algae pond we'd get all wet, and our food would spoil from the dirty water."

"Dad, how did the princess survive if she went down in an algae pond all alone, and came back up with no food?" Rose frowned, eyes scanning the trees around them. "She should have starved, right?"

Gavin laughed again. The unease slid away at his children's words, until he looked at them, until he saw them, until he had to look behind again, and then back, in case they had vanished during his looking.

He forced himself again to breathe. "Perhaps so, Rosebud. But that misses the point of the story."

"The swamp's not our enemy!"

"Bloom gets it," Gavin said. "Her fate was in her own hands, not the swamp's."

The last few bird calls of daytime croaked out between the trees, leaving the swamp to hang in a momentary silence, save for the buzzing of insects, and rippling of his paddle in the water.

"That one's pretty big, Da," Rose pointed at a large black-barked tree with twisting limbs and wide, flat leaves. One of its huge boughs stretched above the river, drooping Cyril vines like flabs of skin.

"It is," he said. "But that's still an Aycmor. We're looking for a Grendle. Look for the color of the bark. Think Grendle Grey."

"Grendle Grey. I'll find it, dad!"

"No I will!"

"Hey!"

Gavin watched with a smile as Bloom and Rose tousled with each other, trying to cover the other's eyes with their hand, laughing together as they wrestled. The loud mirth drew a hiss from a nearby Aycmor, as a Bounder ran down a Cyril vine. Gavin ducked out of the way as it took flight, spreading the flaps of skin under its arms, coming to land just at the edge of the water on the mudbank. It scrambled, kicking up mud, vanishing into another tree.

Gavin swallowed, and looked over his shoulder again. He rolled his shoulders, but he couldn't shake the feeling of eyes boring into his back. *Not real.* If The Wolf's eyes landed on his back, it would be too late.

The river came to a delta, where the dark blue-stained water trailed in amongst the ferns, and the mudbank dissolved into wide puddles. The river lost its definition, spurts of ground rising in the center, wide Wondor Willows dotting the shallow water. A toad hopped onto one of the Wondor Willows, pale blue and large as a human head. It bellowed out a croak as their mudskiff drifted past it.

"Dad it's just like Bubbles!" Bloom pointed, reaching out a hand—

"Nope," Gavin's chest jolted, and he bit back his words from coming off as a snap. He sculled the mudskiff away from the toad. "Careful, he might look like Bubbles but he's still a wild animal."

Bloom pouted. "Bubbles let us cuddle him as much as we wanted."

"Bubbles grew up with you," Gavin said, trying to keep his voice light.

Bloom's eyes tracked the toad as Gavin navigated the delta away from it. The way his eyes burned with tiny little tears reminded Gavin how few petals he had left around his heart. He glanced at the sky. The edge of the small Tuft Rabbit just poked up above the canopy, shining between the Aycmor leaves. He forced himself to breathe deeper, and scull faster.

He led the mudskiff around a bend, pushing through small floating ferns. They emerged into a small pond. A stream led away to their right. A waterfowl beaked water across its wings. It squawked and flapped away as the mudskiff crested past.

"Is that one, Dad?" Rose pointed. Gavin made a show of squinting, following her hand. He knew what he would see. A little ways from the pond, through a scattered, pool filled mudbank, the large trunk of a Grendlewood Tree cut through the Aycmor's, its roots tearing the mud.

"Yes!" He forced a grin, though his skin felt stretched and sallow. "Good spotting!"

He sculled the mudskiff up next to the mudbank, stepping out and hiding a wince as he put weight on his right leg. He glanced around the pond as he pulled the mudskiff ashore. He stomped around to leave a chaotic jumble of markings behind. With the Aycmor's thinned by the long-stretching roots of the Grendle, the Zar'Thul would see a person standing in this clearing for a long, long ways. Time to leave. He stared at the mudskiff, a weight settling on his heart. It couldn't bring them any further.

Gavin nodded to himself. A necessary sacrifice.

"Alright," he whispered. Sweat licked his palms. "I think you guys will love this. It's one of my favorite little secrets in the swamp. But it's gonna be more dangerous. We'll be walking among the wildlife. I'm gonna need you two to be calm, quiet, and follow my directions—the first time I give them, as soon as I give them. Can you two do that for me?"

They both nodded, eyes wide. He leaned over them, checking the clasps on their pack, heaving it over his shoulders. The extra weight sent lancing pain through his leg. He grit his teeth, forcing himself not to wince, and grabbed the oar.

"Rose, grab the two water buckets, make sure to hold them steady, okay?"

She nodded, stepping out of the mudskiff with a squelch, heaving the brimming buckets up by their thin metal handles. She stood with her chin up, little arms shaking a bit at the weight of the water, legs spread wide.

"And Bloom, you grab the plants."

Bloom's nod came vigorous and wide eyed as he hefted the Alimin up next to his chest, clutching the Isingrass beside it, leaning back a little to keep them balanced.

"Follow me," he whispered, stepping back from the mudskiff, ducking under a leaf, eyes trained on the ground. "Step where I step, and don't go in front of me. If you see anything that scares you, tell me as calmly as you can. Got it?"

"Yep!" They both hissed back.

He watched a bit of blue slime crawl off the end of his oar and slip back into the water. The mud cushioned his footsteps, grabbing them with its suction. Every time he pulled his foot back, the earth inhaled. He held the oar in front of him, gently skimming the top of the mud, just in case it could catch anything his eyes failed to spot.

With each step, the swamp came more alive around them. *Slow...* he reminded himself. The weeping whispering on the back of his neck urged his feet forward. *Slow...* The stillness of twilight gave way to the croaking of toads, low and high, their great guttural symphony playing in tones Gavin couldn't comprehend. A bush rustled. His heart leapt. He paused, using the corner of his eye to look. Eyes shone from darkness. He raised his foot with a loud squelch, dripping mud from the heel of his boot. The eyes vanished with a flurry of rustling. He ducked between the low hanging boughs of a couple Aycmor's, stepping over a rotting log, scanning the small clearing around the edge of the Grendle. *Slow...* The weeping pushed him, like a hand on the small of his back.

Quiet. Water sloshed against the shore behind them, plunking and rippling. A nearby toad joined the chorus. A Bounder flicked from the treetops, whisking between shadows. Rustling. Insects buzzed. A bush near the Grendle vibrated in an absent wind, and dark flowers curled around thorn-filled branches.

"Dad," Bloom's voice shook from behind him. Gavin's breath caught. He turned. "There's a really cool looking snake. Can I hold it?"

Under the rotting log, between him and his children, was a little coiled snake with blue rivulets running in stripes along its proportionally thick, stout torso. It looked up at Bloom and Rose with a raised head. Gavin eyed the tail, which remained flat on the ground.

"Don't," Gavin whispered. "That's a Mudstinger. Back away slowly, the way we came, stay on the path we've been following."

They nodded, huddling close together, glancing over their shoulder as they tip-toed back. Gavin felt a weight in his chest, for missing it. *Not slow enough...* Lucky. He'd been lucky. And unforgivably stupid.

He lowered the oar towards the snake. Its head whipped around to look at him, rearing back, hissing at the wood. The tail flicked up, red underbelly flashing in a beam of moonlight. Holding the oar by its very end, he slid the flat head under the snake—

The body uncurled, snapping the tail into the wood with a loud crack.

He stilled his breathing. *Easy there, guy.* He raised the paddle under its body, tilting it towards a large fern growing from the mud. It darted upright, cracking its tail against the wood again. He paused. *Come on now...* He nudged it further. With a final hiss, the snake turned and slithered away into the underbrush.

Gavin waited for a moment, watching it vanish into shadows, holding his paddle by the side of the log. "Alright," he breathed. "Come on, step over the log. No need to go fast. Stay calm."

His kids joined him in the clearing. "Well done," Gavin murmured. "We're almost there," he knelt, pointing to the base of the Grendle tree. It stood large above them, gray roots rising from the mud like uncoiled snakes of its own, wide canopy stretching just above the Aycmors. "See by the roots, where the mud drops off, and there's an entrance?" He forced his breathing steady, eyes locked on salvation.

"We're going in *there*?" Rose's nose wrinkled up. "Aren't there all sorts of creepy crawlies down in the dark holes?"

"Yes," Gavin said, leading the way through the clearing, still sliding the oar along the mud. "But I need you to trust me." With each step, the pain grew. He slid his right foot instead of lifting it, trying to find a more comfortable pattern. Queasiness churned in his stomach.

The oar bumped rocks and twigs. A few times, Gavin caught movement scurrying away. A centipede, legs tripping over themselves in its haste. A tiny frog, hopping from a thicket. A twinge of regret sounded through him as he disrupted their living. But it had to be done.

"Rhondrum thorn," he whispered, nodding to the bush at the side of the Grendle, its dark flowers letting free a beguiling scent. "Don't get pricked."

He knelt next to the opening, peering down. The pale light trickling through the branches of the Grendle started shifting purple. Gavin's mouth went dry, though the extra light did show the expected slope of mud, leading down in a thin cavity below the roots of the Grendle. He slid his oar along the underside of the root. A translucent scorpion darted away from the oar blade, scurrying up the trunk of the tree. He slid the pack off his back, moving in pained bursts, trying to conceal the grimacing as his leg throbbed with the excess movement. He used the oar to test the mud of the slope, waving it through the air, padding the roof of the cavity. No more movement. He let out a breath, sliding the pack forward, dropping it down. It carved a furrow in the mud, coming to rest at the bottom in the near-occluding shadow. He looked around one last time, straining his tired eyes, finding no eyeshine or skittering creepy crawlies. Or, well. *Crawlies.* He didn't like calling them creepy. Plenty of them were nice, if you took time to get to know them.

With that thought, he slid himself over the edge, using an extended left leg to control his slide. He came to rest against the side of the pack, grunting. His backside clung tight and slick with mud, weighing him down. He pulled his hands free, dried them on his pant legs, and stood gingerly in a crouch. The trunk of the Grendle above him made the roof of their hiding spot. Looking up, he could see rivulets of water running through thick translucent veins, vanishing into darkness.

"The buckets," he whispered to Rose, reaching up. He took the first, carefully setting it down, reaching up for the second. "And I can take the plants too," he took them, setting them down. He grinned up at his kids, plopping down into the mud and holding open his arms. "Now the fun part!"

They laughed, looking at each other, before leaping into the mudslide, zooming down and crashing into him. He caught them in open arms, one under each armpit, catching himself on his elbows and laughing as they snuggled into him.

"You both did so well," he tried not to grab them with his muddy hands, relief flooding through him. "I'm so proud."

"I bet I coulda caught the snake," Bloom said, slipping out of Gavin's grasp, falling into the mud. He looked down at his clothes, trying to wipe some of the mud off, but spreading it more as a result.

"I've caught one before..." Gavin said.

"What!" Bloom exclaimed. "Why didn't you, why didn't you—"

"...when I had other adults with me, to rush me back home if I got stung," he finished. "Mudstingers are dangerous. One sting could knock me out, if my body reacted wrong. It's not a risk worth taking with you two around."

"This doesn't look very hidden," Rose murmured, eyeing the open spaces where the roots arched out of the mud. There were five or six gaps, all big enough for a human, and numerous other spots where the now deep purple light of the Carrow Wolf speckled through against the mud. "Is the Bugaboo too big to get in?"

"No, I expect it could fit," Gavin said. "But it won't get us tonight."

"How come?"

"The Zar'Thul comes out soon," Gavin could feel the change in the air, as the Partial Devouring neared. Feel the way the symphony of croaking grew slowly towards a climax, the way the flying insects stilled, the way the humidity christened his tongue. "Even the Bugaboo would be stupid to be out and about while the Zar'Thul hunts."

"The Zar'Thul can't fit in here?" Bloom said, looking around, eyes widening as he craned his neck back to look up at the veins of the tree.

"Nope," Gavin said, undoing the buckle on the pack, taking out more small servings of their rations, preparing one for each of them. "We're quite safe down here. Just keep an eye out for spiders and scorpions and centipedes."

Bloom turned his gaze on Gavin with wide eyes. "Can I hold one?"

Gavin laughed. "Sure, if we see one that isn't venomous. But don't touch anything without asking me first."

Bloom nodded vigorously, crawling up to one of the roots,

craning his head up to look. His nose poked closer to the root than Gavin would have liked. But the truth was, only one kind of scorpion posed any real danger in this part of the swamp. The others would hurt. A few centipedes had nasty bites, but nothing a bit of antiseptic and Ralaf leaf couldn't fix. He sat back, as Bloom squat-stomped around the edge of their hidden cove, and found himself smiling. The petals of his heart uncurled.

"We have food whenever you guys get hungry. You should both eat," he dug into his own, setting their portions on top of the pack. Rose leaned against him, pulling out her sketchbook, flipping through old pages.

"Sorry I got so mad at you before," she whispered.

He blinked, looking down. The seam of the sketchbook had tear marks, leaf-paper ripped along the inside veins. He frowned.

"A bunch of my drawings are gone," she muttered, wiping her eyes with the clean back of her palm. "I don't have any left of mom."

"What happened to them, Rosebud?" He reached around her shoulders, bringing his hand down to feel the torn edges.

"I don't know," she said. "The stupid soldiers must have torn them out. Nell was right. I bet they... they did *horrible* things to Bubbles, too." She again wiped her watering eyes. "For no good reason."

He squeezed her around the shoulders. She buried her head against his chest. His heart curdled, just a bit. *That's how they knew I was in town,* he realized. The journal of a girl with privacy Gavin couldn't bring himself to violate.

Now they paid the price for his respect.

"And I know it's not your fault," Rose continued, shoulders shaking. "I love you so much dad. I know it's not your fault."

His chin quivered. "It's alright, my Rosebud," he rubbed her shoulder. "We're in a tough spot. We're all thorny inside. It's hard to get the thorns out without poking other people sometimes."

Gavin watched as Bloom stared in wide eyed amazement at a centipede crawling up the underside of the Grendle. The toads croaked, the insects buzzed.

"I don't remember what she looks like," Rose shook against him. "I was looking through my sketches and trying to remember but I can't remember."

He rubbed her shoulder, breathing slow and steady.

"Do you remember, dad?"

He gave her shoulder a tight squeeze. "Of course."

"What did she look like?"

He turned down to look at her. She craned her eyes up from his shoulder, wide and impossibly blue. Her nose scrunched on her face, just a little asymmetrical, stretching the skin around her eyes. Her thin wispy hair was tangled and muddy. In the dying light of the Tuft Rabbit, stained with the detritus and exhaustion of the swamp... "I'll take you out on the lake when you're older," Gavin murmured, brushing her hair from her face. "And all you'll have to do is look at your reflection."

She snuggled closer against his chest. "Was she pretty?"

"I thought so," he breathed. "But that's not why I loved her."

"Why did you love her?"

"She couldn't stand the smell of flowers," he whispered. "But when I was sad, she brought me a rose." He squeezed Rose tighter. "She's the one who picked your name."

"Da..." she murmured. "Why do people like that have to die?"

His mouth contorted into a half-smile that felt on his face like a frown. "I don't know," he said. "I wish they didn't."

They sat together for a long moment, listening to the ebb and flow of the swamp. Rose crawled over him, grabbing her dried flatbread and jerky without much enthusiasm, contorting her face as she ripped off pieces with her teeth. Gavin extricated himself, careful not to put pressure on his injured right leg as he moved over to Bloom.

184

"Find anything?"

Bloom stared at the roots with wide eyes, scanning slowly between shadows. "I wanna touch all of them dad," he breathed. "I wanna know what they feel like."

He laughed. "I'm sure we can find you something to hold—"

"What about that one?" Bloom stuck out his finger towards a big spider as it scurried up and hung on the underside of a root, long legs stretching out to cling to the littlest striations of the bark.

"Hm," Gavin breathed, scooting closer to look up at it. Not much of the Carrow Wolf's light curled under the root, making it hard to see the patterns on its back. But, given the smallness of its abdomen, and the length of the legs... "It's a Waterweave spider. You don't often see them out of lakes and ponds, this one must have been scared by the Partial Devouring, and came here to hide just like us."

Bloom vibrated with excitement. "These are the ones that make their webs on the water!"

"Yep! They choose small little ponds and weave right above the surface, so any critters coming to drink will get caught, and down the gullet they go!"

"Do they bite? Can I hold it?"

"They aren't venomous," Gavin said, shifting forward, lifting a slow hand towards it. "It doesn't want to make you angry so it probably won't bite, but they're fast little buggers, let me see if I can—" He brought his hand onto the root behind it, giving the wood a gentle flick. It scurried away from the noise. He placed his other hand in its path, lowering his thumb, coaxing its legs to grab his skin and crawl on... He smiled at the feeling of its little padded feet pressing into his hand. Each time it moved, he felt a little suction. Around the banks of water, these sticky pads helped way more than the hooks that many spiders had at the ends of their feet.

"There we go," he breathed. It started crawling up his arm. He put his other hand in its path, letting it switch hands, crawling over the nubs where his fingers were missing. "Here," he held his hand down. "Don't grab it," he warned. "You might hurt it. But if it tries to crawl again, just calmly put your hand in its way, and hopefully it..."

It crawled around towards the back of his hand. Bloom put his hand out, a little timid. Gavin smiled, coaxing the spider to crawl onto Bloom. The little boy's eyes went the size of the moons as it moved over his small hand, the legs stretching around his thumb and hooking on the back, its abdomen sitting in the center of his palm.

"Woah."

"Cool, right?" Gavin said. "Those sticky pads you feel on its feet help it move around the edges of slick ponds. It's actually a miraculous level of control—when they weave webs, they make them so sticky and durable, even some species of small fish get caught when they swim too close to the surface.

"Woah," Bloom said again, staring at the spider. Gavin had never seen his hand so still, nor his face so full of awe. "Will it weave a web on me?"

Gavin laughed. "Well you tell me, are you a little pond?"

"No, I'm a raindrop!"

"It would really be something, if it could weave a web on a raindrop," Gavin said. "But I don't think so."

Bloom nodded, lowering his hand, shaking it gently. The spider let go and scurried away, back up on the bark.

"You should eat your dinner now, Bloomstalk," Gavin hit him lightly in the shoulder. "Gotta get to bed, so we're well rested for all the cool animals tomorrow, right?"

Bloom kept his eyes on the spider.

"Right?" Gavin whispered a little quieter.

Bloom nodded, squelching back through the mud to the

pack. Another petal tore free from Gavin's heart, fluttering to the ground, color sucked out in the dirt. He watched as Bloom and Rose sat together in silence, and Bloom glanced down at the pot of Isingrass Gavin had brought, and Rose looked out at the slight glimmer of the Carrow Wolf's light in the sky. He stepped over and helped them arrange their bedding over the mud, let them use the pack as a pillow, and smiled down at their small forms under the tree. They snuggled into each other, holding each other close despite the muggy air that hung around them like dewdrops on a dawnlit leaf.

He watched as they tossed and turned, and couldn't sleep. He felt questions in their restlessness. Questions he couldn't answer, at least not for them. He set about removing his makeshift bandage of Ralaf leaves, firm movements smoothing over the turmoil. Again, he had to pry the leaves off, watching little bits of his skin and blood and... Bile rose in his throat, his hands stilling on the bandage. *Moons.* His mind flashed through the previous day. He'd washed his hands. Used Spartippi berry to prevent infection, used Ralaf leaf to bandage. A chill settled through him. It didn't matter.

Among the bits of skin and blood was pus. It clung to the underside of the Ralaf leaf like syrup, squeezing between the greenish swollen skin around the slash in his thigh. His leg hair curled between the ooze, suffocated by the stench that rose to slam against Gavin's nose. He turned away, squeezing his eyes shut. Stupid. *Stupid.* He let out a breath, setting aside the soiled Ralaf bandage, reaching for... The pack, Moons damn it, the pack *he'd let his kids use as a pillow.* His mouth went dry, even as his leg throbbed with pain, and the feeling of that muggy swamp air percolating against the recently exposed skin sent warm shivers up his pelvic region, through his gut. He scooted closer, shaking hands slipping along the straps that kept the pack closed. One of them was stuck under Rose's elbow, which supported her head. He pulled at it lightly, pausing when Rose woke and shifted around, turning over. He reached for the clasp in the moment her pressure relieved—

"Dad?" Bloom muttered, half asleep. "What're you…"

Rose sputtered a snore, laying back down on top of Gavin's shaking hand, throwing her arm over Bloom's ear. Bloom jolted, scrabbling at her elbow, which she threw to the side, hitting Gavin in the side of the neck. She sat upright, twisting around—

"Dad!" She hissed.

"Shh," he muttered, opening the pack. "Go back to bed, Rosebud, I just need to get something from the—"

"Dad what is that smell what's going on—" Bloom crawled over past Rose, staring with wide eyes at the puss covered, greenish skin of Gavin's exposed upper thigh. He froze.

Gavin winced, hands fumbling with the jars in the pack. "Yeah, everything's okay, okay? I just need to get—"

The look on Rose's face stole his breath. A stillness had befallen her, of a different nature than Bloom's. The sort of stillness that begot tremors, cold little movements made at the core of someone when being actually still was too painful to consider. Her breathing stopped and started. For a moment Gavin, too, felt her shivers as if they were his own, felt his hands go cold and the air go still with the weight of words yet unsaid. "Dad…" she murmured. "D-did it, a-are you going to die—" the tears broke, and Gavin broke with them. He reached to her then, hand finding her shoulder, giving it a squeeze.

"Shh, no, I'm not going to die," he pulled out the Ralaf leaf, and Spartippi berry, dropping them on the blanket beside him, looking down at his mud caked hands, and the wound. He turned to their water buckets, dragging one over—

Rose's sobs hiccupped from her throat, heaving and broken and terrified. Bloom just looked on, rigid, like his limbs were sticks.

"Shh," he muttered, grabbing a mug, getting just a little water in it, and cleaning two of his fingers. They shook, the droplets vibrating on his trembling skin. "These berries will fix me right up, okay? There's nothing to worry about, just try to go back to sleep, shh..."

He dipped his cleaned fingers in the Spartippi berry paste, spreading it over his cut.

"Just try to go back to sleep..." he repeated. But neither of them could move. Bloom's face sunk white like the swallowed moon, and Rose sucked in tears, quivering like a leaf in the rain of her own making...

Both of them, staring.

The toads stopped singing. An eerie silence fell across the swamp, nothing but the quiet trickling of the nearby river, and the subtle nearby skittering of the last few insects finding their place to hide.

And then someone shouted. Not in pain, not yet. It was the shouted bellow of someone who didn't realize how the swamp worked during a Devouring. Someone who had just, very recently, realized that they should have been hiding too.

Somebody who hadn't seen a Zar'thul before.

The shout sounded close. Just through the underbrush, where he had left the mudskiff. His throat went dry. *The Zar'Thul will keep us safe.* He finished spreading the Spartippi paste, and with shaking hands lifted clean Ralaf leaves, tying them around his wound. *Not clean enough.* Nothing out in the swamp, in these conditions, was truly clean enough. Dread settled deep, pooling beneath the hot pain that scorched the skin around his wound. He exhaled, and listened to the sounds of fighting in the distance.

"Dad," Rose's voice shook so, so much. "That sounds close."

Gavin grimaced. "I know, Rosebud."

"What if you have to run," Bloom whispered, his eyes still

locked on that spot on Gavin's leg. Gavin tucked it behind himself, but nothing could stop Bloom's stare, seeing through the bandage, seeing that horrible, puss-filled, bloody cut. "Dad you won't be able to run what if the Bugaboo gets you—"

"I can still run, Bloomstalk."

Silence fell across the swamp.

A chill ran up Gavin's back. His breathing paused. Silence could mean a lot of things, but maybe, just maybe... dare he hope the Zar'Thul had won the fight?

"Maybe we won't have to," Gavin whispered. He scooted over next to his children, wrapping them up in a big hug. Rose looked at him, broken and confused. He took a deep breath. He couldn't hide everything. "I set a little trap for the Bugaboo, because I don't think it knows about the Zar'Thul—"

Bloom's eyes went wide against his pale face, some of the color returning. "Is the Zar'Thul gonna eat the Bugaboo dad?"

Gavin rubbed his back. "We can hope, my raindrops."

Screams cut through the night, and despite himself, Gavin tensed. His children curled up against his chest. They breathed fast and shallow. He rubbed small circles into Bloom's back. He squeezed Rose's shoulder. He closed his eyes, and listened.

This violence, and this screaming. That pain, and its keening. All of it could sometimes sound like... sound like...

A hissing screech bore blood across the texture of the sound, razor sharp and vile. It rippled Gavin's skin, drew his eyes wide, and brought forth the searing pain of his leg. He flinched towards the noise, as if it yanked his very soul, as if the swamp itself, and he, a part of it, was bending and breaking and running to go cease that noise, to save the bringer of that noise, to kill the causer of that noise, the evil monster who had brought about the death, death, *death...*

Death of the Zar'Thul.

The thought lanced through Gavin's mind. Hope turned

sour in his gut as the cold wash of necessity shook through his fingertips. He jerked away from his children and snatched up their heavy bags.

"We need to move," he said. "We need to move, *now.*"

12

The Carrow Wolf Moon howled a quarter of the way up the sky by the time Stelli and Dezma reached the delta. Dezma slashed her Longtooth through the last of the slime trail, scattering the drifting patterns in the river. The Partial Devouring would begin soon.

The back of Stelli's head felt skinless, mental blisters popping with each new pulse of the Standwave under her feet. Her legs ached, soreness setting in. Her heel throbbed, bruise forming under the tight wrappings up her ankle. The bug bites on her face urged her to truly rip her skin off, sensation worming its way through her psyche, around the side of her eyes, manifesting as little ravaging dots in her vision. The carnivorous straps of her pack ripped and tore, seeking the meat of her upper arms and shoulders.

"We can slow now," Dezma breathed, ducking a Cyril vine to crouch on the shore, wiping sweat from her face with the back of her hand. The night time air grew thick with moisture, like a suffocating blanket, bringing her to the edge of consciousness. "Gavin went this way," Dezma jerked her head down a side stream to the right, which trickled into a pond. A bird drifted on the water through a beam of purple light, its beak tucked under its wing, eyes open but unseeing. "But let's rest for a moment."

Stelli nodded, stepping onto the bank with Dezma, swinging the pack down by her feet. She eyed a scorpion with a long wicked tail crawling on a branch above their heads. She rubbed the skin of her shoulders, then slid her hands up to massage the back of her head, closing her eyes for a moment. She listened as Dezma threw back a swig from her canteen.

"What is he to you," Stelli whispered, trying to clear the rawness of her head. "That you would do all of this for him?"

"A good friend. A good person."

"He killed my brother," her eyes flickered open, to see Dezma staring at her.

The other woman closed the canteen, crouching to put it in her pack, unfolding a bit of jerky and holding it in her hand. "He had a reason."

"Is any reason worth a murder?"

"Maybe," Dezma whispered, still staring at her jerky. "If it saves more lives than it costs."

"Careful, you're starting to sound like him." Stelli whispered back, staring at that jerky in the larger woman's hand.

Dezma sighed, turning over the jerky. In the corners of her downturned eyes, Stelli found a beautiful and peculiar softness. "When you kill the Wolf," she said. "What of his family? Will it be worth it to you then, to take him out at their expense?"

Stelli swallowed. "His family will miss him," she whispered. "A lot. But they shouldn't. They will be better off without him."

Dezma nodded, slow at first, then finished the motion by popping the jerky in her mouth, and grinding it in her strong jaw. "That's admirable of you. To try and improve the lives of his family."

A cold chill prickled down Stelli's arm. Her stomach churned with sickness. Her hand grabbed her own rations, like rodents scurrying for scraps and morsels of their own volition. She brought the food to her mouth, wiping her eyes with shaking hands. "I guess," she whispered.

Her tears didn't sound like weeping as they clung to the

backs of her hands. They sounded like a heartbeat fluttering to a stop. They sounded like the last leaving gasp of dying lungs. They sounded like the end. Success. Every bit of her cringed away from their possible success.

She chewed, and swallowed, salt coating her tongue with its numbing taste.

"Gavin's children won't be better off without him," Dezma said. "He's not perfect. No men are. But his biggest problem is that he forgets about the rest of us because he's too busy loving his kids." She grunted as she slid the straps closed once more on her pack, hefting it over her shoulders. Stelli watched the movements. Watched the strong muscles tense under her shoulders, watched the tightening of the skin around her jaw. It looked painless. Effortless. A body indestructible in all but her eyes. Dezma had the most expressive eyes. As she hefted her pack over her shoulders and arranged the straps, it was her eyes that betrayed her exhaustion and pain.

Nothing else.

"And he loves them honestly," Dezma continued. "A little selfish maybe, a little shortsighted, but honest. He just wants them to be happy and free," she hefted her Longtooth from the ground. "Personally, I'd fight for more men to have that kind of problem, instead of the other way around."

Stelli's hair plastered to the back of her neck with sweat and grime. She lifted her own pack, closed her eyes for a moment, and stepped back onto the water. Even just a simple Standwave hurt to maintain. She did it anyway.

When she opened her eyes, she found Dezma staring at her, eyes tracing the spots where her hands clutched the straps of her pack, following up her neck, to where the dark stains of bug bites marred her once smooth, full skin. Stelli grunted and stepped past her, onto the river.

The dark purple hues of the world deepened the shadows of

her periphery, as the sky approached Devouring. The toads sure sang this time of night. Their incessant croaking punched her ears like ballistae fire, warbling all around her and making bugaboo's of the tree boughs, spirits of their shadows.

"If they do split up," Stelli whispered. "What then?" Something tickled her heel. She paused and looked down. Thin gossamer web clutched her foot, stretched across the side of the river, strands glistening and warbling with the current of the water. A spider as big as her hand scurried onto her foot, long legged and hairy. She wrenched her foot back, snapping its web, kicking her foot into the water away from her Standwaves. The spider scurried away atop the water, vanishing under a leaf. Her foot dripped with blue slime as she withdrew it. The sticky material clung between her toes and along the exposed skin of her ankle.

"It's harmless," Dezma walked past her. "Unless you drink it."

"Right," she scurried to keep up.

"Assuming the General stays with his scout, we take solace in the fact that some of the soldiers are gone, and we try to split them up further," she whispered. "If the scout and General take different paths, well... Our job is done."

"That won't happen."

Dezma shrugged. "I'm not counting on it."

The stream continued, narrow and plodding, to the right of the small pond. The water glistened and gurgled under the purple light.

The toads fell silent. A prickle spread across the back of Stelli's neck, ears straining. The water trickled under them, their Standwaves playing with the sound of light rapids. A couple snappy buzzings lead her eyes to bugs that flitted through the sky, landing on leaves, or the trunks of trees. Then even those fell still. She looked over her shoulder. Nothing but twisted Aycmor's, broken fallen logs, and an unmoving mudbank.

Dezma stopped moving. "Look," she breathed.

"Why have the toads stopped singing?" She followed Dezma's gaze.

"Their mudskiff," Dezma ran forward, crouching in the mud by the side of a dark wooden boat, pulled up atop a mudbank. She ran her fingers through the groove at the stern.

Stelli put a hand on the larger woman's shoulder, eyes flitting to every small gap in the trees around them. "You're supposed to know the swamp," Stelli whispered. "*Why have the toads stopped singing.*"

Dezma looked up at Stelli, then craned her neck higher. They couldn't see the sky. The tree cover clung thick above them, despite the sparse Aycmors around the clearing.

"I'm not sure," Dezma whispered.

Stelli looked at the mudskiff, up on a mudbank, in a clearing, on the edge of the water right after a pond. Here, in the openness of the pond, the whole swamp could see them.

And it listened.

"A trap," she whispered.

"Gavin wouldn't—"

"He doesn't know we're here it's not meant for us—"

Dezma shouted, lunging forward and *wrenching* Stelli to the side, tossing her out of the way. Her world flipped upside down, blurry vertigo slamming against her, a scream tearing from her throat. She cast Standwaves beneath her, letting the feeling of her drum spread down her arms, legs, feet, everywhere, not sure what would hit first—she slammed against the water, rolling until she hit a mudbank. It gripped her, she coughed, trying to roll free, but the fingers of the mud wanted to consume her— she coughed again, pushing herself up. Dezma. Where...

Dezma stood in the middle of the river, backing up, Longtooth held in front of her towards the darkness of the treeline. Stelli's back ached and stung, numbness preceding pain in little waves of their own across her skin. Anger bubbled in her throat as she pushed herself to her feet, glaring at Dezma—

A thick green vine curled around the base of an Aycmor tree at the edge of the pond. A second wrapped around a branch, then a third, pulling a long, heavy, slender body through the tangle like molasses. Arms, Stelli realized. Great, vine-like arms that preceded a head. A long snout of curling green-scales, with eyes that gleamed in the purple spray of the Partial Devouring, and a row of flickering teeth that curled like thorns in its maw. A yellow pollen tongue flicked through the air, setting adrift flecks of powder that floated down to settle above the ooze.

It locked its eyes on Dezma, and hissed. A low sound, at first, that built and built as its vine arms spread over the tree, down into the mud, pulling its long scaled body into the half-light of the clearing. Dezma's eyes stayed locked with the creature, even as it lifted itself above her, rearing to twice her height.

Stelli stumbled to her feet, back hanging heavy and dripping from her tumble, mud clinging to every bit of her clothing. She slipped the pack off, leaning it against a tree. She stayed crouched low, circling wide, hand down towards the water. The back of her head hurt so much... She grimaced, and split it in half. The water unfolded at her feet into little diamonds, muting her footsteps.

The creature lunged for Dezma, who skipped back, slashing at its snout. It recoiled, testing her, eyeing her. Its vines snaked into the water, reaching across the pond to grab trees on the other end and pull itself forward, looming, encroaching, waiting for the right moment to pounce.

Stelli crouched lower, keeping to the shadows, holding her breath, silent as the wind. Dezma circled around—

A vine split the air, whistling with force. Dezma ducked and rolled—CRACK. Stelli split her mind a third time, and the water rippled with angry triangular Slashwaves, cutting the air and severing the vine mid swing. The severed end slapped into

Dezma, throwing her back, pinning her with its weight. She dropped her Standwaves, splashing under the water, leaving the piece of vine floating on the surface.

The creature's hiss eclipsed the nighttime, shaking the very beams of light that glinted in its eyes. Stelli dropped her Subverted Echowaves, looking up to meet its angry gaze as it turned towards her. Dezma spluttered above the surface at the edge of the pond, throwing off blue slime, staggering onto the blood—

The creature lunged. She heard her father's voice, echoing from a thousand combat drills. *Keep moving.* Duck a vine, hear its whistle—*Keep moving.* Hand to the water, split the rhythm. A new Slashwave. Snapping jaws coming towards her—*Keep moving.* One of the arms skimmed the water's surface, sending up a wall of spray and slime, she turned her head as she rolled through it, coming up with clinging masses of ooze dripping from her hair, under her shirt—*KEEP MOVING*—CRACK. Her arm wrenched to the side, caught by one of the vines. She spun and leapt, her mind instinctually letting go of her Standwaves—*wait,* she held on, as the creature's jaws snapped over the air behind her, as its body splashed towards her in the water. *Shift.* She pulled the rhythm's edges, rounding the corners of the hexagons, yanking them inwards into Boundwaves—

SPLASH. She landed back on the water, crashing through it, thrashing her arms to try and get back above the surface. The slime grabbed her, filling her face, plastering across her eyes, her nose. Something brushed past her leg, she yanked it away, threw her head above the water, sucked in a breath—

Some of the slime got in her throat. She choked, slapping a hand down, trying to conjure a Standwave—

Don't lose focus. That rhythm in the back of her mind still pulled in, pulled in, *pulled in.* She made sure it stayed, crawling onto her wave, coughing up the slime, reaching a finger into her mouth and ripping it out. It wriggled away as she heaved, retching into the water, her throat and stomach convulsing, hot redness filling her. She rolled over.

The creature hissed and thrashed on the water behind her, lunging forward, grabbed back by the very water itself, which surged inwards in the pattern of her Boundwaves, keeping it trapped and still. She scrambled away, but she wasn't far enough, its vine-like arm lashed up into the air, thin like a whip, crashing down towards her—

Dezma stepped above her and caught it, bellowing in pain. She grabbed the vine further up its length and *tore* backwards, ripping it out of the creature's shoulder with a spurt of bright green ichor. She threw it to the side, backing up, reaching down a hand and helping Stelli to her feet as the creature thrashed and hissed, still lunging against the strength of her Boundwaves.

She held the rhythm strong.

"How long?" Dezma gasped, keeping an eye on the thing, bending down to get her Longtooth, which stuck out of the mud where it must have been knocked free in the chaos.

"Not," Stelli coughed again, massaging her chest, hair hanging around her face, dripping. The Boundwave rhythm spiked her head, each beat a hot iron to her skull.

"Then *let's go*, can you move?"

"Slowly."

The creature's hissing slowed as it narrowed its wide eyes towards the two women. It slapped at the Boundwaves with its vines, trying to disrupt the pattern, but that just got it more stuck.

Stelli's vision swam as the absence of hissing left the pond quiet. Quiet and still and tranquil, as the beast eyed them and snaked its head and flicked its pollen tongue, testing the strength of her Boundwaves, trying to shift its weight, move its foot. She felt its cunning movements fighting her rhythm, felt it working to dissolve the patterns that kept it trapped. She grit her teeth, closing her eyes, leaning on Dezma as the stronger woman led her away, dragging their packs with one hand. One step at a time. Slow. *Don't lose focus.* Her father's voice, still, as he kicked at her patterns. *Keep them steady.* Make a circle, pull it inwards. Make a circle, pull it—

Thud. Thud. Thud. Footsteps. The snapping of branches. Splashing.

From all around them.

"Moons," Dezma breathed by her ear. "Surrounded. Don't panic. New plan. On my signal." A prickle went down her neck—

"I suppose I should commend you, Lieutenant," the words washed over her, the voice so tender, as it caressed her heart, working around the barbs of her hook, taking away the pain of its pulling even as the pointed end sank deeper. She shriveled up against Dezma's strong presence, and focused on her Boundwaves. "I meant to kill the tavernkeep because she bothered me. You've corrected my mistake, and made her useful."

Dezma tensed beside her. The creature snapped and hissed against Stelli's Boundwaves, and the soldiers all backed away in a flurry of footsteps. Stelli squeezed her eyes shut tighter. She could feel her father's arms around her, smell his comforting, warm scent, hear his words echoing like a symphony through her mind—

"*Now,*" Dezma hissed. Stelli blinked her eyes open and saw her father, walking towards her, just at the cusp of the creature's reach. He smiled, backlit by the purple reflection in the creature's eyes, holding out a hand—

Dezma yanked her in a run towards the edge of the pond, the soldiers shouted, charging forward with their Canines raised—

Stelli let go of her Boundwaves. The pond burst into chaos. Her father shouted, the water rippling and splashing with shapes and crashes. Dezma plowed her shoulder into the line of soldiers at the edge of the pond, throwing one aside. A Canine cracked against her hip as she ducked another blow, cutting down a second soldier with her Longtooth. Stelli left behind Boundwaves in the water as she ran. A glancing blow took her hip, spinning her, lancing pain up her leg, but Dezma caught her, dragging her onward—

Behind them, a scream ripped into a bloody throat. Stelli shot glances over her shoulder, catching glimpses of the beast throwing a pair of legs back into the air, which kept wriggling and kicking even as it chewed. *Keep moving.* Her father's voice. But it was wrong. Her world stretched, her heart yanking into the back of her throat as the hug dug in deeper, and all the barbs tore her flesh, because her father's voice wasn't there to shield her—

Her father crouched on the water, watching with calculated eyes as the creature decimated his soldiers, lunging, snapping, whipping with its vines.

"Keep moving," Dezma grunted from beside her.

The water around her father cascaded to life, shimmering with subtle Boundwaves that snaked their patterns between his soldiers legs, catching the whipping vines of the beast in targeted locations, locking it down one by one, until—

"Keep. Moving."

They rounded a bend. The last sight Stelli got was her father's piercing eyes, locked onto her retreating form, full of nothing.

Except for numbing regret.

Stelli's legs burned as much as her heart. Tears pricked the corners of her eyes. She kept looking behind her, even as Dezma dragged her forward, arm clamped over her wrist, pace unrelenting. She fell into a familiar breathing pace. Quick inhales in, long inhales out. Quick inhales in, long inhales out. No bugs slapped against her face. They'd all come to rest, hiding from...

whatever that thing was.

Behind them, its hissing faded into pained, air-filled scream-ing. It tore at the fabric of the swamp, the noise itself a Dewclaw digging into skin, pulling free chunks of blood and viscera. The sound curdled and bent, turning over and quivering until not even the silence could erase it from her ears.

Because it echoed. No matter how quiet the swamp fell around them, it echoed.

Dezma led them off the river, ducking around a large spider web. Something skittered by her feet. She leapt to the side as the tail of a snake snapped the air, coming straight for her, missing by a few inches. She stumbled on, ducking a tree branch, avoid-ing a vine, stumbling up to Dezma's side.

Who turned and punched a tree. The muted thump echoed in the silence.

"Moons!" Dezma cursed.

"You were the one who was supposed to know how the sw-amp worked," Stelli spit. "A pretty big oversight, don't you think?"

"Supposed to know?" Dezma spun on her. "I barely go in here, I just know the little things Gavin tells me—great of him to forget to mention that there's a giant man eating plant liz-ard—"

"What great teamwork," Stelli's voice dripped. "Has the plan failed enough for us to try mine?"

"Maybe it wouldn't be if you hadn't hesitated—"

"I saved our lives—"

Dezma's left hand grabbed Stelli's shoulder, yanking her close. She held her right hand up right in front of Stelli's face, palm open and flat. A red welt scarred Dezma's dark skin from fingers to wrist, with small little dotted punctures where dabs of blood pooled out. "For you," Dezma hissed. Her hand shook. The skin around the punctures looked discolored, a little purple. They locked eyes for a long moment, and despite the transparency of Dezma's gaze, Stelli still found something new in them.

Dezma shoved her away, into a tree. She slid down, splatting to the mud, staring at the stains caking her shin-sheaths.

"Stupid," Stelli whispered. Her feet had left indents in the mud. Particulates of wet, moist soil crawled in to fill in the hole, marching forward like a tired company of soldiers struggling to take the next step before nightfall. The mud would keep going. It could not stop.

The words she had spoken echoed in her head, as the chaotic moments of the battle played over and over, snapping through her mind like the hexagons of Standwaves reaching their end and restarting. *His family will be better off without him...* Moons. Her father's Runecasting was *beautiful*. He was beautiful.

Dezma's pack fell into the mud, squashing her footprint. She sat beside Stelli, back to the tree.

"You really will be better off without him," Dezma whispered.

Stelli's eyes jerked up to Dezma's face.

Dezma smiled, softly. "Gavin said he killed the Wolf's son. You said Gavin killed your brother. Not a hard bit of deduction, Lieutenant."

Stelli again searched the woman's strong face, watching the way her mud-filled dreads tangled past her ear. "And you didn't think to kill me? Or let me die?"

Dezma shrugged. "I thought about it."

"But you didn't."

"I don't think you are who you think you are," Dezma whispered. "You think that when this is all over, when my plan fails, and we find Gavin, and we train his children to defeat your father, you'll betray me. You think you'll deliver the children, ready for battle, at your father's feet. And you think his pride will make you happy."

The hook sat dormant in her heart, waiting to yank if it needed to.

"But I think you're wrong about yourself," Dezma whispered. "I think you know, somewhere deep down, how dangerous and manipulative your father is. I think whatever happens, when I need someone to save me from drowning in the lake again, when you need to stay back and watch him as he comes around the next bend again, when you have to let the monster attack him again... You'll do it."

A toad croaked in the distance, a long and solitary note, carrying all the mourning of the swamp. Insects began to buzz, their wingbeats a droning sorrowful melody beneath the croak.

"And if I am just using you to find Gavin?" Stelli whispered. "If I stab you in the back at the last moment? If I do deliver the children to my father, and i-if..." she swallowed. "If his pride does make me happy?"

"Then I am profoundly wrong," Dezma gripped Stelli's hand, and gave it a squeeze. "But I've already been wrong about you once. And I'll let you in on a little secret... I've never been wrong about someone the second time."

Drawn to the smell of blood, yet all they ever do is watch
Black and green feathers that help them vanish in the swamp
Bluotaes Birds
- Listen to their impossible songs

13

Bloomstalk, Rosebud," Gavin snapped, panic crashing thr-ough his limbs. "*Move*. Pack everything up." He closed the jar of Spartippi berry paste, fit it snugly into the fabric, and pulled the straps tight.

Bloom and Rose were frozen in the mud, staring at him.

"Bloomstalk," he looked his son in the eye, who crouched pale as a Sliffitan feather. "Gather up the plants. Carry the Alimin close, okay?"

More shouts echoed up from that not-so-distant distance. The cracking of tree limbs. The pounding presence of soldiers, looking for tracks. Signs. Of Gavin.

Gavin snapped his fingers. "Bloomstalk," he hissed. The boy blinked out of his reverie, hands shaking, and started to do as he was told. "I need you two right now," he whispered. "Rosebud, carry the water buckets."

She nodded, wiping away her tears.

"W-won't the Zar'thul get us if we g-go out, Dad?"

"The Zar'thul is dead."

Bloom whimpered.

Gavin staggered to his feet, hefting the pack over his shoulders, lifting the oar in his free hand like it was a spear. Taking even one step nearly sent him back to the mud. Black spots took his vision. His body sagged with exhaustion.

Rose stumbled with the weight of the water buckets. "Let me take one," Gavin whispered. "Let me take one, here, just like that," he lifted the water bucket in his left hand, putting more weight on his uninjured leg. The black spots swirled dangerously close to blinding him. He swallowed hard, and grit his teeth.

Both his children quivered against the darkness of their hidey-hole. "Keep breathing," he whispered, limping towards a gap in the roots on the far side, away from the sound, away from their mudskiff. "Keep breathing, it will all be okay," he slid the water bucket up over the lip, grabbing Rose's other bucket and putting it up top. He took a deep breath, threw the oar over, and clambered up.

The flesh of his thigh screamed with the excess movement as more blood soaked through his bandage. A tear squeezed out from the side of his eye as he dragged himself up into the open under the light of the Partial Devouring, hands squeezing hardened bits of mud and rock. He let out his pent up breath, reaching down to help Bloom and Rose up with him.

The open swamp air took on a different texture as the Tuft Rabbit whimpered her partial death in the sky. Not too partial, he thought, glancing up. Only a day or so before the Full. The usual moisture blanketed his skin, but the spider-leg tickling of exposure added sinister whispers along his spine, and every sound of every rustling fern and every trickling dew-drop bead on every drooping leaf sneered and glared and ignited possibilities in the grizzled father's mind.

There would be no Zar'Thul to ambush them. The Zar'Thul was dead.

"Come on, Dad," Rose yanked at his sleeve, tears staining her cheeks. "Don't we need to go?"

He looked down at his two children, his two beautiful children. "Yes," he whispered, stumbling along with them. A petal ripped from his heart, fluttering on an unseen wind to go join the Zar'thul in its death.

He flipped the oar around, using the flat of the blade as a

skimmer through the mud, obliterating the tracks as they walked, blinking through the tears that filled his vision, the rage that filled his arms, and suffocated the pain in his leg.

He turned them, leading them between small gaps in trees, eyes flickering between ponds and streams. His foot caught a tree branch, sending it rustling through the underbrush. The heaviness of the sound... *Feltwing fronds...* But could he be sure? He blinked, straining against the post-Devouring darkness. Even the Carrow Wolf dimmed once it ate its fill. Gavin swallowed, lifting his foot, heart hammering in his chest. The swamp was not his enemy. He dipped the tip of his boot to the mud, sliding it forward, stepping down light and slow and careful. He felt the soft skitterings of critters. One passed over his foot. The stray, rubbery leg caught against the slight gap of skin under his trousers, tickling the hair. He froze. The slight hooks on the foot, the narrowness of the touch... *Allcrea Centipede... Venomous... Avoid...* he swallowed again, bending his neck, looking down. He couldn't see his feet. The air was saturated with heavy darkness, flickering leaves above showing the barest glimmers of purple... not enough... not enough... not enough...

The weight left his boot. He let his foot fall down on the mud the rest of the way. He tried to lift his other leg. His right leg. The injured leg. It wouldn't move. Something in the back of his mind hiccupped, revolting, rooting him to the spot. He swallowed. He forced his eyes open. Blinked. Tried to look around.

Darkness. Darkness. *The swamp is not your enemy...* The oar was heavy in his hand, coarse against his palm. His mouth fell open, and he sucked in a breath. The air jerked between his lips, as if a wily frog in his hands trying to jump out, as if a Cyril vine disturbed, his nervous system going rigid and locking his bones. He closed his lips and opened them again, but now his lungs were vines too, vines that connected to the petals of his heart, splaying flat and tugging, tugging until the fibers keeping them whole ripped one by one by one by one and let them flutter to the floor.

The swamp is not your enemy... But the centipede could have crawled behind him, could have crawled over Bloom or Rose's foot, could have found the bare skin under their trousers and found it threatening, could have closed its mandibles over their flesh, and any moment they could scream, or... He managed to turn his head around, blinking in the darkness, but couldn't even see their faces.

He traced the patterns of the swamp in his mind, calculating how far they had walked. Far enough to be invisible from the Grendle, and he'd wiped their trail. It would have to be good enough.

"Rosebud," his voice shook. He felt himself crying, as clear as if he were watching another person cry. He could see himself. Not his face, not through the darkness, not as if looking down at a pond. Just as if—

A three-toned caw sounded above them, piercing the night, and he saw himself in the same way that he heard the noise. One-third guttural, one-third chirp, one-third shrill. "Do you re-member going to those... those Runewave lessons, when you were a little, little girl?"

He felt her bump up against him, wrapping small hands around his arm. Bloom did the same on his other.

"Yeah," her voice was so small.

"Have you used any Runewaves since then?" Gavin said, wrapping his arms around them.

Rose started shaking against him. "You always told us not to..."

"I know, Rosebud, but did you ever do it anyway?"

He heard her breath hiccup, felt her body tense against him. "Only a little..."

"Shh," he rubbed his fingers through her hair, trying to blot out the sounds of the swamp, which for that brief moment overwhelmed his ears and played in the back of his mind like a bludgeon crushing his skull. "Which Runewaves have you used?"

"Am I in trouble?" Her shaking subsided under the soft circles of his fingers.

"No, Rosebud, no, not at all," Gavin whispered. "This might be important right now. Which Runewaves have you used before?"

"N-Nell showed us a few sometimes," Rose mumbled.

"I told him we weren't supposed to but he said it would be fine," Bloom said.

"Okay," Gavin said, his voice thin and weak. Shouts rang out in the distance, excited shouts, like the barking of a dog that picked up its scent. Something tickled the back of Gavin's ankle. A snout? Or just a drop of sweat or blood, sifting through the hair on his leg? "Okay. Can you make the water in the bucket glow?"

Rose's breathing stuttered against him. "Are you sure?"

"Yes."

Bloom and Rose clasped hands. It started slow. But with a burgeoning brilliance, the water in the bucket Rose held glimmered in soft parallelograms, faint purple light growing and growing, casting away shadows, under lighting Rose's face, reflecting off the tear-stains on her cheeks and chin. The light changed the very fabric of the air. It caught the smallest motes of the Carrow Wolf's hue, igniting them to sparkles above the bucket, taking bits of luminance like lightning bugs and bathing the world in its splendor.

It was the most beautiful light that Gavin had ever seen. It made him sick.

"Thank you," his voice fell dead on the air. "Let's go now." He picked out all the details of the swamp around them under the light. Each little sparkle in the air drifted in just the right place, casting a faint light across a translucent spider web hanging between two branches of a tree, or flickering into the shadow under a large fern's leaf to show the glinting eyes of a snake curled beneath.

His limping steps still fell with painful finality. He could feel the terror etched into every movement of his children as they stumbled with him. Bloom balanced the potted plants in one arm, under his chin. His hand linked with Rose's, pressing against the water. Gavin knew Runecasters didn't have to keep contact with the water after the initial casting. Perhaps it simplified the focus, or made it easier to maintain somehow... He tried to smile at them, but his smile felt ghastly, his teeth felt sharp in his mouth, the back of his neck felt mangy, the piercing quality of his gaze picking out the details of the swamp cold and calculating and snide. But the sounds died behind them. He wiped away any trace of their tracks with the oar. The croaking of the toads rose to hide the noises of their movements.

The mud gave way to pools, dark and suffocated by bright green slime. It coated the browns of the mud, like mucus from a monstrous beast, coughed up and left in its own footprints. It wasn't that. *Snotslime,* Gavin's head kicked into gear. *Bogslime's nasty younger cousin.*

"No more light," Gavin whispered. Bloom and Rose pulled their hands back, and the motes of refraction flickered dead upon the air, leaving the clearing dark. Under these mud pools, gaps in the trees showed more light, just enough to see his hand in front of his face, and not much more.

"You're both doing so well," he whispered, feeling a teardrop slide down his cheek. "Just a little bit more, okay? These are the Snotpools—"

"Snotpools?" Bloom whispered, voice too afraid for a giggle. "Who named them that?"

"Probably whoever sneezed them up," Rose whispered. Her cadence didn't carry the joke, but Gavin smiled all the same. A real smile. A necessary smile.

"We need to get across them," Gavin mumbled. "The slime here is a bit different. It'll eat our skin if we come in contact with it—"

"What?!" Bloom hissed. "Eating our skin? You never told us there was slime that could eat our skin!"

"It didn't seem relevant," Gavin said.

"That's so cool!"

Another flicker of a smile.

And then light. Faint and rippling, casting reflections on the trunks of trees in inverse waveforms, light turquoise and dark green and all the shades in the middle. Rose crouched on the nearest Snotpool, eyes wide, one finger pressed cautiously to the surface. From the contact came hexagons, strict and uniform, filling the surface of the water. She looked up at Gavin with those same wide eyes.

"Sorry," she whispered.

Gavin grunted, helping Bloom forward onto the Standwaves. "Come on, stay close, don't step too fast or one of us might fall off..."

They shuffled forward, the three of them huddling as close as they could, Rose doing a sort of half-squat shuffle backwards, Bloom holding on to the back of her cloak, Gavin holding the oar out in front of them, scanning the underbrush, eyeing the shifting and gurgling slime just barely beneath their feet.

The Standwaves shifted as Bloom grabbed on to Rose. Gavin frowned. The hexagons shifted and danced, interlocking and conjoining and swirling. Nell's Standwaves simply *were*. These injected the water with a strut, and felt easier to walk on. Sturdier. More consistent. More *present*.

A cold reminder. In a brief flash, the blue slime turned red, and a green scar loomed in the reflection. He gasped in a quick breath, biting his lip, jerking his head up to scan the area around them. Nothing. Nothing. *Nothing.* But he could hear the panting of the Wolf, as if emanating from the very trees themselves. He saw eyes staring at him from the underside of every leaf.

Nothing. His leg throbbed, and he stumbled. Bloom caught him and kept him upright.

They stepped onto the mudbank on the far side of the Snotpools—

A hiss and a snap, mud flinging. Gavin yanked Bloom and Rose behind him; they shrieked; he dropped his oar and water bucket, rolling to the floor—

Snyrsnout. Warm scales, sharp teeth curling back in a long thin maw, breath dark and staining to his face; he slid his palms up, scales ripping his flesh. His hands found the spot just beneath the creature's neck; he rolled as the creature bucked and threw its weight against him, shoving him into the mud, bearing down on him, snapping just inches from his face. He held it back, hooking a leg over its long thrashing tail, heaving, struggling. His hair sucked against the mud behind him. He could feel slime burning his neck—

Heave, roll—

A squawk screeched in the air, three-parts and discordant—

He grunted in pain as the tail slapped against his wound, sending white dots across his vision—

Heave, roll—

He mounted the Snyrsnout, pressing down as hard as he could on its neck, pinning the head to the mud. He slid his hands forward over the eyes, a jolt of satisfaction surging through him as he felt the slight pop as they retreated into their sockets, eyelids closing. He brought his right hand forward, clamping two of his three fingers under its jaw, the thumb and palm on top. The fingers below found the soft scale-covered skin that hung tight between plates of bone. He squeezed. It bucked again, but his knees were planted firmly in the mud, and his full weight came down on its back. The Snyrsnout swivelled, wrenching his knees through the mud, carving grooves. It jerked its head once. He kept hold of the maw. A second time. He didn't let go.

It fell still. He slid his other hand down, gripping the jaw with both. He lifted the head up towards his chest in an unyielding grip, and breathed out.

"Are you both okay?" He said through heaving breaths into the fading light of the aggravated slime behind him, eyes searching, scanning the shadows. A body, on the ground. Small. Green plumage harsh and unnatural against the brown of the mud and the red of its bleeding. It shifted, trying to drag itself away from the Snyrsnout. Its wing, its beautiful wing, fluttered against the air, but the feathers were broken, and the thin bone looked bent out of shape. *Bluotaes Bird.* "Please tell me—"

"Dad what *is* that thing?" Bloom said, staring at the Snyrsnout as Rose pulled him up from the mud. The Bluotaes bird half-fluttered, half-staggered further away from them, long beaked face turning a reproachful gaze. Rose flung a bit of green slime from off her cloak, recoiling from it, fear in her eyes.

"Snyrnout," Gavin said. It jerked its body around, but he held firm. "Very dangerous. We got lucky."

"Lucky?!" Rose hissed.

"It's a baby," Gavin's breathing started to steady. "I should have seen it, tucked under the mud. Must have stepped too close, scared it."

Bloom stepped closer, eyes wide. "Can I... Can I touch it?"

Sweat slicked his hands. His eyes stayed wide, but they *burned*. He hadn't closed them to sleep in... in... "Better not, Bloomstalk," Gavin whispered. He shifted his grip. "You calmed down, baby?" He whispered, rubbing his thumb up and down the creature's snout. Blood trickled from his palm, down along the small scales of its snout and amidst its teeth. The Bluotaes bird squealed again, wings fluttering against the underbrush.

"Don't worry little guy, I'll get to you in a moment," he breathed, lowering the Snyrsnout's head back down to the mud. He slid his hands up, pressing down on the eyes, still maintaining his full weight over its back. "Back up," he said to his kids. "This is another scary part, I need you two at a safe distance."

They did as he asked. He took another deep breath, steadying himself, maneuvering into a crouch, knees still close at the Snyrsnout's sides. Breathe in... *one*... Breathe out... *two*... Breathe in... *Three*—he tossed the creature as far as he could away from his kids, jumping up to his feet, grunting against the pain as weight hit his right leg. He backed up, staring the creature down. Its mouth opened wide, red tongue flickering between rows and rows of teeth. They glowed with faint striations of green slime which clung between their points. A loud hiss emanated from its throat, mixing with the soft cackle of the slime on its gums. Gavin kept backing up until he reached Bloom and Rose.

He held his hand out, glancing over his shoulder, making sure they didn't stumble into anything. The Snyrnout snapped its jaw shut and settled back down in the mud, watching them with its eyes like little twigs sticking up from the bog.

"Dad you are *so* cool," Bloom said, mouth hanging open, staring at the creature. Even as a baby, it was quite large, long tail trailing away in the mud, long thin snout closed, cupping the earth like a spoon in mud stew. The young boy moved to pick up the fallen Alimin and Isingrass, shaking the mud off their leaves, never taking his eyes off the creature.

"I'm glad you think so," Gavin muttered, mind whirling, half a moment behind. He coughed, turning to look at the Bluotaes bird where it crouched in the underbrush. Its head dipped down to nip under its wing. He knelt at its side.

"Were you trying to clean his teeth, little guy?" Gavin mustered a smile. He turned back to Bloom and Rose. "Remember how the three of us would sit by the basin back at our house, and I would dip you back into the water and scrub out your hair... you guys always liked little circles, right at the back of your heads..."

"Dad?" Rose whispered, voice shaking.

"These birds are like that for their little lizard friends," the words just mumbled out of Gavin's mouth. "They sit by the ponds with the Snyrsnouts and give their bloody teeth little baths in the Snotslime..." He reached a slow hand forward, but the bird hopped to the side, cawing at him. He held his palm up, exposing the blood. The bird paused, cocking its head, letting out another caw.

"That's right," Gavin whispered, shifting closer. In the rippling light of the slime, he could just make out its twisted right wing. A snapped off Aycmor twig jabbed through the green feathers. "I know," he mumbled. "Sometimes you need a little help too. That's okay..." It hopped forward, staring at the blood in his palm, cawing. He slipped his other hand to its wing, bringing his bleeding thumb up along its beak. Its eyes were mesmerized, looking at his blood. They shone red with its reflection.

He pulled the twig out, maneuvering it between the crimped feathers, slow and careful. It came free. He tossed it to the side.

"There you go," Gavin murmured. "Now you're all free. Sorry to interrupt you, little guy..."

He pulled his hand back. It cawed at him again, following him with its gaze. He stood up, looking around. He raised his hand towards his eyes to wipe them, but hesitated. Grime and blood and mud streaked his skin. He swallowed.

"I need some water, Rosebud," Gavin murmured, bleary eyes finding his kids, standing off to the side and looking at him. They looked scared. Rose's skin was pale. He turned to his hands again. Flesh wounds. Flaps of his skin hung off, tangled and dark with grime. He blinked down at them. Swallowed again, and had an idea. He turned and flicked blood into the green miasma. He squeezed his skin a bit, wincing, but drawing more fresh redness to flick into the water. Maybe the General would be careless and fall in, and the slime would eat him alive.

"You dropped your bucket dad," Rose whispered, and pointed. The bucket was half submerged in the slime, clean water drifting amongst the green clumps, integrating with the swamp.

He blinked a few times, trying to get a bit of gunk from his eyelash that he could feel like a hard little rock between the skin and his eye. His vision fluttered, out of control. "You had one too," he muttered. But she didn't. Her hands were empty. "What happened to your bucket, Rose?"

She looked at the ground. "You pushed me..."

He got control of his eye, turning. A second bucket, in the mud, turned over, water percolating with little brown bits of moisture. His heart started beating faster in his chest. He stepped forward, eyeing the Snyrsnout, which still sat docile at a safe distance. He bent to lift the lip of the bucket. But he knew. He could tell from the angle it had fallen. It was empty.

Water sloshed back in as he lifted it. Mud caked. A strand of green slime twisted at the bottom. He ground his teeth together, his insides swallowing themselves. Despair battered him like rain against a flat roof, threatening to cave him in as if every drop of the world's weeping caught atop his shoulders. He shuttered another breath in, leg throbbing, hands stinging, eyelid twitching against that lump of detritus that just *wouldn't. Go. Away.* And he couldn't wipe it out with bloodied dirtied hands, and his eyes stung too, and that stinging spread back through his temples, washing over him in waves of absent pain. The flower in his heart, it tried to grow against his despair, but the roots were so tangled up it was getting harder and harder to tell what bloomed and what wilted.

The last light of the aggravated slime faded from the clearing, and the croaking of toads and buzzing of wings took over his senses. He lifted the bucket anyway, shuffling up to the edge of the Snotpools, filling the bucket about a quarter. "I'll need the two of you to make this water glow again," he whispered. "But don't drink it."

"I'm sorry dad," Rose whispered in the dark. Her voice sounded so small amidst the cacophony of the swamp. So small and weak and vulnerable and terrified. "Is the Bugaboo gonna get us now? Because of me?"

He lowered his head over the bucket of bogwater, its tangy, warm scent hitting his nostrils. "No, Rosebud," he murmured. "Don't go blaming yourself. Come on, light up the water you two. We've gotta move."

"You need to sleep Dad," Bloom said, his voice just as small as Rose's.

"Sometimes we can't get what we need," Gavin grunted. "Come on."

The water flickered, casting strange motes of green and purple light upon the air. His eyes flicked to watch one as it drifted, remaining aglow for a few seconds after leaving the air above the bucket, before fading to darkness. He frowned. Mirrorwaves shouldn't do that. They illuminated, but usually no different than a fire would, just absent the flickering, and absent the heat. These Mirrorwaves seemed to... change the air, spread their rhythm through the humidity itself, like little lightning bugs in the moonlight.

"See if you can keep it going without touching it," Gavin said. Dezma often tapped her brews with Tastewaves, she never had to hold her hand there.

They stepped back, still holding hands. The light remained. Their fingers untwined.

The motes faded to normal Mirrorwave light. They grabbed hands again, and the dancing motes returned.

"Keep holding hands I guess," Gavin said, eyeing their laced fingers. The sight made the discomfort in his eye worse. The Wolf loomed infinite around him, ever encroaching. His claws plucked free the petals around his heart. Its teeth wanted only thorns to remain.

He stepped past them, forcing his eyes to focus on every little detail of the ground. He glanced at the clearing one last time. Snotpools. He traced their path backwards in his mind, to the Grendle, to the river delta, to the trees in their dying embrace, to the town... He blinked a few more times, nodded, picked up the oar from the mud, and then moved into the tangle. He didn't have a map of the swamp, and he didn't think in charted lines or drawn rivers. He held the swamp like a constellation of stars in his head, each landmark and beautiful anomaly a star leading onwards to continue the mesmerizing pattern. He saw the next destination shining brighter than all the rest. *Oasis. Fresh water.*

He felt unsteady as he nudged the oar through the ferns, forcing himself to examine each patch of ground before stepping, trail his gaze across every tree branch and hanging vine. The back of his throat prickled with dryness. Funny how it only came to mind once he didn't have water to drink. *Don't think about that. Scan the ground. Scan the surroundings.* He ducked underneath an orbweaver's web. *Don't waste energy identifying it.* He lifted a log with the end of his oar before stepping over it. He paused and watched the dark gap in the tree bark to make sure nothing lurked in waiting. *Don't step in the deep pools of water. Breathe. Breathe. Breathe.*

Keep going straight. You know where you are. You know where you are going. Oasis. Water.

"Dad," Bloom whispered. "Are we gonna have to drink our pee?"

"No, Bloomstalk," he replied, just loud enough to eclipse the echoing symphony of toads and wingbeats. He nudged a leaf, causing a little pale blue frog to leap away. He didn't like disturbing them. But it had to be done. "It wouldn't help us."

"Would it eat our skin like the slime?"

The faintest smile flickered over Gavin's lips, fighting against the miasma of pain. "No."

"Then why can't we drink it?"

He grunted. "It just doesn't help." He adjusted the straps over his shoulders. The sharpness of them felt like soon it would sever his arms right off.

He stepped, even though the steps hurt. He waited, even though each moment sucked a little more moisture from his tongue. The air felt so thick with it, surely by breathing he hydrated himself. But no. That's not how it worked. *Duck. Sweep with the oar. Scan. Pause.* Pause. Somehow, the pain got worse when he stopped. When he moved, he moved like a stone rolling down a hill, an inevitable descent, each step leading into the next, except he couldn't let it, he had to *stop*. Like a rolling stone bouncing off an uneven ground hovering in the air for a long, impossible moment, scanning the rough terrain and contemplating its imminent erosion.

He swept with the oar in small, light, careful movements. He scared away snakes coiled under leaves. He nudged onward a scorpion on the underside of a vine. He stepped over a trail of large black ants. A centipede. He got it up on the end of his oar, and slid it off into the bushes.

"Dad when can we sleep?" Rose murmured through a yawn.

"We have to keep moving, Rosebud," even his voice felt weak. "We have to keep moving..."

"My legs are gonna fall off," she grumbled.

"Your legs won't fall off."

They squelched forward more steps at their grueling pace.

"Dad—"

His fists clenched, air flashing into his nose. A strange feeling roared inside him, bubbling from his throat as a quick, sharp little laugh that curled his lips into a smile. It *burned* him. It bent his legs. It tensed the muscles in his arms. It pulled tight the skin of his cheeks. It curved his eyes.

"Dad why can't we just sleep here?" Bloom asked. "Isn't the swamp not our enemy?"

"It's still dangerous," he said, fighting the damn laughter that boiled his insides and tried to force itself out over his words. He swallowed it down, and the heat of it burnt up the petals of his heart. "We just need to keep going. Okay? Keep moving. That's all. That's all! Come on. Stay right behind me. *Right* behind me."

They kept walking. Excruciating step by excruciating step.

"But how much longer do we have to go?" Rose whispered. "We've been walking for so long—"

"I don't know!" Gavin snapped, his limbs going rigid, that boiling sensation burning his tongue as the words left his mouth. He forced himself to take a deep breath, but even that hurt. "I can't deal with you two right now. Just walk behind me. No more questions."

As they kept going, not even the swamp noise could quite manage to be louder than their silence.

SLASHWAVE

The only Runewave that can make opponents bleed. Slashwaves can cut through bone, and could murder armies if the blood they drew didn't undo their own power.

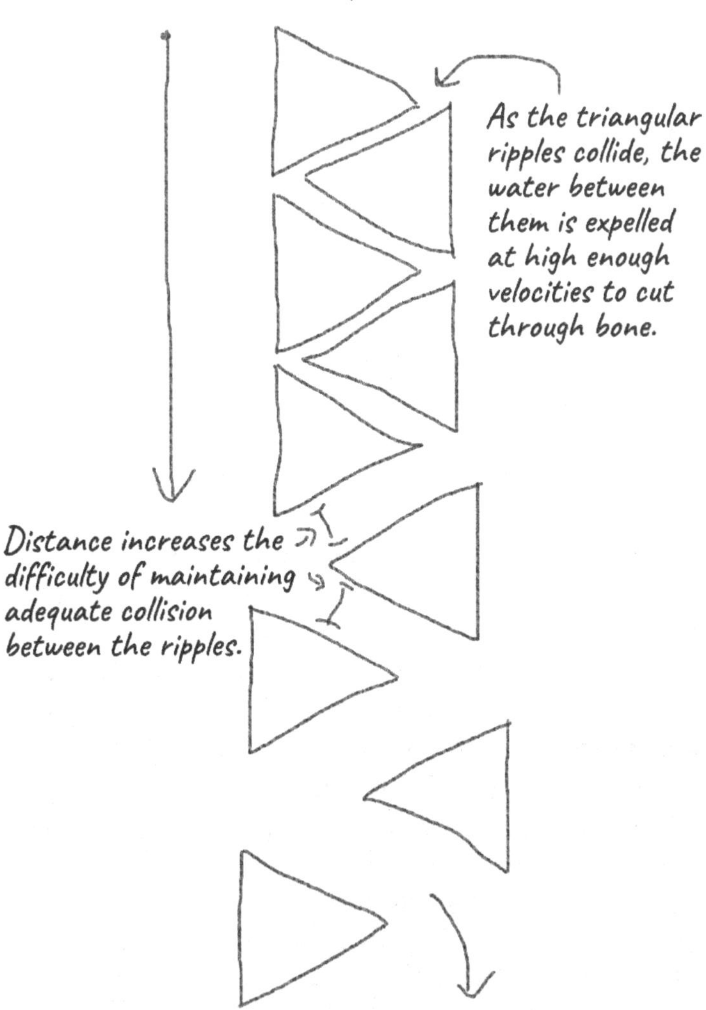

14

The great monster lay dead. Half-submerged in bogwater, its head severed from its body, its pollen tongue limp, its thorn teeth savage and still, its vine arms drifting in murk. The mudskiff lay overturned and cracked in half. A trail of footsteps led away from it, still fresh in the mud. Stelli and Dezma followed those footprints, coming up on a great gray tree, its roots carving the mud in waves of bark. They paused behind one of those roots, barely daring to breathe as they peaked out into the clearing.

Stelli's eyes flicked between shadowed movements, as the General's men stepped across the swampland, vanishing one by one into the darkness of the Aycmor tree's branches. Her ears picked out the soft splashes and ripples of Standwaves as the soldiers stepped, until that too faded with distance.

Dezma ghosted forward at her side, Longtooth flickering just ahead of her, right above the tangled trail left by the ragtag, haggard, tired, wounded company.

Stelli clutched her Canine in a slick grip. The weight brought her comfort, but it felt woefully inadequate in the swamp. In this strange realm of vines and beasts, avoiding blood felt secondary to slicing through obstacles.

Stelli grunted, foot slipping on mud. She caught herself with a hand down on a rock, its slick surface leaving behind a thin veneer of slime on her palm. She wiped it on the hem of her cloak, though it made little difference. The grime hardly felt like grime anymore. The pain, hardly like pain. The exhaustion, hardly like exhaustion.

The Rabbit didn't stop running, so the Wolf didn't stop hunting. Which meant Dezma and Stelli couldn't stop either. She blinked away caked gunk in her eyes, shaking her head. The weight of everything pulled her forward. A promise, tugging, tugging, tugging at the hook within her heart, and forcing each foot to land after the last.

"What trail are they following?" Dezma muttered, kneeling down, checking their footprints, using her Longtooth to sift through the crushed underbrush that marked the soldiers' passing. "Maybe they've swallowed it, but I see no sign of Gavin..."

"He's moving with two children, *at night*," Stelli breathed, scanning. They didn't have much room to stand. The Aycmors pressed from all sides, their drooping leaves tickling her hair. A thick bead of Aycmor... water? Sap? Splashed against her arm. She flicked it off, shaking the stickiness from her hand. "Is he that good?" The question sent a queasy twinge through her stomach. *He killed your brother.*

Dezma stood, ducking forward. "He knows the swamp better than anyone."

"He's exhausted."

"What are you implying?"

She shrugged.

"He is *not* dead," Dezma growled.

Stelli just shook her head, plodding onward.

"Gavin would sooner burn the swamp down than let his children get hurt."

"So you keep saying," Stelli murmured.

A toad croaked right next to Stelli's ear. She tensed, shifting forward behind Dezma, eyes trained on the critter. It sat placid and docile, a big flap of skin hanging down beneath his wide lipped mouth and beady eyes. Its tongue snapped the air above her shoulder, retracting in with a big squirming bug.

Stelli moved on. Here, away from the rivers and ponds, the swamp cover blotted out light. She pulled out her canteen, popping the top off, sticking a finger in the mouth and wincing as she slammed the beat of a Mirrorwave against her cranium. A beam of light shone out of the mouth of her canteen. She used the stopper to direct the light, lowering it to her hip.

Something flashed, reflecting off a leaf to Dezma's side. She nudged the other woman's side. "There," she breathed.

Dezma grunted. Stelli knelt next to the leaf, her light pouring across the small pores of the leaf and illuminating it in all its detail.

A spot of dark, fresh blood dripped off its end, down to the mud below.

"Sooner burn the swamp down, eh?" She breathed.

Dezma glowered at the blood as she pressed onward. Stelli scrambled to keep up, turning her light back and forth, using its beam to scan the ground. Eight eyes gleamed under the shadow of a leaf. A snake coiled tighter under a log. A large spiderweb hung across the path, the queen hanging rotund and bristling in the center. The web quivered as a bug slammed into it. The spider picked its way across the web, unhurried. She grabbed its body, turned it over, and reared her front fangs to snap off a chunk of the insect's head.

Dezma and Stelli ducked under the web, keeping their eyes on it, watching it feast as they continued onward.

"I wouldn't step in that..." A shaking voice drifted back to them from up ahead.

"Moons, you come by here earlier and sneeze?"

A guffaw. "I wish I was this good."

More laughter.

Dezma held up a hand, poking her Longtooth through the underbrush. Bits of Aycmor sap caught against her shoulders as she shoved through the thicker patches of leaves. The banter made Stelli uneasy, setting inside her a deep and guttural sense of wrongness. She shook her head, trying to still her breathing, ducking lower and eyeing a lizard clinging on the underside of a branch, whose long orange frills pulled back from a sharp looking snout. Dezma poked her head through a gap in the leaves. Stelli came up beside her.

The company of soldiers stood in a gaggle around the edge of a clearing. Dark pools of green-slime infested mud dominated the space in front of them. It really did look like snot, the way it clung to rocks, stringing out until it split and congealed anew with another drifting globule.

Stelli's eyes landed on two of the soldiers in particular, who stood apart from the rest. She could see only a sliver of them between the hanging fronds around her, their visages bisected by the very swamp itself. Yet she knew. She knew by the squareness of his shoulders, the mottle of his cloak, the fierce gaze of his staff. She knew by his very proximity. Next to him, a shorter woman. Stelli knew her, too. Knew her by the slightness of her posture, and the firmness of her stance. The confidence and surety in every detail of her movements.

The swamp squeezed around Stelli, constricting her. The hook burned through her, searing her heart like the pain of flavor shining through too-hot soup. Her body shook with the pain. Tears reached her eyes.

Her father raised the staff, pointing it at the soldiers behind him, and jerking it forward. They quieted, moving forward together. Hexagons rippled between the clumps of slime, setting the ponds aglow with bioluminescent flickers. Only six soldiers remained, timid and scared.

Stelli's hands curled into fists, gripping the rope attached to the hook in her heart. If she didn't grip it, soon it's yanking would be too much. Her father would step, and it would yank her forward, and she would drown in the snot of these pools.

"Change of plans," Dezma whispered. The soldiers had made it about a quarter of the way across the slime. Her father and Tess stepped onto the slime behind them, staying a few paces back.

"What?"

The soldiers approached the halfway point. The one in the front paused, but the guy behind him bumped his back. He stumbled forward a few steps—

"There's—" his words cut off in a scream as his foot sank through the Snotpool, his step unsupported. He bent forward, hands slapping at his leg, but that only made him scream more as he pitched forward. He thrashed, trying to swim, but the slime clung to him, drifting through the water towards him, grabbing his shoulders, grabbing his neck, weighing him down.

"Was there blood?" Stelli breathed, squinting, trying to make out what had caused the fall—

"Gavin must have left another trap," Dezma whispered.

The soldier crawled up onto the shore, skin red and raw and bleeding. He slapped at himself like he was covered in bugs, trying to throw the slime off, but every time his hands touched his skin new noises of deteriorating pain wailed from his throat. She could see muscle and bone beneath the skin, beneath the slime, except not beneath the skin, because the skin was gone, sloughed off *into* the slime, hovering in fragmented pieces within the green blobs. The noises broke into a whimper, and then silence, as his contorted body fell still on the shore.

In front of the company, his blood filled the pools of mud.

"We can take them out," Dezma whispered. "They're stupid. Make them bleed, and they fall in."

The soldiers standing in the middle of the pools looked down beneath them, started to scramble back towards the shore.

"There's still—"

"*Go*—" Dezma lifted her Longtooth, standing up from the brush, rushing forward, feet snapping branches as she moved—

Gah, Stelli grunted, lunging forward, heart hammering. *Skin, pulled off*—That green scar, curving across her father's staff. It stared at her. Taunted her.

The soldiers came up short, staring at Dezma with wide eyes. Stelli scanned their faces, for a brief moment her heart spiking with pain and loss when she didn't find York among them, and her mind jumped to all the horrible ways he could have died at the hands of that monster—

CRACK. One of the soldiers ran forward, Canine swinging. Dezma caught it on her Longtooth, deflecting the blow as a second and a third rushed forward, scrambling to get onto the shore, past Dezma's flickering blade and wide reach. She swept the Longtooth low, keeping them back, but there were five pressing forward, chaotic, straggling, but *five*—

Stelli caught up, throwing a hand to the slime infested water, taking on the angry beat in the back of her head. Slashwaves. *A stupid name,* her father's voice echoed. It didn't slash. Like any other Runewave, it—

The water *surged* as those small triangles oscillated forward, interlocking like fingers laced together, the spaces between them launching water into the air. She slammed the rhythm in her head, playing with a frequency her ears couldn't quite follow, sending the water spurting with enough force to...

Some of the slime kicked up with the waves, splattering across the soldiers, forcing screams from their throats as they duck and spun, trying to avoid her Slashwaves, slime splattering against their clothing, their necks, hissing as it tried to eat their flesh. They threw it off, formation scattered, giving Dezma time to—

Her Longtooth lanced one of the soldier's legs. Blood

poured out, coating through his Standwaves. The man screamed as he fell in, writhing in the pool while the slime devoured him.

Three of the soldiers staggered back, blood flanking them on either side. They looked back at Tess and her father, who stood still together at the center of the pools. More unease settled in Stelli's gut. Her father had his hood up. Why would he have his hood up?

One of the soldiers leapt the blood, staggering through the last little bit of blood-slime mixture, shouting in pain as the slime grabbed his feet. He staggered to the shore, the wrappings around his ankles disintegrated, feet red and bloodied, but his Canine was raised, striking at Dezma—

CRACK. She caught it, spinning him to the side, lunging forward with the Longtooth in two hands and slamming the hard wood into the man's skull. He collapsed to the mud, unconscious. Dezma spun back to the remaining soldiers in the middle of the mud pools, blood flanking them. The soldiers eyed the sides. The Snotpools stretched wider than they were long, but the blood didn't cover the entire length. Stelli could see them calculating. One edged towards the side. Stelli flicked the water, and a burst of Slashwaves cast slime into the air, right across his path. He cringed back away.

Her father kept standing still. *Don't make an opponent bleed...* Stelli edged further, eyeing her path across the pools, along the edge of the blood... *Unless you are ready to kill them...* the soldiers couldn't move. She just had to—

"We surrender!" Her father called. "You got us!"

The words hit her like a bucket of cold ice water. The voice. It sounded like the squeak of a raindrop, rolling down a polished steel chestplate. Like the laugh of a kid, scared but trying to lighten the mood. Her father reached up and threw back his hood.

Stout countenance, unkempt beard. Scared eyes. York. Wearing her father's cloak, carrying her father's Wolf staff. With his face, the staff suddenly appeared comical, the scar like a child's scribble. The cloak hung heavy and awkward around his shoulders. Stelli's breathing hiccupped through her exhausted throat. The water twisted and turned under her hand, little gouts of slime kicked up by her angry Slashwaves. Her fingers curled. Her hand shook.

"Where is he?" She hissed.

"You're too late, anyway," York said, swallowing, holding his hands in the air, staff horizontal above him. "He told us to kill you if we had the chance. But it doesn't matter if we do or not—he said that too."

"WHERE IS HE?" She shouted, another burst of Slashwaves launching just past York, a bit of slime catching his cheek. He slapped it off, shaking it free of his hand, cringing away from her. "Tell me," she hissed.

"Stelli," Dezma warned.

"I'll kill you," she hissed at York. "You know I will, just like he would—"

A hand clamped her shoulder, giving it a squeeze. The flickering Slashwaves under her palm dissipated.

"Toss your weapons into the slime," Dezma called. "And walk to shore."

The soldiers clumped tighter together, stumbling away from the blood, which only spread further in the water. They glanced at each other with uncertainty, looking to York, before remembering he had no more authority than the rest of them.

"If you don't," Dezma said. "*Then* we kill you."

Even York turned his head, like he was waiting for orders. He held the Wolf head staff with the green scar out to the side, hand shaking—

Stelli launched her Slashwaves just past him, slime kicking

up and missing him by mere inches. He yelped and dropped the staff. She watched as its green scar turned up to the sky, fading down into the murk, green slime crawling across the carved snout and ears, drowning it. The four other soldiers still standing dropped their Canines, sidestepping the blood, making their slow path around the spreading redness, eyes flickering between Dezma's staff and Stelli's hand, just above the water. The air mugged them all with its moisture, clinging to them, the sounding of the toads rushing up and down against their ears. A branch above them bounced under the weight of a landing bird, its long green plumage effusing amidst the canopy. Its beak parted, releasing a three-toned caw.

Dezma met the soldiers as they came to land, Longtooth held ready. She separated them, patted them down, checking them for weapons. Stelli kept her gaze locked on York, and the other cloaked figure, who thus far had been silent.

"Take your hood off," Stelli whispered.

Hands curled up from beneath the long sleeve. Long fingers, hair on the knuckles. Stelli grit her teeth.

"Sorry, Stelli," Seban threw back the hood. A haunted look hung in his eye.

"The two of you," she whispered. "Here. Now."

She let the Slashwaves fade, starting up a new rhythm in her head. Hexagons pushed out through the mud. She breathed past the nausea, putting mental brackets on the rhythm of the Standwaves. The ripples extended, their shape stretching through the murk, working around the expanding pools of blood. By the end, a winding path of repeating hexagon ripples lead from the two fakes to the shore.

She pushed her lip through the back of her teeth, the mud beneath her pulsing, as if she stood atop her father's Standwaves, her worries gone, her hook steady. The total comfort that came from helplessness. She saw those same emotions playing on

York's face as he walked forward. Something cracked inside her, and the ground felt solid again. Any moment. Any moment she could let her rhythm falter...

Right at the shore, she washed the Standwaves away, watching his eyes shift to pure fear, terror, his arms coming up to flail, his mouth falling open, and in that briefest moment of realization playing across his face, she felt more okay than she had ever felt—

She rounded the edges of the rhythm, pulled it inwards, shaping the Standwaves to Boundwaves, locking the two in place right at the edge of the Snotpools. She stepped right up to them, her feet on the solid mud of the bank. "One wrong answer," she murmured. "That's all it takes."

"He'll hunt you down," York's voice shook. "After he captures the kids, he'll hunt you down."

"I know," Stelli said. "So you'd better tell me where he is."

York's eyes darted around the edges of the clearing, as if expecting to see the Wolf snarling under every tree branch. "He guessed," York said, starting to babble. "Where his quarry is going. He split off to get there quicker. Did you think he forgot about you two? We're the decoy. Kill you if we can, he said. But even if you kill us, it'll be too late..."

"*Moons*," Dezma cursed. Stelli looked over. The four conscious soldiers also stood stuck in Boundwaves, though Dezma had been nicer, finding small puddles for them to stand above, empty of Snotslime. Dezma wasn't with them, though. She had picked her way over the Snotpools, kneeling in the mud on the far side, looking at something.

A mud-covered bucket.

"He's going for water, isn't he?" York said. "To one of the oases."

"He won't have a choice," Dezma called, voice grim.

"Tess thinks she knows which one he's going too, based on

his patterns so far. She has a map of the swamp that she found in an old military atlas, and she thinks she can cut through the swamp to get there faster than Gavin will expect." Seban whispered. "She thinks that by the sun's zenith tomorrow the fight will be over."

Stelli affixed him with a hard look.

"She told me to tell you something," Seban said, though his chin quivered just a bit. "Before it's all over."

Stelli stepped up, face to face with Seban. That Moon cursed chin wouldn't stop quivering, even as the rest of Seban stood calm.

"She says that she should hate you," he whispered. "But she doesn't."

A flame burned in Stelli's gut. It withered on long-blackened charcoal.

"If you make it back to her," Stelli growled. "Tell her that it's okay if she does."

Seban bowed his head, watching the Boundwaves flicker beneath his fee. York's eyes were squeezed shut, face pale. Seban reached over and squeezed his hand.

Stelli stopped watching, a sick taste in her mouth.

"Why are none of you running away?" Dezma's voice, raised, sturdy, cut the air, cut the fire, cut the swamp. She picked her way back across the Snotpools, well away from the blood. "I haven't gagged you, or bound your hands. Spit blood on my Boundwaves, and run away into the swamp. You'll probably die. But some of you may have picked up enough to make it out."

"Loyalty never crossed your mind?" One of the soldiers, a man with a chin-strap beard, called out.

Dezma snorted. Stelli's mouth went a little dry in her presence. A bit of a smile tweaked the edge of her lip.

"I'd like a single one of you here to look me in the eye and tell me you don't resent him," she called. "If you did, I still wouldn't believe you. He's dragged you through hell. Your friends are dead. You're exhausted, and far from home, and it's all his fault. So go ahead. Tell me you don't resent him."

Chinstrap looked away. "I've lost friends to Cindeere's armies too. We all will, soon enough."

"It's a waste of time, Dez—"

She held up a finger, silencing Stelli. The flame kept burning in her gut. But somehow... somehow she trusted the woman, who stood in the swamp with broad shoulders and surety, who clutched her Longtooth with a tenderness that whispered calming balms in her ears.

"Who is it?" Dezma whispered, crouching down to look Chinstrap in the eyes.

"Wh... huh?"

"Who's heart leaps whenever anyone walks past their front window?" Dezma whispered. "Who brews just a little bit more tea than they want in the morning, hoping you'll stumble in through the door after the war and need tea to calm your frayed nerves?

Stelli repressed a snort, the fire burning up her neck, swirling with such scalding heat it made her fingers curl in and out of fists. *Nobody. Nobody. Nobod—*

"Don't tell me there's nobody," Dezma whispered. "There's always somebody. It's why you're here."

The trust withered in Stelli's gut, and the hook twisted, cutting up her heart. Venom dripped in her mouth, sour and sick. *Always somebody...* She was right. She was right. She was right. The hook yanked her, yanked her, yanked her, egging her on deeper and deeper into the swamp, towards her somebody, the only somebody she'd ever had.

Chinstrap spat on the ground, still cowering away from Dezma's gaze. "He don't even know about me," he muttered. "Won't be no different for him if I never come back."

"Might be different for him if you did, though," Dezma whispered. "That's my point. You aren't gonna run. None of you are. Not because you're loyal to that abusive General, but because there're people you care about somewhere in this world who don't have anyone better than you to fight for them."

The toads croaked in the silence that followed, as Dezma stood and looked around, her eyes shining under heavy brows.

Chinstrap guffawed, and spit on the ground. "You're doing a good job of convincing me to punch you in the face, woman."

The other men chuckled, growing into a roar of laughter, fueled around the four of them.

"Here we were surrendering, not even thinking about ma and pa back home," another man laughed.

Dezma blinked, mouth opening to speak—

"Not even—"

"It doesn't have to be the General," Stelli said, her voice slicing their laughter to ribbons. Everyone turned to look at her. The hook ripped her. The pain glowed like sore muscles after a workout, hardening her posture, bringing bile to her throat at the same time as gratifying her words. "I plan on killing him, yes. Killing him by *training* the children. They have the power necessary to do it. And then when he's dead? When he's dead, they'll be mine. I can use them just the same as him. To save all of our someone's from Cindeere and his army, from all the threats the horizon brings. But it will be me—be *us*—calling the shots. Not him."

None of the men spoke. Dezma glared at Stelli, mouth a firm line. Her grip on the Longtooth no longer looked so tender. Her broad shoulders no longer looked so sure.

"Fight for that vision, instead," Stelli commanded, stepping next to Dezma. "Where your loved ones are safe. From the Horizon, *and* the Wolf."

Behind her, something thudded into the mud. She turned

to see York, squatting on the Boundwaves, head bowed, dark mud squeezing between the fingers of his planted fist. He lifted it into a two-fingered salute. "You're better than him," he whispered. "You always have been."

"Moons," said Chinstrap. "Beats gettin' killed."

The second man saluted. The third joined him. The fourth man only hesitated a second longer.

Stelli turned to Seban. He looked down at York with a strange expression. Something looked wrong about his face. It took a moment for Stelli to realize what. His chin. His chin wasn't quivering. He spoke without looking at her. "You think it's possible?"

Stelli nodded, then swallowed, and said... "Yes."

He looked up at her. His chin started to quiver again. "Just don't let the General kill York for this," his voice warbled. "Please. The person I'm fighting for is right here. I can't lose him." He squeezed York's hand.

Stelli nodded again, holding back tears. They held their gazes for a long few seconds, listening to the crescendo of toads in the distance. Seban gave her a firm nod in return.

She pointed at the Boundwaves beneath their feet, yanking the corners into hexagons. York and Seban stepped into the mud, and she let her Standwaves go.

Moons, her head hurt.

"I need you to try and catch up to him," Stelli said, trying to put together some semblance of a plan. She glanced at Dezma, but the woman wouldn't meet her eyes. "You know which way he went. When you find him, tell him we're dead."

The man with the chinstrap beard snorted. "Probably will be."

"Not your concern," Stelli snapped, the pain in her head whipping out through her words. "We have to hope that Gavin is clever and fast enough to get water and leave right away. He's not an idiot. We can do this."

Chinstrap man rolled his eyes, looking away. She glared at the other soldiers. "Any questions?"

A few mumbles in return.

York caught her eye. "We'll do it," he whispered, face heavy.

She nodded. "Then go. And we'll find Gavin." She turned to Dezma—

Dezma's eyes stormed, her knuckles white against her Longtooth. Stelli moved up next to her, jerking her head across the Snotpools. Dezma followed half a step behind. Her presence was like lightning against a dark sky. They made their way around the blood, around the fallen bucket, the tangle of disturbed mud, the couple flecks of red. They ducked through the underbrush.

And then the thunder crashed.

"*What was that*?" Dezma hissed, spinning on her.

"I saved your ass," Stelli hissed back. "Be grateful."

"Now we're committed to a plan that *I never agreed to*—"

"Your plan failed," Stelli cut her off. "Twice now? And we agreed—"

"That we could train them to kill the General, not that we could take them away to fight in a *war*—"

"You're just so smart, aren't you," Stelli grabbed Dezma by the front of her shirt, their faces inches apart. The fire boiled over through her hands, across her fingers, playing in the air between them, snapping at the Aycmor branches around them. "Always able to tell what people are feeling, read them like a recipe book and take them for all their ingredients. Do you even *care* about what you find in people's heads or is it all just a little game to see how well you can predict the future?"

Dezma grabbed Stelli's hands, squeezing them white. "You're the one willing to *use* children," she whispered. "Your words, wolf cub."

"At least in my world Gavin is the last father to lose his children to war," Stelli hissed. "You backwoods folk are all the same. You'll die for nothing but yourselves."

Dezma threw her back. She stumbled up against the Aycmor tree. They glared at each other, the gazes alone enough to stoke the fire between them. Dezma's eyes were full and storming, all the recipes of her soul on display. Stelli could taste them. They tasted warm, and full, and kind. They tasted determined. They tasted sure.

They tasted bitter.

"At least we're willing to make the sacrifice ourselves," Dezma spat. "Instead of getting other people to make them for us."

She turned and stalked into the swamp, leaving Stelli alone with the phantom flame that flickered unfulfilled in the space between her, and emptiness.

Hound Hornets

They use their blue aromatic poop to leave communication trails through the swamp

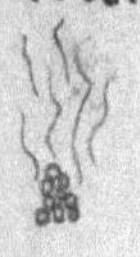

Do Not Approach Hornets if you Have Recently Handled A Flower
- Scent sends hornets into murderous frenzy

15

Pain and thirst moved rapidly into delirium. It beat against his eye sockets, sending little dark flecks over his vision, assaulting his focus, pulling the granules of his sight apart and forcing the world to be blurry. He blinked. And blinked. And keep looking.

Aycmor's.... Bark hole... Bounder den... He ducked the Cyril vine on some far back instinct. *Allcrea Centipede*, perched on a root stretching across their narrow path. He flung it aside with the oar. *Orbweaver's Web.* Avoid. *Snyrnout, poking up from a pond.* Avoid. *Hound nest, perched between two branches. Mudstinger, coiled under a log. Wild Wandering Warrighast Toad, eyeing them from the shadows.* Avoid. Avoid. Avoid.

His lips cracked a little more with each inhale. Bloom and Rose stumbled by his side, heads down, hair tangled around their faces, mud and dirt and grime caked over their skin. With each breath, Rose let out a little gurgle of a whine. Bloom barely picked up his feet.

Almost there... The muted mumble buzzed in his head. "Almost there..."

Another wheeze whine from Rose. Bloom bumped into him, catching himself on Gavin's sleeve, feet splashing in a shallow puddle. So many sounds, from a footstep. Land in a puddle, it splashed, but more than splashing, it sent a subtle whisper of tiny water critters scattering, and followed with the muted squelch or thump of foot on mud or stone. Land on the ground, and it never felt quite solid. The ground of the swamp wanted to grab, to hold on, to never let go. It wanted to drag down and protect, to make sure nothing could ever leave again.

"Almost there," Gavin mumbled. His bleary eyes picked out a gap in the trees in front of them. He tried to speed up. Each step felt like a swarm of Vargus biting at the skin of his thigh, little tingles representing millions of individual legs, the pain amplified by the presence of their biting. He wanted to scream. Wanted to rip and tear at the cloth that wrapped his leg. It squeezed so tight. His foot tingled. Had the Vargus found him there, too?

"Almost there," he mumbled, raising the oar, nudging at the space before him as if to clear leaves. There weren't any leaves. Just the absent croaking of frogs, and a couple Hounds, hovering with their heavy bodies in front of... in front of...

He let out a choked laugh. Bloom stumbled against his good leg, grabbing his arm. Rose held herself like a bundle of sticks, tired, woeful eyes nothing more than shadows between the knots in the wood, hair like Wondor leaves in the mud. But something shifted in her eyes. Reflected in them, as the little motes of light above the bucket she held flickered, brightened, and darted forward into the clearing. She tipped it forward, casting a beam of firebug Mirrorwaves...

Gavin's ears adjusted to the new sound. Water gurgled and trickled with merriment, pouring over rocks that glowed beneath the vibrant and clear water. Frazzle Moss ringed those rocks at the water line, sitting placid and smooth and frazzle-less. The silent rays of early morning cast through the treetops, finding patches of water to set ablaze with blueness, refracting in the subtle sun patterns that whisked across the surface of the oasis. Green lily pads drifted in the soft current, carrying pink flowers that bloomed with sharp petals, and drifted a scent like warm stew crackling on the fire of Dezma's tavern. A great tree sprouted from the center of the oasis, standing tall and reaching far above, bathing the clearing in its ochre presence. Thick roots broke up the pond like the back of a mighty serpent, forming a miniature landscape of ponds and waterfalls in the weaving bark. The leaves shifted and cut the air above like scales. Drops of brilliant clear water danced between the offset tiers, plopping from one to another like some great natural rain chain, until they flickered in beams of morning light and sparkled to the water below. One of the firebug lights from Rose's bucket caught a drop of falling water, twirling in a silent waltz.

Watching the water, in all its glorious forms, the way it trickled down across the roots, the way it swirled with absent wind, the way it dropped from leaf to leaf, the way it shone with dawnlit beauty, the way it rippled up against his feet, and stole a bit of mud from his toes... It made his mouth burn. A redness choked the back of his throat. His hands trembled.

Rose took a slow step forward, the toes of her boots tickling the water. She looked back at Gavin, her eyes wide and exhausted. He tried a smile, stepping forward with her, stumbling a few steps into the water, waving Bloom to follow. Rose fell to her knees, careless of her soaked pants, planting her hands down into the silt and sand and mud of the oasis floor, squeezing her hands to fists, chin quivering. She cupped her hands, filling them with the glorious clear water. It trailed between the mud caking in her hand, percolating little bits of the brownness, finding the gaps in her fingers and sifting through to sprinkle down as droplets. She breathed like she hadn't before. She looked at him with a half open mouth like opening her mouth hadn't been possible until now. Her red rimmed eyes glowed. They glowed, and made Gavin's heart glow with them. He smiled. He let out a laugh. He plopped down on his behind in the shallow water, cupping some of it and throwing it at her.

She shrieked, ducking away, laughing, skimming her hand

across the surface right back at him. The water caught his face, trickling through his beard. So cold. So delicious on his skin. Like the first morning drizzle of the summer. He smiled at Rose, washing his hands in the oasis, feeling the grime melt away.

"Not too fast," he croaked at Bloom, who sipped water from his cupped hands. "You'll get sick."

"It's so good," Bloom whispered, getting another handful. Gavin scooped some of his own, puckering his mouth, forcing himself to take small little sips. His eyes fluttered closed. The water hurt, stinging his lips with its coldness. Swallowing seared him. But the sensation of liquid coursing down his throat, trickling between the cracked and dry crevices of his body... It forced a shudder out of him. He wrenched his eyes back open, glancing around with drowsy awe, sparkles somehow brighter than they had been before. His gaze landed on the Frazzle Moss that rimmed the rocks.

"Can we finally sleep, dad?" Rose whispered.

He tried another smile. "Yes, Rosebud," he heaved himself to his feet with a splash, stumbling towards the nearest rock. He slowed as he approached it, kneeling down and reaching forward with the tip of his oar. He only needed a little, and an oasis was the best place to harvest it. He made sure to scrape under and not prod the moss's soft skin-like rolls. Even exhausted, his hands didn't slip. He'd done this before, to make the sponges Dezma used in the tavern.

The smell of the flowers tickled his nose again. He blinked new moisture from his eyes, secured the moss on the end of the oar, and made for the nearest root, which formed a natural bridge among the oasis.

"Come on, up we go," he scrabbled at the side of the root, grunting as he pulled himself up, using only his upper body. He paused for breath at the top, reaching a hand back down. The pack hung heavy on his shoulders, biting his skin. At least they hadn't lost it. His leg throbbed. *Spartippi berry paste... clean water...* He would be fine. *He would be fine.* He hauled Bloom up next to him. Rose looked at them, then grinned, raising her foot, poking the water with it. Her poke sent Standwaves rippling out— normal ones, in the absence of Bloom. She stepped onto the pattern, one hand up on the tree root, as if expecting the water not to hold her weight.

But it did.

"Rosebud, could you please come up here with—"

She laughed, running forward along the edge of the root, her feet casting out more merry little hexagons with each step. Gavin sighed, watching her with heavy eyes.

"Come on," he whispered to Bloom, half-crawling along the root, making slow progress towards the tree. Keeping the oar steady proved an extra challenge as he made sure not to drop the moss. Little droplets from the leaves above caught his cheeks and beard, plopping with enough force to sting. He felt them tearing through the grime caked on his skin. It tickled. Bloom grunted behind him, still clutching the two little plants, which looked muddied and worse for wear. *Clean water...* It solved everything.

Rose waited for them, leaning back on the tree root, kicked back and smiling, bucket sitting next to her. "Can we just stay here dad?" She craned her neck up, eyes going wide as a droplet of water landed on her nose, and traced its way down her cheek. "It's so pretty."

He laughed under his breath. One moment ready to sleep, the next vibrating and ready to bounce. "Maybe for a little while, Rosebud," he whispered, looking out to the edge of the oasis. The Aycmors around the edge loomed like the death of gloaming, heavy shadows hanging under sad leaves. A dread filled him looking at those Aycmor trees, and the dread brought him a deep sadness. Once he would have watched the bog sap drip between the Aycmor trees with longing. But the echo of the Hounds buzzing stayed in his ears, and the horrible screams of the Zar'thul tore his heart, and the aching of his leg, and the pounding of his head, and the looming fangs of the Wolf which seemed to shine in the eyes of every hidden creature, and and and... and he couldn't quite feel excited about returning to the swamp anymore.

And that made him sad.

"Hopefully the Bugaboo has no idea where we are," he whispered. "Hopefully he won't find out."

"He?" Bloom whispered.

Gavin just shook his head, eyes drooping. "It's time to sleep, Raindrops," he murmured. He glanced around again. He didn't like how exposed they were, up on the root. But where else... Where else... The oasis was hard to see from outside... He knew that without a map, without knowledge, someone could wander for days without finding one... he blinked, as he realized the sound of trickling had faded in his ears, like a gentle whisper. He could feel the distance between him and the noise, as his ears reached out and grabbed the sound in slow motion, pulling himself along an invisible rope... He blinked again. "I can't keep going much longer," he mumbled, taking the pack off, laying it safely between a crook in the roots. He slid himself down, finding a nice crevice to sit in. He brought the oar down at his side, prying off the moss with shaking hands. It folded wet and heavy between the crooks of his fingers. He laid it flat on his knee, rolled up his torn sleeve, and laid his bare arm on the moss.

It was like a little bed. A little bed that would spike him if the slime started glowing.

"Come on," he mumbled. "Stay close, okay? We can eat... when, when we wake up."

Bloom set the plants down carefully on top of the pack, curling up on a flat section of bark. It wasn't very comfortable bark.

Bits stuck out, jabbing his shoulder blades, his knees. The pain, too, seemed to come to him from far away. Far away, and stretched out, like a Cyril vine pulled through his fingers, but an endless vine, one he could endlessly pull, letting it caress the rarely touched skin on the inside of his fingers...

He blinked, trying to find Rose. She slipped into the crevice with him, tucking her legs up against her body, resting her head on his shoulder. He smiled. He couldn't quite register the moment when the smile faded. It happened like the water that rolled across the moss-covered rocks. Like the sun-stains on the water's surface, as they rippled, split, and re-linked into complex, beautiful patterns, formed with the symmetrical rippling.

"Dad," Bloom whispered from above him. Gavin tugged that vine, and found what the words meant somewhere in his jumbled head. "Can I ask that question I was going to ask now?"

"Sure, Bloomstalk," he muttered, breathing in and out, slow and steady. "Sorry I snapped at you earlier."

"It's okay dad," he said. "I was just wondering why you brought Isingrass with us."

"Oh, right," Gavin hummed under his slow breath. "I promised I would show you."

"The pretty flower it turns into during the Full Devouring?"

"Yeah..." Gavin breathed. "I wasn't sure if we would make it home in time for the Full Devouring. So I brought one with us, just in case we're still out here, I can still show you..."

Amidst the plopping of the Oasis Tree's great dripping, Gavin heard a lighter trickle of water on bark, little individual teardrops. It sounded like...

"I love you so much, dad."

"Love you too."

* * *

Sharp frazzles jabbed into his arm, spiking through his skin. His eyes shot open.

Aycmor trees, still. Shadows, still. Everything, still. Still, despite the light of the morning, still despite the light breeze that brought bumps to the skin of his arms. The rocks dotting the oasis water were still too. Still, and chock full of agitated Frazzle Moss. It had uncurled, stretching the soft skin as tight as it could go, displaying sharp corkscrews to the air. He squeezed his left hand to make sure Rose still lay beside him. He looked up, and saw Bloom.

A flicker of sick-blue light played through the Aycmor branches, and he knew why the moss was agitated. Rivulets of nausea ran through his arms and stomach, bile rising in his throat as the pain of his leg caught up to his consciousness.

"Up," Gavin hissed, shaking Rose, dragging her to her feet, "up, come on, Bloom, Rose, *up!*"

The water in the oasis moved, shifting like molten glass pulled by a glassblower's tongs, rippling in concentric circles, perfectly symmetrical, pulled inwards towards the tree. Lily pads congealed to the surface of the water, bending with it, *contorting* with it—

His children blinked blearily awake. Gavin grabbed the pack, threw it over his aching shoulders, pushed Rose up next to Bloom. He couldn't spot any figures in his rapid backwards glances. Just shadows. Leaves shifted, rustling. The birds fell quiet. He squeezed the skin around the puncture wounds from the frazzles, getting as much blood out on his arm as he could. It trailed out down his elbow.

"Da, what—"

"You need to run, use your Standwaves—"

Bloom rubbed his eyes, glancing behind them— "dad, dad!"

"*Run*" Gavin hissed, shoving Bloom and Rose away. They stumbled to the edge of the root. Bloom slipped off, landing on the water, caught in the sticky rippling that took over the entire oasis.

Rose grabbed the pack, staggering under its weight, "Come *on*, Dad—"

Gavin turned. The Wolf. Running forward, on a thin strip of Standwaves between the rippling adhesive oasis. Those eyes. Small, beady, black against pale skin, but somehow just as purple as the Carrow Wolf Moon, purple not in hew, but in the sinister, inevitable, unstoppable way that a perfect hunter was purple.

Gavin grabbed the bucket and tossed it. The Snotpool water flung out, the heavy wood of the bucket flipping end over end towards the charging Wolf. The Wolf ducked, throwing his cloak up and stumbling, catching the slime against the dark fabric as the bucket hurdled above him, slamming into the oasis and sticking to the Boundwaves. Gavin swung his arm, splattering droplets of blood through the air towards the General's feet. They landed in the water, taking to the ripples and tearing them apart, deconstructing their rhythms. The General crashed under the pond and vanished.

A strong hand grabbed Gavin's arm. He stumbled backwards and fell off the root, crashing down next to Bloom. His blood attacked the Boundwaves, and he felt himself sinking—

The water hardened beneath his back. The same hand grabbed him and lifted him. "Dad come on," Rose yanked him to his feet, but his leg didn't want to hold his weight— "Lean on me," Rose hissed. He stumbled forward on one leg. Blood oozed from the edges of his soiled bandage, spreading in the water in a pool around them.

The Standwaves didn't care. They kept spreading with the blood, working as a team. The blood dissolved the General's Boundwaves, and Rose's Standwaves rushed in to replace them.

Bloom grabbed him from the other side. "We've got you

dad," he whispered.

Tears jumped to Gavin's eyes as they stumbled into a run. A hand slapped up from the water, forming a burst of fizzling Standwaves. Gavin wrenched them to the side, stumbling over the hand, his blood dissolving the Wolf's attempts to resurface. Muted thumps rose from beneath them as the General beat his hands against their Standwaves, unable to cast his own. Then the sounds stopped.

They kept running. "Come on dad," Rose huffed, half-pulling him onto the shore. "Come on—"

"TESS," The Wolf roared from behind them. He'd hauled himself up on a root, hair hanging around his angry, piercing eyes. A force slammed into Gavin, and he lost his children. He wasn't holding them anymore. They weren't holding *him* anymore. He rolled in the shallows, getting up onto his arms and looking through his tangled hair. Rose kicked and screamed in the grasp of a cloaked woman, who had a knife raised to sink itself into Rose's flailing body—

Gavin screamed—

But the woman hesitated. The knife didn't swing. Bloom grabbed her wrist, clawing at her fingers. Rose twisted around and got a hand on her face, going for her eyes. The woman bucked, growling, wrestling Rose's hand away with minimal effort, throwing Bloom aside—

She wasn't looking. Gavin heaved himself forward into her legs. She went down. They grappled. The image of her knife above Rose flashed through his eyes. Rose's frightened eyes. *Determined* eyes. *Come on dad...* He pinned her knife hand to the mud, raised his right fist, and decked her across the face. He felt her nose break under him. He punched again. Her head snapped to the side into the mud. He raised his fist again.

"DAD," Rose screeched, pulling at his arm. He slumped back away, the woman groaning on the ground. "Dad we need to go." She said it with tears streaking down her face, hair a mess around her head. She was staring over his shoulder at the oasis. "Come *on*—"

She hauled him to his feet. He staggered. "This way," he wheezed, as Bloom supported him from the other side. "Come on, this way."

And they ran. Each step demanded he fall to the ground, demanded he clutched his leg in both hands and moan and roll and do anything to try and get rid of the red hot pain drilling up through his leg, towards his groin, nauseating his stomach—

But Rose held his right, and Bloom held his left, so he didn't fall.

They ducked a Cyril vine. He reached up and yanked it, letting go the moment he felt its stiffness as one end snapped and flung across the gap between two trees, lashing out and twisting up into a strange sort of noose. The Wolf growled behind him. Gavin caught glimpses over his shoulder.

The Wolf, stumbling to the side, hitting the tree to avoid the Cyril vine—

—right next to a dark hole in the wood—

—eyes gleamed, and a Bounder hissed, lunging out at him—

Gavin dragged Bloom and Rose to the side at the last minute before they slammed into a large orb-web, ducking a tree branch, heaving in breaths as they broke into a full run.

He heard the pained squeal of the Bounder, coupled with a meaty smack. Gavin flinched.

Footsteps.

They broke through a patch of thick ferns, into a mudbank, a river toiling forward in front of them, more mud than water. A long, narrowing log floated in the water, half-submerged—

"We have to jump—" Gavin wheezed. "We have to—" Rose and Bloom pulled him up as they jumped and his one good foot pushed off, slipping on the mud. He rolled forward, losing his grip on Bloom and Rose as they tumbled into the mud river, just shy of the opposite bank. His hands scrabbled at the slick mud, pulling himself forward. The current tried to drag him back, drag him away. Rose grabbed his arm, pulling him. Something hissed behind him. He turned around. The log. Snyrsnout. Maw open, eyes angry—

Bloom lunged to grab Gavin's hand and help Rose yank him from the river. He staggered as the Snyrsnout's hiss grew in volume. They all backed away from the river, scrabbling up the mudbank.

They staggered together into the heat of the swamp.

"This way," he led them at another run, as fast as they could go, but even with their support his legs were going numb. Bloom and Rose heaved in desperate breaths, but neither complained, and he didn't feel their support flagging.

"Just a little further," Rose said between breaths. "You can do it dad, come on."

He huffed, glancing over his shoulders. No Wolf. He heard another hiss from the Snyrsnout, a bellow of surprise from the Wolf, followed by a tangle of splashing. His heart soared—

A noise, like he had never heard before. A hiss torn in half. He turned forward. Broke through another bunch of underbrush. He dragged Bloom and Rose with him, stumbling free into another clearing.

Water lapped their feet. But not the clean crystal water of the oasis, or the mud filled water of the river. This water was green and slick, algae coating the surface like bark on a tree.

The final petal drifted free from Gavin's heart. Another landmark, another shining star in the constellation of his mental image of the swamp. He'd brought them here. His leg screamed, and he wanted to scream with it. He glanced over his shoulder, then back at the algae pools, then at his kids. Rose and Bloom looked up at him with wide watery eyes.

"Is this the pond where the Princess hid?" Bloom whispered.

"Two days," Gavin said. "The air at the bottom of the pond should last you two days. If I'm still not back, you know how to get out of here. You know everything you need to—"

"Dad," Rose whispered.

"Look for Grendles at night," he said. "Remember the river we followed. The oasis, the Grendle, the river. The delta. The two Aycmor trees with tangled up branches. Follow those landmarks, you'll be able to get home—"

"*Dad.*"

"Dezma will help you," Gavin whispered. "The town will help you. You have to go to her, to them. Okay?"

"Dad you can come in with us and hide too dad," Bloom pulled in a half-hearted tug towards the algae pools, stepping into the shallows. Gavin shook his head, and planted his feet. Bloom uncurled his arm from around his shirt, showing the potted plant he still clutched there. Isingrass. "I carried it all this way dad. You promised."

"I'll do everything I can to keep that promise," Gavin whispered, reaching forward and plucking a single pod from the Isingrass plant. He held it up between them. "But I need to hide our tracks and lead him away, or he'll find us here, and there's a chance I won't be able to come back for you and if that's the case I need you two to be strong and make it back to Dezma, okay? Be strong."

He pulled him into a tight hug. "Be strong," he whispered again. "I love you both so so much."

Branches cracked behind them. He shoved them into the pond. They didn't protest anymore. They splashed through the algae, gripping the pack with white knuckled hands and wide terrified eyes. That's all he saw of them. Their terrified eyes. Before they were gone. The algae muted the ripples, bringing the water's surface back still.

He turned around. Footsteps pounded—

He shouted in pain, loud and piercing and obvious, darting around the algae pools, dragging his feet to carve deep troughs in the mud, shaking free blood from his hand onto the ground. He ducked under another spider web at the edge of the clearing, roaring with more pain as he tripped over a log, stumbling up against a tree. A Hound's nest buzzed above him. He ducked past their large airborne bodies, making his way along the edge of the clearing, more and more tears building in his eyes.

Cracking of footsteps. Two sets. Closing in from either side. *Coming for...* For *him*. Good. He glanced around surveying the terrain. Cyril vine. Spider web.

He kept moving, ducking tree branches, shoving through underbrush with abandon. It didn't matter anymore how scratched his clothing got, how much blood he left on the leaves. The throbbing in his leg, the black spots in his vision. None of it mattered. He ran. He turned between two trees. *Spider web—* he fell, jarring his shoulder into the ground and rolling under it, staggering back to his feet. Thick foliage rose in a tangle before him. Behind it, the sluggish trickling of a mud-river. He checked over his shoulder.

The Wolf, closing in, rolling under the same web. Gavin's leg throbbed, half-buckled beneath him. Sweat poured down his face.

The Wolf locked on Gavin's form, charged forward, lunging—

Gavin leapt at the underbrush and crashed through it. The heavy ferns stuck against him, giving way to a sharp bush full of thorns that tore his flesh. He gasped, screaming as the Rhondrum dug into him, sending jitters through his muscles. He squeezed his eyes shut, rolling out of control down the slope, tearing through the plants, splashing down hard into a mud-caked river. His shaking hands came down on the riverbed. He heaved himself to his feet, glancing up at the fall he had just taken.

Footsteps crashed down the river to his right. A woman, hood up, Dewclaw jutting out from her hand. Gavin stumbled through the river's shallows away from her, his steps pulling through the river like a leaf slowly buried by dirt. Black spots swam past his eyes. Thoughts buzzed with each spot like Hounds ramming through his skull. *Safe. They're safe.*

The footsteps stopped behind him. In the ecstasy of his pain, he felt free. Free amidst the singing birds, which now that he thought of them, had fallen oh so very quiet. Free amidst the one place he had ever felt truly safe. The great Aycmor's above him, in all their dark, bog-filled dripping. The river at his feet. Wildlife, pure untainted wildlife existing around him.

A weight slammed against his back. A scream tore from his throat. He went down, face first into the mud at the edge of the river, hands crashing into the water. He tried to crawl, but he couldn't feel his legs anymore, couldn't quite make the thought of movement pass through his body and reach the rest of him. He coughed up blood into the river, watched with delirium as the blood drifted through the brown water. The weight hadn't left his back. He realized as much in a faint and distant epiphany. The weight felt sharp. Like a knee. Pressing him down.

"Got him," a woman's voice shouted.

Another thump and splash, of feet in water. Gavin twisted his head, blinking eyes and seeing in only the barest of slits between his lashes.

The Wolf's legs. Strong, wrapped high with fabric stained red and brown. The water of the river twisted into hexagons with his landing. He stepped forward towards Gavin, whose blood slowly drifted in the current of the river to meet him. It infused his Standwaves, and his steps thunked down into the mud.

"Yes," growled the Wolf, kneeling above Gavin, gripping his

face between two fingers. "But where are the children?"

Gavin laughed, grinning through bloody teeth.

"Where did you hide them?" The General whispered.

Gavin gathered the blood in his mouth and spit it across the General's face.

16

The swamp made distance intangible. When the horizon was far away, Stelli could pretend she was small, and convince herself that her choices didn't matter. What was one woman against the horizon? Nothing, unless she followed the hook yanking her along with the General, whose dreams would save the world. Here in the swamp though, with the Aycmor trees bearing down black branches above her, and the water fowl croaking their sad melodies in her ears, and the insects attacking her face and neck, and the ferns and fronds and canopy blotting her world with shadows... She felt enormous. If she extended her arms, she could reach across all the space there was and touch the horizon which should be untouchable. She felt enormous, and so, so alone. Haunted by the way that Dezma looked at her, convincing her that she might be able to make a difference. She winced, swatting a bug on her neck. It stung. Her elbow brushed a drooping Aycmor leaf, catching some of its sticky black sap. She jerked away.

But she couldn't reach across all the space there was. She couldn't bring herself to spread her arms enough to try.

Screaming echoed through the swamp.

Her head whipped up. High shouts of pain whirred through the trees, which caught the sound and rippled with the movement of disturbed swamp creatures awoken from their slumber. For the briefest moment, the guttural, primal pain of that breaking voice turned her into an awoken swamp creature too. All the exhaustion and loneliness of her bruised, bitten, rash-ridden body twisted, bleeding her nightless sleep out from her fingertips, startling her to full attention, overwhelmed with adrenaline, with presence, with *fear*.

She took off through the underbrush, instincts honed with the swamp. She knew which vines to duck, where the gaps in the branches were, and how to avoid spider webs. She knew to leap the logs, pulse Standwaves from her feet for any would-be puddles she might step on. She plucked free images from the shadows with each tree she passed, each fern she pushed through.

Another shouted scream, lower, visceral. The shout had blood in it. Something bubbling under the noise, boiling and torn.

Silence.

Stelli crashed through a thicket, half-stumbling half-sliding down a mudbank, feet crashing into water. *Standwaves.* The rhythm kicked her mind, keeping her up as she tripped over a hard edge of the newly solidified water, rolling, coming to a stop at the side of a lily pad. It drifted up to her, beaching itself on the edge of her Standwave, until another ripple washed it away again. She pushed herself to her feet, heart in her throat, looking around.

Clean water. A tree, its branches doing what she could not, reaching out and touching every end of its horizon. Drops of clean water fell between tiered leaves. *Plop.* One fell on her head. Cold. Pure. It washed down past her cheek, tickling one of the insect bites on her chin. It hung on the lump, before plunking onto her Standwaves. She glanced around.

The oasis. Lily pads, with pink lilies. Beams of blue sunlight, through bright green leaves. Sunlight. When had it become daytime? She'd been walking alone for so long...

Something else drifted up, beaching itself on her Standwave.

A bucket, overturned and empty, save for a bit of green slime that twisted in the otherwise clear water. Bits of blood tainted the clear water around the roots, slowly diffusing.

Blood. Gavin's other water bucket. *Screaming.*

She let her Standwaves fade beneath her. She slipped into the shallow water, knees kicking up silt, hands falling to her lap like fallen leaves. The soft chill brushed the folds of skin between her fingers and brought goosebumps to her arms.

She cupped her hands, lifting crystal clear water from the oasis, staring down at it as it soaked into her skin, and escaped between her fingers. There was a small cut in her hand that she didn't remember getting. A bit of the blood seeped through the water. It picked up granules of dirt and grime, obfuscating the liquid little by little as it drained from her grip, slipping away from her even as she defiled it.

She drew in a shuddering breath. A tear pricked her cheek. Her traitorous lips twisted up at the ends to catch it, even as her chin quivered, and her breath shuttered. She couldn't quite breathe through her nose anymore, so her mouth parted, battling the strands of saliva that would have kept it shut. The tear, first one then a deluge, found her tongue, tainted and salty and earthy. She heaved in more breaths, but she couldn't tell if it was breathing or laughing. Because, Moons, she felt so *light*. Her hand gripped the skin in front of her heart, curling into a claw, even as her chest glowed with visceral joy, and her arms shook with the realization that her father had done it, he had succeeded.

I'm proud of him. Her chest bucked, shoulders rolling inwards as the tears crashed into the oasis around her, joining the joyful trickling of the Oasis Tree's rain. She listened. Moons, did she listen.

The tree, and its dripping. Her tears, and their rippling.

All of it sounded so much like laughter.

Footsteps sloshed in the water behind her. She couldn't

bring herself to look around. She was caught. Caught tainting the pureness of the oasis with her pride.

An unceremonious splash, at her side.

"It's not over."

Stelli shook her head, glancing up at Dezma, taking in her presence. Slumped shoulders. Jawline holding just the slightest quaver. Her muscular arms and wide chest squeezed tight to her body, one hand playing with the now-wet hem of her cloak. The other hand held a pink lily, from one of the pads. It just rested there, on her knee, almost comically small against her muscular frame.

Stelli couldn't bear to speak. She just looked away, off in the direction of that last scream.

"Here," Dezma grumbled. Something brushed Stelli's arm. She jumped, jerking her hand away. Dezma had the flower held out, frozen in the motion, eyes a little wide, lips dry. "I... thought it might help."

Stelli uncoiled, letting herself settle, letting Dezma set it on her arm. She took it in her hand, staring down at it. The smell caught her, just a little sweet. Somehow, it overpowered her own sweaty, swampy musk. "You think you know how I feel," Stelli whispered, staring down at the flower.

"No," Dezma said, a defensive note entering her tone. "Not at all."

"You do," Stelli looked up at her. "You think you know."

"You said you didn't want—"

"Maybe it would be just a little bit nice to know that someone understands," she whispered, gazing at Dezma. The other woman met her eyes. The horizon extended forever in Dezma's eyes, yet it never managed to blot out the foreground of her beautiful irises. She made Stelli feel so small and so meaningful all at once.

"But I don't," Dezma said. "I don't understand, Stelli. I can see the look in your eyes, I can guess what it means. But unless I've had the same look in mine, I..." She shook her head. "Knowing isn't the same as understanding."

Stelli looked down at the lily in her hand. It had heft to it. Bright pink, with thin, sharp looking petals, which spread wide to reveal a greenish powder that coated their bases. She spun it a little, back and forth.

"I'm not afraid of you anymore," Dezma said.

Back and forth. Back and forth. The petals clacked together a bit, with the movement. "Stupid."

"Maybe."

The water lapped at their legs. Stelli kept her eyes on the flower, even though she could feel Dezma's warmth, right by her shoulder. Little goosebumps played on her arm.

"Just because I don't understand how you feel," Dezma's voice was like a tickle in her ear, full of gravel and heft, yet light as the pinkness of the flower. "Doesn't mean I condemn it."

"If we had waited for him to come around the bend in the river," Stelli whispered. Back and forth. Back and forth. It tickled her fingers, where the base of the flower spun between them. "Maybe I wouldn't have helped you."

"What if we are the ones coming around the next bend?" Dezma whispered. "What then?"

"If he's waiting for us," she replied. "He'll kill us."

"I'm not asking what *he'll* do. I'm asking about you."

The flower stilled in her hand. The pads of her fingers tingled with the recent movement of the stem.

"Depends on who's right about me," Stelli whispered. "My father. Or you."

The long droning of the birds returned in slow measure, hesitant and confused.

"I wish I hadn't said that," Dezma grunted. "It doesn't matter what I think. Or your father. Only you can be right about you, Stelli."

One bird in particular caught Stelli's ear. A long, and sordid note. Its cadence carried with it grain, like grit on shorn wood, that broke the sound like a drumbeat. She looked at the flower in her hands. In her dirty, bloody hands. A bit of grime stained the back of one of the petals. She lowered a shaking hand into the oasis, rubbing the pads of her fingers together, watching the muck sift away. She lifted a dripping hand, and reached to scrub off the grime. She hesitated. She gripped the petal in her fingers and plucked it free, leaving the smudge on the backside. She cast the flower back adrift on a passing lily pad, before tucking the petal behind her ear. It tickled her skin. Grimy and gross. Her mouth flicked towards a smile.

She stood up, looking to the edge of the oasis, where the scarred branch led. The underbrush was smashed and broken with the obvious signs of desperate flight.

"Let's go, then."

Dezma grabbed her hand, stepping up onto her Standwave. They locked eyes for a moment. Dezma gave a firm nod. Stelli returned it, afraid to grip the other woman's hand, but letting their fingers hang tangled, reflexively curling just enough to keep their skin in contact.

They made for the crushed underbrush. Stelli felt hollow. Carved free. A peculiar sort of lightness, where the edges of the lightness felt heavy, but left the center empty. A tangible void. A forgotten whole. It felt so easy to breathe. It felt so easy to see. Beaten. Bruised. Bleeding. Exhausted.

And so very *not* alone.

She stepped over a snapped branch, eyeing the torn landscape. A tangle of footprints marred the mud, leading off into the swamp. A Cyril vine hung, looped around a branch. On the ground, a dark, furry creature lay splayed in two parts, a smear of dark blood and intestines ripped and splattered between the head and legs. She stepped over it, her footfall thudding like a corpse to the soil. The lightness became heavier with each step along the detritus she took. Each one felt final.

A gurgling brown mud-filled river broke through the tangle of ferns. Footsteps clumped around the mudbank. A red smear coated the river's surface, trailing downstream. Bits of brain matter and muscle drifted and jerked in the rapids, caught on the edges of sharp rocks. She wrinkled her nose, stepping up stream onto Standwaves that heaved with heavy rhythms thr-ough the murk and mud. More footprints. She pulled herself up the mudbank on the far side of the river, hands falling into grooves carved by other hands. The mud stuck between her fin-gers, almost molding and hardening with the pressure of her grip. She turned, reaching down to help Dezma up.

Dezma took her hand but didn't pull on it to get up the mudbank, vaulting up beside Stelli. They locked eyes for a mo-ment. Dezma's face was laced with tension, eyebrows furrowed, mouth a thin line. They both looked away to scan the shadows in the trees around them, pricked their ears to listen for any snapping of any branch, for any abnormal caw from any bird.

The petal slipped behind her ear, its coarse texture sliding along her neck, leaving the skin bare, abandoned. Her arm jerked up towards it as it drifted in the air—

Dezma caught it between two fingers, reaching up and slid-ing her hair back to make room for the petal, which she pressed firmly in place. Her fingers rubbed along the cartilage of her outer ear. The warmth of them paused Stelli's breathing. She stood up, not quite looking at Dezma. The lightness in her sto-mach once again battled the heaviness. She swallowed a bit of nausea, eyes picking out the trail of footsteps, leading through the swamp—

Bzzzzzzzt. Something heavy landed on her cheek. She froze, looking at Dezma.

"Hornet," Dezma whispered, staring. Stelli's heart pounded in her throat. She reached up with a slow movement as she felt the legs of the hornet crawl across her skin, picking across the tiny hairs of her cheeks, the bumps and blemishes... The petal shifted. The hornet stopped moving. She grabbed the petal between her fingers, pulling it back. The weight of the hornet left her face as it clung to the petal, curling itself over the side.

Long angular body, turquoise abdomen, vicious looking stinger, cone-like eyes. "You're one of the friendly ones," she whispered, glancing up at Dezma. "Right?"

Bzzzzzzzt. Another one landed on her thumb, legs coming up to play with the end of the petal. *Bzzzzzzzt.* A third. She drew in a shuddering breath, shifting her thumb—

The pain hit her like the turning of a key in her flesh. She felt the stinger under the muscle at the base of her index finger. Her lungs convulsed, but she didn't have time to open her mouth, so the sounds of pain just buckled into her cheeks as she stumbled, shaking out her hand. She saw the hornet, body curled across her finger, its stinger stuck in her skin. She had to get it out. Had to get it out. Had to—

She shouted, a fast, staccato exclamation, dropping the petal, staggering as a second jab came in her wrist. Buzzing eclipsed her. She hardly heard it over the pulsing of venom in her forearm. She *felt* it in her blood, working its way up through her, resisting the pulsing of her heart, each beat sending new waves of nausea and pain. She waved her hands, swatting at the hornets as they swarmed her—

Another sting. She could hardly breathe, one of them found the space behind her hood, she felt it on her neck—

Another staccato shout escaped her. She wriggled her shoulders, trying to twist, squirm, as if she could jump out of her own skin to avoid those jabbing stingers, to avoid the creeping of the venom which spread and jolted razor sharp through her veins, all across her body—

Strong arms grabbed her around the torso, sweeping her feet out from under her. Her world spun, her limited horizon becoming a whirlwind of movement. The sky. The sky. She could see the sky through the leaves. It gleamed hot and painful. Moisture racked her skin. Had the stinging stopped? She couldn't feel the individual jabs anymore, just the encroaching venom, with its pulsing gouts of pain running through her, and the buzzing, the buzzing in her ears, it still sounded like it was all around them, careening, terrible, overwhelming. The sound itself hurt. Like fingernails clawing at her ears. The arms around her, holding her, ground into her skin, sturdy and painful, the fingers pressing into her shoulder where she'd been stung, making it worse, making it so so much worse—

Splash. The sky vanished. The sound vanished. She forced herself not to breathe, to squeeze her eyes shut, because the water around her dug into her eyes with its little particulates, green, and algal. The arms were still around her. She didn't thrash. *The arms were still around her*. Wrapping her, holding her around the waist, pressed close against a solid chest, a wall of muscle. She felt Dezma moving, kicking, keeping them buoyant. Water roiled in her ears, bubbling, pressuring. Anything to focus on. Anything but the pain. She couldn't feel the fingers on her right hand. That whole limb just flooded with pulsing pain, as if her blood had been replaced with a swarm of biting insects, crawling on the inside of her skin and nipping at her nerve endings—

Her head broke the surface.

"They're gone," Dezma wheezed, clutching Stelli close, dragging her as she kicked them to the shallows, splashing to her knees. "Are you okay?"

Stelli tumbled into the mud-caked edge of the pond, left hand slipping on the shore. Green algae covered everything, sliming between her fingers, making it hard to hold. She tried to lift her right arm. It came in front of her face, but moving it, Moons moving it... she bucked forward, expelling the meager contents of her stomach across Dezma's lap, falling into her own mess. She shook, forcing herself to look at her hand, to hold it, gripping the elbow in her left arm. Numerous spots bulged around her fingers and wrist, tiny pinpricks of blood mixing with a pale blue translucent liquid that leaked from the edges of each sting. Her hand swelled, her veins bulging through her skin. She forced down more bile, the nasty flavor coating her mouth. Sticky expulsion stained her cloak, plastering it against her skin.

Dezma's arm came around her, holding her close, firm. "Talk to me, Stelli."

Stelli turned over her hand, using slow movements to examine every inch of her skin. She opened her mouth, taking in small little breaths. "Yep," she got out. "Not dead."

Dezma relaxed against her, shoulders falling just a bit. "Moons."

Stelli twitched her fingers into a fist. The contact came to her in fuzzy disconnection, as if a phantom finger brushed against a phantom palm. She flexed the hand a few times, huffing another breath. She tried to talk, but the pain surged, and all she got out was a little growl shout of pain. She puffed the air out through her cheeks fast, the quick breathing somehow making the pain easier to bear. Her vision swam, just a bit. She growled again, bringing her closed right fist to her forehead.

It felt like she was being touched by someone else. Another quick shout of pain escaped her lips, between her huffed breaths. "Moons," her voice snapped the air, forced out by the escaping air from her lungs, which she tried to suck back in. "Moons!"

Dezma squeezed her shoulder. "Try—"

"Wrong," she hissed, squeezing her eyes shut, feeling a tear leak out. She punched the mud, visceral hot pain in her chest expanding, demanding, spiking up through her throat, but it only hurt more. She let out another shout through caught, stuck lips. The pain subsided a bit. There would be another wave. Always another wave. "Not even here," she hissed, sucking in another breath, breathing it out through puffed cheeks. She couldn't open her eyes. "He still finds a way."

"The swamp is just dangerous," Dezma whispered. "You'll be okay. We'll still figure things out—"

"Dangerous," Stelli hissed, trying to slow her breathing, squeezing her nails into her palm, trying to feel something in that skin other than hot venom. "But not for him—" another breath. "For him—" another breath. "He walks right through them—" exhale. "Not a sting—" another breath.

"Something must have made them angry," Dezma murmured.

"The flower—" another breath. "They went for it—"

Dezma tensed against her. "I'm sorry."

"Don't be," Stelli managed to take a normal breath, deep in, deep out. Then another. "Would've been a stupid way to try and kill me. Could've ran me through at the oasis. Would've let you."

She felt Dezma shaking her head, the motion shifting her shoulders just the slightest bit, rocking Stelli in her lap. Nausea and euphoria roiled together through her gut, up in her throat, giving her a headache. "I didn't know," Dezma said.

"I know."

"I didn't know—"

"I know."

Another deep breath, a full one. The air tried to jump away from her, to spark through her lungs like wildfire, but she held it back, kept it steady. Her arm tingled now. More like burning than biting insects.

"Aunt Dezma?" The high, uncertain voice of a young child played in the air behind them. "Did Gavin send you to come get us?"

17

Gavin woke up suffused in pain. A dull and aching pain, throbbing underneath his cranium, lining the soft, torn tissue of his upper arms and shoulders, pounding his sweat-drenched thigh. He caught the first glimpses of his awoken vision through slitted eyelids. Black branches tangled above him—

Aycmor... native to the swamps... Black bark, often conceals Vargus...

A fern bobbed against his cheek, light feathery offshoots tickling, bulbous, weighty—

Feltwing fronds... strong root systems keep the mud from flowing away... poisonous...

He felt a drop of sap hit his cheek, sticking in his unkempt beard. He shifted. More drops hit him, forcing his eyes to blink, hand raising... something held it back. He pulled harder, but the something tightened, hardening, going rigid against his wrist and compressing it, forcing a gasp of pain from his lips as he fell back limp—

Cyril vine... Used by Bounders as a snare... goes rigid when force is applied...

He blinked, squinting, contorting his cheeks, trying to see through the blurriness, through the stinging of moisture and mud and detritus that stained his eyelids. An image refocused in front of him, bright and pristine, like the Tuft Rabbit alone at its apex in the sky. Brown bark, gashes torn free to reveal pulsing blue veins—

Oasis Tree... A natural water filter... The best water you will ever drink...

Clean water, dripping into a beautiful pond, sending abstract ripples out beneath green lily pads, rocking the sharp pink lilies in peaceful circles—

Oasis Knife Lily... Don't bring them outside of the oasis, or the Hounds will attack...

His head fell down, looking at his legs. They were submerged in the oasis, right at its edge. The coldness of the water hit him as he saw it, washing up through his thighs, intensifying the pain of his wound. He swallowed down bile, eyes squeezing shut. His body leaned forward against his will, tugging on the bindings. The vines snapped tight, yanking him backwards. He slammed against the trunk of the Aycmor, the bark digging into his back, taking the wind from his lungs.

"Glad you could join us for dinner." The voice sneered as much as it growled. Gavin felt as if he was beneath the tavern bar again, his limbs jabbing the wooden slats, his insides screaming for his children, his children who were missing, who...

This time he knew where they were. *Not here.* Thank the Moons.

He craned his head for the voice, squinting against the falling sap. Sounds percolated into his ears: the patter of raindrops hitting the Aycmor canopy above, the muted ebb and flow of flying insects, the song of the toads, the soft bubbling of Steamwaves. He picked out the column of steam, rising up and twisting among the leaves along the edge of the oasis clearing.

He forced himself to suck in a breath, felt its rasp as it passed through his throat, and tried to ignore the pain. There was a small campsite, set into the border between the bogwater and the pristine pond. The underbrush was cut and crushed, cleared away from the immediate vicinity. The edge of the oasis rippled with Steamwaves. Two figures sat around it, hoods up, warming their hands in the steam.

Gavin shifted his torso, raising his head, sliding his elbows back a little to support himself. The movements grated him. His muscles screamed. He glanced between the figures. Familiar. Both, but the smaller one... slight frame, particular mottling on the fabric, and she had two knives at her belt... Her nose was crooked, with caked blood around the nostrils. His knuckles were still bruised from those blows. *I've fought her twice, this same woman*, Gavin thought. Then, with a slight and selfish thrill. *I've won both times.* His leg throbbed with his infected wound. *Kind of.*

The General shifted forward, up to Gavin's side. Gavin tracked the movements with his pupils, not wanting to turn his head. The General really did move like a wolf. Silent. Purposeful. He held out a pouch, plucking free a berry from inside. "You do want to eat, I imagine? You've been unconscious for days."

Gavin's heart thudded, eyeing the berry. Black, ovaloid, and pointed. *Spartippi berry. Used for disinfectant when applied as a poultice. Bitter, but edible.*

His mouth watered, ghosts of the berries aftertaste playing on his tongue. His throat was so dry. The berry would burst, when he bit it. Burst with juices that would run down his mouth and trickle along his pallet...

For days... Smiles flickered in the back of his vision, melding with the pain. They... they were... *For days...* starving? D...de— he blotted the word from his mind, closing his eyes, swallowing down his dry throat. Venom throbbed in his blood, setting in a deep and paralyzing soreness along the inner muscles of his shoulder. It felt stiff, hard to move, but not impossible.

Rhondrum thorns... Fast acting venom... targets muscles, leaves them paralyzed within a few days... Fast... Fast acting... If it had been days without an antidote, Gavin would be paralyzed by now. The General likely didn't know how to make the anti-venom, which meant he was lying about the timeline.

Gavin opened his eyes. He coughed a laugh. The dryness in his throat didn't seem so unbearable anymore. The gnawing hunger receded. "Untie my hand," Gavin grunted. "I'll eat it myself."

The General stared at him for a long moment, then shrugged a single shoulder. He reached down with a blade, sliding it between skin and vine. The cold steel chilled Gavin's wrist. The vine severed with a snap and release, its green blood hissing free as it decompressed.

Gavin raised his hand with jerking movements, wincing as his muscles screamed from the Rhondrum venom. He forced his palm up, his fingers apart. His three fingers. The General's eyes locked on those three fingers, and Gavin caught the barest hint of a smile under his cowl.

The General dropped a couple Spartippi berries in Gavin's hand. Gavin looked at them, passed one into his mouth, bit down, and felt the beautiful juice coat his tongue, roll down the back of his throat, trickling through the dryness, inflaming every taste bud with brilliant bitterness. He ate the second one, trying not to chew too fast, trying not to let the ecstasy show on his face.

The General shot a look back at the other figure crouched in front of the Steamwaves, and held the pouch out to her. She grabbed a couple of the berries for herself. The General followed suit.

"Don't eat them all," Gavin croaked. "Save a few."

The General eyed him with a weary glance. Seeing him in the dim swamplight, backlit by steam, his cowl catching the drips of Aycmor sap and rainwater that dripped through the canopy, he looked alarmingly human. His beard was a scraggle, unkempt, uncut. His eyes drooped with deep, sallow, dark bags.

The juice of the berries stained his lips, dribbling a little from one corner. That telltale scar cut across his right eye. But new wounds accompanied it. Bug bites along his jawline, which swelled it, discolored it. A fresh cut on his cheek.

"They're used to disinfect wounds," Gavin grunted. "The berries."

Another long pause, as the General stared at him, and the rain dripped through the leaves. "We have no wounds," the General finally said.

Gavin leaned forward and stretched out his right arm, fighting the pain and paralysis. He could only move in sporadic bursts. He grabbed the hem of his pant leg, dragging it up, fingernails scratching the hair that clung in matted clumps to his skin. He hesitated, sucking in a breath as he pulled the pant leg up and over his wound, exposing it. His Ralaf leaves were damp and brown. The skin felt strange touching the air, strange and cold. A droplet of Aycmor sap fell on his leg, just under the wound. He flinched.

The General stared at it. Jerked his head. The woman maneuvered around the Steamwaves, crouching at his side. She worked tender fingers around the Ralaf leaves, lifting them off his skin. "All of this, with a wound like this," the woman muttered. There was a touch of disgust and anger in her voice, but underneath it, admiration. "I assumed I had missed." Pus clung to the filaments at the edge of the Ralaf leaves, stringing out and resisting her movement. He felt the strands like rubber bands of flesh, yanking at the corners of his wound.

The woman grunted. "It looks like some of the skin is dying."

Gavin shook somewhere deep in his core of his mind, where there were no muscles to actually shake. On the outside he glared. Glared a silent, numb, fierce tug of war with the Wolf who stared back at him. He burned with the memory of his children.

The thought of them alone in that lake, deep below the surface, terrified, waiting. He burned, because the memory hurt him. Because he had to return to them as soon as he could.

Because he was the only one who knew where they were.

The General glowered, breaking his gaze. "Give him the paste, Tess. Treat the wound."

Tess nodded, her face impassive under her hood. She took a few berries, grinding them in her hand—

"Stop," he grunted.

She paused.

"Throw those out."

She looked back at the General.

"They're useless ground in a dirty hand," Gavin coughed, turning to spit phlegm into the underbrush. "Worse than useless."

She tossed them into the mud, taking out new berries, looking at him with a raised eyebrow.

"Hot water's good," he grunted. "Wash them in your Steamwaves."

She did as he asked, soaking and scrubbing her hands in the hot water of the oasis. It should help. A little. Better than nothing. Maybe. He watched her hands work the berries, their bitter aftertaste fresh in his mouth. He swallowed.

"Squeeze some of the juice onto my wound."

"I thought you said they had to be a paste," the General growled.

"Hands are too dirty for that," he grunted back. "The juice should work a bit. Better than dirty paste."

Tess squeezed the juice over his wound. It tickled his torn flesh, adding to the cold tingle that the air already provided. The way his wound oozed and mixed with the juice made him *feel* it's oozing, like skin turned mush and placed on his tongue. He coughed again, turning to the side, rotating his shoulder a bit.

As much as he could.

"You probably don't have Ralaf leaves," he grunted.

"What?"

"Just wash the old ones," he said, picking up the soaked, browned leaves between his thumb and two fingers. They dripped with pus. The leaves congealed together in a singular, uniform mass. Tess took them at their very edge, holding them away from her, moving to the Oasis water—

"Steamwaves," Gavin grunted. "Boiling water is better."

The woman turned her slow, piercing gaze on him.

"Or you could let me die," Gavin shrugged, finding that only one shoulder obeyed him. He felt a strange pressure in the side of his jaw, tensing up his forearm, down his neck, like he was trying to swallow when there wasn't enough moisture—he twitched the right shoulder, just a bit, but it was enough for him to focus, bearing down, finding... finding his muscles...

He sagged back.

"Wash the leaves," the General growled.

She dunked them in the Steamwaves. The water hissed. She turned over the makeshift bandage, pulling it through the water. Pus and blood and viscera trailed behind, leaving rivulets of red in the pure blue bubbling water. The red separated, swirling, breaking apart and conforming to the pattern of the Steamwaves until it unmade them. The water stopped bubbling, and the steam trailed off into the sky, and the last little tendrils found their hiding places in the scaled canopy of leaves above.

Tess turned with the still browned, but much cleaner bandage, and pressed it to his wound. He gasped as it scalded his skin and steamed in the cold air. He grit his teeth at the new wave of pain that shot through his wound as she tied the bandage in place.

He sagged back against the Aycmor, head lolling against the bark. He stared up at the canopy. It really did look like scales, or feathers. Like the infinite plumage of a bird.

"Thank you," he grunted, the words dying in his tone, almost making him laugh.

He blinked against the falling of Aycmor sap, which caught his cheeks and eyelashes with heavy droplets. The patter of rain above the canopy had a lulling effect. It muted the buzzing of the swamp.

"I understand, now," the General said. His voice, too, sounded more human under the drizzle of swamp rain.

"What could you possibly understand," Gavin muttered, lifting his right hand to shield his face from the sap. He looked at the canopy through the gap of his missing fingers.

"How you managed to kill my son."

Gavin grunted, bringing his thumb in to rub the bone-stubs, which pressed uneven against a thin layer of skin.

"He asked you," the General said. "He asked for your permission to train them."

Gavin's laugh broke into a cough.

"Of course he did," the General continued. "He believed that disagreement was just a failure in explanation. That if things were taught well enough, everyone would agree."

Gavin closed his fingers over his stretched thumb, then opened them again, eyes shifting focus between the emptiness of his severed fingers, and the canopy of feathers above. "You would have done the same thing," he whispered. "If it had been my children, threatening to take yours away forever, threatening to turn them into weapons of war, nothing more than a means to an end..."

The General's face hardened. "Not if it was for the greater good," he whispered. "I would turn my back and let my children get dragged away screaming if it would save the world. I don't miss my son. He died telling me about your twins, and now our salvation is promised thanks to his sacrifice."

Gavin sighed and closed his eyes, hand falling to his chest. "I would kill a thousand more sons for my children."

The General grunted, but said nothing more. The patter of rain hitting the leaves washed over Gavin as droplets trailed between the feathers, finding the air, warning him moments before the sap tap, tap, tapped his face. A tear squeezed out from between his eyes, trailing along his cheek with the sap. It might as well have been another act of nature. He might as well have been the mud.

Time didn't pass the same for mud. Nothing changed, until footsteps stomped scars for the mud to heal from. A twig snapped. He blinked open his eyes. Dark shadows pressed forward through the underbrush at the edge of the oasis. Three gritty, grime-covered figures, wearing the torn remnants of soldier's uniforms.

"You're alive," came the General's voice.

The soldiers stumbled forward, collapsing to the mud at the edge of the oasis. Gavin caught a glimpse of one soldier's face. Narrow, high-strung, and afraid. The skin of his unscarred cheeks dappled with moonlight. They locked eyes for a moment, and Gavin could see him shaking. Something wriggled inside Gavin. His arms tensed, the Cyril vines like sharp rocks against his veins. He felt Bloom in his embrace, shaking as he wept over Bubbles. He saw Bloom's shaking in this soldier's shaking. It shook him, too. Sent little tremors that he couldn't imagine would ever leave.

"It's done, then?"

The Shaking Man nodded. The General winced to the side, exposing half of his face to Gavin's vision, the slit of pale skin clammy in the dappled light. One eye blinked in the shadows of the hood. The eye with the scar across it, the eye that looked so small and imperfect, above a corner of a tweaked nose, and grizzled beard, and a mouth twisted with pain. A shining droplet painted the General's cheek as he too began to shake.

For a flash, Gavin wanted to hug him. The feeling made him want to claw his skin off. He turned away and squeezed his eyes shut. But closed eyes couldn't stop him from listening. Always listening. Always listening.

The oasis, and its raining. The General, and his grief. All of it could sometimes sound like weeping. Right now it sounded a little too familiar.

"Leave," the General's voice graveled in the air, low and rumbling. Gavin uncurled his fingers, feeling the indents in his palm left by his overgrown, torn nails. "Search until you find the children."

"But sir—"

A smack, a snap, a stifled shout. Silence for another moment.

"Yes sir," the Shaking Man warbled. "We'll find them, sir."

Twigs snapped and branches swayed before their exit, and silence entered the clearing again. It crept like Vargus over Gavin's exposed skin, endless tiny legs and mouths clawing at the air.

"How many more," the General whispered. His presence loomed above Gavin, a buzzing outline of tingling colors against the inside of his eyelids, half real and half imagined. "How many more have to die for you to care?" His voice warbled, just the slightest bit, behind his unnerving calmness.

Gavin swallowed, and didn't answer.

"Your friend was among those my soldiers dispatched," the General continued. "The tavernkeep."

Gavin's heart went cold, prickles of frigid fingers pulling themselves along the outside of his skin ripped and tore at his composure. He kept his mouth shut.

"I killed the man with her too, at your house. The fisherman."

Gavin's body strained to curl itself together. His bindings

held him back, leaving him open and exposed, his head twisting against the bark, the skin of his cheek conforming to the rivulets of empty space. No tears found his eyes. Only sap. And mud. Dragging him down, plastering him amongst the mud until he could no longer feel clearly the distinction between his tailbone and the hard root that dug against it.

A three-toned caw sounded out across the swamp. Gavin still did not speak.

"You grieve them. Yet they did not have to die. All around the Kingdom, thousands of others join you in their grief. But you don't care. Will nothing make you care? Or will you insist on holding true until even your beloved children succumb to the swamp and abandon the rest of us to suffer?"

A toad croaked from under a nearby leaf. A longer note, low and fluting. *Wandering Warrighast Toad... The lowest register of croak... They make good pets.*

He fluttered his eyes open and turned his head, finding the little guy under the leaf. A dark leaf, the size of his hand, just in front of his nose. It had pale veins accenting its shape. It rested on the toad's head like a little hat, its point landing just between the toad's eyes. A tear slipped down over the lid of Gavin's eye, cutting between the built up sap. Then another.

The toad croaked again.

His right hand fell over his upper chest, finger slipping into the pocket sewn there. A crinkled, ruined paper brushed his finger. A bit of liquid shocked him: the juices where the creases in the paper had snapped the membranous material. Something shifted under the paper. He let his palm fall flat over the outside of the pocket, feeling that round shape pressing back. Pressing into his skin, both palm and chest.

Isingrass pod... Great for making tea.

More tears pooled under his lids, catching on sticky sap. "I don't care about your war," he whispered, voice choking. The pain burned in his right arm, contracting his muscles over his chest, fingers squeezing into that Isingrass pod in his pocket. "I just want my children to be happy and free."

The toad croaked again, and hopped away.

A bird fluttered from a nearby tree, flying away.

Something shook the underbrush, and then fell still.

The General grunted. "Happy and free," he echoed. "So close to the goal you've come."

A cold chill spread through his core, mixing in with the pain. His right hand clenched tighter on his chest, squeezing that Isingrass pod. He felt it with the finger in his pocket. Felt the coarse little hairs, the slight bump on one side.

Time became tapping, like sap. Dripping through a canopy of scales, falling between the tiered skin of the swamp in slow moving molasses, constant, inevitable, breaking, and whole. It moved in bursts. Each trail down each leaf took an eternity, each fall an instant.

Movement passed around him. Footsteps. Quiet voices. The crackle of new Steamwaves. The rustle of crushed underbrush. The groaning of a tree, from the jabbing of a Dewclaw, from the hanging of a cloak, which caught the sap. They didn't cover him. In time, he felt buried. Buried in sap and mud, as deep as his pain, as wide as his weeping.

Another drop of time fell between the feathered skin of the swamp, and he couldn't tell if his eyes were open or closed. Sap built in the corner pockets of his eyelids and felt like rocks digging through his skull. He couldn't take it. He rubbed them. The rocks shifted. In one eye, they bit like gravel. In the other he created a second rock. He blinked. Blinked. Bit his lip so he didn't scream, dug his nails into his palm just to give him something else to feel. He thrashed against his bindings, aggravating the Cyril just so he could know for sure he couldn't move again. Sometimes he would try to look. He hit his eyes with the back of his dirty hands enough that he could blink a bit of vision through the haze of sap and tears. There was some light. Dim light, from a dim Mirrorwave trickling in a pond at Tess's feet. Tess, who was awake, crouched in front of the General's body, who leaned against a tree, under their makeshift canopy, his eyes closed and shadowed in the darkness.

She watched Gavin like a Bounder perched in her tree.

The dark noises of night time sifted through his mind. He forced himself to lie still, with his arm across his eyes. The sap fell there, instead, sticking his cloak to the hairs of his arm, pulling at them like little blades yanking through his flesh. His arm got tired across his face. He tried to lean it sideways against the bark, to let his arm rest atop his head, to save him the energy. His bent neck started screaming. He tried to shift. The Cyril vine yanked his left arm back down.

He breathed.

So close to the goal you've come... A rock pressed against his right shoulder. It would bore through him. Dig a hole in his flesh. He knew it would dig a hole in his flesh. *Succumb to the swamp...*

Rose's face, blue and breathless, floating in the water—

The tang of blood entered his mouth as his teeth came down on the inside of his lip. He bent the fingers of his left hand, trying to grab the side of the vine, reaching, reaching—

Bloom, wide eyed, picking up a centipede, its hooked maw twisting into his flesh—

He breathed out, flicking his eyes open. The woman had her head between her knees, eyes on him. Were her eyes on him? Her hood was down. Short hair stuck to her face, but her eyes were visible in the pale light of her Mirrorwaves. Her eyelids drooped. She blinked, rubbed them with the back of her hand, rested her chin between her legs again.

His heartbeat stuttered.

He forced his breathing steady. He looked through just his lashes, and watched the canopy above. So strange, how the feathers of the swamp worked. To his eyes, infinite layers showed at the edges of each overlap the faintest outline of purple from the Carrow Wolf above, forming little patterns like sun-stains on rippling water, shifting and transforming as the breeze bobbed the leaves up and down, up and down...

He blinked his eyes back open wide, gritting his teeth, forcing his breathing to stay consistent.

Rose would think the leaves would make a good painting. Bloom would want to touch them. He could. He could climb a tree and touch them. Rose could climb the tree beside him and rearrange the leaves so they really did make a painting, a-and...

Drifting algae... The pack... The pack... Rations, thrown in tainted water... *An air pocket, suffused with the bodily fluids of children who ate food soaked with contaminants, forced to drown in their own rebellious stomachs—*

So close you've come—

Breathe in. Breathe in. *Breathe in.* He focused on the pain. The pain in his right arm. At some point it had fallen against his neck. He left it there, tracing the edges of his fingers in his mind, trying to pinpoint the exact place where the pain in his finger ended and the skin of his neck began. Like pulling apart the pieces of a puzzle never put together—

Breathe out. Breathe out. *Breathe out.* On the last exhale, as his shoulders slumped, he let his head fall to the side, keeping his eyes as slits, glancing through the barest lashes at the woman keeping watch. Her head rested between her knees. Her hands lay still. The Mirrorwaves trickled, nearly silent in the pond next to her.

Her eyes were closed. He watched her until his own eyes burned. And hers were still closed.

He lifted his right hand from his neck. Silent. Slow. He

could feel the burning toxins in his shoulder and arm like steel pegs driven through his bones and into the mud. But mud was malleable. He pushed through it, reaching across his body. His right hand found the vine that gripped his left. Tiny leaves trailed along its rough surface, twisting under his fingers.

The vine trailed down the trunk of the Aycmor tree, falling across a dark hole. Gavin blinked. He remembered this hole, and the Bounder's eyes he had seen within it. He heard it scream, and felt it die all over again.

He swallowed.

He slid his right hand up the Cyril vine, glancing again at the woman. She hadn't moved. Eyes still closed. He took a deep breath, turning his thumb inward, feeling with his nail along the leaves of the vine, pressing with slow, light, precise movements until he felt...

A vein popped against his finger, sliding back and forth as he adjusted the pressure. He held his breathing. Squeezed his eyes shut. Grimaced.

And pressed his nail through the outer skin of the vine, into the vein. It popped with a soft hiss, liquid pouring over his hand. He slid his nail down as the vine's water coated and stuck to the crevices of his thumb. Pressure released from the whole system as the vine tried to pump more water through it to stiffen itself, instead rushing out of the hole poked by Gavin's finger, splattering down across his arm.

He glanced at the woman again. Still no movement. He worked his left hand free, slipping it out of the loop and leaving the deflated end in the mud. He pushed himself to his feet, sucking mud and sap and detritus with him—

He bit his lip against a scream, air slamming against the inside of his cheeks. He fell against the Aycmor tree, hands clasping at the bark, entire body shaking. He glanced at the woman. Still asleep. He squeezed his eyes shut for a moment as his injured leg throbbed, throbbed, throbbed—

He took a step onto his better leg, away from the campsite, still gripping the tree for support. Black spots danced in his already black vision.

He pushed off the tree, stumbling over his bad leg and landing on his good one. Stumble-step. Stumble-step. He shot a couple glances over his shoulder. Shadows. Darkness. Not a rustle. He crunched over the underbrush. It was all he could do to move. Surely they would wake. *Stumble-step. Stumble-step.* He caught himself on another tree breathing in low gasps and muted groans. His feet splashed in puddles and kicked aside logs. A snake hissed at him.

Mudstinger. Venomous tails. He stumbled away as it bared its red underbelly.

He glared up at the tangle of the swamp before him, taking a deep breath through his nose, grasping the fabric above the pocket of his tunic, feeling the Isingrass pod inside.

And took another step.

His skin squeezed as he moved. Squeezed between the bones of his fingers, where he grabbed the Isingrass pod. Squeezed along his arms where his muscles tensed and burned red hot. Squeezed along the chord in the back of his ankles as his feet rose and fell, rose and fell. *Thud. Thud. Thud.*

He stumbled, ducking away from a Cyril vine that hung in the path. He slipped. His knee hit the mud on a slight decline and he slipped forward, crashing through a Feltwing frond, crushing the leaf under his weight as he—

He grabbed an Aycmor root, fingers clamping through the mud, holding him in place. His momentum pitched him forward. He stuck out his foot, jarring it against a rock. He couldn't hold in the gasp of pain. It rocketed from his mouth, hissing like Steppe wind pushed between a wound in the rocks. He clutched his stomach, prone across the mud, hurting and queasy.

Below him, the river of mud gurgled forward, lazy and placid. His head fell to look at it, turning through molasses up the river, and then down the river... *broken mudbank... handholds...* he registered the details with a bleary mind. The Snyrsnout was gone.

He let go of the root, sliding down and splashing through the mud river. He pushed himself to his feet, stumbling forward, injured leg giving out after just one step. He fell to his hands and knees, shoulder-deep in mud, craning his head up above in the clear air, kicking his legs to try and move, move at all—

He got his good leg against the bed of the river, pushing himself to his feet, roaring out of the mud, throwing himself forward, collapsing onto the far bank.

He stood up again, scrabbling up the other side, gripping fistfulls of the embankment, making progress little by little until he rolled to the top.

He stood up again, staggering a few steps. His leg couldn't hold his weight anymore. He fell, elbow landing on a rock, another gasp of pain escaping his lips.

He... he stood up again... Arms pushing and lifting, the three fingers of his right hand splayed like tree roots shaking in a windstorm. Left leg... left leg beneath him... he stumbled forward... his foot caught a log. He fell. He threw his arms down to catch himself—his arms gave out. The mud stung his cut palms and wormed into his ear where the ground pressed up against him, where the ground extended out from that small spot where his small body lay, his hands scrabbling in vain to grasp for handholds in the endless texture of the swamp floor.

Through the barest sliver of a gap in the great tiered feathers of the Aycmor canopy, a Bluotaes bird watched as the tiny speck of Gavin's body stood up again.

He stood delirious for a moment, with half-bent knees and

a bowed head in the half-space between moving and falling, standing the way a tree continued standing for just the briefest moment after a lumberjack cut through the trunk. His right eye couldn't open, it was too caked in mud. But his left eye saw. His left eye saw the small details. The little Vargus, somehow all alone and away from its colony, hunched on a black root, tiny antennae prodding the bark. The lone green Wondor Willow, growing alone in the mud, miraculous and melancholic, far from its river home. The Bluotaes bird, pitched at the very top of the canopy, looking in all its plumage like it was the very swamp itself.

His mouth flickered to a smile. He took the Isingrass pod out of his pocket, looked down at it.

Saw it.

Put it back in his pocket.

Stumbled forward.

And fell back down.

He clawed through the mud, crawling, raising his head as much as he could, staring into the shifting shadows in front of him. He didn't have the moisture to cry anymore. The mud caked his eyes too much, his throat too dry. He grabbed rocks, dug knuckle deep and *wrenched* himself forward. The venom in his right arm surged with each motion, locking up his muscles. He jerked through it. Reach. Grab. Reach... Grab... r-reach... reach... his head fell into the mud. He squeezed the fingers in his left hand, feeling the ground break and split between his grip. *G-grab...* He sucked in stuttering breaths, jolting his right arm forward, kicking with his legs. They didn't respond right. He... he couldn't... couldn't feel where they ended, and the mud began... c-couldn't...

He felt his legs start curling into his torso in jerking movements. He coughed, trying to jumpstart air into his lungs. His knee hit his chest. He heaved.

R-rea-reach...

His body just couldn't do it.

Footfalls broke the mud and underbrush, crushing detritus. They stepped up to Gavin's side. Knelt. Slipped arms under his torso, and lifted. His head lolled to the side, falling against a thin, wiry chest. It smelled of sweat, and dirt, and blood. He felt the chest rise and fall. Felt the breathing break, the same way his own breathing had broken when hugging Bloom and Rose and telling them that Bubbles would be okay...

"I thought you loved them enough to get back to them," the General whispered, soft and haunting. "If only I'd been right. It would have saved us both so much pain."

18

Bloom and Rose huddled on the shore under Dezma's cloak, hair plastered around their faces, eyes dim, scared, and wet. Some of their natural blondeness shone thr-ough the dye. Streaks of black mixed with mud and green algae on their faces and shoulders. Their smooth skinned cheeks and innocent faces were dirtied and weathered.

Stelli sat on the shore, massaging her hand. Every few minutes the pain surged again, and she gripped her wrist in white knuckles, clenching her teeth, forcing herself to breathe until the wave of pain subsided.

"Dad's coming back, right?" Rose whispered, shivering. "He told us he would."

Dezma's eyes softened. "I hope so."

The two children huddled closer, so tiny in the oversized cloak. Bloom's eyes filled with tears. Dezma hesitated, glancing over her shoulder at Stelli. Her small eyes looked panicked, unsure. Her large, muscular frame looked inadequate and small. Stelli grimaced, giving a little half shrug.

"Okay," Dezma grunted. "Here, why don't... why don't we," she swung the pack from her shoulders. The fabric was covered in mud, unrecognizable. She fumbled with the straps, pulling them loose. "Eat some food, drink some water," Dezma said. "The adults are gonna talk real quick, alright? We'll be right over there."

Stelli watched her back up, half-smiling half-grimacing at

them. They pulled closer together, hugging the cloak with weak hands. They turned to pick through the pack at their feet, fingers slow and uncertain. Stelli saw the barest shine against Rose's cheek, tracing through the muck.

Stelli grunted as Dezma knelt beside her. "Would've guessed you'd be good with kids."

Dezma slumped into the mud, hands pressing against her forehead, pulling up her brows, showing the whites of her eyes. "It still hasn't hit me," she whispered. "How am I supposed to tell *them?*"

"I don't think your friend is dead."

Dezma's jaw twitched. "Right. Because your angel father didn't rip him apart the moment he got his hands on him—"

Stelli shook her head. "I don't think he did."

"His son—"

"Died a hero, in his eyes," Stelli murmured, feeling the skin of her bicep, feeling the hardened muscle beneath. Little tremors of pain moved with the pressure. "This isn't about revenge for him. It's about *them*. What they can do." She jerked her head at Bloom and Rose. They looked defeated. Broken. Trapped in the maw of the looming black Aycmor trees behind them. "And he doesn't have them," she continued. "He doesn't have them, but he has someone who knows where they are. Where they were, at least. Until we found them."

Dezma remained silent, staring at the twins.

"You told me at the start," Stelli whispered. "That if we used a child as a weapon, we would have already lost."

Dezma bowed her head, looking at the mud.

"If we take them and run away, my father will eventually find out," Stelli continued, staring at the side of Dezma's face. Her heavy black hair hung in thick chords, tangled and messy, down past her firm jawline. "Then he *will* kill your friend. The children will finish growing up without their father. And they won't be free, either. They will have to hide. Because my father won't stop hunting them. Not for anything."

Dezma looked up at her, meeting her eyes. Red-rimmed. Exhausted. Stelli swallowed a lump in her throat. She opened her mouth. Something twisted in her gut, at the redness of Dezma's eyes. She swallowed again. Opened her mouth again. "There is a part of me," she whispered. "That wants to say that our only choice is to train them, because I know that if we do, I can go on to use them the same way my father would have."

She scanned Dezma's eyes for any sign of contempt. She found none.

"But what if," Stelli whispered. "What if that really is our only choice? What if that really is the only way to kill him?"

"They wouldn't have to kill him," Dezma croaked. "Just trap him in Boundwaves long enough for one of us to do it."

Stelli blinked. "You're considering this?"

Dezma shook her head, breaking eye contact, looking back at the children. "I'm out of ideas, Stell."

"You aren't afraid that I'll take them myself, once this is all over?"

"I told you," Dezma whispered, pushing herself to her feet. "You aren't your father. You aren't me. Make your own choices."

Stelli followed Dezma, holding her arms close to her chest. She could feel another wave of pain coming. She breathed through it, trying a light smile as the children looked up at their approach.

"Where is he?" The young girl said, chin raised. She pushed herself to her feet, glaring up at the two taller women. "You aren't gonna tell us, are you?"

Dezma blinked, glancing at Stelli. She opened her mouth, kneeling down—

The young girl backed up, hands in fists, glaring at her. "Don't do that thing!"

Stelli cocked her head. Now it was her turn to look at Dezma. And Dezma's turn to shrug.

"Where you kneel down to my height and look at me like I'm so cute and innocent," Rose stomped her foot. "I'm not cute and innocent! W-we a-almost..." She hiccuped into tears, chin quavering. "We've been running away from the Bugaboo for so long now," she whispered, voice cracking. "We've been doing a really good job. Dad said so himself."

"I think the Bugaboo got him," Bloom whispered, tears pouring down his cheeks. "Did the Bugaboo get him?"

Stelli nodded, glancing at Dezma again. She nodded back, smiling a bit. "It did," Stelli whispered. Bloom and Rose paled. "But don't worry," she said. "The Bugaboo didn't..." she swallowed. "Didn't eat him." She glanced at Dezma, who gave another nod. "We have to go get him back," she said. "And we need your help."

Rose nodded. "Anything."

Bloom sniffled and nodded.

Stelli's heart jumped. She opened her mouth. Glanced at Dezma, who still stood, half a step behind. She raised an eyebrow down at Stelli. She looked back to the children, swallowed again, took a deep breath.

"Are you sure?" She said, meeting both of their eyes. "It'll mean a lot of danger. And fighting. Maybe even hurting. Things you... things you won't be able to take back after doing them."

The tears broke over Rose's eyelids, contorting her mouth. Her expression warbled, like the aftermath of a single raindrop on the taut surface of a windless lake. "We'll have to use Runewaves?"

"You'll both have to," Stelli whispered. "You'll have to use them to hurt someone."

"But it will get dad back?" Bloom whispered.

Stelli nodded.

"Okay," Bloom said, voice a tiny pinprick amidst the miasma of the swamp.

Rose wiped the tears away with a tiny hand. "We can do it."

Stelli gave them a smile, pushing herself back to her feet, eyes falling to the pond. Her arm throbbed with that dull ache. The back of her mind felt raw, exposed, bloodied. She closed her eyes. A Standwave... low, consistent... she could find the rhythm, but it hurt, and the pain in her arm crept in, tumbling over the patterns, blotting them out...

Dezma's hand fell on her shoulder. "When did you two last sleep?"

Stelli blinked her eyes open, trying to get the black spots to leave her vision.

Bloom and Rose shared a look. "At the pretty place," Bloom whispered. "With the good water. Where the Bugaboo found us."

Dezma looked at her and mouthed *oasis.* Stelli nodded.

"I think he found us because we slept," Rose muttered. "And he didn't. That's how he caught up."

"Well," Dezma murmured. "I'm exhausted. We'll rest here, and then start—"

"Is here the best place?" Stelli said, those few words leaving her out of breath as another wave of pain trembled in the muscles of her arm. Dezma paused, mouth half open. She frowned for a moment, raising an eyebrow. Stelli raised both of hers, squishing her mouth together. Realization dawned on Dezma's face. She shook her head.

"You don't have to worry about that."

"You're sure?"

"Positive." Dezma gave her shoulder a squeeze, sliding out of her cloak, stepping to the edge of the clearing and eying an Aycmor tree. She took her Longtooth, jabbing the sharp end into the bark and the blunt end into the mud, leaning her cloak over it as a makeshift lean-to. They squeezed under the cloak, which spread out quite wide, shielding them from the blue light that trickled through the opening in the canopy above the pond. Stelli tossed her own cloak down over the ground, the skin of her arms and neck bruised and muddied, discolored by stings. She didn't recognize her own hand. Her stomach couldn't muster any more nausea.

She leaned her head back, letting it rest against the tree. The slightest aberrations of the bark slipped around her hair, digging their wooden fingernails in amongst her locks, against her scalp. If it weren't for the pain, she would have drifted off right away. But the pain interrupted her breathing, made the air come in random jolts and jumps. And the inconsistent breathing interrupted her sleep.

She forced the breaths in. And out. Any time the pain came creeping through, she made her chest rise, and made her chest fall, made her shoulders stay in the correct pattern, consistent, constant...

"Aunt Dezma?" A hissed voice.

In... and out...

"Is she asleep?"

Like a Runewave...

"I think so, Rose."

Just another pattern...

Stelli could barely hear the next words above her breathing. "You'd better watch out, Aunt Dezma. She's one of the mean soldiers who took our house."

Nothing more than another pattern...

Dezma laughed under her breath, a soft sound, like the bubbling of a pot of tea. The sound alone took some of Stelli's pain away. "Don't worry," she whispered. "I know."

She'd lost the pattern, her mind distracted by Dezma's voice. It left a warm afterimage on her brain. A bundle of fuzzing, that let the sleep finally find her and whisk her away.

* * *

Stelli walked the algal pond, her right arm in a makeshift cast, affixed by the muddy fabric of her cloak looped around her neck. Beneath her, tenuous Standwaves pushed aside algae, sifting their small ripples across the surface, coming to rest in a neat hexagon around her feet. The soft noises of twilight croaked all around them as the swamp woke up.

She turned, waving Bloom and Rose forward.

Something buzzed inside of Stelli. It reflected the murmur of the insects that lit the air aflame. It reflected the twitching of the Carrow Wolf's nostrils, as the Tuft Rabbit made its way into the sky. It reflected the Standwaves on the heels of her feet, soft vibrations thrumming through her bones, through the twilight air, between her and these two innocent, eleven-year-olds.

"Which of the tones do you already know?" Stelli prompted, kneeling down on the water, placing her palm flat in front of her. The drifting ebb and flow of her Standwaves tickled her palm with algae as it was pushed up and away by the pattern. Her eyes traced their muck-streamed faces with bated breath.

"Tones?" Rose cocked her head.

"Patterns," she said. "Runewaves."

Rose frowned. "Um..."

"The standing ones," Bloom said.

"The glowing ones!"

"I think Aunt Dezma uses one of them to make tea taste better?"

Stelli blinked. "Right," sighed. "Okay." She took her thumb and forefinger, pressing them down at the edge of her Standwaves and dragging them to the side. In the back of her mind, she modulated the rhythm, expanding it and creating a gap. The pattern erased as her hand passed over it, leaving an empty hexagon of still water amidst a honeycomb of Standwaves. The algae settled atop that one hexagon

"Woah," Rose breathed.

"There are seven Basal Tones," Stelli said, pushing her rhythm wider, expanding her honeycomb. The hexagon ripples passed underneath Bloom and Rose, who both looked down, watching with wide eyes as their ripples constructed with hers, growing frantic, splashing over their feet before integrating with Stelli's. She cocked her head, bringing her left hand forward again, thumb and forefinger tracing stillness in amongst her Standwaves. The entire pond subsumed to her honeycomb, leaving only that one hexagon of normal water between her and the twins.

"The most basic are Standwaves," Stelli said. "You know about those. Try casting them into this hexagon. Not loud, don't attack it. Just let the rhythm hit the water. Try and focus on how it feels in your head. Like a... like a drum, almost, that you hit with your mind."

Bloom and Rose lowered their hands to the water in that hexagon of stillness, their fingers lacing together. Stelli watched them with eyes sharp as Dezma's Longtooth, tracing the tiny fingernails, the slight bumps on the joints, the smooth skin that was still unmarked by the hazards of time. In the moments before those hands touched the water, she felt her world start to spin.

Her father's voice echoed in her head. *Who stops the horizon, which swallows them both?*

The water came alive. Patterns spread across the surface like drops of ink, catching the algae, pulling it apart in tiny strands that rearranged with the movement of the ripples, soft, small hexagons interlocking and spreading from a thousand minute points, like the puncturing of raindrops. Stelli reached forward a tentative hand, hesitating, bringing just her index finger down to touch that scintillating pattern—

It felt like her fingers slipped into the grooves of a storm-cloud.

"What does it feel like for you?" She breathed, pulling her hand back.

Rose laughed. The patterns swirled around the tips of her fingers, the hexagons so small and precise they might as well have been brushstrokes. "Like I'm painting," she said. "But it's so much easier, like the paper wants to look like the things I want it to be."

"I feel the drum," Bloom's eyes were wide as saucers. "I never noticed it before."

Stelli glanced between the two of them. Rose, eyes affixed on the pattern. Bloom, eyes distant. "If you stop holding hands," she whispered. "Does it stop?"

Rose nodded. "They go back to normal if we aren't holding hands."

"Yet Bloom still does nothing... Fascinating." She watched their Standwaves dance in that center square for a few more moments. The patterns, the complexity... it made her honeycomb look boring and drab by comparison.

She blinked, swallowing. "I suppose I should start by explaining that..." she trailed off. *The common names are misnomers.* Her father's voice echoed in her mind. But these children didn't even know the common names. "Runewaves don't just have a singular effect," she said. "Right now, your Standwaves are making the water solid, so we can stand on it."

Rose and Bloom nodded.

"Most people might see that effect, and assume that's just what Standwaves do. But it's more complicated than that. What people call *Standwaves* are actually just this basic hexagon Runewave shape, or the shape of the first Basal tone—which don't automatically make the water solid. They just alter the water's *solidness*, allowing us to make it so solid that it supports our weight."

Bloom and Rose looked at her with glazed over eyes, and blinked.

"I'm getting ahead of myself, aren't I?"

They blinked again.

"Right," she took a deep breath, glancing to the edge of the pond by instinct. No encouraging nod. No smile. She blinked, turning back to the children, fighting back the slight sweat that swept across her neck and behind her ears. *She's out scouting the oasis.* Stelli knew that. Still, she missed the encouraging nod, and the smile. "Sorry. We'll get there." *We might not have time to get there.* "Try out a Mirrorwave."

Rose frowned. "What's a Mirrorwave?"

Moons. "The glowy one."

Rose's face brightened. The dancing hexagons jolted, swirling together, twisting and turning the way a crowd of dancers might adapt to minstrels taking up a new song. The air above the Runewaves started to glow, motes of dust lighting up in the air like glowbugs, flitting this way and that, light fading as they passed from above the square, always replaced by a new glow flying in from the other side.

Stelli leaned back, both eyebrows going up.

"The drum feels different this time," Bloom said, looking up at the glowbugs. "More... swirly."

She snapped her jaw shut, realizing it had been hanging open. "Are you doing that on purpose?"

"Doing what?" Rose asked.

"The... the glowbugs," she whispered. "The motes of light."

"The glowy things!" Rose said, grinning. "Yeah! Isn't that what it's supposed to look like?"

Stelli shook her head, lowering her hand towards the hexagon filled by their Mirrorwaves, which danced and sparkled in a miasma of movement. Stelli tried to pick it apart. To *see* the Runewaves, see them objectively. She found traces of the classic Mirrorwave parallelogram shape, but tiny, interlocking, ever moving, ever shifting. The shapes would hand each other off, spinning and shifting and changing and reconstructing. Like the shapes found in the intersection of the ripples left by the first drops of rain upon a still surface, like the moments before those shapes closed, swallowed by the expansion of the rain-drops, only to be remade again as they passed each other. She couldn't even begin to imagine how she would deconstruct such a shape. The complexity. The controlled chaos.

"Not at all," she whispered. "Let me..." the Mirrorwaves faded. Stelli tapped the surface. From where her finger touched, parallelogram ripples emanated, singular and concentric, until they faded away at the edges of the hexagon. The border behaved oddly. In the back of Stelli's mind, to maintain her honeycomb of Standwaves, she had to keep part of her mind playing that rhythm. To begin the Mirrorwaves, another part of her mind had to play a different rhythm, in syncopation. To watch the borders of the empty hexagon, she had to disassociate from the chaotic discordant deconstruction caused by the collision of parallelograms and hexagons. To focus on the collapse would throw off her careful balance.

The lines made by her Mirrorwaves glowed a faint green, brightening and darkening a bit with each pass of the ripple.

"That's boring," Rose said.

"You're telling me," Stelli whispered, looking at Bloom and Rose. So small. So young. "Try a Boundwave now."

"What's that?" Bloom said.

Stelli smiled. "These are my favorites." Her heart thumped. Something surged in her gut. *Excitement.* It didn't make her feel like throwing up, for once. "They change how attractive or repellant the surface of the water is. It's the one Runewave where the common name is actually accurate—well, kind of—because it encapsulates both the basal and subversive tones of the wave: the runes either bind the target to the water, or cause them to rebound off of it. Sorry, anyway, we'll get there," *maybe*. She took a breath, and shifted the pattern in the back of her mind, pushing out the edges of the parallelograms, pulling the beat backwards from her drum instead of pressing it forwards. The Mirrorwaves shifted, bending circular, and rippling in towards the centerpoint of the hexagon. Maintaining this twice-cast came easier. As each new pulse of the adjacent hexagons pushed up against the edge of the Boundwaves, she blended their shapes together, continuing the momentum of the Standwaves to fuel the inwards drift of the circular Boundwaves.

"Oh oh oh, I know these! Nell showed me these," Rose elbowed Bloom. "The best ones for cheating at..." her face fell, shadows passing under her eyes like feathers falling from a bird's plumage. She bit her lip, hair falling down around her face, hiding her eyes. Bloom reached over and pulled her into a hug. She fell against him, their small heads nestling together.

Stelli let her waves fade away. In slow crests, the water became still. She swallowed. Her gaze flicked to the edge of the pond without her thinking. She forced it back to the children. Forced herself to breathe, and wait.

"Are you two willing to try?" She whispered. "This is an important one."

"Dad gets so scared when I use them in Zvaloor," Rose whispered, wiping her eyes.

"We're getting him back," Bloom whispered.

"I know..." Rose whispered. "I know." She shook her head, little strands of hair flying around her face. She grabbed Bloom's hand, and together they touched the water. It remained still for a moment. Rose closed her eyes. A few ripples played out from around their fingertips.

"Grab the rhythm," Stelli murmured. "Yank it towards your hands, not away."

The water sloshed, kicking up a bit of algae onto Stelli's Standwave. It got pushed off with the next pulse, back into the miasma of the empty sloshing square.

"I don't wanna yank it..." Bloom muttered, scrunching his eyes up. "My head hurts—"

Tears squeezed out between the scrunched folds of Rose's eyes. She shook her head—

"I thought you just said you wanted your father back," Stelli whispered.

Bloom winced. Rose grit her teeth. Stelli could see sweat against the smooth skin of their hands.

"The bugaboo has him."

Rose shook her head, gritting her teeth. Bloom whimpered a little. "It hurts—"

"The bugaboo will hurt him."

A sound boomed, like the shattering of a sea glass shard between teeth. The water *bucked*, the pattern of her Standwave shrieking into oblivion in the back of her mind. Her body pitched forward. She tried to catch herself—she slammed into something solid, pain wrenching up her arm, throbbing, reinvigorated. She gasped, rolling sideways—she couldn't roll. The water pulled back on her, sticking her in place. She couldn't budge. The water had no give, it's sticky surface somehow...

She blinked, looking down at the water below her. The algae hung frozen and still, like stringy green stars in an empty sky. She had seen a frozen lake before, in the coldest nights of winter; dead fish caught in the pale blue permafrost, covered by the tiniest fractals of ice.

This water had no sheen. It simply stopped, caught between moments. The only movement that betrayed its nature as water came in wide, silent crests, which pushed Stelli up as they passed underneath her. Like she was resting on adhesive rock that bent against her torso, rolling like dark clouds in a storm. She blinked again. The crests. They were hexagonal. Her Standwaves weren't gone. They were subsumed, captured by these new Boundwaves, and washed along with them.

She turned her head up to look at the twins, who sat with wide eyes, hands on the water. A couple lines of clean skin marked tear trails on Bloom's cheeks. Both of them trembled.

"Sorry," Rose mumbled. Stelli blinked. She heaved another breath out, relaxing the lines of her face, trying for a smile.

"Don't be sorry," Stelli murmured, eyes gleaming. She could *feel* them gleaming. Gleaming with tears. Gleaming with awe. Gleaming with fear. "It's beautiful..."

Bloom and Rose pulled their hands back. Rose grabbed Bloom into a big hug. The waves beneath Stelli faded, water soaking into her pant leg—she rolled forward and filled the pond with Standwaves.

"This doesn't look as happy as I would have hoped," Dezma called from the treeline, stomping through the mud, throwing her pack down next to their lean-to. A tear plopped from Bloom's chin onto Stelli's Standwaves, picked up by one of the pulses and pushed to shore.

"That's probably enough for now," Stelli breathed, picking herself up, adjusting the sling, grimacing at the dull ache. Any movement set the pain in motion once more. Bloom and Rose didn't respond. "Come on, let's go talk to Aunt Dezma..." She paused by them, her left hand gripping her right arm across her torso. She thought about reaching down to touch them, hug them, help them walk to shore. The thought froze her. She turned back to Dezma instead, and walked off the pond.

"I didn't want to scare them," Dezma whispered as she reached the shore. "But we have a friend."

Stelli's eyes flicked up past Dezma's shoulder, ears picking out the slight rustle of the leaves. Her mouth hardened.

"You brought them here?"

"He found us," Dezma said. She jerked her head back towards the children. "Are they okay?"

Stelli grunted, massaging her arm. "They could render all traditional forms of warfare obsolete."

"Yes but are they *okay?*" Dezma's eyes burnt through her.

"You should go talk to them," Stelli whispered. "I don't know how."

Dezma nodded, moving towards the algae ponds. "Say hi to our friend for me. Don't let him stick around."

She left Stelli standing on the bank, alone, her soggy vestments still dripping from their ends. She felt like a leaf, moments after being dropped from its tree. The wind wanted to carry her away, but the branch above her still looked down with such a warm, affirming gaze. The branch didn't care where she drifted.

She ducked under an Aycmor branch, into the darkness of the swamp, and the hook returned, yanking firm through her heart.

York hugged himself in the shadows of those branches, shifting his weight back and forth in the fallen leaves and mud. He looked up as she approached. His eyes flashed wide. Lumps streaked his face, bug-bites mixing with clumps of detritus. She couldn't make out the division between his sleepless eyes and the voids of his cheeks. "I don't want to be here," he whispered.

"Then run away," Stelli said. "Leave the swamp. Leave the General. Go make a life somewhere. There's nothing wrong with the coward's way out, York."

"Running isn't the coward's way out," York spat, hugging his cloak tighter around his arms. "Compliance is the only way for a coward. It's all I do, Lieutenant. Complying with the draft when the King said he needed every able bodied man to defend their homes. Complying with the General, because at least in his company I wouldn't have to fight on the front lines. Complying in your unit, because at least you didn't take pleasure from bending our skin closed like the others did. Now I'm in the middle of a Moons cursed *swamp* surrounded by deadly bugs and vipers and Wolf knows what else and on top of all of it you're asking me to *stop complying*. But I don't want to be here. I don't want to be here…" tears slipped down his cheeks. "I already lied to him once, Stelli… I see him in every shadow… He can smell my fear, I'm sure of it…"

Stelli stepped closed, her footsteps breaking the gossamer thread of silence that hung between them. Seban's voice drifted in her head. *Don't let him kill York for this…* She gripped his shoulder. After a moment, he looked up to meet her eyes. "Does the General know where you went searching?" She whispered.

He gulped, his blink displacing another tear from the side of his eye. He nodded, sucking in a snot filled, gasping breath. "I h-have to go back to h-him, d-don't I?"

She squeezed his shoulder. "One more lie."

He nodded, the tears falling in earnest now. She pulled him into a hug. His shaking body and heaving breaths rocked through her form. For a moment, they were one.

"I'm starting to learn something beautiful," Stelli muttered in his ear. "There's a world where you can make a different choice, and people won't hurt you for it. Where you can mess up, and someone brings you a flower anyway. Everything is just as complicated, and maybe even just as painful, but it doesn't matter. It doesn't matter, because you have a flower, and you know that someone cared enough to give it to you."

"That sounds so nice," York's breath started to steady. "Are we almost there?"

"We're so close," Stelli whispered. "So so close. Just one more lie, York. One more lie, and you and Seban can run off to find your flowers. Okay?"

"One more lie," York took one final deep breath. He stepped back from the hug. "I can do it."

"You can do it," she smiled at him.

He smiled back. He looked small and frail in the framing of the dark Aycmor branches. As the swamp tried to swallow him, the smile reached his eyes, and it didn't matter how small he was. "Thanks," he whispered. "I'll see you there, okay?"

"Yeah," she whispered. "See you there."

He turned and marched into the darkness. It tried to swallow him, and couldn't. Stelli watched the spot where he disappeared for a long, solitary moment, before returning to the algae ponds.

She plopped down to the mud beside Dezma's pack. Dezma knelt by the children, one arm around each of them, holding them close. They shook against her, heads angled inwards. Stelli kept her distance. She had pushed them. Too hard, maybe. Not hard enough, maybe. She distracted herself by plucking out a strand of jerky from the pack, grinding it between her teeth, feeling the little strands that held it together snap and twist. Snap and twist. The more she ground her teeth, the more the meat broke, her jaw forcing it to conform, forcing it to meld to the gaps between her molars. One little bit got stuck. She worked at it with her tongue, the angry, frustrated desire to force that little bit free, to make it go where she wanted it, where it was *supposed* to go—

She swallowed the jerky, teeth slipping down over her tongue, drawing a little bit of pain. She grunted, taking a sip from her canteen. Dezma made her way back over, helping the children duck into the lean-to. She was muttering something, a kind look on her face. But there was a tension behind her squat, a tightness in the placement of her jaw, and the contours of her skin. She stayed there for a while, turned away from Stelli, speaking in a low voice that Stelli couldn't hear. She didn't mind that she couldn't hear. The pain didn't feel so bad, one hand braced in the mud, with the algal pond lapping at her feet.

She watched Dezma. Couldn't take her eyes off. Her neck had a large vein, running down the right side, which bulged against her skin, trailing down to where her undershirt covered the edge of the broad muscle in her shoulder. The skin felt taut to Stelli's eyes. Taut and ready to snap.

Dezma stood with a smile, giving one of the kids a hair tousle, before stepping over to Stelli.

"You're doubting the plan," Stelli whispered.

Dezma plopped down in the mud beside her. "They're just kids," she whispered. "Scared little kids."

Stelli brushed her finger through the mud, just to feel the warmth of the earth.

"You think they can do it?" Dezma asked.

Stelli's finger curled, pulling a clump of mud against her palm. She felt it invade her fingernails. She swallowed. Opened her mouth. Closed it, and bowed her head. "Yes," she whispered. "But not soon enough."

"And if someone bled?"

Panic jolted up in Stelli's throat. She shook her head, hardly able to hold on to her words. "Nobody could beat them if there was blood in the water."

Dezma broke eye contact, giving a slow nod, and a slight smile. They sat in their separate silences for a long moment, held together by a tension that reached through the air and bound them tight like a spider's cocoon.

"Gavin would hate me for this," Dezma said.

"Will," Stelli said, all of a sudden yanked by the fire burning away the webs between them. "Will hate you for this."

Dezma laughed under her breath, and it stoked the fire. "Gavin never let them use Runewaves, back home."

Stelli nodded. "I know."

"But do you know why?"

She stared at the mottled, muddied cloak of the lean-to. She could almost see through it. Almost see those two tiny bundled figures, upon whose shoulders rested the world. She felt the same weight. The weight of everything, tugging her on a string attached to the hook in her heart. "Yeah," she whispered. "Because they're different."

The lean-to shifted. Bloom stumbled out. They watched as the little boy craned his head upwards, staring at the sky. The canopy blocked his vision, so he stumbled forward a few more steps, right up to the edge of the algal pond.

Dezma nodded. "He's afraid it will consume them."

The purple light of the Carrow Wolf started to eclipse the pale white of the Tuft Rabbit, casting the algae in a sinister pearlescent lavender sheen that sent the natural green askew. Faint ripples lapped at the boy's feet, his form effused in the light. In front of him, the pond reflected the sky, colors and flashes playing in the drifting gaps between the algae. A crescent of water shifted bare. It reflected the last sliver of pale white glow as the purple eclipsed it. Iota, by iota, by iota. Until only the barest sliver of the Tuft Rabbit remained. She vibrated in the reflection. Vibrated with the shifting of the water. Vibrated with agony. Vibrated with hope.

"Rose thinks she can handle it. She's not afraid."

The algae drifted over the image, pulling it apart. The rest of the story played out in the boy's eyes, as the Tuft Rabbit came unbearably close to being devoured, and survived.

The Full Devouring is tomorrow night, Stelli reflected idly, watching the boy's face. She wondered if Bloom had ever been allowed out at night to see one before.

"Bloom is afraid. But not of The Wolf," Dezma whispered. "He's afraid he won't have a home to go back to after this."

The little boy fell to his knees, curled forward, and wept.

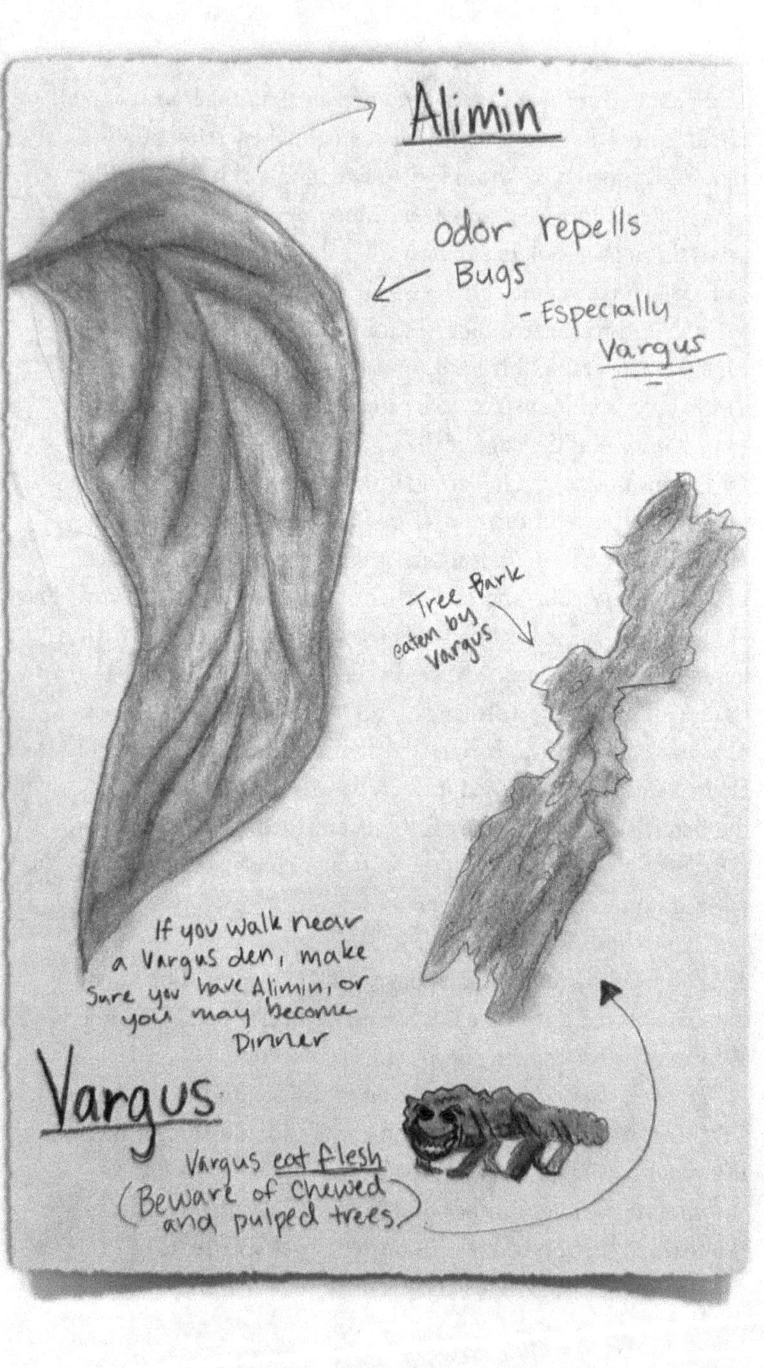

Alimin
odor repells Bugs
- Especially Vargus
Tree Bark eaten by Vargus
If you walk near a Vargus den, make sure you have Alimin, or you may become Dinner
Vargus
Vargus eat flesh (Beware of chewed and pulped trees.)

19

Gavin's next moments of consciousness filtered through him like warm Gurrengie leaves wrapped tightly around his mind. He became aware of his breathing first. Slow. Steady. Then the discomfort of a knot of wood against his lower back. Thick, rounded. *Decayed knot.* It felt loose. A dead branch, mostly shorn off. The tree must have grown around it.

A dull ache in his leg. Far away. Coupled with the pain, a strange clamminess warbled against the skin of his thigh. He shifted. Thick cords around his arms, subtle leafage. *Cyril vines.* Tight. Too tight. Breathing was... hard.

His shoulder. No pain. He twitched it up. It moved. He blinked his eyes open.

A cloak, stretched tight between branches, over his head. Droplets plop, plop, plopped down on top of it, sliding off to the side. He grunted, grateful for the cover, remembering the discomfort of sap in his eyes. He squinted down at his right leg. The trousers that once covered it were ripped, just below his waist, leaving the skin open to the air. That explained the clamminess. He flexed his fingers, unable to move them much against his bindings. His nails picked up mud.

Around him sprawled the decayed swamp. The Aycmor trees looked sad and sallow. What vines hung between their boughs did so with an air of defeat, like the furs of dead Bounders hung up to dry. He swallowed a heavy glob of mucus and pain, craning his head around. A toad croaked nearby. A Hound passed by his head. He squeezed his fingers more, digging them into the ground. His fingernail scraped a root. A large root, a bark-covered root. It peeled off against his finger, chipping under his nail, jabbing him with quick pain. He flipped the splinter onto the pad of his finger. Definitely Aycmor bark, from its rough texture, and small scales. But something didn't sit well with him. Something in the way that the bark crumbled, just a little bit piecemeal, as if clawed into fragments and stuck back together with sap...

He bucked against his bindings, to no avail.

"You're the one who ran into the swamp," a voice whispered behind him, teasing. "Why so suddenly afraid?"

Gavin clenched his hands into the mud and roots, craning his head up to look at the sky. He couldn't see it. The cloak kept the droplets off his face, but it hid the sky, so he couldn't see it, so he didn't know. Vargus came out at night. Came out to swarm and devour... *Vargus nest... when Vargus are hungry, they chew up the bark and paste it back together with their saliva and sap...* A chill settled deep in his bones.

"Poetic, wouldn't you say?" The General continued, out of sight. "I could think of no better ending for the villain of my quest. Dead by the very thing he claims to love."

Gavin closed his eyes, forcing himself to breathe. "You really think you're a hero?"

"Oh, not yet. But I will be. Once you realize the predicament you're in, and tell me where to find your children."

A tiny pressure alit on the underside of his knee. Probing legs scratched at his skin. The weight moved up his thigh, clinging to his thick, tangled hair. He bucked against the bindings again, trying to twist and squirm away. He couldn't. Not even a little.

A second pressure joined the first. Then three more. Thousands of legs pulled thousands of Vargus up from the mud and the roots and the bark, clamoring across his flesh. He felt their mouths, like tiny knives. They probed and prodded, gnawing on his hair, seeking flesh.

He clenched his hands, his entire body shaking. "Get them off me," he croaked. "Get them off me. You can't let me die. If they kill me you'll never find my children so get them off me—"

"You're not the only one who knows the swamp's tricks," the General sneered.

A smell wafted up to his nose, as his entire body tensed away from the ground. A scent like age old mildew, intensely organic and rotten. He tried to bend his right leg. To bring it closer towards his chest, towards his head and neck where that smell must be coming from, where that smell kept the Vargus from chewing through his vital organs and killing him. His right leg didn't budge. A thick vine tied around his ankle held it fast to a tree-root. He bucked, trying to rip the root out of the ground. He couldn't.

"All it takes is a location," the General whispered. "And I can move that Alimin for you."

One of the Vargus found the wound on his upper thigh. It pushed under the bandage, rooting around in his infected flesh. The first bite took a strip of skin off the edge of the wound. It stung, like a scrape after falling down on the rocks. The second bite jolted him from another part of his leg. Then a third came. He screamed. They swarmed his flesh. It peeled away beneath their teeth in curdled clumps. His eyes shot open, and he couldn't close them. The Vargus carried his skin like trophies on their backs, scurrying with it back into the mud, leaving behind welts of red. His stomach expelled itself. He choked on the bile, unable to stop screaming even with the putrid drippings coating his teeth and falling from his lips.

"The swamp will kill them too, you know." The General said over Gavin's choked screams. "They won't survive alone."

The words didn't register. Pain throttled him. His vision, back. Senses, off. The Vargus wriggled under his skin, pulling out the meaty chunks of his thigh, searching for the juiciest morsels to rip off. It felt like they were in his brain.

"Would you let that happen? Let them *die*, just to keep me from saving the world?"

His entire existence. The pain. The tearing of his flesh. And that voice.

"Is this what it means to be a good father?"

Pain. Tearing, ripping, screaming. That voice.

Something else. A weight against his heart. The weight of a small brown pod in his pocket. As he felt it there, he smiled, and the pain couldn't overwhelm him.

The swamp is not their enemy... Were his lips moving? *The swamp is not their enemy...*

"Is this really your choice?" The General growled, right in his ear.

"The swamp is not their... their enemy..."

The General's growl grew to a fever pitch of anger. The pain overtook him.

* * *

Gavin moved his leg. It was the first thing he became conscious of, in the filtering blackness of his pain-suffused eyelids. His head pounded. His throat was parched. His stomach roared and churned. His bowels were raw and empty. The space between his thighs was wet and soiled.

But he moved his leg. It throbbed with the phantom rivulets of a forgotten pain, far away, distant, yet *pounding* against the inside of his head. He shifted it back and forth. His heel scraped the stone ground. He frowned. He didn't feel any bindings. He bent his knee. Up. Down. Reached out and touched it, felt the caress of his hand, felt... felt... his hand *was* bound. He felt the coarse vine, little tingles of bloodlessness in his fingers. He rolled his head over, trying to pry his eyes open, blinking through broken eyelids. The world was blurry. Dark greens and blacks, a mess in his vision. Swimming figures, figures swimming in his tears. He blinked. Things rotated. Rotated things. He squeezed the toes on his foot. What did that feel like? He couldn't... couldn't quite remember... Trying to conjure the feeling just brought back phantom tickles of Vargus under his skin, their tiny mouths moving, pulsing, *squirming*.

He blinked. The haze settled just a little more into uniform shapes. He looked down at his leg. He bucked away from the tree. The bindings wrenched him back. Spittle carried the meager contents of his stomach down his chin, dripping under his shirt. He blinked.

He didn't have a leg. Halfway up from his knee, the skin was red and boiled, melded and stretched over a rounded stump. He heaved again, but had nothing to expel. His head crashed back against the tree, and his vision flashed. He swallowed the foul taste of bile.

He blinked. His body felt cold and jittery and tingly. He could still feel his leg. Bright blue light filtered through the cloak stretched between the branches above him. The light of daytime. He had hours, at most. Drips of clear oasis water fell along the edges of the cloak, painting rivulets in the mud. One of them landed on his... not his leg... not his leg... *not his leg...*

He forced himself to look back down, taking deep breaths. A tiny weight pressed above his heart. He twitched his remaining leg. It shifted in the bindings. The stump of his severed leg wouldn't respond. He couldn't... couldn't quite tell... couldn't quite feel, with his mind, that the rest of it... rest of it wasn't... he felt the bile rising, took a deep breath, and focused on that tiny, singular weight.

310

His little Isingrass pod.

He closed his eyes. *Breathe.* Let the swirling stop. Let the bile sink back down. *Breathe.* His heart rate settled. *Breathe...*

He opened his eyes, and scanned the surrounding trees, blinking through the black spots and dizzying unfocus. A huddled figure crouched nearby, face obscured, cloak wrapped tight. A sliver of dark hair curled out from the edge of the hood. A twin scabbard hung at her belt. One of them was empty. A flash of light reflected off the blade, which rested on her knee.

They stared at each other for a long time. He looked away first, eyes falling to the mud below. It was red. Churned up and disturbed by a thousand tiny creatures. *Remember...* his own voice, somewhere far in a distant memory. *When the mud is churned up, and the bark looks chewed, don't go near it at night time...* His hands clenched into the mud and blood. It squeezed between his fingers. *At night time...* The sun shone through the cloak above him. Was it getting dimmer? Did the blue light of the sun look paler than it had when he woke up?

He shut his eyes, bowing his head. He shouldn't think about it. The General needed him alive. The General didn't know where his children were. His little Bloomstalk and Rosebud were safe.

In his missing leg, phantom Vargus burrowed through his skin, dug themselves into his muscles, nestled under his knee cap. The light faded against his closed eyelids, turning white. Fear lanced through him. He shot his eyes open, arms jerking against their restraints. He tried to roll his body over to see around the cloak. He couldn't move.

Crawling, on his leg. He looked down. He had no leg. The bile rose in his throat again. He closed his eyes. The crawling continued. It infiltrated him. Burrowed into him. Took chunks of his flesh. He thrashed, yanking, pulling. Maybe he could rip the roots out of the ground, the roots that the vines were tied too. He strained his arms up, pulling as hard as he could. He felt the ground shift a bit with his effort. The vines dug into the soft skin just above his wrists, cutting off circulation to his hands. The tingling grew too much. He collapsed back against the bark and mud, back drenched in sweat, eyes prickling. His head whipped from side to side.

His children were safe. The General needed him alive. His children were safe. The General needed him—

"Where is the sun?" He croaked, eyes landing on the woman. The woman who sat and watched with her broken nose, broken under his hand. "Where is the sun, just tell me that much, where is the sun?"

She turned her head away.

"Going to stop watching me?" He shouted. "And what if I escape? What then? You know I won't tell you where my children are so at least tell me where the sun is—"

"Have you ever heard a child scream?" Her broken nose made the violent whisper nasal and rough.

He fell entirely still. The words washed over him, prickling his arms. "Is that a threat?"

"No," she said. "It's context."

He kept staring at her.

"You look at us like we're monsters," she said, voice low. "You think I *want* to be fighting for him? My town burned, and by the time the embers died both armies had left. I heard my own little sister scream herself to death, while a beam of our broken house trapped her in the flames. I don't want to be here, doing this to you. I want to be back home watching my little sister grow up into a world that won't rip families apart. How many more children have to die for you to want to live in that world too?"

He stared at her for a long time. A toad croaked, and he listened. His vision swam again. "My children," he said eventually, shaking his head, delirious. "My children…"

"*Your* children," she whispered. "What about everybody else's?"

He looked away, eyes falling on a scorpion that clung to the trunk by his right shoulder. It locked claws with a beetle, whose horn jabbed the scorpion in its chitinous face, the two of them stumbling up and down in a powerful tug-of-war.

"If you looked at yourself," she whispered. "Maybe there you would see a monster too."

The scorpion lanced its tail down, jabbing it against the beetle's armor, failing to find a gap. The beetle gave a shove, horn hooking under the scorpion's head, flipping it backwards. It fell down the trunk, catching itself sideways on one of the roots, before turning and scuttling into the shadows once more.

Gavin shook his head. A slow, defeated movement. His grizzled, bearded, unkempt chin fell down to press against his chest. His gaze locked on a bit of blood that pooled by his hand. It trickled through a trough in the mud, catching in the soft lines of his thumb. A tear slid down his cheek. Then a second. Through all the strife and tangle of his beard, they kept on trickling, until they met at his chin, paused for a moment, took a breath, and fell down to join the blood.

He couldn't muster the energy to listen when it hit the ground.

He lifted his head to look at the treeline. He saw the world through a new filter. It washed out some of the color. Muted the greens of the Aycmor leaves, muted the blacks of the trunks, muted the flashing dark blues of Hounds in the air. Even the slight presence of wind, with its whittled whistling, felt damp and heavy on his ears.

He stared, but he didn't. A bird fluttered its green wings as it landed on a black branch. It reared back its head, and opened its beak. Three tones. Discordant. Syncopated. *Correct.* Gavin didn't see it. Gavin didn't see it, because when it looked down at him, it saw him. And his eyes were seeing past it. Seeing something far, far away.

He looked so small, to the bird. A small sack of meat. Lopsided. Weakened. And the smell of his blood...

Gavin shifted. The branch shook under the weight of the departing bird. His eyes found the branch a few moments later. It took a bit for his ears to find his eyes to find the branch. He coughed in his bindings, shoulders shaking. He bent forward just to feel something, to try and get the redness of a stretch to shake free the tingling in his arms and legs from the tightness of the vines.

Time, to Gavin, felt muted too. Muted and far away. Endless and instant. *Tonight is...* the woman got up and left at some point, another guard replacing her. The shaking man from before. He brought food with him, and placed it on Gavin's eager tongue with gentle fingers. Bitter berries. Dried meat. A few sips from the canteen. *Tonight is the Full Devouring...*

He tried to look at the sky. He sat for so long. It must be night by now. They must cut free his bindings soon. Or bring more Alimin. They would, he told himself. Because his children were safe. Because the General needed him alive. So they would cut him free, soon, or bring him more Alimin, and when they did the squirming bodies of the Vargus that still ate his nonexistent leg would finally go away, and he could hug Bloom and Rose again, and he could... and he could... He squeezed his eyes shut.

His heart thumped against the Isingrass pod in his pocket. A new tear fell down his cheek, and out leaked the water he had just drank. The thumping of his heart grew intense. So intense it hurt. He swallowed, letting his head fall to the side, chin bumping his shoulder. The woman returned, exchanging brief words with the Shaking Man. He shook his head. She grimaced, looking at the sky. Even such a simple look jolted him, dried his throat.

She left. He strained his eyes to the sky, and saw nothing. Time felt as flexible as his severed leg. Able to move. Able to bend. In his control, yet forever out of reach.

The General's voice chilled his spine like frozen rainwater. "How have your musings been, oh loving father?"

Gavin shut his eyes, squeezing his hands into fists. His body couldn't curl into a ball, but his insides did. They curled so tight he could almost squeeze the memory of the Vargus away.

"I did some musings of my own, today," the General continued.

Footsteps squelched through mud. Gavin forced himself to look. The General walked up to the Shaking Man, clapping a hand on his shoulder. The Shaking Man jumped, bowing his head.

"And I've realized that you are not like other selfish men, Gavin."

The General led the Shaking Man towards Gavin.

"You see, York here, he's a selfish man," the General said. "He's afraid of being hurt, so he follows the rules. It's a simple thing to understand, really. A fair and honest relationship."

York nodded up and down. Gavin watched York's throat bob as he gulped. Something twisted in Gavin's gut. A desperate plea, broken resignation, a horror. He exhaled through dry lips.

"But because of you," the General whispered, reaching under his cloak with his free hand, and withdrawing that savage, straight-edged Dewclaw. "Selfish, cowardly, innocent soldiers like him are being massacred by the thousands."

The General slashed the Dewclaw through York's shoulder. York screamed, red blood pooling through his torn jerkin, down his torso. He bucked and twisted, trying to get away, but the General's arm locked around his neck. The flailing only made it worse for him as his blood splattered down into the mud. Skin pulled back around the soldier's pale eyes, eyes that *screamed*, eyes that feared, eyes that regretted. The General moved the Dewclaw down York's arm, slicing through the sleeve.

Gavin closed his eyes and turned away as York screamed again. He felt his extremities drain of sensation and warmth.

"Watch," the General growled. "Or I'll kill him."

Gavin opened his eyes. York begged. He begged with words that weren't words, muted sounds and pleas so overwhelmed with panic they barely resembled language. No matter how much the bucking and twisting must have been hurting him, he didn't stop. He didn't stop. The Dewclaw came down again. He didn't stop.

Gavin's eyes glazed over. He drew back into himself and hid in the squirming of his missing leg. He embraced the feeling of the Vargus devouring his skin. At least it wasn't York's screaming. At least it wasn't that horrible choked begging.

"He represents but a fraction," the General whispered, breathing labored. "Of the consequences of your silence."

The fields of Gavin's vision split out of focus. He let the colors separate from the shapes, let the bright reds and browns smear across his world.

"His life is in your hands, loving father. What will it be? Him, or your children? Ten thousand soldiers, or your two children?"

"Please," York found his tongue, his voice slobbering and straining. "Please I'll do *anything* please..."

Gavin saw one side of York as nothing but a cascade of red. But he didn't see. He didn't see. He saw past. He heard the three-toned caw of a far away bird, listened to it grow closer, hopping through the bushes.

"You really would watch him die," the General whispered, his voice tinged with awe. "You would watch them *all* die."

He pressed the Dewclaw to York's neck.

York screamed. "NO PLEASE I KNOW WHERE THE CHILDREN ARE!"

York's body dropped, collapsing in a heap. He rolled himself over to look up at the General, blithering words escaping his lips at breakneck speeds.

"I'm sorry I'm so sorry I lied to you I never should have lied to you you always find out but I'm sorry, I did find them, they're hiding by some algae pools nearby I can lead you to them but *please stop hurting me...*"

The blurred fields of Gavin's vision snapped into focus, and he saw the terrified face of the young man who was bleeding out on the bark. Gavin couldn't draw in breath. His extremities were cold again. And something was wrong. More wrong than it ever had been. His leg. He couldn't feel his missing leg. No pain. No itch. He couldn't bend it. His missing leg had been the only limb he could bend, and now he couldn't bend it.

The General knelt by York's side, cupping his chin. "Oh dear," he whispered. "I'm so sorry I had to hurt you..." he hoisted York up against him, clutching him tight, letting his blood spill out across his torso. York groaned in pain, head lolling into the crook of the General's neck. "There you go, that's right," the General cooed. "Algae pools, you say?" The General murmured. "Where are they? I'll never cause you pain again, you'll be free, if you can just tell me where..."

"Not far from the oasis..." York slurred, voice cracking. "Go from the oasis and cross the river of mud and you'll find them..."

Understanding dawned in the General's eyes. "You've done so well, York," he whispered, rocking the soldier forward and back in his arms. "So so so well..." the General lifted the Dewclaw towards York's neck. The young soldier had his eyes closed, face buried against the General's shoulder, shuddering breaths in and out. "No more pain, my friend," the General whispered. "No more pain."

The General slit York's throat.

Gavin flinched to look at the tree line. None of him could move. He was suffocating. Light played between the branches of the Aycmors. Blue light. On the horizon. Tinged with white. The sun was setting. *Twilight.*

The General stood, moving towards the edge of the clearing, carrying York's dead body like a child scooped into his arms.

"Wait," Gavin said in a hoarse voice.

The General turned around, raising an eyebrow. York's blood drained across his torso.

"I need Alimin," Gavin croaked. "The leaf you used earlier, I need it, the smell only lingers for about eight hours and the sun is setting and the Vargus will come back out soon and y-you need me alive, so get me more Alimin."

The General smiled. It reached his eyes, and looked so sweet. "I told you earlier," he whispered. "It's almost poetic."

He stepped into the shadows of twilight, and left Gavin alone. Two twin tears trickled at the corners of Gavin's eyes. He bowed his head, and awaited his devouring.

20

A gain," Stelli whispered, maintaining her honeycomb of Standwaves to fill the algae pond. Bloom and Rose stood in front of her, hands clasped, eyes determined. Stelli left two open hexagons in the water for the children to cast into. At her word, they began, and the water rippled. Their skin whitened at the intersections of their grips as they squeezed tighter.

The ripples in both hexagons remained fuzzy, the crests and troughs snapping over one another, formless. Bloom's little body shook.

Stelli's heart lurched. She swallowed. "You have to let them be different."

The ripples fuzzed, the way that a painting might if a fist wiped the pain into a smear, and then somehow wiped back into clarity.

"It feels wrong," Bloom muttered.

"I know," Stelli whispered. "But it's okay."

"It doesn't feel okay!" Bloom grit his teeth. The ripples in the left hexagon surged, becoming circular, bubbling, chaotic. Steam rose from the water. The ripples in the right hexagon shimmied towards a similar shape, with less definition, parallelograms whispering between the edges of the hexagons, failing to find individuality.

"Shh," Stelli murmured, lowering a slow hand towards the right hexagon, bringing her middle finger down to tap lightly at its center. A droplet of the water clung to her skin, flickering in a shaft of light. She let a rhythm leave her fingertip, playing in the back of her mind. It helped the parallelograms that were there, guiding them, pulling them away from the shape of the Steamwaves.

The Steamwaves in the left hexagon started to shift, rotating inwards towards—

"Focus on the Steamwaves," Stelli murmured. The Mirrorwaves glowed a soft blue, lighting them from beneath. "Feel the pattern. Warm, eclectic. Right?"

Bloom nodded. One of his tears caught his chin, falling down to slam hard against the solid water beneath them.

"Hold on to it," Stelli continued. "Let it be. Let it repeat. Let it exist."

Bloom's breathing steadied. Stelli pulled her hand back from the Mirrorwaves, as slow as she could, holding her breath. She let the rhythm fade from the back of her mind, handing off her burden to the small boy and girl crouched in front of her.

The water kept glowing, next to the steam that kept rising. Stelli held her breath, watching as the little boy and girl inhaled, and then exhaled, inhaled, and then exhaled. A sensation passed down Stelli's arms, up her torso, across her neck. The honeycomb beat its standard Standwave rhythm, and the patterns of its movement washed across her. More than that. The patterns of its movement interlaced with the patterns of the Steamwaves and the patterns of the Mirrorwaves. The soft noises they made in the air, the crash of trough over crest, the syncopated whispers of parallelogram on hexagon, of circle on rigid edge, all of it meandered in the open clearing of the swamp, and created a feeling in Stelli. The feeling that she had stepped down into the center of the music. The feeling that she had found the core of distortion and discord, and it couldn't vibrate her to pieces. The feeling that this was okay.

The shapes blurred beneath her gaze. Bloom gasped. A tiny

squeal escaped from Rose's mouth. Their hands squeezed, and Stelli felt her own concentration slipping, a new pattern breaking through her carefully curated Standwaves. She couldn't hold on to the new pattern. It washed too clean across her mental drum. She blinked, leaning back, shifting all her focus to maintaining the Standwaves beneath them as her hexagon flickered away.

Between them flickered a new pattern. Stelli's stomach flipped. Circular parallelograms. But no, that was impossible. A circle, made of parallelograms? Not quite. Her mind struggled to find the pattern in the minute ripples, eyes seeking the tiniest details in the mosaic of water. Steam poured off the crests, obscuring her view. And then it all began to glow. Not in the way that a Mirrorwave would glow, rather each individual *wisp* of steam glowed, as if a billowing flame, a wildfire of luminescent purple. Stelli grinned. And inside, the hook dug deeper.

"Beautiful."

It faded away. Rose jumped up and down. "We did it!"

Bloom just looked relieved.

"You both just did something impossible," Stelli said. They looked back at her, scared. The pattern played in the back of her vision, and she couldn't deconstruct it.

"I let them be different," Bloom whispered, staring down at the water.

Stelli smiled.

"What about the one that hurts people?" Rose's voice mumbled over the moment.

The feeling drifted away into goosebumps on Stelli's arms. "Slashwaves?"

Rose nodded, hair bouncing around her head. "The Bugaboo won't hold back, will he? The purple steam was pretty but it won't stop him from hurting us."

"No," Stelli whispered. "No it won't."

"So show us the Slashy wave."

Stelli drew in a deep breath. The back of her neck prickled with eyes. She turned back towards the treeline. No Dezma. She'd gone out to look for fresh ingredients to make a stew. Stelli's mouth watered at the thought. The last time Dezma had made them stew...

Moons. All the way back in those twisted, tangled trees. It felt so long ago.

"I'll show you," Stelli whispered. "But I need you both to promise not to try them yourselves."

"What?" Rose glowered at her. "I thought you were teaching us!"

"They're dangerous," Stelli muttered. "And I'm not sure what will happen if you two try."

Rose heaved a sigh.

"That's okay," Bloom whispered. "Just show us."

Rose glared at him.

He shrugged. "Dad isn't going to let us use Runewaves at all once we get him back." His words hung in the air. Rose looked down at the water, her face reflected and distorted amidst the algae. "And we're *going* to get him back," Bloom whispered.

Rose's eyes brimmed with tears. She nodded. Her chin quivered. *Plunk...* The water rippled as a tear fell between strands of algae, the circular divots in the water uneven and broken by the tangle of green. "I'm just scared," she whispered. "Why shouldn't we be able to do whatever it takes? To get him back?"

"Hurting yourselves won't help anyone—"

"But what if we need to hurt the Bugaboo?" Rose seemed to shrink even further into herself, as Bloom and Stelli stared at her. "Nell says that when people want to hurt you, sometimes all you can do is hurt them back," her voice started shaking. "I don't wanna hurt anyone. But what if it's the only way to save dad?"

The asymmetrical ripples cast by Rose's tears interlaced with one another, shifting and reforming into a complicated, un-followable pattern. They brushed up against Stelli's Standwaves, the sound barely audible above the background buzz of the swamp.

"Alright," Stelli whispered.

Rose blinked. Bloom paled.

"You can try it," she said, standing, moving behind them, stepping into the mud at the edge of the pond. "I'll stay over here. I'll be right behind you the whole time. But I need you two to focus. Alright? I need you two to focus, and remember. These waves are different. They leave the surface of the water. They break things. Cut things. Namely, skin and bone. Focus on directing it *outwards*. Away from me, away from yourselves. Bloom, when you cast the pattern, make the triangles wide and spread out. Rose... I'm not sure how to direct you. I've never felt what you feel. But control it. Limit it. And don't lose control of it."

Stelli tapped the water, just to their side. Between her Standwaves, a new pattern formed. Triangles rose from the water and lanced forward, straight and angry. In their wake, tufts of spray and algae kicked up, drifting in the air before settling atop her hexagons.

The children watched with wide eyed focus, and nodded. Rose sucked in her tears, wiped her nose with the back of her hand, and set her mouth into a thin line. She closed her eyes. Bloom swallowed a lump, reaching with shaking hands to interlace their fingers

Their hands touched down on the water.

A soft hum. The water buzzed, popping and snapping like a swarm of insects crawling across flesh. Gouts of water sprayed up at uneven intervals, slicing through the air and leaving it somehow emptier. Stelli watched as a wasp got bisected by a stray burst, its body flying apart, falling onto her Standwaves.

She sucked in a breath. "That's enough," she whispered. The triangle patterns surged forward and *slammed* against the edge of her Standwaves, carving chunks free from her patterns with the very force of them, leaving her ripples chaotic and broken. "That's enough!" She said louder, reaching forward and grabbing Bloom and Rose's shoulders, giving them a squeeze. "Stop. Let go."

One last stray burst of water lanced through the canopy above them. A bird squawked. A few leaves spiraled free of their branches, falling through the air. A silence fell across the clearing. Stelli heard Bloom gulp.

"The only reason these Runewaves don't kill entire armies," Stelli whispered, voice shaking. "Is that once one man dies, his blood prevents the Slashwaves from killing the rest of the company. The two of you have no such restrictions."

Rose's breathing shook. "You're saying we could kill entire armies."

"Yes."

Rose pulled her legs up against her chest, hugging her knees, staring at the edge of the swamp. Her eyes were haunted, distant. Bloom played with the edge of his pant leg. Stelli closed her eyes for a moment. Against the back of her neck, she could feel the prickle of a stare. A disapproving stare. The stare of small eyes, on a hard, well-defined face. She swallowed bile in her throat, forcing her fingers to rub against the sweat of her palms.

"You only have to fight one monster," she whispered. "That's it. And Dezma and I will be right there to help you."

Rose nodded, staring without seeing, crying without tears.

"Come on," Stelli whispered, stepping back out on the pond. "Let's practice, okay? Let's spar. I'll be the Bugaboo. Grrrrrrrr," she curled her fingers, bringing them up next to her face, sneering. Rose picked herself to her feet, dragging Bloom up with her.

Stelli stalked forward, pressing her heels to the water, contorting it with the rhythm at the back of her mind. She stepped with her right foot forward, and used her heel to stamp down Steamwaves between her Standwaves. She shimmied with her left foot, and as she moved, she split her mind a third time, layering in Mirrorwaves, twisting the pattern, twisting the light. *The steam, the canvas...* The green scar, across the hideous face of the wolf, swirling in the steam. She cast the image with each step, different, wild-eyed, hectic. *The Mirrorwaves, the brush.* Her head started to hurt, as the three distinct patterns beat in discordant syncopation behind her skull, separate, unique, uncombinable. She hefted her Canine, relieved to feel its weight once more. The heavy, blunt weapon was designed for fights against other Runecasters, not for navigating the tangles and brambles of the swamp. Now she had use for it once more.

The light faded out between the leaves above them. Stelli stalked forward.

And they sparred. The first lunge went poorly. Bloom wasn't ready. He scrambled backwards, face paling, as Rose stomped her foot and tried to conjure some type of wave in the water. But as they split their intentions, their hands came unlaced. Bloom fell onto his backside in the shallows of the water, Standwaves gone. Rose accomplished nothing more than hitting her foot against her own Standwaves, yelping in pain. Stelli stopped her swing inches from the young girl's head.

"Again," Stelli growled, backing up. Bloom scampered to his feet, grabbing Rose's hand.

She lunged. Rose yanked Bloom to the side. Stelli's swing missed. The twins knelt, Bloom still white in the face, their hands coming down into the water even as Stelli whirled with another strike—

The Standwaves at the twins feet—*normal* Standwaves, Stelli noticed, emanating from only Rose—obfuscated with wild patterns, the hexagons pulling inwards and rounding at the edges, before sloshing back and forth in miniature spirals—

She redirected her momentum so the strike slammed through their ripples, passing into the algae and sending up a splash. The water caught on their pant legs, dripping down as if they had wet themselves. Stelli let her wolf-illusion drop.

"What happened?"

"I was gonna bind you!" Bloom said.

"But we could do the cool thing she's doing and make our own illusion—"

"Which would have needed *Steam*waves not just Mirror-waves—

Stelli snapped her fingers. They both redirected their glares from each other to her. "You have to work together," she said.

"Duh," Rose snorted.

"No, I mean, in a different way than most teams," Stelli continued. "You can't cast if the two of you intend to cast *different* Runewaves. Bloom gives the pattern for one, and Rose..." Stelli bit her lip. Teaching... teaching... her father always brute forced it, drilled until she figured out how to get it right. *A thousand bruises...* She felt Dezma's eyes on her, glancing over her shoulder. Empty. She shook her head. "Which one of you is the artist?"

Rose blinked.

"Is it you, Rose?"

The little girl nodded.

"Alright," *painting... painting...* "When you're trying to make it look like something, you have the image of it in your mind first, right?"

Another nod.

"That's normally how it would be with Runewaves, too. Except I think Bloom is the one making the image for the two of you. You're gonna have to learn what image is in his head, so you can paint it."

Rose blinked.

"Bloom could just tell you," Stelli said. "A shout, when he casts the patterns. But then you'd be telling your opponent what you're about to do, which is a bad idea..."

"I could say the *wrong* things!" Bloom said. "But Rose will know what the wrong things actually mean. Like, if I say Boundwave, that means use a Steamwave, and if I say Slashwave—"

"No, no, no," Stelli shook her head. "*Way* too complicated. You'll forget. Or you'll have so little time to remember that your instinct will betray you. Or, if you had the time to drill that for days and days until the code was perfect, it would work for about a minute before your opponent figured out your code, and you might as well be shouting the real plan from the start."

Bloom deflated.

"What I'm curious about," Stelli continued. "Bloom, if you try to cast a wave, and Rose does nothing... will the pattern exist without the effect?"

He shrugged, glancing at Rose. They knelt to touch the water. Ripples drifted from the edges of their fingertips, sloshing over top of themselves, struggling to find definition. Stelli narrowed her eyes. There was *some* sort of pattern to them... Some vague repetition in the disorder, some complicated miasma of shape.

"Steamwave," Bloom whispered.

Rose cocked her head, frowning. Little by little, like the blinking away of early morning dew, like the emergence of a single raindrop from the cascade of tiered shingles, the back-and-forth, uniform pattern of Steamwaves emerged from the disorder, and somehow Stelli's eyes knew they had always been there. White steam pulled itself off the surface of the water, twining and twirling like blades of tall grass in a windstorm, somehow tranquil despite the chaos.

"Fascinating," Stelli mumbled. She stood again, stepping

back. "For now, try just talking to each other. Call out your Runewaves, Bloom. We'll try and think of a better way to communicate it later."

Beneath her right foot, the Steamwaves. Beneath her left, the flashes of the wolf. Unfair, she thought as she stepped forward, her visage crackling and snapping to the left and right. She tried to mimic her father: the way his strikes would flash from three spots at once, arching from the steam as if he had six arms and six maws, all snapping and striking and biting. She was but a weak facsimile. A thrice-casting imitation of her father, who kept his illusion going on top of casting Slashwaves, and Boundwaves.

Rose and Bloom jumped backwards, feet coming to the edge of the pond. She struck forward, willing the shadows in the rapidly billowing steam to strike left and right, while she struck in the center.

"Boundwave and Steamwave!" Bloom shouted.

"What?" Rose yanked him to the side. They staggered away from her real blow, her mist strike passing through them harmlessly. Bloom left behind chaotic, undefined ripples as he stepped.

"Do both!"

Rose's eyes were panicked, confused. She glanced down at the ripples, which congealed, focusing, sliding into place like the Aycmor leaves when the wind stilled—

She felt the moment their waves overtook her own. Like a snap in the back of her mind. Her Canine flashed for the twins. She stopped it in the air in front of them. And then looked down.

Her feet weren't stuck. She could move them. But her Steam was gone. It clung to the water, pooling and billowing around her ankles. Her Mirrorwaves still cast their dark lights into the air, but with no steam to catch and befuddle, all the light did was illuminate. She lowered her stick, kicking her feet through the pooling mist.

Somehow, it stuck to the water, as if... as if bound.

Stelli grinned, twirling her Canine, crouching low. Rose's mouth flickered towards a smile. Bloom looked down, eyes wide and thoughtful. Stelli opened her mouth, ready to announce the next match—

She lunged, even as they looked up at her to listen, her stick flashing through the air. Rose shrieked, stumbling backwards with Bloom. This time, they could get out of her way much quicker, no illusions making her next strike hard to follow. But back up too far, and they would hit the edge of the pond—

"Boundwave," Bloom grunted, filling the water in front of them with unfocused waves. Stelli jumped even as the water pulled inwards, grabbing the algae, even grabbing the edge of her ripples—

She dropped her Standwaves while she was in the air, watching the pond beneath her *surge* and spiral. She started the subversion before she even landed, taking the clean, crisp, rounded Boundwave rhythm and shoving it outwards, each hit of the pattern touching only the very bottom of her mental palm, snapping clean and precise. The moment her feet hit the water, she felt them stick, felt them *lock* in place like vice grips over her ankles, but she cast out her pattern, her inverted pattern, and her waves deconstructed with...

But they didn't. She jerked her feet back as the twins lunged for her, but her leg wouldn't budge, because her subversive tones got subsumed into the Boundwaves, the strange Boundwaves that didn't quite look the same—

Hands wrapped around her legs as light bodies slammed against her, grabbing her cloak, squeezing her. *Strange Boundwaves...* She adjusted the pattern in the back of her head, hit with quicker strikes, cast her subversive pattern smaller, tighter, felt her right foot snap free, then her left. She disentangled herself from the twins, spinning away, Canine ready, standing on hasty Standwaves.

"No fair!" Bloom shouted. "We got you!"

She steadied herself, heaving a breath, focusing on the consistent normalcy of the Standwaves at her feet. "One moment," she heaved. "Won't be enough." She pushed herself off her knees, rolling her shoulders, wincing at the headache coming on. The back of her head buzzed with the echo of her subverted tone alteration. It just felt *wrong*. Like speaking sounds without words or purpose. "Again."

This time, Stelli didn't strike out towards them. She waited, circling, crouched low on nothing but Standwaves. Her Canine flicked in her hand, ready to lash out if they got too close. But they didn't. They circled too. A few times, Bloom called out waves, trying steam, trying steam and light at the same time. At first they had some success. The light twisted in their bursts of flame-like steam, working together, as if the steam itself could conform to the shapes Rose wanted them to appear as. A big plant monster, with a pollen-tongue, and thorn-teeth, and vine-arms. Stelli skirted around their tricks, eyeing the water at their feet, studying the chaotic, yet still uniform patterns...

She subverted them in her mind, and cast their opposites, wiping the water to stillness. Once she had seen their Runewaves for long enough, the subverted tone stuck in her head, and she knew how to outcast them. The children just didn't have the speed or coordination or skill to counter subverted waves. A trained Runecaster would know to adjust their waveforms, to never stop moving, to twice-cast in subtle ways that hid their true intentions. But the children had none of those advantages. They had to *talk* to one another, giving her warning. And they didn't understand the Runewaves, so much as they cast them by instinct.

Rose stomped her foot. "Stop doing that!"

"The Bugaboo won't stop because you ask," Stelli growled, pulling her blow a fraction of a moment before it crashed into Rose's neck. The light of day vanished above them, and the pale-white of twilight snuck in to replace it. "And he won't still his weapon—"

"Slashwaves," Rose spat.

Stelli's eyes widened. The water vibrated. Her Standwaves shook. She dropped them and dove under the water. Algae spun past her face. She thrashed, righting herself, squinting through the green-tinged water to see the whirling of the space above her begin to calm. She came up to the surface, gasping for air, shoulder and arm stinging from exertion, pulses of pain reawakening and snapping across her muscle. She threw a hand up, slamming it down onto the water and forming a small Standwave as a handhold, pulling herself up from the algae.

"You could have killed me," Stelli grunted, throwing her other arm up, glaring at the twins through strands of algae that hung across her face.

"The Bugaboo isn't going to avoid Slashwaves just because they might hurt someone," Rose whispered. "Boundwaves."

The water twisted under the grip of her hands, like rock shifting and moving between her fingers, pulling inwards and locking her hands in place. She kicked with her legs, still submerged, but couldn't make any upwards progress as the water around her torso clung to her, binding her. She couldn't lift her hands. She ground her teeth together, glowering up at them.

"Let me out."

Rose crossed her arms, raising an eyebrow. Bloom looked away.

"Let. Me. Out." The prickle on the back of her neck returned. The prickle of those kind, translucent eyes. She closed her eyes, trying to breathe.

"Think we can beat him now?" Rose said, voice hard.

"Unlike me," Stelli growled. "He'll be expecting you to try and hurt him."

"We wouldn't have hurt you," Bloom whispered.

"Yeah well," Stelli tried to pull her hands free of the molasses water around her, and failed. "Good job showing that."

A clap pierced the air. It froze Stelli's spine. The second clap choked her. Bloom and Rose looked up, their faces contorting with confusion. A third clap, and then a fourth. The prickle of those kind, translucent eyes turned sinister, dark, foreboding.

She turned around.

"You've done a wonderful job, daughter," the Wolf stalked from the shadows of the swamp.

"Who is he," Rose said, her hands in fists.

Stelli's cheeks flushed red, heat rising along her neck. A part of her withered. A part of her glowed.

"Don't be scared," her father whispered, stepping out onto the algal pond, his hexagonal Standwaves pushing out through the murk. They twisted as they came in contact with the Bound-waves in the water, rebuffed for a moment by the swirling circles. Only a moment though. In the second moment, the General's hexagons shifted as they reached their end, rotating into the inverse of the children's pattern, and wiping the water smooth. "I'm Stelli's friend. She thought we might need some help saving your father. You can trust me."

Rose and Bloom shared a look, eyebrows creased, mouths unsure. They looked at Stelli.

She scrambled to her feet, onto her father's Standwaves. They washed clean the vibrations of her mind, lifting her, keeping her calm and steady. She swallowed a lump in her throat. Footsteps crunched by the edge of the clearing. Her eyes flitted towards the noise. Dezma walked out. Too slow, too calm, hands empty. Tess stepped out behind her with a Dewlcaw to Dezma's back, carrying Dezma's Longtooth in her free hand.

Stelli's throat went dry. Near imperceptible tremors vibrated over the top of her skin.

Dezma met her eyes, and raised her eyebrows.

"Leave her alone," Stelli whispered.

"Don't worry," her father smiled a smile so sweet it picked her up and supported her along with the pulses of his Stand-waves. "You've done such a good job for me. I wouldn't hurt your friend."

"Dezma," Rose said, voice warbling. "Y-you said you knew her. These are the mean soldiers from back home and Stelli's one of them, but you said you knew—"

Dezma's gaze hardened as she looked at the young girl. "I know, Rose," she whispered. Stelli couldn't tell what her voice sounded like. Defeat? Fear? Confidence? Some strange sort of burning entered her heart, hot and melting. "I meant it."

The burning flipped, and she felt the hook ripping her again. It hurt. She loved how much it hurt. "He's my friend," she whispered. "I thought we might need help saving your father. You can trust him."

Rose looked at Dezma, whose gaze was trained on Stelli with that strange mixture. Rose followed her gaze to look at Stelli. Her voice came out so small. "Okay," she whispered. "Where is dad? Can we go get him back now?"

21

Dried excrement caked Gavin's groin. The smell overwhelmed the ambience of the swamp. When it found his nose again, he heaved, but his stomach didn't have anything left to expel. What used to be there now chunked and sloughed against the skin beneath his shirt.

He sat in his filth. He watched the hue of the world change with the coming of the Full Devouring. He waited to die.

The weight of the Isingrass pod in his pocket ripped his chest open and spilled him further on the mud. It bored into him, whispering its toxic floral aromas into his ears.

Bloom's face, eyes stretched wider than the sky. Both moons shone in his irises, the Carrow Wolf bloated and full, the Tuft Rabbit not but a trail in his sated wake. Rose didn't look in the sky. In her eyes reflected a flower. The petals sifted like the entire canopy, swamp scales, feathered plumage in the palm of her gaze, so sweet and innocent and small.

He coughed as he felt the first Vargus pull themselves across his skin. Never. Never. His fingers felt with feeble flickers against the fringes of the Cyril vines, but he couldn't even grip them. They somehow felt tighter. Biting him. He had a vein in his wrist that protruded blue under his stretched skin. After losing his fingers, he had sat for hours moving his thumb, watching that vein in his wrist pop side to side. It brought lead to his thumb, even now as he remembered the sensation. As if he could move his thumb back and forth enough times to rupture the vein, as if his blood would pool beneath his skin and bleed it purple, taking his hand, his arm, his shoulder. He always stopped moving his thumb. He knew it wouldn't kill him, to keep doing it, to keep feeling that strange little pop. But he always stopped. If he kept moving it and the vein did break and he did start bleeding, then he would die, and who would make sure Bloom and Rose knew not to move their thumb back and forth long enough for their veins to burst? So he always stopped.

He whimpered as the biting began. It started on his right leg at first, near the feet. One of them dug into the chunk of flesh just beneath his big toe. The legs curled under his nail. It didn't hurt. A million bites from a million bugs could have filled him from the inside, could have swarmed through his throat, pulled at his heart, and it still wouldn't have equaled a fraction of the pain he felt before they came.

As the hands of the swamp took him, Gavin felt impossibly alone.

A bluotaes bird cawed. Its tri-tonal form could sound many different ways. Grating and coarse, overlapping and discordant. Rough and hard-edged, uncompromising, unadaptable. Each note could hurt the eardrums, falling separate and syncopated. To a trained musical ear they might even be insulting. A hopeless mockery of beauty, of truth, of cogency and wholeness.

All of it depended on who listened.

A dying father listened. To him it sounded beautiful. He tried to find the originator of the noise up in the branches of his horizon. His vision blurred with the shrieking of his skin, as the Vargus burrowed deeper. The colors splayed, a canvas wiped by Rose's little fist. Greens and blacks, pale purples. He blinked, straining, as the Bluotaes bird cawed again. It didn't sound like it came from the distance. None of the branches bobbed under any weight.

He lost the strength to lift his head. It fell back against his chest. His field of vision bounced, settling still and blurry on the stretch of red mud around him. A clump of green and black hopped into the red. It stretched further, taking over his vision. His eyes focused.

A bird, favoring its left leg. The plumage looked small and frail against the backdrop of the mud, with no sprawling branches and scaled leaves to accentuate its presence. Its right wing looked injured. As if, not so long ago, a stick had been stuck between its feathers, until kind hands had removed it without a second thought. It hopped closer, feet unfamiliar with the terrain.

Gavin groaned, a low and broken sound of pain, squeezed out of him as the Vargus squirmed deeper against the bone of his toes. They grew more confident, with time. A few dug towards his groin, crawled along his waistline. Miniature flowers of pain spread petals across his lower stomach.

The Bluotaes bird flapped its wide wings to aid its hop. It landed on Gavin's stomach. The claws dug into his skin. He coughed, stomach muscles contorting and hardening at the pressure—

The bird lowered its head, opened its beak, and dropped a leaf on his stomach.

Alimin. Its aroma burst across him. The Vargus wrenched themselves off his skin, twitching and rolling through the tangled hair on his legs, scrambling through the mud to vanish back into the swamp.

Silence fell. The Bluotaes bird cawed its beautiful three-toned caw, and hopped away. Gavin's limbs shook with an invisible tremor. He breathed. His shoulders shuddered, body spasming with the exit of the squirming.

Then he jolted to action. He bucked against his bindings, straining his arms, trying to rip the root free of the mud. The vine around his ankle gave as his foot twisted. He screamed. His foot felt smaller than it used to be. He yanked it towards him, bending his knee, wriggling it against the vine. As soon as it gave a little, the dam in his mind broke, and he *had* to get it free. He wrenched and tore and screamed in pain as the blood flowed freely from the holes in his skin. But the vine couldn't hold his chewed foot. It slipped free, and with a glorious final shout, he bent his leg up against his chest. He straightened it and bent it again a few times, just to feel the brilliant pain of his muscles at work.

He brought his foot up and kicked at the vine by his wrist. His heel bounced off, scraping against bark. He growled, kicking again, trying to hook a toe under the vine. He got a bit of leverage, squeezing his fingers together, squashing over the rigid bone endings of his missing fingers. The protruding bone of his thumb roared in protest at the pressure, his leg pushing, pushing, his arm pulling— *SNAP*. He screamed as his hand came free, little pinpricks running along the outside of his thumb. He couldn't feel it to move it. He couldn't unbend it away from his palm—

It twitched, shaking like a leaf in a rainstorm. He peeled it away from his palm with sheer force of will, and went after the bindings at his other hand. Digging his nails into the underside of the knot, groaning through the pain, he wrenched it undone, and then got to work on his torso.

And then he was free. He shoved himself to his feet, put his weight forward on his right leg, and collapsed. It took him a moment, hands stinging against the mud, to realize why he had fallen. He sucked in another shuddering breath, hands scrabbling for the fallen bit of Alimin. He got to his knee. He grabbed the trunk beside him. He tried to shimmy. Not fast enough. He fell forward and crawled, kicking off behind him, falling over himself to make progress.

His mind felt sharper than it ever had. The woman, with the

knife. The guards. A rotation. The main base, the oasis, must be close. The algae pools, they must be close too, then. His ears picked out the nearby trickling of sludge, just before his arm crashed through a Feltwing frond, and pulled his head forward to see a heavy stream. *The* heavy stream, into which his leg had sunk during that frantic run just days ago. *Just days.* He glanced at the sky. The sky that he could now fully see, and let the purples warble over the whites of the light that trickled through the leaves.

The far edge of the mudbank was savaged and torn. He threw himself over the uneven ground. With each jerk of his leg, sharp bursts from deep inside wanted to escape, wanted to batter him and force him to scream. He didn't. He crawled as silent as the Carrow Wolf in the sky, crossing the river, sliding through the fronds and under the vines.

And then he heard the voice.

"He's my friend." Defeated. Shallow. Broken. Full of conviction. "I thought we might need help saving your father. You can trust him."

Gavin crept up to the edge of the clearing, low to the ground, seeing through the gap between two drooping fronds—

Dezma. Her presence staggered him, curled him into half-breaths of disbelief and wonder. Tess stood next to her, holding her Longtooth, pressing a knife to her back. His frantic eyes scanned past the pair of them. The General. His arm rested on the shoulder of a woman, mud-covered and frail, her arm clutched close across her chest. She looked tiny beside him. Like his hand could crush her or carry her at his leisure.

Then his eyes found what they were looking for. Standing in the middle of the algae pools... "Okay," whispered Rose. "Where is dad? Can we go get him back now?"

A cry tore from Gavin's throat, and he was helpless at the force of his love. "I'm right here, Rosebud," he threw himself forward, flopping through the mud, dragging himself free of the underbrush. "I'm right here, I'm right here."

He fell into a coughing fit at the use of his voice, muscles spasming as his missing leg exploded with wriggling. He curled, carving a trough in the mud, even as his hands splashed into the algae at the edge of the pool. His two Raindrops saw him and squealed, running forward—

The General uncoiled, lunging for the pool of algae, his foot touching the edge. A note played in the air, more silent than nothing, more singular than anything. The surface of the water churned with Boundwaves, the tightest Boundwaves that Gavin had ever seen. His hands stuck fast. Bloom and Rose toppled forward with their momentum, falling onto their arms which stuck just as strong, leaving them prone.

"Ah," the General said in the stillness that followed. "He saved himself. How wonderful."

"Dad what's going on," Rose cried, kneading the water with furtive movements, trying to pull herself free, to no avail. "We're trapped dad *what's going on*—"

"Shh," the General's voice cut through her cries and brought the clearing to silence. It carried the timbre of words that were meant to be obeyed. "No need to worry. Look! Your father is back, and now we can all have a little conversation. We can all be friends here. Isn't that right, Stelli?"

The woman he called Stelli stood stock still at his side, as if the very force of his presence stripped away her flesh and carved her in stone. A tear sparkled on her cheek. She nodded.

Gavin smiled at Bloom and Rose. In the twilight stillness of the swamp air, he knew how he appeared. He saw as if he were doubled, himself looking with all the love in the world at his two children unreachable in front of him, himself also looking down from the canopy and seeing an emaciated half-body curled in the mud. This time though, the himself looking from above knew how much the himself curled in the mud cared. In his desiccated smallness he was infinite.

"I promised I would show you, I..." he coughed, contorting over the Boundwaves. "I p-promised..."

The General stepped forward towards them across the pond. The Boundwaves parted in tiny hexagons around his feet, allowing him to stand. "Most people misunderstand the moons," he whispered in that voice that demanded attention. "You call me a Wolf, and you think that makes me a monster. But the Wolf and the Rabbit... they're in the same sky."

The Full Devouring began above them. In the swamp, it appeared as a bespeckled miasma of warring light, purple's eclipsing whites in the beams of light that flashed between the feathers of the canopy.

"Every night we both get swallowed by the horizon," the General continued. "Yet what if we could stop the horizon? You, little Raindrops, *you can stop the horizon*. Your father still isn't safe. The horizon is coming for him, and it will devour him clear as day unless you stop it."

"Stelli," Dezma called. The General bit back his words, turning to look at her. Tess grabbed her shoulder, pulling her tight. Dezma didn't resist, just straightened her back, raised her chin. "If this is your choice," Dezma said. There wasn't a hint of conflict in her voice, stance, or eyes. Just confidence. "I trust you."

Stelli bowed her head.

The General stepped closer. The water around Gavin bubbled, remaining Boundwaves by his hands, but sparking into angrier triangles under his neck and chin. Little bursts of knife-sharp water shot up, not quite high enough to reach his neck. "Do you... *want*... to save the world, little Raindrops?" the General said, looking directly at Bloom and Rose. "Do you want your father to survive the coming war?"

Another step closer. He loomed above the trapped children

now, his shadow stretching and flickering in the light of the Devouring.

"Do you want to have a home to return to?" The General whispered. "Do you want to know your mother's face again?" He looked at Rose. "It's all on the table, little Raindrops. All you have to do is embrace your power…"

The water shifted. A note played in the air, less loud than anything, less multitudinous than nothing. The ripples around the General's feet broke and washed away, his hexagons subsumed as inverse ripples deconstructed them and replaced them with Boundwaves. The warpath of inversion took the water beneath Bloom and Rose, leaving them crouched atop Standwaves instead.

The General twisted around, a look of pure shock on his face.

"Dad," Stelli whispered, standing at the edge of the pond. Her posture was that of a leaf in the wind, its stem broken and snapped from the tree. "Stop."

Shadows passed across The General's face, leaving his cheekbones hanging and sallow, his jowls taut and angry. "I say the word, and she dies," he whispered, jerking her head towards Dezma. The broad-shouldered woman raised her chin, meeting Stelli's eyes.

Gavin saw Dezma as if he were doubled, himself seeing her standing so tall and strong and confident, himself also seeing her from above surrounded by enemies with a Dewclaw pressing into her back. The himself looking up at her from the ground saw in her eyes how much she cared. In her confident helplessness, looking at Stelli, she was infinite.

"You don't know what it feels like to love someone," Stelli said to her father, shaking. "You can't have them."

The General raised his hand towards Tess and Dezma, face contorting into an order—

The clearing broke into chaos.

Gavin threw himself to the side as the water whipped into frenzied Runewaves. Someone screamed. A splatter caught him across the face. He flinched away, blinking, trying to see through his blurry vision.

Dezma roared as Stelli crashed into Tess, throwing her away. Bright blood spurted across Dezma's back, but she stayed up, twisting to grab Tess and grapple over her Longtooth. The three of them collapsed to the mud, a tangle of limbs and blades.

He whirled around. His heart caught in his throat. He wanted to cry out, tried to run forward, but he didn't have a leg. He slipped and fell, chin into mud.

Bloom and Rose stood on the water alone with the Wolf. Concentric circles swarmed towards their tiny forms, rippling for them in angry, tight crests. They locked hands. The Standwaves beneath them *bent,* hexagons pulling apart into a honeycomb of pulsing ripples, hard edges catching the incoming Boundwaves like an ocean cliffside. His two children knelt in the center, hair streaked a glowing blond where the dye washed out, and looked up at the General looming above them. They had wide eyes and clenched teeth. Terror etched in their eyebrows, their pale skin, their sallow cheeks.

They didn't flinch.

The General's Runewaves bore down on them, eroding their hexagons—

SMACK. He spun at the last moment, catching Dezma's Longtooth just below the blade as she charged him. He twisted it, rotating the blade down towards the algae—

"Boundwaves, Boundwaves!!" Bloom shouted—

Dezma threw her shoulder into the General, knocking him back as Boundwaves surged in around his feet. He stomped his foot. The water clung to his foot as he tried to raise it again, bending the surface of the pond to an angle. Gavin's heart soared, until the inwards circles reversed, blasting outwards. The General launched into the air. Dezma staggered, arms wrenched up from the force. She lost her grip on the Longtooth, and the General carried it with him, flipping over her head. The Boundwaves rippled to completion under her, sticking her in place.

Dezma twisted around, throwing a punch before he even landed, timing it perfectly to slam her fist into his chest as he came down behind her. He staggered back, coughing, eyes wide.

"Slashwave, Slashwave!" Bloom shouted. The water exploded in front of them, little triangles launching for the General, sending up angry, sharp gouts of water. He leapt to the side, stumbling along the edge of the pond, dropping the Longtooth to focus on casting Slashwaves of his own. They *caught* the approaching blades of water, slowing them, reversing their motion and sucking the droplets back where they had come from. Bloom and Rose pressed him back, pushing closer and closer as wave after wave of piercing water crashed towards him. He caught them all, casting his counters moments before they reached him, face contorted with intense concentration, eyes *locked* on the complicated patterns of the Runewaves—

His right hand twisted, piercing the water like curled claws, dragging backwards. The air itself shifted as the algae water *stilled*, angry triangles fitting together and settling like the leaves of the Aycmor canopy when the wind stopped.

The General grabbed the Longtooth from the shallow water, and lunged—Dezma slammed into him. She got an arm around his neck, squeezing, squeezing—he spun the Longtooth, whacked the back end into the side of her head. She staggered. He stomped to the side, casting Boundwaves. Her foot stuck to the water. She grunted, losing her balance as her feet refused to lift. The sharp end of the Longtooth swung towards her head this time—

She caught the blade in a closed fist. Blood spurted between her fingers. She stood up, grabbing the shaft with her other hand, spinning it from his grasp. She flicked her hand towards the water, casting blood across the Boundwaves at her feet. She leapt away. Red spirals took the water, claiming the Boundwaves, claiming the General's Standwaves, forcing him to backpedal—

But he didn't. He lunged *forward*, over the blood, landing with the barest fragment of his foot on clean water where his Standwaves could take, running forward, each foot leaving the water moments before the blood disabled his Standwaves. Dezma swung the Longtooth towards him, right as Bloom shouted "Slashwave!"

No no no no—

Rose's face was contorted and angry. Her lips sneered, the whites of her eyes showing behind blotted red lines.

*Nononono—*Gavin's limbs betrayed him. The mud slipped under his single leg. He splashed down into the water at the end of the pond, weeping into the algae.

Rose screamed. The water around the twins *boiled*, cascading forward like liquid flames, straight for the General's back as he rolled under Dezma's Longtooth strike. He turned behind him at the last minute, face stricken—

Rose's scream pierced the clearing, pierced the swamp, sent birds squawking from the branches above, even as its cadence shifted from anger to horror, as the mist cleared, and the General was nowhere to be seen. It was only Dezma, spinning and crashing into the pond with a heavy splash.

Red filled the water. The algae hung heavy with blood. All fell still. Gavin forced himself onto his knee, splashing through the water towards his children.

A wordless, broken voice snapped through the air. Angry. Terrified. Stelli, thrashing beneath the weight of Tess, who had her pinned, with that terrible Dewclaw at her throat. Tears stained her cheeks. Desperation writhed in the twitching of her fingers. She was staring at the blood in the water. Where both Dezma, and the General, had disappeared. Her face struck something in him. The slight quirk of her nose, the way her skin pulled back around her eyes, the small, flat lips... The features reminded him of a man he had killed, long ago.

Gavin could not tell for whom she was afraid: Dezma, or the General.

"Dad?" Rose whispered, tears streaming down her cheeks. "Dad, dad, dad—" her little feet splashed towards him in the shallows, forgetting Standwaves. "Dad—" her voice cut out in a scream as a hand lunged from the side, grabbing her ankle. She went down in the mud, Bloom falling a moment later as a second hand grabbed him. A figure crawled from the water on top of them, wrapping them in a tight grip, pulling them close against his chest. He looked up between their squirming heads, glaring towards Gavin with that sinister, twisted scar across his eye. His hand curled over Bloom's neck like a claw, pressing the skin white. His nails dug into the boy's esophagus. They looked ready to rip and tear. Bloom sniffled in the grip, squeezing his eyes shut.

Gavin shoved a hand in his pocket, pulling out the Isingrass pod. It sat small and fragile in his hand. He lifted it—

The General growled and uncoiled over the twins, snatching the Isingrass pod from Gavin's hand and throwing him backwards into the mud.

"No more tricks," the General spat. His free arm locked around the children's necks. He heaved them backwards out of the water, staggering onto the bank. Bloom and Rose screamed and kicked, but the General's grip could not be resisted.

"Tell them to obey me," the General said through heaving breaths. "Or the boy dies."

Rose kicked and screamed in his grasp. Bloom hung limp and shaking. That terrible claw of a hand snaked back around Bloom's tiny neck.

The General's gaze flicked over to Tess and Stelli, as if an afterthought. "Tess, kill the traitor."

Gavin's arms and leg shook as he got to his knee, raising his head back up to look at the General, to look at his children. His hair hung heavy across his face. Mud clung and dripped from his unkempt beard. Above them, in flickering bursts, all semblance of light faded, and the world bathed purple.

SNAP.

The General didn't have time to blink. The Isingrass pod in his hand cracked down the middle. Translucent petals pushed off the casing, flickering like eager tongues upon the air. They twisted, irregular and unique, syncopated and discordant and tiered. Each petal shone in the purple light of the Full Devouring above, reflecting it, like water itself bent into the shape of a flower.

The General turned a curious gaze down upon it. "A flower?" He said, voice snide.

Gavin coughed, getting his leg beneath him. He looked at Bloom and Rose. "Isn't it pretty?"

Bzzzzzzzzzzt. A Hound landed on the General's hand, front legs reaching for the Isingrass rose. *Bzzzzzzzzzzt.* A second. A third.

Gavin jumped forward, slamming into Bloom and Rose.

The General screamed.

Gavin yanked his children free, falling backwards into the shallows of the algae pool. He scrambled away with them, holding them tight as the swarm descended on the General.

The General thrashed, dropping the Isingrass rose. Too late. The damage was done. He fell backwards into the mud. His voice tore, and broke, and snapped in a thousand places as scream after scream after scream rent free of his throat, terrible and visceral and bloodied. He leapt for the water, hands slipping on the slick bank.

"Standwaves," Rose muttered, slapping the pond over and

over again. "Bloom, Standwaves. Standwaves, now!"

Bloom shifted in Gavin's grasp, his entire body shaking. He grabbed Rose's hand. The General rolled towards the pond, about to crash through to safety—

A honeycomb of hexagons *flashed* to life across the red algae ponds, and the General's body flopped with a thunk against the hard surface. He slammed his hands down, screaming as the hornets stung him. His Runewaves couldn't do anything. The pond was full of blood.

Gavin hugged Bloom and Rose as tight as he could. "It's gonna be okay," he mumbled. He felt their shaking. "It's gonna be okay..." He rubbed his fingers in their hair, pressed his forehead up against theirs, drank in the dirty, bloody, rank smell of them, the smallness of their bodies against his, and just hugged them. Hugged them as if maybe a good enough hug could hide them from the horror of the screams. Hugged them as if maybe a good enough hug could erase what they had just gone through.

Hugged them as if maybe they had forgotten how much he cared about them, and he couldn't let that be the case, not in a thousand more Devourings. Not in a million.

"It's gonna be okay, it's gonna be okay, it's gonna be okay..."

And still the General's screams continued, even as his throat filled with blood.

"It's gonna be okay... it's gonna be okay... it's gonna be okay..."

22
───

Stelli watched the swarm attack her father with a Dewclaw at her throat, and waited for her throat to be slit. Her father had ordered her throat to be slit, so her throat would be slit. Her throat would be slit. It would hurt and she would crumple and she would be dead. She wasn't upset. It's what her father wanted. For her to be dead. What her father wanted. For her to be bleeding out in the mud, screaming, screams gurgling, screams fading, screams dying.

Her father wanted her to be dead.

Her father screamed, and his screams gurgled. No pain laced Stelli's throat. No blow landed.

"You did this to him," Tess whispered in her ear, broken. "You did this to him, *you did this to him—*" the Dewclaw shook against the soft skin of Stelli's neck.

Stelli stared at her father's writhing form in the mud. A thousand Hounds stung him, in every bit of bare skin they could find. Tears filled Stelli's eyes. She knew how much pain he was in. She felt it echoing through her own body. Her father didn't have anyone to bring him under the water, to save him, to hold him close. Instead the water kept him out, full of Standwaves despite the blood. Stelli had Dezma. Dezma... Dezma was under that water, and she was bleeding. Stelli gripped Tess's hand and redoubled her efforts to hold the blade away from her throat.

"He was gonna make the screaming go away," Tess choked out in Stelli's ear, strings of mucus slurring the words. "You always seemed to get it."

The screams peaked as the swarm built. *My father ordered me dead.* A part of her wanted to help Tess complete the order. *My father is dying.* A bigger part wanted to break free and run to her father's side, to drag him free of the swarm.

Stelli stood on the edge of everything, and realized that her everything wasn't just in front of her anymore. Her father was not her everything. He couldn't be. Not anymore. *There's a world where you can make a different choice... And someone will bring you a flower anyway...*

"I just don't understand," Tess whispered. The arm around Stelli's neck was weak. The hook wrenched and jiggled in her heart, spiking pain with each scream that left her father's lips. The hook tried to slip out of the flesh of her heart. The hook had barbs. The barbs caught. If she didn't run after the hook, it surely would rip her apart. She wanted to run after the hook. Wanted it more than anything. But the rope... t-the rope—

She felt so small. Her father stood above her. Her tiny cheeks were wet with tears. His screaming voice bled into ringing. *You did this!* She gasped for air but she couldn't find it. Because her father's hands were around her heart, and they were squeezing, and they were pulling, and they were tearing. *You did this!* And she was screaming. Her father had left and she was alone and she was screaming, screaming because she needed him back, screaming because she wished he was dead.

—She was holding the rope. She had broken it and snapped it. And now she held it.

"I think you do though," Stelli whispered. "Tess. I think you do understand."

Tess's cold cheeks pressed against the top of Stelli's head, and shook. Back and forth. Back and forth. "No. No, no, no. He was gonna make the screaming go away."

Stelli pried Tess's fingers away from the Dewclaw, taking the hilt into her own hand. "You're right, I do get it," Stelli whispered. "But the screaming child in my head, Tess? It's me. If he took away your screaming it would only be by making someone else scream louder."

Tess fell to her knees, eyes locked on the screaming, writhing form of the General.

Stelli opened her mouth, hesitating, palm sweaty against the Dewclaw's hilt. Her hand twitched up.

She turned and leapt into the algae pond instead.

She couldn't feel her heart. The hook no longer tore her and yanked her, so she couldn't feel it. The water crashed cold around her, striations of warmth running like vomit in patches where the blood spiraled, catching in her hair, her eyes, her mouth. She stroked downward, Dewclaw still in hand, eyes wide open, fighting the brine, the blood, the algae, trying to pick through the green haze... Her hand hit silt. She clawed at it, spinning herself, searching.

To one side, the water was greener, thicker. She swam for it, sending up gouts of spiraling detritus into the water. Her hand passed through a membrane. Water cascaded from her fingers in tiny droplets. Her head pressed into the algae wall, the soft fuzz-like follicles filling out the nooks and crannies of her face, before she made it through, and breathed. Heat. Hot air. Her hand hit something hot and sticky, viscous, warm, *too* warm. She gripped fabric and skin. Dezma. Eyes closed. She squeezed the woman against her, pushing off the pond floor, throwing herself towards the surface. Blood filled the water around her as she ascended, trailing and spiraling like strands of hair with unending length, strands of hair that just pulled and pulled and pulled, twisting and curling in every direction.

They broke the surface. Stelli grabbed Dezma under the arms, hauling her back through the mud. Algae clung to her cheeks, mixing with tears. Dezma's cloak was in tatters. A gash ran down her chest from shoulder to groin, blood clinging to the torn fabric of her robe, mixing with algae and water and mud, a milieu of muck. Stelli gagged, chin shaking. She dropped the Dewclaw. She pressed her hands to the wound, trying to staunch the blood, trying, trying... It just pooled around her fingers, it didn't care, it... it just...

Her father's screams roared in her head. The buzzing of the swarm started to die.

"Let me," someone pushed her hands off Dezma's chest, picking out algae and torn pieces of fabric. She blinked, paralyzed, shaking... One of the hands had three fingers... Gavin's face swam in her vision. Beside him, Bloom and Rose, staring with wide eyes and pale faces.

She started breathing again. "C-can they boil the water, burn the wound shut—"

"Doesn't work," Gavin muttered, the cloak already soaking through with blood. "Water evaporates before it gets hot enough to cauterize—"

"Not for them," Stelli whispered. "Standwaves and Steamwaves at the same time. Keep it together while it boils. It can stay liquid as it heats up."

"She needs stitches, not Runewaves—"

Bloom and Rose clasped hands, pressing their palms to the water. It flashed solid, a hexagon rippling out from their touch and leaving behind the translucent stone of solid water. The Standwaves balked, rolling on each other, becoming effervescent and conflicting. It all looked fuzzy, as if no pattern could emerge from the chaos. Until it did. In just the smallest edge of the pond, around their hands, the water clarified. Little bubble shaped patterns roiled together, forming a hexagon in the negative space between the fading edges of the bubbling Steamwaves.

Not a smidge of steam rose from the surface of the water. The pattern sped up. Bloom and Rose's eyes widened as the water started to hiss, a silent scream. The algae in the pattern started to blacken, curling in on itself. Bloom and Rose yanked their hands back. The pattern remained.

Gavin looked at it, cursed under his breath, and looked back at Dezma. He shifted closer, hesitating. Stelli bent down, scrabbling at Dezma's hip to rip free her canteen. Gavin grabbed it from her hands and dipped it in the water, careful not to let his hands touch the roiling patterns. He cursed, gritting his teeth, holding the canteen with as little contact as possible.

He poured it over the wound. Slow. Steady. The skin blistered and boiled, pulling tight, and the wound *did* close, it did, it did—Dezma's body bucked. Gavin tossed the canteen to his left hand, shaking his right. He refilled the canteen, and continued the job. Stelli grabbed Dezma's hand through the process, squeezing it so tight. The water poured like liquid steam, free and unfettered by the viscosity of Standwaves, held as a superheated liquid. It should have been physically impossible.

For Bloom and Rose, few things actually were.

Dezma bucked awake as more water hit her wound. She screamed. Stelli's chest contorted. She pressed her hands down on Dezma's shoulders, planting her legs over her lower torso to hold her still. As slow as he went, Gavin's pouring hit her uncut skin too. It boiled and blistered and burnt. But it... it was working... Right? It was working...

Dezma's screams eclipsed the General's. Stelli still heard him in the background. Heard him like an echo in her head, heard the pull of his pain, the roiling of the hook... the hook... the hook... she could still feel the hook.... She bent her head and held Dezma down. Bent her head and watched the wound stop bleeding. Bent her head and *stayed with Dezma anyway.*

Dezma shut her mouth, body contorting into the mud as Gavin finished burning her shut.

No more bleeding. With one final, tense exhale, Dezma fell

back flat, head lolling to the side, once more losing consciousness. Gavin's hands were on her neck in moments, feeling for a pulse. His fingers were raw and red from holding the canteen.

He smiled and nodded.

Moons. He nodded. *A pulse.* Bloom and Rose let the water fall back still. Dead, burnt algae drifted in the aftermath of their Runewaves.

The General no longer screamed. His whimpering begot the silence of the absent swarm.

"Don't you see how many lives they could save?" Tess whispered. She stood in the shadows of the swamp's edge, staring at the four of them.

Stelli pushed herself to her feet, grabbing the Dewclaw. The lingering venom in her arm didn't like the pressure. Emptiness lingered in her torso. She stumbled in front of the family, planting herself between them and Tess.

The two women locked eyes. Tess had hard, angry eyes; eyes that had a hundred times soothed Stelli and demanded a hug. Stelli felt those hugs closing in around her as she looked at Tess, taking in her broken nose and muddy, blood-covered frame. The hugs didn't feel warm like they used to. They felt... purposeful.

Tess took a step forward. Stelli jerked the Dewclaw up between them. "Don't make me," Stelli whispered through tears. "Please don't make me."

Tess stared at the Dewclaw. The skin around her eyes clung tight and weathered. Her arm dripped with blood. She looked up past the Dewclaw, and saw Stelli. Saw Gavin. Saw the twins.

"You're all monsters," she spat. She had no weapons. Blood dripped from her torn open forearm. Her chin quivered, tears building on her cheeks. In the pain and chaos of the moment, she looked ready to lunge. Stelli took half a step forward.

Tess turned and fled into the swamp.

Stelli watched her go. Turned, and looked at the huddled family above Dezma's body. Gavin met her eyes. Gave her a nod.

She let the hook yank her to her father's side.

A body, in the mud. Curled and contorted, legs pulled up against his chest. Swollen. Neck twice its normal size. Spots along the arms and legs burst through fabric. What skin she could see was red and puffy. The layers were disconnected, drooping like the deflated belly of a toad. Off-yellow liquid dribbled from the center of the sting sites, squeezed free of the crevices in his swollen skin like pus wrung out of a soiled bandage. His eyes hung open, the skin of his left lid torn apart and punctured, venom spider-webbing through his iris. His lips pressed together, compressed in their swelling by the limitations of his jaw, skin puffing back over his tongue and throat. Laying at his side was a flower full of reflected purple, petals curling open from a small brown pod.

Stelli knew that her father would stand up again.

She moved towards him. The handle of the Dewclaw pressed in her palm, slipping with her sweat. She clutched it tighter, feeling every prick as the skin of her knuckles pulled taught, as the sharp edges of the pommel grated the top of her hand. She held it out in front of her as she approached, eyes trained on his bloated, curled body.

Because she knew he would stand up again.

She fell to her knees at his side, staring down at his face. His destroyed face. She brought the Dewclaw down, pressing it against the side of his swollen neck. She nudged him with the flat of the blade. The skin bent with the pressure, his chin rocking up. She withdrew the Dewclaw. His chin flopped back towards the ground. The swollen skin didn't move like skin should. It was stiff. Stiff and tight. A coldness trickled between her lashes, down her cheek.

He would stand up again.

She nudged him again, with her hands this time. His body rocked, jostling, falling back still. Another tear met the first at the end of her chin, falling down, landing on her father's body, mixing with a bit of leaking venom from one of the stings.

He had to stand up again.

Her shoulders heaved, jerking forward. She bent low over him, shaking him, shaking him, shaking him, only to watch him fall back still in the mud. Tears poured down her cheeks now. A cascade. A rainstorm. They washed the grime from his face, cleansed the venom from his skin. Her chin quivered, snot building under her nose, stringing out across her mouth as she heaved in breaths between desperate choked sobs.

He always stood up again.

She stopped shaking him. Her body curled low over his. Her hands bunched in the remnants of his cloak. She felt every bruise he had ever given her, set deep in her skin. They throbbed with pain. Her ankle was broken again, because he had knocked her down with his staff again. Her cheek was swollen and purple again, because he had elbowed her in the head again. Her head was fuzzy and hurting again, because he had knocked it against a wall again. Her heart was fuzzy and soaring again, because she had landed a blow on him again. Her mind was calm and empty again, because he had been proud of her progress again. Her breathing was easy and full again, because he had given her a hug again, because she had done what he wanted again, because she had been a good daughter again... She looked into his eyes. His angry and desperate and screaming and very dead eyes.

And she knew that he wouldn't be standing back up again.

You're not your father... Dezma's words. *Make your own choices.* But she couldn't. Couldn't choose not to miss him. Couldn't choose the loneliness of her back without the prickle of his gaze. Couldn't choose the coldness of her neck without his braying breath. Couldn't choose the empty ripped out part of her carved from the love she felt for a monster whom she'd helped to kill.

Shaking, she pushed herself off his body, stumbling away from it, feet splashing in the pond. She wiped her eyes with the back of her hands. Like a leaf in the wind, she felt untethered. No rope pulled at her. No hook jabbed her heart. Only the blooming pain of the hole where the hook used to be, which throbbed with every heartbeat. Pain, but not a rope. She felt it, and she felt free.

"You're his daughter," Gavin murmured from behind.

She turned, arms hugging her torso, and nodded.

"I'm sorry."

Stelli shrugged, a tight movement that pulled her shoulders up tight around her neck.

"You care about her," Gavin jerked his head at Dezma.

Stelli convulsed as a new hook tried to jab her.

"She's a nice soldier, dad," Rose whispered. "Not like the other ones."

"She would never hurt Bubbles," Bloom added in a low voice. "She would fight to save him."

Stelli's gaze fell, finding a stray speck of darkened, reddened mud by her feet.

"We need to get her back to town," Gavin continued. "Her wound could reopen. Her burns can get infected."

Stelli kept staring at the darkened bit of mud. He knew she cared about Dezma. He needed her help. *He knew she cared about Dezma. He needed her help.* She squeezed her eyes shut, fingers curling against her palms. Her skin flaked like scales, slick with sweat. His hook tried to find her tongue, invade her heart, and yank her down to lift Dezma. She stood numb for a moment.

I trust you, Dezma had said.

She ripped the hook out of her heart, and bent down to lift Dezma anyway.

23

Come on now, there you go," Gavin ran his fingers through Rose's hair, squeezing suds between the locks, feeling its coarse texture bleed smooth. He had to be careful not to move his thumb too much, which was still healing from when he'd broken it escaping his bindings. He smiled anyway, watching the dye drift away through the water of their large stone basin. He glanced up at the drooping dark leaves of the plant hanging above them.

"I think I wanna keep mine dark, da," Bloom said from where he sat perched on the edge of the stone basin, kicking his legs. They made soft thuds against the edge. "I like it."

Gavin gave a thoughtful frown, nodding. "Alright. I guess I should have asked. You too, Rose?"

Rose wrinkled her nose in thought, then shook her head, tossing the wet hair and sending droplets up to splatter against Gavin's neck. He laughed. "Okay, okay, I get the point."

He helped her lean back into the water again, sweeping up more suds with his hands and dribbling them over her head, squeezing out all the dye. Her natural blonde shone like Sliffitan stalks fresh in the morning sun. He worked his fingers in, smiling as Rose closed her eyes, letting the water go over her cheeks and mouth.

Three days. Three whole days back, full of water and washing. There was no sign of Bubbles. Gavin, Bloom, and Rose had operated in a daze of recovery, silent and paralyzed. Dezma had yet to wake up from her injuries. The Vargus hadn't eaten deep enough in Gavin's remaining leg to cause any permanent damage. He was bandaged, treated, and though putting pressure on it hurt, he could still do it. His missing stump had sealed over; they found traces of a strange paste that sealed his skin, which Stelli explained was a kind of berry used in the military to stabilize wounds. She'd helped him affix a peg leg, cupped around his skin. Apparently she had seen people attach peg legs before in the General's company. With the help of a few other healing-minded townsfolk, they'd made it work. He shuddered looking at it. He shuddered at the feeling of the straps digging into his still raw flesh.

It would, he thought, take a thousand baths to be clean again.

He pulled Rose back up, moving on to Bloom, shifting on his one knee. He could still feel the second, pressing against the floor. Painful wrigglings continued in the crook of his absent kneecap. His fingers twitched to knock free the Vargus, but there were no Vargus. They remained only in his head, leaking out from the undefined edges of his missing self.

Bloom gave himself over to the familiar ritual, a tremor of a smile coming across his face. Gavin curled his stained fingers into claws, jumping forward and grabbing him by the back of his head, tousling his hair. The boy gave not a squeal nor a screech. He didn't cringe away like he once would have, or laugh as Gavin brought his head down into the water. He just gave that slight little smile.

Gavin smiled back. He worked his fingers along the back of Bloom's head, not squeezing as he had with Rose, but rubbing gentle circles, working his way down to the back of the boy's neck. He helped Bloom sit back up, reaching for his mortar and pestle, pulling free a dark and drooping leaf. It ground under the quick jerks of the pestle just the same as it always had, became powder just the same as it always would. But somehow it felt heavier on the tips of his fingers. Heavier and coarser, as if his fingers had learned to feel with extra precision, as if his hands had already forgotten what it was to lift any weight at all. He worked the powder into Bloom's hair, picking through to find every little spot of natural blond, smearing it away. The movements came so easy. So familiar. There was a comfort in familiarity. But also a heaviness that extended beyond his fingertips. A heaviness in the action's lack of necessity, coupled with the fear he felt deep in his heart, despite the Wolf's breath no longer whispering on his neck.

Now, as he listened to that whispering, he heard the weeping of three dead men. Nell's weeping eclipsed the other two, and broke Gavin's heart.

"There," he whispered, wiping free a bit of old dye that stained the back of Bloom's neck. He smiled at them. A stretched smile, that cracked apart the weak scars of dryness left upon his lips. "You both look great."

Bloom groaned, hopping down from the edge of the basin, stumbling a little into Gavin's leg. "You'd better not make us look," he mumbled.

Gavin laughed. "You can do whatever you want, Bloomstalk."

He stretched up, reaching for the ceiling, hooking two of his three fingers through a Cyril vine that draped loosely in the rafters. At the touch of his hand, it went rigid, pulling him up to his foot and peg leg and giving him better control. He used the vine to pull himself out of the bathroom in short little steps. The peg leg gave him enough balance to walk around, if he had handholds like the Cyril vine to support himself. Perhaps someday, when the wounds healed over better, and when he got used to it, he would be able to walk again with just a cane. *Perhaps.*

His upper back and arms burned with an unfamiliar soreness. He puffed out a sigh as he eyed the rest of the house. What little cleaning he had managed so far still left wilted and broken detritus strewn in the corners. Shriveled brown leaves hung off dead stems, some detached and decomposing in the dirt around the edges of the pots. About half his supply still looked healthy. The succulents, his one cactus up in the far corner. A few species of flowers that didn't need water. A heavy fog settled over his brain. So many mundane chores to get done. How to change the soil of the plants on the higher shelves? How to water them? How to clean their beds from death?

He blinked, and shuffled himself further into the room. The fog swirled in his head, heavy on his eyelids, heavy on his temples. It weighed him down like condensation on the bottom of a leaf.

Bloom scampered past him, scanning the rafters. The little boy's eyes watered, but he quickly wiped the tears away. The corners of Gavin's mouth twitched in a forlorn smile. The kind of smile that pulled itself out of you to run away from something inside.

Rose paused, looking at the front door. She trotted over to it, feet sending up light *taff taff taffs* of dust. She pulled on the handle, looking back at Gavin.

He nodded, even though it broke him. "It's safe, Rosebud. Go where you want."

"I'll just be right outside," she whispered with a slight smile. A smile that told him she felt a little bit broken, too. She slipped out the door, closing it behind her with a gentle click.

Bloom walked over to the fireplace, plopping down by the hearth, falling into a cross-legged sitting position like a bundle of sticks. He stared into the unlit embers. He grabbed the fire-poker, jabbing it amongst the coals, moving them around. Gavin pulled himself as close as he could, crouching next to his son. They watched the coals together. Bloom scraped little circles in the charred stone brick. The sound played without accompaniment, soft scrapes coming alone and irregular.

"Is it okay to hurt people?" Bloom whispered.

Scraaaaaape, scrape scrape.

Gavin sighed. "Sometimes we have to."

"You told us the Bugaboo was a monster," Bloom whispered. "I thought monsters were cool. Big, with thorn teeth, and vine claws, and pollen tongues. The Bugaboo was just... a man. Someone's dad."

Scrape. Scrape.

"The scariest monsters are like that," Gavin said, wrapping his arm around Bloom's shoulders.

"It's not fair," Bloom whispered, still scraping away. "Monsters are supposed to be cool scary. Not actual scary."

Gavin rubbed the boy's shoulder. "You don't have to be scared of the Bugaboo anymore, Bloomstalk. He's gone for good."

Bloom set the poker down, turning to lean into Gavin's arm. Gavin brought his other hand up and around, pulling him into a full hug. He felt the boy shaking, little trembles deep under the skin. "I know," but the voice was so small, so squeezed. "I know, dad. B-but I can't remember what home feels like anymore. What if home doesn't feel like how this feels like. What if it's different."

Gavin squeezed him tighter. "Do you remember that spider?"

Bloom sniffled against his neck. "The one that weaves its web over the water and catches little fish?"

"Yeah," Gavin said with a slight smile. "They actually build their webs to be destroyed. Did you know that?"

Bloom shook his head, eyes wide.

"When the fish gets caught, the web gets tangled in its fins. All the spider's hard work building the web gets thrown away, gone for just a single meal. But the spider doesn't mind. Because now, on top of a tasty dinner, it gets to build the next web even prettier than the first one."

"You think we can be like the spider?"

Gavin ruffled his hair. "I don't see why not, Bloomstalk."

"Okay," the boy whispered, looking up at Gavin with wide eyes that reflected the fire. "Yeah. Okay. That sounds like it could actually... be fun?"

Gavin smiled, and nodded.

A knock came at the door. Gavin tensed. Bloom's head whipped around. He pushed himself to his foot and peg leg, groaning a little as his muscles protested, reaching up to grasp the vine in the rafters, letting it support him. His arms felt tingly and sore already from the constant lifting. He pushed himself over to the door, turning the handle, cracking it open, peering outside through a small slit.

Rinna. Nell's wife. Tall and thin, wearing a dress made of scrapped cloth, woven with rope salvaged from old fishing nets, dyed and cleaned. Her hair hung low past her shoulders. Her head was bowed, looking at something in her hands that Gavin couldn't see. Her shoulders were tense. Her right arm slid up her left, bunching the fish-net rope over her shoulder, squeezing a bit of her skin. He caught dark hanging bags under her eyes, a quirked strong nose, and a straight-line mouth.

He pressed his lips in a smile, heart catching in his throat. He pushed the door open the rest of the way. "Rinna," he whispered, trying to make his smile wider, the corner of his lips quivering under a tear. "Good to see you, I was planning on coming to visit..."

"I thought the young ones might appreciate this," she cut him off, returning the smile, lifting the item in her hands. A cage, made of rope and wood. A large pale blue toad sat inside, perched up on its hind legs. It saw Gavin, and its eyes bugged out, tongue shooting between the ropes to slap into his face. He laughed, reaching up a hand, touching the toad saliva that dripped down into his beard. He still hadn't shaved. He should shave soon... Another task that needed doing. The morning dew on the underside of his brain built thicker.

"Bubbles?" A high pitched squeal came from inside behind him. Bloom slammed into his leg, sending a burst of pain up through his gut. He pushed it down, smiling and blinking back the tears as Bloom's eyes lit up at the sight of his toad, hands stretching out through the bars of the cage. The tongue shot out, slapping against the skin between Bloom's fingers. Rose came up from around the edge of the house, smiling at the scene from the side, waiting her turn.

"Bubbles Bubbles Bubbles!" Bloom screeched, grabbing at the cage. Rinna let him hold it, and he lifted it up in front of his face, the tongue slapping around his cheeks and eyes. "What are you doing in a cage?"

"I found him when Nona and I got the house back," Rinna whispered, looking back up to Gavin. "I'm not sure how he ended up there. But he's been keeping us company, helping us..."

"Yeah," Gavin whispered.

Bloom struggled with the cage, turning it around. "How do I get him out?"

"I got it," Rose trotted up, slipping behind Gavin, stepping next to Bloom. "Here, gimme some Slashwaves."

Bloom and Rose knelt together, hands clasped.

Gavin nodded. "That's a good idea."

They both spun around, looking up at him with surprised eyes. Gavin shrugged. "It's your choice," he whispered. "I trust you both."

They stayed immobile for a long moment, incredulous. Bloom lifted his free hand, glancing at his palm, stretching his fingers wide. He looked back up at Gavin and gave a tentative smile. He nodded again, and they both turned back to the cage.

Water jolted up from the lake, just missing Rinna, chipping

off a bit of wood from the deck before slicing through one of the ropes on the back side of the cage. Bubbles let out a long croak, glaring at Rose. She rolled her eyes, shaking the rest of the trap apart. Bubbles tumbled out into her arms, back legs scrabbling at her forearms as he leapt, sliming up Rose's torso, before landing in Bloom's outstretched hands.

"There you go Bubbles," Bloom laughed, wincing away from the toad's tongue. "All free now."

"Would you be free for a quick walk?" Rinna said to Gavin.

Gavin glanced down at his peg leg.

"Oh—Oh no, I didn't see—"

"No," Gavin shook his head, looking around the entry way with bleary eyes. He grabbed his cloak and swung it around himself. Dezma's Longtooth rested against the wall where the cloak had just covered. His mind recalled the delirious walk back through the swamp with Stelli and his children and Dezma's body, each step a new bolt of fire through him, as he leaned all his weight on that horrible weapon.

He grabbed it from the wall, using it as a crutch as he shifted from the doorway. "It's alright. It'll be good for me," he turned back to the kids. "You two have fun with Bubbles, alright? I'll be back soon."

Bloom nodded. Rose looked up at Rinna, hugging herself around the torso. "When can we see Nona again?"

Rinna jolted, turning away from the Longtooth, on which her eyes had been unblinkingly locked. She smiled at Bloom and Rose. "Aye," she whispered. "Tomorrow? That work for you, Gavin?"

He nodded through the pain, smiling anyway. "Yeah," he paused to catch his breath. "You can play all you want tomorrow. All *week*, even."

Rose nodded. "Thanks, Dad. Thanks Rinna."

"I won't be far," Gavin said, making another shuffling movement away from the house, leaning on the Longtooth. "Holler if you need anything."

Rinna helped him move down the deck, across a small rickety wooden bridge spanning between houses. The fresh air was nice on his skin. The slightest of breezes crested between strands of his recently washed hair, tickling through his beard. He looked down, and saw beautiful blue water. Looked up, and saw a brilliant sky, filled with twilight. His eyes still trailed to the left, to where the swamp loomed out of the lake. The bristling black Aycmor boughs. The dark muddy water, with its hidden critters, and striations of slime. He missed the feeling of a sculling oar in his hand. He missed the mugginess of the air.

Still. This was nice.

He cleared his throat after a while. "I'm..." he coughed, taking another step. A bird sang a mid-day song. Three overlapping tones and textures, existing together in discord. The water lapped at the edge of the hodge-podge boardwalk, the breeze kicking it into a silent, slow ripple. The water reflected the twilight sun. The ripples reflected its infinite color. "I don't know what to—"

"Shh."

Rinna led him around in slow, shuffling progress. He just kept watching the ripples. Watching the way the water sang like a chorus of birds when it caught the light of the dying sunset. Each step hurt a little more as the cup of the peg leg dug into his skin. The Longtooth grew heavier in his grip. It became too much, eventually. He paused, grimacing, lowering himself to the planks. Rinna sat next to him. She let her feet dangle down into the water, disappearing into that vibrant song. He felt in the air as her shoulders shook. Felt in the air her tears as they joined the song. Watched in the ripples, as the teardrops fell amidst the rocking twilight reflection, lost in the lake, their presence casting ripples that would never be symmetrical. Not in the back and forth cresting of the lake. Not in the rising and falling song of the sun. Not in the grief of the widowed.

He looked up, towards the horizon. He saw something out there, as real as his missing leg. The silhouette of a ship, with a man kicked back on its deck and a long fishing rod curving over the side. When he blinked, the shadow had gone. The song the sun sang sounded more like a symphony.

"Do you regret it?" Rinna whispered at his side.

"Which part?"

"Any of it," she said, voice cracking. She swallowed, and cleared her throat. "Coming here. With them. Knowing you were being chased. Staying when the soldiers came. Leaving when the battle started. Getting Nell..." she cleared her throat again. "That's not fair. That's not fair of me."

"Getting Nell killed," Gavin murmured. "And abandoning my neighbors to fight a battle I started. I know."

"Do you regret any of it?"

Gavin swallowed, a tear tracing his cheek. "If it was for Nona," he whispered. "Would you?"

The breeze picked up, rustling through his hair. The sound of the water grew frantic. The breeze changed the pattern of the ripples. The waves broke across one another.

"You can't ask me that," Rinna whispered. "Please don't ask me that."

He let his head fall down to watch the water. He listened to the music of the waves. His chin quivered until his eyes broke, and more tears came. "I hate that Nell is dead," he whispered, his voice like a silent reflection of twilight. "So much. And it's more than just Nell. My children have a gift with Runewaves. They could slaughter armies. End war as we know it. Thousands more fathers are dying now, because I won't send my little children off to fight..." He shook his head. "But I would do it again," he swallowed. "To keep them from bearing that weight. Maybe

I'm selfish. Maybe I'm a monster. But Moons, Rinna. I would do it all again."

She drifted her feet forward and back in the water, casting out more asymmetric troughs in the rippling color. More tears fell amidst her own little storm on the water's surface.

"You don't have to forgive me," Gavin said.

"I know."

He shifted on the wood of the deck, his leg starting to tingle as he kicked the peg through the water. He thought he could feel the touch of cold water on his foot. His absent foot. As if it, too, dangled through the waves, and cast its own ripples. He picked at the wood of the Longtooth's handle with his fingers.

The wood shook as Rinna got to her feet, ankles dripping with lake water. "I should go," she said, a little too quickly. "Can you make it home?"

"Yeah," he looked up and met her eyes. He tried a weak little smile. "Thanks for offering."

She wiped her eyes, smiling back, just as weak and little as his. Weak and little. But not fake. And not brittle. "Of course."

"Let me know if you need anything," Gavin said. "I'll be there."

She nodded. "Thanks."

"Yeah."

She smiled one last time, before hopping down onto the water, casting Standwaves, and vanishing between the shadows of the town. He turned back to the twilight. He stared at it for a long time. He dipped his hands in the water, and cupped his own small part of the brilliant reflection.

"Now you've seen me tired, buddy," more tears brimmed in his eyes. "I hope you think it was worth it. I really hope you think it was worth it." His tears fell into the water in his hand and washed it through his fingertips. The droplets caught the lake, rejoining the melody. A raindrop caught the side of his face.

Then a second fell on his leg. The lake found a new rhythm, as a thousand more raindrops plunked through the surface of the water, like tiny wounds sealed and reopened a thousand times in a single moment. He listened, his tears joining the rain.

All of it sounded like weeping.

He wiped his eyes, using the Longtooth to prop himself up anyway. His arms groaned at the weight of himself. His hair hung heavy across his face, unkempt and uncut after days in the swamp, matted down by the rain. His progress home went slow. Laden with pain, etched in the leg he didn't have. Laden with a fog-like condensation under all his thoughts.

Laden with the knowledge of the monster that he couldn't think he was.

He paused at his doorway, glancing at the creaking wooden slats of the small walkway around the outside of his house. He jabbed the Longtooth into a crook of the wood, stifling a groan at the pressure of it against his armpit as he struggled forward on his peg leg. He passed the doorway, and kept going.

Rose sat on the edge around the corner, staring at her reflection in the lake. Her golden hair shone sleek and wet in the rain. Her face warbled and twisted with the ripples.

"Mom's hair was like this," Rose whispered without looking up. "Right? Or did she dye it too?"

Gavin's heart lurched, head too full of condensation for more tears. He smiled. "It was just like that."

Rose kicked her legs. They didn't even reach the lake below, just swished through the raindrops. "Dad..." her voice shook a little. "Can I ask you something?"

He pulled himself forward, plopping down with a rattling shake on the boards next to her, wincing at the impact. His one foot hung low next to hers, brushing the lapping water. Twilight had faded. In the reflection, a million stars. He only looked at Rose. "Of course, Rosebud. Anything."

"Do you think..." Her feet kicked in the air. "You know how Bloom and I could use the Runewaves to keep Aunt Dezma alive?"

"Yeah..."

"Do you think we could bring Mom back too? Like we did with Dezma?"

Gavin's breath caught in his throat. He reached around, giving her a hug from the side. "Oh Rosebud," he whispered. "Dezma wasn't gone. Not like Mom is."

"I know, I just," her hands were little balled fists at her side. "We can do awesome things dad. Why not that?"

"I don't know," he said. "Water can't undo mistakes, no matter how it ripples. But it *can* make the aftermath of the mistakes a little more beautiful, sometimes."

"Well why can't we go prevent more mistakes then?" Rose said, voice really small. "Go out and... and... I dunno! Do something! Bloom and I can do something! We could have stopped all this, trained sooner and fought the General so Nell didn't have to..." Her breathing hiccupped, cutting her off. She leaned against him, clutching at his cloak. "I'm scared, Dad."

He stroked his hand through her hair, holding her, holding her... "I'm sorry you're thinking about all of these things," he murmured. "You're too young to be thinking about all these things."

"Will we have to fight the Bugaboo again next time?" She shook against him. "We should, right? We're—" she hiccupped again. "We're good at it? So we should?"

"I'm going to try and trust you both more, going forward," he kept stroking her hair, rubbing in small circles with his thumb. "I won't stop you from practicing with Runewaves. You're responsible. But... it's also okay to still be a kid."

Her next words barely drifted on the drops of rain to reach his ears. "What if I already feel old?"

He leaned back, running his hand to her cheek, wiping away a tear, and smiling at her. "How are you supposed to grow up if you never give yourself the chance to be young?"

A couple raindrops landed on her cheeks, mixing with the tears as she smiled.

"If you want to save the world one day, then Moons above, I know you'll do it. I won't try to stop you. Okay? But for now..." he grinned. "Think you can beat me in a game of Zvaloor?"

Rose laughed. "Dad you *suck* at Zvaloor!"

"Hey!" He reached up, heaving himself to his foot, stumbling against the wall. "I've been practicing!"

"In the swamp?"

"You don't know!"

Rose hopped to her feet, running for the front door, holding it open as Gavin leaned forward to grab his vine. "Bloom!" Rose shouted. "Dad's gonna play Zvaloor, let's get him!"

"What?" Gavin lowered himself down, sliding free the board. "A two on one? That's not how the game works!"

"Game works how the judge says the game works, and I'm the judge!" Rose tossed the little buoy into the center.

"Who made you the judge?"

"Me!"

"Ach!" Gavin slapped at the water, trying to keep the buoy from his goal post as Bloom slid over next to the board, tapping the water. Bubbles balanced on his head, sliming up his hair. The toad threw its tongue down, helping the kids spin the buoy towards Gavin, who couldn't keep up with the onslaught of splashes. He skimmed his hand across the top of the water, spraying Bloom and Rose. They shrieked, falling over each other to avoid the splashing. Giggles filled the room. Bubbles hopped off Bloom's head, slamming into Gavin's chest, sending him back against the floor. Bloom and Rose piled on top of him, their laughter a tempest of warmth.

"We got him! We got him!"

The rain grew stronger against their roof, pattering amidst the carved shingles and passing through the rain chains into the lake below, twinkling with a noise that joined the families in laughter.

This rain, this pattering. These moments, and their giggling. All of it could sometimes sound like weeping. Whether it did or not, of course, depended on who listened.

Gavin listened.

And even though he heard the weeping, he heard the smiling, too. Discordant. Syncopated. And no less present.

That, Gavin thought, was worth it.

TASTEWAVE

I can't believe I even spent time drawing Tastewaves. They are useless. Father doesn't even teach them, but something compelled me to complete the collection. These Runewaves do nothing but slightly alter flavor.

Tastewaves are not simple. The shape is complex, and from what little time I've wasted figuring them out, it seems that the star shapes need to be quite precise.

I suppose I should remember not to underestimate anyone who has trained to use Tastewaves. Time wasted, but it still shows skill.

24

Stelli walked alone through the rain. No matter where she set out to walk, she always found herself arriving at the same place: a tavern, imbibing the swirl and patter of droplets through its gutters and rain chains. It was the fourth day since her return from the swamp, and she'd been here every night. The General's company had left for the Steppes days ago, but Stelli couldn't leave. Not now, not yet.

Dezma hadn't woken up yet. She would. She had to. She'd stirred yesterday, just enough to squeeze Stelli's hand. So Stelli walked alone to go visit Dezma, her heart yearning for the other woman to be awake this time, even just enough for a few words.

"Stelli!"

She froze, turning to scan the shadows. That voice shouldn't be here. He should have left with the rest of the company... "Seban?" She whispered. He sat on Standwaves underneath a house, leaning against a wooden stilt. A pit expanded in her stomach at the sight of him, a wriggling echo of the hook, as if it still dug through the hole in her heart. "I thought you left, with the—"

"No." His face was caked in mud and streaked with tears. His clothing was filthy. "I couldn't leave."

"You..." Stelli swallowed, afraid to ask her next question. She crouched down next to him. "You didn't want to go with York? You'll be reassigned to someone else, someone far less brutal than my father, I'm sure. Not all generals are like him, and—"

"York's dead," Seban whispered. "I couldn't leave because I needed to find him and I found him. In the swamp today. Throat slit, worms burrowing through his eye sockets."

Stelli's heart broke. She reached out a hand to him. He flinched away, but when her fingers touched his chin he turned and fell against her, letting her hug him. She sat down on the water and just held him as he wept. "I'm so sorry, I—" Moons, she'd promised. The one thing she had promised that day in the swamp, that she wouldn't let York die. Now York was dead. "I'm so sorry. Moons, Seban, I—"

"Don't be sorry," Seban's grip tightened around Stelli. "Please don't be sorry. I'm sure there was nothing you could have done, Moons, we all almost died and it's a miracle we made it out of there and it's a miracle the General is dead—"

"You don't have to focus on all the good things right now," Stelli whispered. "It's okay to grieve, Seban. It's okay to be mad. I..." she paused. "I know how you felt about him. About York. I do notice things, as your Lieutenant. I know what you two were, to each other, and I always..."

"Always thought it would get in the way of our duty, I know."

"No," Stelli whispered. "I had to act that way for my father. But inside, I was always jealous that you two could get away with it."

Seban buried his head into her shoulder. His hot tears trailed down the skin of her collar bone. She closed her eyes and held him so tight, as if somehow she could stop the pain from breaking him apart. He shook.

"I just wish," he choked out. "I just wish I told him how bright he made the flowers bloom. H-he never... never believed it about himself, a-and I was too scared..."

Stelli rubbed his back in small circles, holding him, tears falling from her eyes, too.

"It's the most beautiful feeling in the world," Seban said. "York was scared of everything. I never knew someone more scared of the world than York. But he still looked at me and decided to kiss me—Moons damn the consequences if the General found out. I don't know when I'll next feel okay now that he's gone, but I can't bring myself to regret it, not a single part of it, because York taught me how to be brave enough to kiss him back. And even just that was worth it..." Seban started weeping again, and Stelli pulled him into a hug.

She stared off over his shoulder, watching the underside of the stilted wooden houses creak and groan in the rain. She shook too, now. She felt a warm hand grabbing hers, fingers laced just enough to not pull apart when she walked. The shaking snuck under her skin, into her bones. Her heart ached. A strange sensation wriggled within it, like a hook, but made of fire, burning her.

"I have to go," she said a little too quickly. "I should... I should go."

Seban looked at her, untangling himself from her arms. He nodded. "Sorry, I just..."

"It's okay," she said. "Are you going to be okay?"

He shrugged. "Yes. This town is... nice. I'll figure something out."

Stelli swallowed, and nodded, standing up. "Take care of yourself. I'll be... around. I'm so sorry."

"It's okay."

She paused, frozen in the rain. She nodded. "I'm still sorry. I'll... see you."

"Yeah."

She smiled at him through her tears, wrenched herself away, and sped towards the tavern. She paused at the doors. *She probably won't be awake yet.* Stelli took a deep breath, but couldn't still the shaking. She wiped her eyes. *She probably won't be awake yet.* The thoughts did nothing to prevent the surging hope inside her, which had pulsed and flickered and flamed like a candle on an endlessly dying wick for four days now.

Another deep breath, and she pushed through the front doors. Empty. No patrons. Of course not, Dezma hadn't opened the tavern for business. She couldn't. She was still—

Dezma sat behind the bar in front of a large bubbling cauldron. Stelli froze. Dezma looked up and smiled.

"You're awake," Stelli said.

Dezma eyed Stelli up and down. "You're covered in mud."

They stared at each other. Stelli did her best to shake her mud off just outside the door. Dezma's smile wafted warmth around her, calming the quaking beneath her skin. The echoes of the rope that had for so long yanked her heart tangled up against her, knotting in a thousand places, rooting her to the ground in the entranceway.

Until Dezma's gaze burned through the knots, and Stelli ran forward and threw her arms around her, burying her head into the crook of Dezma's neck. "I'm so glad you're awake." Stelli whispered. Dezma's large hands pressed into Stelli's back, holding her close.

Dezma grunted and squeezed tighter, then winced and stepped back, balancing herself on the cauldron.

"Sorry," Stelli whispered, leaning back against the bar. "I didn't mean to—"

Dezma waved the words away. "Worth it," she said. She grabbed a mug from under the bar and dipped it in the cauldron. Stelli hopped up onto the bar and tucked her legs beneath herself, peering in and watching the bubbling pink liquid disturb at the passing of the mug. Dezma poked her finger into it, sending out flurries of Steamwaves and Tastewaves. "You've never had my tea before, have you?"

Stelli shook her head, settling down cross-legged on the long, thin countertop. Dezma handed her the mug, then grabbed one for herself. Stelli took a sip, and shivered. The flavor swirled down her throat, coating it with a comforting balm.

"What do you think?" Dezma grunted, nudging her leg.

"Tastes like grass," Stelli said. "And hot water."

"Moons," Dezma went to lean over the counter next to where she sat, but winced, squeezing her eyes shut and pausing to breathe. She turned sideways and leaned back instead, folding her arms across her chest. "You don't like it?"

Stelli shrugged. "It's better than canteen water."

"I should throw you out of my tavern."

"Good luck," Stelli grinned.

"You think I can't just because I'm hurt?"

"Remember what happened last time you tried to stab me?"

"Wasn't trying. You think I wanted a dead body in the swamp? Vargus would have eaten me alive."

Something lurched deeper into Stelli's heart: that hook of fire again, formed from the heat that burned in the air between them. She took another sip. "I think you were just tired."

Dezma chucked, the sound breaking off into a fit of coughs. Stelli reached up a hand to grab the other woman's shoulder, but Dezma waved it away, a foul look on her face. "Wouldn't be so bad," she wheezed. "If it didn't feel like my chest was ripping open every time."

Stelli raised her eyebrows. "And you still think you'd beat me in a fight?"

"Easy," Dezma closed her eyes, sipping her tea. "I tell the town I'm back on my feet, ready to run this place again. People flood in. I tell them you hate my tea. They beat you up."

"All that muscle, and you need other people to do it for you?" Stelli smirked through another sip of tea.

"You're pushing it, Wolf Cub."

She withered, just a little bit, that new hook crawling up the inside of her throat. She swallowed, forcing it down until the hooked end found itself back amidst the tangle of her heart. Stupid heart. It always found more ways to tie more knots, no matter how many of them Dezma burned away.

"Well," Dezma grunted. "Don't drink it if you don't like it. More for me."

Stelli pulled her mug away as Dezma reached for it. "Thief!"

"Oh so now you like it?"

Stelli shrugged, the hook flickering aflame. "I want to see if it starts tasting better as I drink more."

Dezma glared at her for a long moment. "Well, keep waiting," she growled. "I hope it puts you to sleep before you get to taste the rest of it."

Stelli snorted, sipping again. She could almost feel the pinkness in the water on her lips. The slightest graininess, like miniscule beads under her tongue. The grass taste grew a little sweeter with each sip. It was the warmth that made the moment pleasant, though. The warmth of the mug against her palms, the warmth of the cauldron bubbling beside them, the warmth of the new hook in her chest, the warmth of Dezma leaning against the counter beside her.

"Does any part of you think your father was right?" Dezma said. "About any of it?"

Stelli tensed, hands going clammy against the mug. "Why?"

"Something you said to me," Dezma said. "Back in the swamp. 'You only die for yourselves'. You're right. I'd die for anyone in this town in a heartbeat, but for someone like you? Had you been in my way during that fight, I would have killed you, just as quick as your father killed Nell."

"Dez..."

"I don't regret anything," she continued. "Your father needed to die. Bloom and Rose need a childhood. I just..."

"What *are* you saying?"

Dezma's hand rested on her mug, which sat on the counter, untouched. "I don't know, Stell. I've been happy here for a long time. My tiny little world, where the corrupt men of the Steppes with their unjust violence and murder and careless warfare maybe don't matter so much." She turned to meet Stelli's eyes. The hook of fire churned in her heart. Dezma spoke with the kind of voice that dragged from word to word, lulled the listener into the next breath. "But I'm starting to learn something beautiful. That bigger world, despite its terrors, isn't just full of corrupt men. It has people who I can be wrong about, and they still make the right choice," she shifted closer to Stelli, reaching out a hesitant hand.

The fire burned up Stelli's throat. She grabbed Dezma's hand, and let the woman's huge fingers wrap tight around hers.

"People who..." Dezma continued. "Who teach me that love is about more than understanding. Sometimes it's about not understanding, and that being okay."

Stelli examined Dezma's eyes, unable to look away. She needed to look away. But Dezma's eyes had little lines in them, a dark brown amidst a lighter hazel. They almost glowed, just like the tangles of Bogslime in the swamp, just like lightning bolts in the sky. She needed to look away. But Dezma's eyes crinkled a bit at the edges, like clouds that framed the sun.

Stelli looked away, and as soon as the contact broke, tears found her eyes. "I don't know how to tell what I think anymore, Dez," she whispered. "I don't know how to tell what I feel."

The patter of rain drummed on the roof. Dezma's gaze caressed her.

"I can't be caught on my father's hook any longer," Stelli continued. "But there's still a hole where the hook used to be. And it's bleeding. And I want to fill the hole, to stop the bleeding, but I can't tell if I want that because it hurts and I want it to stop hurting, or if I want that because my father told me not to bleed."

Dezma squeezed her hand.

"Who stops the horizon, which swallows them both..." Stelli whispered, looking at the rain streaking across the tavern window. "I'm glad it's not my father. I'm free of feeling a hook rip my heart when I say that. But someone might still have to stop the horizon—and do it the *right* way. For the sake of everyone in the sky. The rabbits. The wolves. The stars."

"I don't know how to even start trying," Dezma said. The caress of her gaze shifted warm and whole in timbre. The prickle of skin-on-skin where their fingers laced together rumbled with a soft thunder. "But I want to try. I feel like... like trying is the most important thing I'll ever do."

The most beautiful feeling in the world... "I want to try and figure it all out with you," Stelli blurted. She looked back and met Dezma's gaze again. The warm and whole timbre filled her, flushing out from her cheeks, down her entire body.

"I thought you didn't know how you felt," Dezma breathed.

An image floated to the front of Stelli's mind. A beautiful yearning in the eyes of the terrified soldier who was braver than Stelli had ever been. *Something beautiful...* Her heart was so tangled still, so caught in knots that tied themselves even as they unraveled and burned away, burned away in Dezma's warm hand—

Maybe I can do that too.

Stelli leaned forward and grabbed Dezma's face, kissing her. The other woman went rigid, but then her hands slid around to Stelli's back and she gripped her so gently that they could not be pried apart. The new hook burned within her, but she didn't mind. It didn't scare her. Its flame couldn't undo the bleeding hole in her heart, but it could cauterize the wound, just a little bit.

She pulled away, staring deep into Dezma's eyes, smiling a little. "Maybe we'll never understand," she whispered. "Maybe we'll never do the right thing. Never make a difference, never be sure anything can even be changed. But I don't care about understanding. I care about feeling. This. With you."

"I want to try," Dezma whispered. "This. With you."

Stelli examined Dezma's eyes, and this time she could look away. She just didn't feel like it. They maneuvered closer together, intertwining their bodies atop the tavern bar, holding each other with gentle, curious hands.

Not many sounds made their way into that moment with them—merely the whispering of the rain on the roof tricking through the gutters into the rain chains outside. The sound of that rain depended on who listened.

Two living lovers listened.

It sounded like millions of raindrops cascading to an unshielded lake. It sounded like the roof above their heads catching a smaller number of millions, and the rain chains rushing with quite a bit fewer. But more than the imperfect shielding of the village, more than the imperfect flow of water through the rain chains, more than the imperfect mosaic of ripples, it sounded to Stelli and Dezma like love.

Which to Stelli sounded pretty close to perfect.

Author's Note

I keep an envelope in my wallet everywhere I go. That envelope has a short letter in it, written for me by a screenwriting professor in my first year of undergrad. As he handed them out—one for each of his students—he told us that writing often feels lonely; that it involves long nights of being frustrated at the sentences that you just can't quite get right, wondering if your words will ever mean anything.

He told us that if we ever felt that way, we should read his letter. I read it frequently. It's short, a mere 45 words long, and consists entirely of words that I wrote: a quote from a short film script assignment, written back to me in neat penmanship on sunset-colored paper. Ironically, the quote is about loneliness, and yet when I read it in that context, written by my professor, with his kind and supportive words echoing in my memory of that classroom, it is impossible for me to feel lonely.

Because writing is not a lonely activity, and neither is reading. When I read that letter, I remember my professor's words, and the words of my classmates who gave me feedback, and the words of my friends who sat with me as I wrote that screenplay and bounced ideas off them. I might be alone most of the time that I spend writing, but writing is the process of choosing words and sentences out of the infinite variety of possible meanings that language can create, and I choose the words that I choose because of the people that I love. I tell the stories that I tell because of the way that the people that I love have changed me.

Just as language is the infinite recombination of words, stories are the infinite recombination of shared memories.

So I thank each and every person with whom I share memories. This story would not exist without you.

Of course, a few more specific thanks are in order. To my mother, who forever has chosen to fill my memories with support and love; who has poured over my book more times than I can count to find typos and formatting errors. To my close friend Colby, who has, despite working a more-than-full-time job, spent his free time reading my stories, encouraging me, and providing me with sound business and marketing guidance. To my close friend Kate, who offered her brilliant sketches which you can find in this very book. To my writing group, Danae, Ian, and Olivia, who have seen this book from start to finish, and who have directly and profoundly improved its quality at every step. More than a few of the horrible things that happen to Gavin in this book are their fault—they were right, it is better for the story, so get mad at them, not me. To my friends who so graciously gifted their time discussing with me the complexities and nuances of lived experiences that I do not have, so I may more accurately and considerately portray those experiences in this story: you know who you are, and I thank you immeasurably. This story could not have existed without your council and friendship.

To you, my reader, I leave you with this: I hope my words have reminded you that you aren't alone. Your rain might sometimes sound like weeping, but the sound of rain is never singular, and it is always you who listens.

Glossary

Alimin: A wide-leafed plant which emits a foul odor that the insects of the Zenithian Swamp cannot stand. Those journeying through the swamp should always carry Alimin, especially if they aren't trained to avoid Vargus dens.

Allcrea Centipede: A venomous centipede, native to the Zenithian Swamp.

Aycmor trees: The most common kind of tree in the Zenithian Swamp. They grow with black bark and twisting limbs.

Berlyrr Bird: A semi-aquatic bird species native to the Zenithian Swamp.

Blood: Blood disables the functionality of Runewaves.

Bluotaes Bird: A bird species drawn to the smell of blood. You must listen to them sing.

Bogslime: An amoeba species that lives in the waters of the Zenithian Swamp. It bioluminesces a brilliant blue when activated by abnormal movement.

Bounder: A mammal native to the Zenithian Swamp. Bounders cannot swim, so they navigate the swamp through the trees, spreading flaps of skin beneath their arms to glide between branches.

Boundwaves: A Runewave which alters adhesion.

Burria: A leafy vegetable that grows in the Steppes. When ground up and dissolved into water, Burria helps ease nausea and fever.

Canine: A blunt weapon, favored by military Runecasters who can't afford to draw blood in battle.

Cindeere: The King of the conquering army. To most folk, his name is only relevant to invoke as a distant threat.

Cyril Vines: A vine species native to the Zenithian Swamp, which is often found hanging low over rivers and pathways. Cyril vines go taut when disturbed, making them natural snares– Bounders make use of them to catch prey.

Dewclaw: A long straight-edged knife.

Echowaves: A Runewave which alters the resonance of water.

Feltwing Fronds: A frond species with strong root systems which grow through mud in the swamp to hold it in place. Feltwing leaves are mildly poisonous to ingest.

Frazzle Moss: A moss species with a peculiar relationship to Bogslime: when the Bogslime lights up, Frazzle Moss senses the light as a warning and displays sharp frazzles to defend from predators.

Full Devouring: A monthly occurrence where the Carrow Wolf Moon fully eclipses the Tuft Rabbit Moon, creating the appearance of the Tuft Rabbit being devoured completely.

Grendlewood tree: Also known as Grendles, this nearly-extinct species of tree grows tall and sturdy in the Zenithian Swamp. It is known for its grey hue, and large root systems, which leave alcoves beneath the trunk that many creatures use for shelter at night.

Gurrengie: A bush with leaves as long and wide as a human torso. The leaves are soft, and absorb the warmth of the sun, though the heat releases an odd-smelling stench.

Harrywick Beans: A folk bean, invented by storytellers and invoked in the common idiom "harvesting harrywick beans in Vaelor," which simply means 'wasting one's time.'

Isingrass: A species of grass, which grows in clumps of a thousand hair-thin strands, each carrying a small brown pod. Isingrass Pods bloom into brilliant flowers under the light of the Full Devouring.

King Arnall: The current sitting King of the land in which the Zenithian Swamp is found. His rule has little effect on people living in small and forgotten towns.

Lake Vithim: The purewater lake which surrounds the Zenithian Swamp.

Longclaw: A polearm weapon designed for hooking opponents with its curved blade.

Longtooth: A polearm weapon designed for wide sweeping slashes with its long blade.

Mirrorwaves: A Runewave which alters the reflectivity of water.

Morri: A poisonous stalk from the Steppes which numbs nerves, and can be used in small doses to take away pain.

Mudstinger: A snake species with a highly venomous stinger at the end of its tail.

Nurrii: A drooping stalk that excretes incredibly sticky slime. If you add water, the slime loses its stickiness, and is actually quite delicious.

Partial Devouring: The colloquial term for the partial eclipse of the two moons: the Carrow Wolf Moon and the Tuft Rabbit Moon. The term comes from the appearance of the Carrow Wolf eating the Tuft Rabbit as the light fades during the eclipse. This occurs every night, as more and more of the Tuft Rabbit Moon is eclipsed, until the monthly Full Devouring.

Ralaf: A bush with long, thin leaves. Their smooth and bendable texture, coupled with their shape, makes them useful natural bandages.

Rhondrum: A thorny bush in the Zenithian Swamp, whose venom will leave those pricked with a temporary paralysis near the prick site.

Saxtile Passage: A thin strip of water that narrows between two mountains about a ten-day travel from the Zenithian Swamp. According to rumors, it marks the front-lines of the war between King Arnall and Cindeere.

Sensiili Magdolin: A beautiful flowering bush, a favorite for wealthy people living in the Steppes.

Shin-sheathe: A garment worn by most Runecasters, consisting of a long strip of cloth wrapped around the foot, ankle, and shin, leaving a small sliver of skin on the heel exposed to the water below for easier Runecasting.

Silverscales: Delicious fish that live in Lake Vithim.

Slashwaves: A Runewave which alters pressure.

Sliffitan: A grain that grows well in water-logged environments, cheap to grow and easy to store.

Snotslime: An amoeba species that is highly acidic, capable of melting through skin. It bioluminesces a sickening green when disturbed.

Spartippi berry: A sour-tasting berry found in the Zenithian Swamp. When ground into a paste, its juices have an antiseptic quality.

Standwaves: A Runewave which alters solidity.

Steamwaves: A Runewave which alters temperature.

Steppes: A land where rivers pool in the spaces between waterfalls, and the site of the largest city east of the Saxtile Passage.

Swamp Hound: A hornet species that lives in the Zenithian Swamp. These hornets are friendly, until they smell a flower... at which point they enter a murderous frenzy.

Tastewaves: A Runewave which alters acidity.

Twitillic: A tree that grows in the Steppes with highly poisonous sap.

Wandering Warrighast Toad: A toad species found in the swamp. They make good pets.

Waterweaver Spider: A spider species native to the Zenithian Swamp. Waterweave spiders weave webs over rivers and trap fish for sustenance.

Wondor Willow: A tree species that grows in the rivers of the Zenithian Swamp, spreading branches and leaves just above the waterline.

Wyllinic Bugs: A tiny waterbug that lives atop Lake Vithim. They sing a harmonious, hissing song.

Vargus: Flesh-eating parasitic bugs who live in the bark of Aycmor trees. They are repulsed by the stench of Aycmor.

Zar'thul: A half-plant, half-beast that lives in the Zenithian Swamp. There is only ever one Zar'Thul, which hunts only at night under the light of the Devouring. It reproduces asexually when it dies, releasing spores that regenerate its body slowly over the nights after its death.

Zenithian Swamp: A terrifying, tangled swamp, which few dare to enter. There is a small, nameless town which sits beside the swamp and listens to the rain.

Content Warnings:

This story contains depictions of abusive family dynamics, including emotional manipulation and physical abuse.

This story contains depictions of insects and infestation, mostly swarming hornets and flesh-eating beetles. There is mention of spiders, centipedes, and other creepy crawlies, though these do not feature prominently.

Chapter 19 contains depictions of torture.

Joseph Langley is a fantasy author based out of California. He writes stories because they might matter to someone, and because thousands of other people's wonderful stories have mattered to him. He believes that fantasy enables the whimsical to reach out and touch us, and in the process, we all might be just a little bit changed for the better. Find out more about the author at www.josephlangley.com.